Reliquary

BOOK ONE OF
THE PEREGRINUS TRILOGY

PRUE BATTEN

Darlington
PRESS

Contents

Characters v

Part One *The Journey...* **5**
Chapter One 7
Chapter Two 21
Chapter Three 32
Chapter Four 50
Chapter Five 78
Chapter Six 92
Chapter Seven 109
Chapter Eight 123
Chapter Nine 138
Chapter Ten 151
Chapter Eleven 168

Part Two *The Finding* **181**
Chapter Twelve 183
Chapter Thirteen 197
Chapter Fourteen 210
Chapter Fifteen 220
Chapter Sixteen 237
Chapter Seventeen 252
Chapter Eighteen 272
Chapter Eighteen 288

Chapter Nineteen   304
Chapter Twenty   324
Chapter Twenty One   340
Chapter Twenty Two   357

Author's Notes   375
Acknowledgements   381

Characters:

*- denotes historical characters

Prieuré d'Esteil

Gisela of Peslières – Prioress of Prieuré d'Esteil which is a
Benedictine convent

Soeur Cécile – Obedientiary of Prieuré d'Esteil

Soeur Canna – head scribe within the scriptorium of
Prieuré d'Esteil

Soeur Melisende – infirmarian within Prieuré d'Esteil

Soeur Benedicta – aged nun of Prieuré d'Esteil

Gervasius de Mons – a merchant

Geltidis de Mons – wife of the above-mentioned merchant

Venezia

Henri de Montbrison – former soldier in Philip II's crusading forces and now mercenary guard in the Gisborne house

Ariella ben Simon – daughter of Saul ben Simon and 'wife'
of deceased Guillaume de Guisbourne

Saul ben Simon – Merchant and Ariella's father, survivor of Jewish pogroms, most notably York

Lucas de Guisborne – infant son of Guillaume and Ariella

Tobias Celho – occasional troubadour and *espie* for Gisborne-ben Simon

Sir Guy of Gisborne – disenchanted English knight and purveyor of secrets and exotic merchandise

Lady Ysabel of Gisborne – wife of the above knight

William of Gisborne – five-year old son of Guy and Ysabel

Adam of London – Master at Arms of the Gisborne house in Venezia

Ahmed – Gisborne's shipmaster, based in Venezia

Lyon

Amée de Clochard – wife of deceased Lyonnais merchant, Jean de Clochard, whose trading house in Rue Ducanivet was bought by Gisborne-ben Simon

Jehanne de Clochard – daughter of Amée and Jehan

Michael Sarapion – Byzantine merchant married to Jehanne de Clochard, and head of the Lyon branch of Gisborne-ben Simon

Herviet – guard of the trading house in Rue Ducanivet, Lyon

Goss – ditto

Raol – ditto

Petrus – possibly once a Varangian guard and now an occasional employee of Gisborne in Lyon

Odo – steward of the Gigni house in Rue Trammasal, Lyon

Alexandrus Gigni – head of the Florentine trading house of Gigni and resident of Lyon

Other players:

Robertus de Mercer – cloth merchant travelling to Lyon from Toulon

Erembouc de Breguet – his companion, also a cloth merchant

Gilbert de Tremelay – Templar knight

Amoury de Poitous – a fellow Templar knight

Jean de Laon – de Tremelay's serjeant

Historical figures of note:

Phillip II of France

Richard I of England

Reynaud, Archbishop of Lyon, formerly the Comte de Forez

Henry VI Hohenstaufen, Holy Roman Emperor

*Eleanor of Aquitaine

Bertrand Drac, seigneur de Châteauneuf, Esteil

George II Xipphillinus – Patriarch of the Byzantine Christian Church

Part One

Suffer the Little Children...

We passed a small village near Jaffa, a nondescript place with no name and no value to our lordly commanders. There were maybe a handful of villagers, nothing more – you could imagine it might have been where Jesus or his disciples walked. Perhaps it was, which makes what happened all the more despicable.

There was a Templar commander who was chivvying us, urging us on despite that Saladin and Richard Plantagenet had agreed to terms. I don't know who this man was, just that he rode a Saracen stallion of immense beauty and that perversely, the man had a voice of gold.

But he had a heart of Greek Fire and if the Templars were men of God, this man was the very devil. As we passed this village, he ordered us to wipe it from anyone's memory and he galloped in and slashed down any who stood in his way. With each swipe of his blade, as blood sprayed across the belly of that magnificent horse, he yelled at us to follow if we wanted to see our homes again.

We had thought we were marching to the coast to sail away from years of brutal turmoil and yet this man, in the face of a treaty that had been agreed to between Richard and Saladin, killed the defenceless – the old, the women and the children.

Because it was *only the old and women and children. All men of fighting age had long since departed.*

There was a child – a precious little boy.

A small child, a beautiful boy of four or five years. Soft of face and a fluff of dark hair lifting in the breeze. He had wide, innocent eyes that reached into one's heart. He was crying for his mother who lay dead at his feet. What harm had she done any of us? A jug lay shattered and I suspect she had been carrying water from the well.

Just water.

Not a weapon, nothing sinister.

This little child stood in his bare feet, a tear rolling through the dirt on his cheek, a trail of sadness. Sometimes I see that tear and nothing else. Just rolling through the dirt leaving a trail of suffering behind. A tear of such poignant virtue and in my mind it travels slowly, just drifting down with the most god-awful sadness over his tender cheek. In my mind, that tear always magnifies the bloody carnage all about, as if my sight has been uncannily sharpened.

The Templar, vulgar, brutal man of God, wheeled his horse, spurred it so that it reared high, screaming as the barbed metal at the knight's heels dragged over its flanks.

Then he rode at the child at a gallop, raised his sword and…

My confrères and I were silent, stricken with the horror of what we had witnessed.

The Templar galloped on upon the wings of his evil. I swear his white cloak was only a figment of my imagination. In truth it was black and feathered, the appendage of a foul swamp creature from Hell.

I cursed him.

Every curse I could lay my hands on, filthy-mouthed, as my own sword dropped to the ground. I could not look at what remained of the child and for sure, no life remained of the people of the village. The vomit came then – hot, acrid and I puked until my stomach breached my teeth.

The shaking started and on the bad days, it continues still, but I hide it from all. No one knows the anger and sadness that rots my soul. And so it shall be...

A priest walked back and forth amongst us in that village, carrying a cross and chanting the Paternoster as though it would cleanse us of the horrible destruction and I wanted to throw him and his cross to the ground, to bash his face in the dirt with that crucifix so that he would be beyond recognition.

If he died, so what?

God wasn't even within earshot!

If God had been present, Saracen or no, He would surely never have allowed this massacre.

For a little child to die like that?

Or any other child?

Suffer the little children...

The Journey...

*'Help me to see and understand the path
that you have opened for me...'*
Saint Benedict of Nursia

Chapter One

Soeur Cécile
Prieuré d'Esteil
1196 AD

'We need a relic.'

'Pardon,' the Obedientiary put down her mug of watered wine and stared at the Prioress.

'We need a relic,' the Prioress replied. Younger than the Obedientiary, she had blue eyes. One could almost say guile-less, had it not been for the veil of iron behind the heavenly colour. The Obedientiary had observed those eyes harden to moulded steel, and as strong, many times. Especially when senior prelates had visited the priory with the express purpose of wanting it closed because of its small population and lack of fame and fortune. As the Prioress spoke now, her eyes darkened – a tint reminiscent of the forge as the smithy honed blades for those who sought to arm themselves.

'Something to bring the pilgrims,' she continued, rubbing the worn edge of the table as if the smooth rhythm might settle the uneven nature of her thoughts. 'In short, to bring us monies. We are only a few leagues away from the Chemin de Compostelle…'

In fact, the Obedientiary knew this. The Via Arvena, beloved of pilgrims, passed through Jumeaux, following the river that trickled and sometimes flowed, not far from Esteil.

'I cannot fight off these crows of canons for much longer. I have been communicating with Mother Abbess at Fontevrault and she agrees that we must find a way to improve Esteil's fortunes. In between times, she has said she will do what she can, but in my view, it will be little, perhaps nothing.'

Esteil was situated within Fontevrault's purview. Occasionally, the mother house dispensed funds to smaller houses in times of distress. It also kept a weather eye on the spiritual wellbeing of the houses, but most small convents were expected to contribute to their continuance – temporal and spiritual. Survival of the fittest, thought the Obedientiary.

Outside, the wood pigeons cooed and the hens that lay smooth brown eggs pecked and clucked as if they understood the Prioress's concerns. Someone walked past in clogs, the beat of their steps on the stones of the cloister the only sound apart from the birds. Perhaps the midday meal was done and the sisters were beginning to file out of the refectory to attend to their yard duties – the physic garden, the provender garden, the hens or the orchard. Or perhaps some of their small number were copying in the scriptorium, or stitching within the solar. Right now, the Obedientiary should be there, checking that her three stitching novices had begun their afternoon's work on a cope while there was any sort of light.

'And what *is* our value, *Mère* Gisela?' she asked. 'Are we any better or worse than other such small houses like ourselves? How do we argue our value when we are less than twenty sisters?'

'Indeed, and despite what we do every day, what we accomplish in the scriptorium and with our threads, it is apparently not enough.' The Prioress sighed and rubbed at the smooth skin of her hands. One folding over the other, rubbing this way, rubbing that as if her young bones ached.

'God help us. Despite the quality of our scribes and the skill of our needlewomen, such work is not enough to plead our cause. Which is why I say we need a relic.'

'*Mère* Gisela,' the Obedientiary said, 'we have no money with which to purchase a relic, even if we could find one. What coin we have must be put to daily survival. We are a poor house.'

'And likely to remain so until our establishment is removed from us and we are sent to other places. Perhaps far from here.' The Prioress slapped both hands on the arms of her chair and the crack of palm on wood resounded round the chamber.

Soeur Cécile's stomach flipped over. The convent of Esteil was all she had known since she entered as a postulant, twenty-five years previous. It had provided her with warmth and succour and under God's Divine Grace, she had become educated…

'But I have a plan, *Soeur* Cécile,' the Prioress's voice had softened like butter left in the sun.

They sat alone in the Prioress's dour chamber, a wooden platter of bread, cheese and watered wine between them. The Prioress, Gisela of Peslières, had broken the community rule of eating together in the refectory in this instance, *and* she had broken the rule of silence that accompanied eating. Cécile shifted, uncomfortable with the baldness of the meeting, hating the hard truths of the discussion, wanting life to continue its God-given rhythm. She moved her feet again. Her toes were cold in the worn sandals she wore around the priory. She hated clogs and would only slip them on when she had to venture to the gardens or the orchards.

She looked down at blue toes and uneven toenails. Underneath her sandals, the floor was rough-hewn – no rushes, just cold stone. Stone floor, stone walls and with warmth usually emitted by a brazier that filled the air with throat-catching smoke. Today, it remained unlit for which she thanked God. She preferred chill to smoke any day. She smoothed her hands over her coarse robes, faded black wool that offered a kind of protection in winter but when wet, became as heavy as the mud over which the sisters would walk in their clogs. In summer the rough-made robes were prickly and unkind, but then, God help me, Cécile thought, wasn't that what being a sister was about? Suffering for God's love?

She frowned and broke off a piece of the bread that was still warm from the kitchen fire. It was good bread made with quality wheat flour, donated by *Le Seigneur* de Drac. He bought himself indulgences to pay for that terrible crime from his past. And for his loose pizzle. He so often strayed that the sisters no longer blushed as they kneaded the bread. In the beginning, it had seemed that they worked with something lewd, something forbidden, but now they were used to it and they all benefitted from his misdemeanours. Besides, his father had built the priory and they must not think unkind thoughts.

The bread smelled of the hearth and had a whisper of the honey that was gathered from their own woven skeps at the bottom of the orchards. It was rich and golden and of great value in the simple food that was their lot. The truth was that it was not often they had good white flour, normally just rye or barley flour but this was true bread – le Seigneur must have sinned greatly for this to have come their way, thought *Soeur* Cécile as she chewed and tried not to enjoy it. The sin of indulgence sat badly and she strove to ignore this light-as-a-feather bread with its crisp, flaky golden crust. Thankfully Gisela was talking once again, deflecting any self-indulgence away from the table.

'I have a cousin, Cécile. She is a joint owner of the Lyonnais branch of the trading company of Gisborne-ben Simon. The company has an agency in Constantinople, a city renowned for having relics in the marketplace.'

'You say so?' Cécile had no idea. It seemed odd that relics were traded as merchandise, like spices or cloth. Besides, the relic at Conques had been stolen from the abbey at Agen hundreds of years ago so that wealth would flow to Conques instead – no buying or selling there. It seemed perverse that something stolen from one abbey to belong to another should have any value at all.

She had thought there was an inordinate lack of morals in respect of relics and that must surely negate their value to Christendom. Did not Prioress Gisela feel the same way? Besides, why would she engage with a trading company that had the lick of the English in its name, let alone the label of a Jew? Was Gisela's cousin English perchance? Cécile didn't know. Indeed, she knew very little about her superior, not least because it had no relevance within the walls of the nunnery. What mattered was piety and application here, not what happened outside.

'Yes', the Prioress continued. 'My cousin shall stay with us for the month of May. She wishes to go into seclusion for a time, some peace and prayer, and it is highly fortuitous for us that she does so.'

'But how will we pay for a relic?'

'I have thought on that. My cousin and I have been communicating about her visit since she lost her husband some time ago. A series of devastating events happened to she and to her business and she is very tired and in need of succour. Which of course, we are liberty to provide.'

Cécile was taken aback. Their *dorter* was spartan, enough for any pilgrims and travellers that tripped accidentally upon Esteil. But for a wealthy merchant to stay for a month? There must be a better chamber. She, Cécile, would have to make sure…

But the Prioress continued, breaking Cécile's train of thought. 'During our communication, I proposed to my cousin that she pays the convent for her time here with the purchase and donation of a precious relic. She agreed quite readily.'

'What sort of relic? What does your cousin bring our house that is so important?'

Everyone knew that relics could be anything from a saint or somesuch. A splinter of bone, some hair – body parts. Cécile shuddered. It was all too macabre. She wanted to cross herself – forehead, chest, left and right, but she refrained because she did not want Gisela to see her fear and concern. She supposed she must be prepared to accept the divinity of these objects, their sanctity, despite that they worried her sensibilities.

She reminded herself that yes, once in extremis she too had prayed before the Saint Foy relic, but the grim nature of such things sent the shivers down her spine like snowflakes in a flurry. Saint Foy had been tortured to death with a red hot poker because she would not recant the charges of paganism against her and in time, her skull became a sainted relic. When Cécile had trudged the road to Conques before entering the priory and becoming a nun, she had done so to show gratitude and to ask for guidance, never really convinced the journey might turn her life around. And in the end it wasn't the Saint Foy relic that had helped her.

It was something else entirely…

Cécile was betrothed to a miller, an older man, not someone that a young bride would want as a husband – with his greasy long hair and a monkish bald circle on the top of his head. But then Cécile was no beauty and her family were keen to see her gone from the home as she grew beyond marriageable age. One less mouth to feed.

The miller's first wife had died of an ague, drowning in her own fleum. There were two grown sons who had become men at arms for the Seigneur de Drac but who had, perhaps through dint of acquiring their father's temper, been killed in a drunken and violent tavern brawl. In consequence, Cécile's betrothed had a face as sour and bitter as a bad apple and an escalating temper built of shame and anger. Simply, sourness was ingrained, like creases in leather, and she dreaded their marriage. The miller however wanted to wed her sooner rather than later. He wanted a woman to tend his hearth and bake his bread, to clean, cart grain, stitch up hessian bags of flour, grow vegetables, tend to the goat and pig. And to mount regularly…

Every night before settling on her cot, she prayed to the Virgin Mother to save her from her fate. She would attend the chapel of Esteil daily, pleading to the Virgin for help. As she hurried back to her father's small leather stall this day, to where scraps of leather goods would be laid out for all to see and hopefully buy, a shrill voice called her.

'Cécile, Cécile! Have you heard?' It was her friend, Marie, whose father was a hunter who sold skins on to her father for tanning.

'What?' asked Cécile, pushing at the hood of her cloak which had slipped over her shoulder.

'Jean the Miller!' Marie danced on her toes with excitement.

Cécile's heart sank to her toes. She did not want to talk of the man. He was a blight on her life. 'And so?' she replied heavily.

'He's dead.'

Cécile's eyes widened, a wave of giddiness rolling over her. Almost joy, she thought. But mindful of her state as the dead man's betrothed, she crossed herself.

'Deus,' she whispered, not entirely acting because she was shocked. She had learned blessings and prayers in her frequent church visits, liking the mellow sound of the words and how they fell from her tongue with ease as she became more familiar with them. 'How?' She was flustered, unsure of what might happen next, disappointed that Marie had told her the news in the middle of the village where people stared at her.

Poor Cécile! *She bet her life it was what they were thinking.* Where will such a plain face find another likely husband at her age?

'He died in his sleep, it seems. They found him this morning at Dawn when...'

'Marie, my thanks to you for telling me. I am shocked...' she began to back away from her friend. 'I must go home immediately. Please excuse me.' She hurried away, her head down, acknowledging no one and thanking the Virgin for heeding her prayers. Now that she thought on it, she cared nothing for what her future held, as long as the miller was no part of it.

Her mother wept with the unfairness of the miller's death. What would they do with Cécile? What would people say? It mattered so much more than her daughter's health and welfare.

The miller was buried, his business taken by his dead brother's son, his family turning their backs upon Cécile the Betrothed, and whilst her own family thought on what to do with her, she informed them she intended to make a pilgrimage to Conques, to ask for guidance from Saint Foy. As she told of the pilgrims whom she would accompany from Esteil, she had seen the covert but relieved glances exchanged between her parents.

She was a quiet and thoughtful presence amongst the pilgrims who welcomed her within their number so that she may travel safely. A matron took her kindly to her side and together the two rocked along in a cart pulled by a rough-coated rouncey. They talked of embroidery and of life and the matron patted Cécile's hand when she mentioned that her betrothed had died in his sleep.

'Ah, my dear. We survive without men,' the lady had said. 'More often than not they leave us on some fool's errand anyway and we must carry on. God willing.'

Cécile prayed before the gold reliquary within the abbey at Conques, unimpressed with gold and enamelled largesse of it all. She prayed for strength, for clarity of mind, for knowledge. For a sign... for a blessing through the windows above the altar. Such was the light within the nave, the soaring effect of the columns so newly carved, the stone still fresh and clean that she felt breathless, tight in the chest. She wanted a visitation, a bolt from on high, anything.

But there was nothing.

Nothing except the murmur of the pilgrims who were on the path to Compostela – a gentle hum like bees in the skeps of Esteil's orchards. The occasional cough, a sigh, all heightened by the soaring emptiness above.

Behind her, a nun prayed to the Virgin. Cécile thought it was Saint Augustin of Hippo's prayer, she wasn't sure, but the rhythm of the Latin thrilled her.

'Take our offering, grant us our requests, obtain pardon for what we fear, for thou art the sole hope of sinners. Through thee we hope for the remission of our sins, and in thee, O blessed Lady, is our hope of reward...'

She grabbed at the prayer like someone who is starving and stepped aside for the nun. The religieuse moved forward, bowing her thanks with a tilt of her veiled head. Her eyes glowed, filled with fervour. Whatever the nun had been praying for, she was receiving back tenfold, a shaft of light illuminating her rough linen wimple.

There! There it was!

The answer she craved stood before her clad in rough dark robes and veil and with an oaten-coloured linen wimple, adoration drifting from her very fingertips.

Cécile sucked in a breath and clasped her hands tightly, whispering the Paternoster to herself to steady her excitement.

She would seek a vocation.

And the oddest thing was that she knew it was exactly what her parents would want to do with her, failing marriage to the miller. See her behind the stone walls of a convent out of their way. An acceptable outcome within the village where her family would be admired because their daughter had chosen God above all. She wondered if they had money for a dowry. Would it be the same dowry they offered the miller or much less? She thought she knew.

She didn't care. Bliss coursed through her. As long as the Church would take her it was all that mattered. Besides, she had skills. She could sew, was known for her skill within the village, and she had an ability to learn, evidenced by her familiarity with and love of Latin prayer.

Thus at twenty-five years of age and a virgin, she wed Christ, and twenty-five years later, still a virgin, she was the Obedientiary of the Benedictine Prieuré d'Esteil. Skilled, organised, literate and in charge of the postulants.

She also kept the ledger, managing to keep the house's head above water.

Just…

The Prioress sat back, a smile playing around her youthful face, like a young cat who had found the cream. One more moment and Cécile was sure she would begin preening her whiskers. But then that was unkind. Unlike *Soeur* Canna in the scriptorium, *Mère* Gisela did not have whiskers sprouting from her chin. In fact, she had skin as smooth as said cream. It was in fact a wonder she was a nun at all. Out there, beyond the walls, she must surely have had a lover, a husband, a life… For sure, she was from a noble family and had secured her position by knowing someone at Fontevrault…

'Something precious, Cécile. Something so memorable to the Church that we could almost have Rome beating a path to our door when they hear about it.'

'I am filled with suspense, *Mère* Gisela. Do you know what it is? Has it been purchased already?' Something slid down Cécile's spine and her shorn and bristled hair lifted on her scalp beneath wimple and veil. Perhaps she might have to rethink some of her thoughts on relics. If this was something truly remarkable, then did she not owe it heartfelt veneration? For perhaps it *was* genuine and it had belonged to a saint who had bestowed upon it the very spirit of the Divine, just by being beatified. She crossed herself and reached for the mug of watered wine, throwing it back as *Mère* Gisela toyed with her expectations, rather like a cat playing with a mouse.

'*Soeur* Cécile,' she made a small moue, neither saying yes or no. 'I gather from my cousin that she can secure a relic that will have pilgrims flocking to Esteil. She is confident of it. Imagine...'

Prosperity and the continued existence of the priory would always rank uppermost in Gisela's mind and such a relic was indeed bound to bring monies, Cécile knew this. She had seen how Conques glowed with wealth. But what type of relic could be any more special than any other piece of decayed flesh or bone? Enough to encourage pilgrims to divert from the Chemin de Compostelle.

'Please,' she begged of Gisela of Peslières. 'Don't keep me in suspense.'

The Prioress stood and placed her mug on the table, then walked to the horn window which allowed a bland amber light to fall across the floor. Attached to the wall directly opposite, was a wooden, age-darkened crucifix, rough-carved. Christ's face hung in elongated pain. Gisela turned back to her Obedientiary and Cécile held her breath.

'Cécile, my cousin has said that the company can provide us with something that will save us.'

'*What?* Bone fragments? A finger? Some hair perhaps or a piece of the Cross?' Cécile refused to countenance the idea that their own relic could be so valuable. It was impossible. 'I hardly think pilgrims will divert from their path to Compostelle to see some splinter or other.' She knew the Prioress well enough to speak plainly, fully aware that *Mère*

Gisela saw her as a rigid woman of elder years, following the Benedictine Rule to the letter and without the slightest visionary bone in her body.

So be it, she thought. Someone has to keep their feet on the ground.

'Cécile' Gisela said in a swift *volte face*. 'We have five novices currently, do we not, due to move forward next year? And we are not to receive any new postulants until the autumn?'

Cécile nodded, confused at this digression from their conversation. She had met the three prospective postulants and their families. Two were plain girls from artisan families and they would bring a small dowry each, not enough to create any kind of insurance for the priory. The third, a very distant cousin of the noble Forez family, would be trouble from her long silken hair to her fine leather-shod toes, and Cécile had cringed deep within her soul. The girl would require watching – a hard hand perhaps. She was the kind of postulant she hated admitting through the doors of the nunnery. But the dowry was large – obviously not large enough though for a distant cousin of Archbishop Reynaud to be admitted to a larger priory. It made Cécile wonder just how difficult this young woman would be. But the dowry would enable the roof to be repaired and for a younger ass to be purchased for pulling the priory's small cart. But after that, their coffer would again be bare enough to see the aged wood at the bottom. Once again, they would have to hold out their hands to Fontevrault.

'And so, Cécile,' the Reverend Mother continued, dragging the Obedientiary from her deep concerns. 'Whilst we have this reprieve before the postulants arrive, I propose that you travel to Lyon and meet my cousin, judge whatever relic she is purchasing and determine its potential for us, and then return with Amée as her companion and chaperone. I cannot travel because the canons prowl too frequently.

I have written to ask for a dispensation from the Mother Abbess and she has agreed that you may go. I have papers accordingly. You understand I must do this to protect our house and the sisters?'

Cécile's heart stopped.

Of course the Prioress was right. The church men needed very little excuse to transport the sisters to another more prosperous house and close the doors on Esteil. It was proper that the Prioress stay at such a fragile time. But Cécile's own security lay within these walls, had always done. How could she possibly go to faraway Lyon? Besides, there were her postulants, they needed her guidance.

'But the young sisters, Reverend Mother. They will have no instruction...'

Travel? Her palms became slick with sweat and her heart fluttered like a butterfly caught in a spider's web. Away from here? She was not traveller, had travelled nowhere else but Conques in her fifty years and then only to view a relic.

How ironic...

'I will be here to oversee the stitching and *Soeur* Melisende and *Soeur* Canna are competent in the scriptorium. Cécile, you look very pale...' Gisela scrutinised her Obedientiary, unaware that she had not just rippled S*oeur* Cécile's comfort but torn down secure walls. Sometimes Cécile wished there was less glibness, less confidence about her prioress. Less business and more empathy perhaps. She bit her lip, guilt flushing through her. Unkind thoughts! There was no doubt that since Gisela had assumed the position as the head of the priory, some of the cracks that had appeared in the future of Esteil had been repaired, even if only temporarily.

Gisela managed to put the prelates on the back foot every time. She didn't charm them as such, but she managed to divert their train of thought. Whether it was with a new illumination which was always well-received, or whether the sisters had embroidered a cope or an orphrey in the style of *Opus Anglicanum*, it diverted them enough to save the house for another month or three. It would be a fool, however, who thought it wasn't just a temporary state of affairs.

As Cécile worried on what Gisela had said, she realised with shock that the fine linens used for their embroideries had come from Lyon, from Gisela's cousin. And because she, Cécile, handled the house's ledger, she knew that the price of such remarkable linens had been far lower than if they had been purchased from a less sympathetic cloth merchant.

Another point in Gisela's favour.

'Pale. Am I? I do have a headache. I have been working on a cope the last few days and the work is quite fine, the thread not behaving at all and with the lack of sunshine lately, the light has been bad.'

'Then you must see *Soeur* Melisende and ask what she has in the infirmary to ease your aches. Go now and I will talk with you again before you leave.'

Chapter Two

Henri de Montbrison
Venezia
1196 AD

The shadow moved.

Henri stiffened. He had no expectation of shifting shades. Not on the edge of the laguna and on an islet removed from the centre of Venezia. There was no breeze to shift the olive branches set hard against the villa and he had thought to be alone. His heartbeat gathered pace and the sweating began as he reached for the dagger sheathed at his belt. A subtle movement born of years of a desperate need to be secretive, unobtrusive. One didn't survive the crusade otherwise. Although he *had* been captured – a slip of movement revealing him behind a tumbled and bleached rock wall near Arsuf. By God, he had learned from that mistake.

The Saracens had pierced his shoulder with one of their hideous barbed arrows and he had collapsed, lying in the sand and almost dead with blood loss and no water. Some young pups, swaggering as if they were Saladin's army, found him, pretending they were their fathers and uncles, beating his back to a bloodied pulp with sticks that were make-do scimitars. They had perhaps been eight years of age and they had gloried in what they did. He could not condemn them as they watched their lands and homes razed. And a flayed back and pierced shoulder were surely better than being cut in half he thought and fainted, eyes rolling back into his head, limbs loose. The young boys left his bloody form, thinking him dead and he lay drifting for a night, shivering and sweating in turn.

How could he blame those children? Had not the Caput's and Lionheart's men showed equal lack of bloody restraint? Two thousand Arabs beheaded in a day?

Christ, war stank. In so many ways…

But an Arab field doctor found him and cared for him – a kind man who treated everyone, infidel or otherwise if he was able. He pulled the barb, dressed the suppurating wound with an unguent that smelled of Paradise and fed him poppy. When Henri, lacerated and in pain, croaked, 'Why?', the man had smiled and replied as he gently rolled Henri to his side so that he could swab his back. 'The *Quran* says the reward for goodness is nothing but goodness.'

'Then why do your men fight?' Tears coursed through the dirt on Henri's cheeks as the poppy began to claim him, inch by inch.

'Why do yours, my friend? We are just small men with ideas beyond our station, I think. You are as like to convert your king to a more amenable pathway, than I to convert my lord Saladin. They believe the truth of their ways. I, and I think you also, just believe in the truth of life.'

When Henri had been able to stand without collapsing, the doctor urged him away behind the fighting forces, telling him to run to the coast to escape. But being a Frenchman, and loyal to King Philip, he found Christians on the coast near Jaffa and set to, his shoulder a bloody mess and his back congealed with scabs that seeped through to his tunic. Each night, no matter his exhaustion, he would find a solitary space, strip off his clothing and wash his wounds, as the Arab physician had exhorted him to do because Death came so easily in filth and war. He knew it was that sound advice, that 'goodness', that had saved his life. For the rest, the slashing and killing, his mind sat far away, somewhere in the vales of France, where it didn't have to think.

But that was then, and this was now as he peered into the night gloom.

Fortuitously, he had left his cloak and leather gambeson on his cot in the villa before coming along the edge of the water for a quiet piss. He wasn't on duty and had merely grabbed a dagger on the way through the gate – force of habit more than anything. Once a warhorse, always a warhorse. But he knew a cloak would have inhibited him now and a gambeson might have creaked, despite that the leather of his was old and worn. He stood unencumbered, taut with expectation.

He lowered himself to move with stealth toward the sedge, easing the dagger from its tooled leather sheath. No point in disappearing into the water grass because it would shiver and crackle as if a herd of swine battered its way through.

He waited, listening – his heartbeat crashing against his chest so loudly it reminded him of Saracen drums and a something like lightning flashed through his head. He shook the fear away and listened.

Footfalls approached.

Soft. Probably goatskin without a hard sole. Someone wealthy. But clandestine? A man, for sure. There was purpose there, steady and even. A woman would have hurried through the night, her skirts grabbing and fussing the undergrowth. There was none of that. And a woman would most like have not been out at night anyway.

He slowed his breath to nothing, causing his heartbeat to ease. It was the skill of the archer apparently, to still themselves and then loose with swift and deadly precision. He had learned that much from fellows in the field, because he himself had been a swordsman. But they gathered and talked around the fires and water butts and he had learned much. Later, it was that stilled breath that sometimes eased the night terrors when they came.

Waiting...

His scalp tightened with a spreading chill that sent any thought but that of the Holy Land fleeing from his mind. His hands moistened, hot as if passing through flame and then a rush of something – battle-lust, courage, fear – tore through his veins.

The footfalls shushed forward. One, two, three, four...

He sprang, the dagger in his hand, screaming in the face of whomever came on.

Behind Henri, the gates of the villa slammed hard shut, the bars shoved into place.

The night shade fell back into the sedge, grasping at its chest and yelling, 'Christ's bones, Henri!'

Henri froze, dagger strike in mid-air. 'Tobias!' He shook his head, his sight clearing, a sharp reality drying the sweat on his palms and warming the chill that had swept through him. He thrust his dagger into its sheath and reached to help his small friend stand. 'Jesus wept! Why didn't you sing? Something to identify you? You're supposed to be in Constantinople!'

In the gloaming, Tobias, minstrel and *espie* for the house of Gisborne-ben Simon, master of disguise, able to charm his way across the civilized world with a singing voice like the angels, stared back at him. The fellow jerked his gambeson back over his diminutive frame with an indignation substantially bigger than his height.

Henri always thought his friend was blessed – Tobias Celho of Liguria, the disguised dwarf troubadour loved of royal courts mostly as the Spaniard, Sens di Dia, but there were other names.

Who was he now? By the sounds, merely a much-affronted Tobias...

'The ship moored earlier today. I saw Gisborne at the docks. Did he not say?'

'I haven't seen him at all, you little horsefly!' Henri brushed grasses from Toby's hair, feeling guilt rush in to replace the fear. 'I could have pierced you.'

'And had Gisborne, William and the Lady Ysabel to deal with. Rather you than me,' Toby grumped. 'Look, you've made me damage my new gambeson! I found an excellent leather man in Pera and paid a fortune for this…'

'Too pretty by half. A gambeson needs to tell a story, Toby.' They fell into step and headed toward the Gisborne villa.

'Then you had better scrape and scratch your own. I had one made for you whilst I was there.'

Henri slapped Tobias on the shoulder and grinned. 'That's very kind of you…'

'Then perhaps you should show your appreciation a little better.'

Henri laughed and the two pushed through the now unbarred gates, acknowledging Julius of Cyprus and Leo, the big man from Khorasan who guarded this villa on the far edge of the Venetian laguna. Both men welcomed Tobias into their midst, the little man lost in the circumference of Leo's arms.

Leo put Toby down and the gates were barred shut. 'By the stars, Henri, your yell shredded down to my backbone.' Leo said. 'I shivered when I heard it. I still have nightmares of the galleys.'

Leo had been a galley slave, sentenced for some religious misdemeanour by men of his own faith. What was it? Because he had been a follower of a sect… a Sufi? Was that it?

Henri grimaced. 'I apologise…' He knew he'd been in the grip of a terror, and sometimes at night he dreamed the shriek of battle and then sticks thrashing across his back, seeing the dead with arrows through eyes and throats, others disembowelled. He dreamed it all too often. 'Maybe in my soul, I wanted to scare whomever moved. I didn't expect it to be Tobias.'

He would never admit that if he heard the words '*Allāhu akbar!*' he trembled. The Arabic cries were forever in the deep recesses of his mind. As well, the sound of drums and trumpets would curl from his ears to his throat, threatening to choke him, whenever he recalled Saladin's noisome mounted archers sweeping down the slopes like an army of desert djinns, picking off the Christians like flies.

Some things stayed with one after war…

The large hall of the villa filled with shouts and excitement as the household welcomed back their favourite person. William, at five, not much shorter than Tobias and Gisborne's heir, held on to Tobias's arm as if he were conjoined. Henri admired the ease with which Toby interacted with the young boy – not a shred of patronising affectation.

Ysabel of Gisborne drifted down the stair, as perfect as the holy Madonna. Henri could almost have loved her himself if Gisborne hadn't claimed her. Sometimes his own singular status pained him and he would long for a wife, a hearth and a child. The years were in his favour but the life he led erased such a likelihood in a moment. As a guard and occasional *espie*, it would always be a brotherhood of men and he must live vicariously through his lord and this strange family of misfits.

Misfits that fitted together like hands in gloves. From across the Middle Sea or as far northwest as the English vales, from the French countryside and exotic Khorasan, home of precious lapis and pigments for the church scribes. Oft-times, Henri would sit at table, with a trencher before him and a glass goblet no less, of good wine from Liguria,

Prue Batten

wondering how they could all be friends when in truth they had all sprung from war of one kind or another. There was a moral there he was sure, if he took the time to unpick it from the fabric of merchants, trading and business. But in the Gisborne-ben Simon house, there was never time. Business was a constant; energy and mental acuity prodigious.

One step ahead in this game.

Always.

News of something rare and exotic would arrive in coded messages from any of Gisborne's men at any time and if he thought the investment was worth the expense, he would send forth a ship and men to retrieve the goods and bring the merchandise safely back to Venezia to be sold on later to an expectant and voracious market.

Lady Ysabel was accompanied by another vision and this time, he allowed his eyes to linger. Whilst Ysabel of Gisborne was softly beautiful, like a lush spring day, Ariella ben Simon simmered like a summer thunderstorm. Hair the colour of good Burgundian wine, eyes with sad, even grim stories to tell. She talked little with Henri and then only about business, a metaphorical shield between she and men, he thought. But with Ysabel and William ... Christ, even Tobias and Gisborne, she bloomed.

She visited her Gisborne friends frequently from her father's home closer to the city and he became accustomed to her being a constant. He'd heard her laughing with young William and feelings that had laid dormant began to rise from stagnant soil. When she had looked his way one day, whilst she was kneeling with William, examining some crawling bug, his manhood had throbbed and he quickly walked away, flushed with unease that this woman should disturb him so.

He knew she'd lost a betrothed. Gisborne's half-brother,

27

they said. And he knew that up the stair, in one of the chambers, an infant son lay sleeping, a son who would never know his father, the archer, Guillaume de Guisborne.

He watched her twitch her gown away from her toes as she descended the stair. Fine grey wool, the fabric of a successful merchantwoman and better than a widow's black. It fell in sculptural folds, elongating her body and clinging to hips about which she had clasped a damascened pewter girdle. The candlelight sparked on the metal medallions, as if she radiated her own light from within.

'Toby!' she ran down the last stair, crossing the hall in a waft of rosewater to hug the minstrel, her white veil flying over her shoulders.

Ah, thought Henri. This has been a sad day for her. She wears her veil, concealing her outrageous hair and once again a *widow*.

'Oh, you're back!' she cried. 'How I have missed you!'

Tobias, ever the minstrel, held both women's hands and kissed each with much play and innuendo. 'To Constantinople and back, I have seen much that is fine, rare and remarkable, but I have seen none to equal the two ladies before me. You are visions beyond belief.' He extended his leg in a courtly bow, releasing their hands as Ysabel of Gisborne laughed.

'And you, Tobias,' she said. 'are beyond belief with your compliments but we thank you anyway because God knows, if we had to wait for sweet words from Sir Guy and anyone else, it would be Doomsday. Come…' she moved to the long table. 'Let's eat. Sir Guy and Saul will be an age at the docks and I find I'm starving. Biddy!' she called in the direction of the kitchens, and in moments a robust little woman, part of this family that had mostly travelled from England, began to carry in platters of bread and fragrant edibles.

'Ariella, Lucas is still asleep?' the housekeeper asked, and when Ariella nodded, said, 'Then eat. If he wakes, I'll fetch him and deal with him.' Biddy was the house mother to everyone, even infants.

'As if it's a trial to *you*, my little hen,' Toby blew a kiss to Biddy. 'Christ's blood, your bread is remarkable!' He broke off a piece and a small waft of steam eddied skyward.

Henri had been content to let all the attention fall on Tobias. It enabled him to study Ariella which would give him something better to dream about in his cot at night, where whitewashed walls and no hangings exacerbated the feelings of monkhood.

Chaste. With no heirs…

And yet he valued his position within the Gisborne company. He had travelled to Constantinople with Gisborne and with Adam of London, Gisborne's master-at-arms. The vessel on which they sailed was jointly owned by Gisborne and an Arab called Ahmed. Henri called him doubtful and yet his loyalty and perspicacity in business was without question. Indeed it was Ahmed who encouraged him to look for the secrets in trade, to foster contacts in shoreline taverns, to keep an ear on all kinds of gossip, eyes wide open. The find of the voyage could often eventuate, or so Ahmed said.

'Frenchy,' he never called Henri by his name. 'You have a skill in spotting rarity. Methinks there's more to your little story than you are telling, *and* you can bargain in Latin and Arabic! Tell me how you learned my mother tongue…'

Henri briefly alluded to the Holy Land but his cool tone of voice was enough to warn Ahmed away from that conversation which, strangely, the Arab let go. Instead,

'I suspect you may prove yourself rather quickly to Gisborne. *In shā᾽ Allāh!*'

The truth was that Henri took great pleasure in working for the trading house. He liked his fellow guards and respect soon grew to become friendship in a short space of time. Despite the oddities of personalities and types, the trading house existed as a band of brothers. And sisters. There was no doubt though, that Guy of Gisborne and his business partner, Saul ben Simon, were the heads of the family.

Gisborne was known to yell and heave things about if he was angry, to show little patience in the face of fools. But he had the capacity to listen, requiring his men to deliver information in detail, with not a facet missing. Henri had learned quickly. Already mindful, for how else did he survive the crusade, he developed an eye and ear for nuance. It might be the tip of one man's head toward another in a tavern, it may be a wink or a raised eyebrow, it may be a nugget of information about political gaming that may seem like idle gossip to some. Or not…

Henri learned to digest it, sift it, pull out the flaws and discard them and then to deliver a concise report that enabled Gisborne-ben Simon to sell information to the highest bidder, to source spectacular goods to deliver to a voracious western market, to satisfy the whims of a world that was changing by the day.

He slept well on the night of Tobias's return and dreamed of Ariella. The fact that such a dream kept him warm in his cot was not lost on him. He rolled over in bed and hiked the woollen blanket up round his shoulders, pushing at the goose-feather pillow that was a luxury. Gisborne treated his men well.

Henri liked his chamber – it had been years since he could call a space his own. Life between Montbrison, the Holy Land and Marseille, when he had set foot once again on his homeland, had been lived in creaking barns with rats and spiders, in corners of *dorters* with foetid air and snoring. Very occasionally under canvas but mostly beneath the sweeping, starlit sky of a Holy Land that was surely created by God. He often thought he should be more grateful to God than he was but it was hard to show gratitude when he had seen Saracen and Christian beheaded, cut to ribbons. Women and children killed as a by-product of war.

He carried a level of bitterness toward his Creator and felt little guilt for doing so. He still crossed himself though and occasionally muttered the Paternoster.

Old habits died hard.

Chapter Three

Soeur Cécile
Prieure d'Esteil

Leave?

'*Mère* Gisela, it is surely unseemly, nay, forbidden for a religieuse to travel alone. And when am I to depart?'

Gisela placed the mugs and platters on a battered pewter tray. 'Indeed. And I did think on that. I would perhaps send Melisende with you, but as our infirmarian, she is needed here. Those who work in the scriptorium and with our embroideries must stay to keep up the supply of the only things with which we can barter with the canons. It is why I wrote to Fontevrault for a dispensation for you to travel. And the reply, with your papers, indicated that it will be allowed as long as you travel with another woman.'

Cécile opened her mouth to indicate the difficulty of this decision, but…

'Wait,' the Prioress, held up a hand. 'I have recently had word from a small group of merchants who ask for shelter in our *dorter* tomorrow. They plan to leave for Lyon the following day. I understand there is one such accompanied by his lady wife. I asked if you might accompany them. They agreed.'

And not a word to me. About anything. Not even the extra numbers to stay in the priory or the supplies needed? This decision of hers to pluck me…

'I've spoken to the kitchen about supplies and I'm taking this opportunity to ask if you can make sure the *dorter* is clean and free of mice and that there is bedding for four men. The goodwife shall sleep in the infirmary.'

Cécile inclined her head which now felt as if it was weighted with boulders. 'Of course, Reverend Mother. I shall lock the cat in overnight and the sisters shall scrub the floor and strew fresh rushes first thing in the morning. I will also have them refill the mattresses. We have a small amount of clean straw...'

Gisela patted Cécile's arm. 'You are so reliable. We could not have a better Obedientiary. Can you inform *Soeur* Melisende to prepare a bed for a lady guest for tomorrow night.' The Prioress stood and smoothed down her folds, bowing her head in a half obeisance, looking at Cécile with confident eyes the whole while. 'I thank you for the strength you give us here and I thank you for the fact that you make my job a lot easier. We will save this place, *Soeur* Cécile. Against the odds, we will prevail. I shall see you in chapel at None.'

'*Soeur* Adela,' Cécile called to one of the novices carrying a pail of vegetable slops to the pigs. She gave the raw-faced young woman instructions for the *dorter* on the morrow, telling her to fetch another of the novices to help catch the cat and lock it within the sleeping quarters this night.

'But the scriptorium, *Soeur* Cécile. I am supposed to go there after I take this to the pigs. We...'

'I'm aware of the psalter. But we have merchants arriving, *Soeur* Adela. I'm afraid that because they bring immediate monies, they must take precedence. Find me when you are done. Have you seen *Soeur* Melisende? She is not in the infirmary.'

The disgruntled novice replied with a face like bitter lemon. 'She tends *Soeur* Benedicta.'

'*Merci.* Go with grace, my child.' In other words, take the grimace from your face, Cécile thought, or the wind will change and your expression will frighten the angels. But in truth, she could not remain angry with the novice. The girl was a competent copyist in the scriptorium, always diligent and rarely wasting pigments or parchment. Like all of the sisters, though, she resented a change in their ordered day and visitors were an intrusion upon their peace, their routine, their daily journey through the Hours with their Holy Family. No, if she was angry with anyone, it was the Prioress. How dare she! Mary Mother, that this should happen to *she,* Cécile. Her life was here, inside – not on the road.

As she walked to *Soeur* Benedicta's cell, she thought what great comfort there was in Divine routine. Her mainstay, her joy. But she was concerned that Melisende visited Benedicta. The oldest nun in the priory, everyone loved her, saw her as a fixture in their daily life – her soft face, the slight sideways tilt to her head wrought of a neck bent over parchment in the scriptorium for so many years. Her gentle smile. Nothing ever rippled her calm, nothing was ever too much trouble.

But winter had sent her to her cot too often and it was possible to hear her coughing, even above the wind and priory noise. But then, by the grace of God, she would rally and totter back amongst them, bestowing her benevolence upon all, engaging with anyone at speech-times. Shaky of hand, fragile, maybe not quite as wit-sharp, but always cognizant of whom she was with. And she was wise.

Benedicta and Cécile were not that many years separated in age. They formed a friendship early on, when both were postulants. Over the years they worked together in the scriptorium or sitting peaceably in the solar, Benedicta reading the Gospels aloud whilst Cécile stitched. When they were able to speak, they debated a little of life, of their past and their hopes for the future within the Priory. Invariably this led to a simple wish – to do God's service. In another life, Benedicta might have been the older sister that Cécile might have craved.

When Prioress Gisela had informed Cécile of her imminent departure, she knew there was only one person with whom she could speak, unveiling her insecurities and asking for wisdom. Perhaps she should be asking the Virgin in the chapel, but Benedicta had a clarity of view that would set Cécile's mind at rest and she was sure the Virgin would not mind.

Benedicta's cell was at the very end of the vine-clad cloister. The sun had begun to slide from its apogee in the torn-wadding sky and a half-hearted glow warmed the stones. A breeze tossed leaves before Cécile – crisp, dried little things that had been shucked from the boughs as buds swelled in the new season.

There was something mournful in their haphazard passage along the cloister, as if it were their last chance and Cécile stooped to pick one up, her beads clacking against the cobbles. The leaf was an aged, frilled oak leaf, dry and the colour of mud with half of it already skeletonised. As she held it in her open palm, the breeze picked it up and floated it away.

As insubstantial as a soul.

She stood very still, a feeling creeping upon her as *Soeur* Melisende stood at Benedicta's door, her fingers flicking over her prayer beads, her mouth moving as she prayed. She looked toward Cécile and her eyes sparkled with unshed tears.

'Mary Mother!' Cécile's hands flew to her mouth.

'She slipped away…' Melisende wiped the corner of each eye. 'She was so tired…'

'Benedicta, my loved sister in Christ!' The words slipped out in a choked whisper and Cécile's heart ached with a ferocious pain.

'Stay with her, Cécile. I must inform the Prioress.'

'*Soeur* Melisende, was she in pain?' It mattered. She was such a good person, so filled with compassion.

'No. Methinks her heart may have been worn thin and just stopped, so she just drifted away. She drifted off with that smile…' She twisted her head a little sideways to indicate the departed sister in the cell and then hurried off, sandals clapping on the paving stones until all that was left was birdsong.

Soeur Cécile pushed at the pain spreading through her chest and, taking a breath, walked into the cell. She left the door open so that the lowering sun could lighten the space and the birds could sing praise.

Benedicta lay with her hands folded across her middle. Her wispy hair, thin and short, uncovered and as white as snow, fanned in a halo on the linen-covered pillow Melisende had slipped beneath her head.

It was true. She had the faintest smile upon her face – an expression of calm acceptance.

'Oh, my dear Benedicta.' Cécile knelt on the cool paving stones, her dark robes spilling round her, the wide sleeves falling back as she laid her own hands upon her saintly friend. 'Can you forgive me for not being with you? I would have…' Benedicta's hands were still faintly warm and Cécile smoothed them, noticing the translucent skin and the way the blue veins that had been so noticeable as she aged, had sunk away in death. 'Ah, I wanted so much to talk with you. I had so much to say, so much to ask.'

She wondered at the propriety of speaking thus to a person whose soul had departed. Surely she should be devout, praying for Benedicta's deliverance into Heaven. But there was something comforting in the old nun's expression and Cécile continued, telling her of what was to come and that she doubted she would cope with leaving the priory for such a long journey.

Simply she was afraid.

Cécile closed her eyes and squeezed them tight to prevent

the tears from rolling but when she relaxed the tension a little and when the flashes of light had ceased, she imagined her friend counselling her.

'Cécile, I am just beginning the greatest journey of my life. To something unknown, but for which I have been praying since I entered the priory. I'm not afraid. Neither should you be. You are chosen, after all.'

'What?'

'Indeed. You have been chosen to approve this relic that will be the saving grace of our priory. Without you, our home might cease to function. Go with joy, my sister, and trust in the Lord.'

Cécile opened her eyes and gazed upon Benedicta's face. The smile was filled with trust. There was no fear frozen into any part of her body as if at the vital moment, she had seen someone approaching her and was welcoming of the fact.

Take notice…

Feet could be heard clapping along the pavers of the cloister. Fast but not running because running was forbidden. In moments, *Mère* Gisela had turned into the cell and *Soeur* Cécile stood, brushing down her robes, tucking her hands into her cuffs.

'Oh my dearest Lord. Sweet Benedicta,' whispered Gisela. She reached out and gently smoothed the woman's brow, then stood for a moment, eyes closed, lips moving – some prayer for herself and Benedicta alone. Then she turned to her two senior nuns, collecting herself, a woman commanding the ship that was their convent.

'Melisende, can you begin the proceedings please? Lay her out, wash her with the finest oils and herbs we have. Cécile, find our best linens for a shroud. Fetch them here, please. She must be given every gentle honour. We will say a Mass tonight.

'*Ma Mère*, the travellers…'

It was the first time Cécile had seen Gisela confused.

'Travellers? Oh, the merchants. Of course. Tomorrow. Melisende, can we prepare Benedicta for her funeral and then wait two days until we can honour her in peace and quiet?'

Melisende's mouth straightened, perhaps a little disapproving but unlikely to dispute her prioress. 'Yes, *ma Mère*. It is cool and if we leave her in here…'

'Then it is what we must do. Cécile, fetch the cross from my chamber and set it at Benedicta's head. And, the chamber already smells of death so bring fragrant flowers and herbs, as many as you can find, and place them around her. She will understand the delay.'

But I won't be here to honour her. I will be treading a road toward Lyon.

'And Cécile, would you care to keep vigil through this first night?'

Of course she would. Benedicta was her dear sister and how else would she farewell her?

Soeur Cécile's knees ached, angry pain coming from deep within her legs and she was cold.

The largest proportion of the night was spent with her kneecaps pressing into the unforgiving stone. At one point she had pushed herself up to sit upon a stool at Benedicta's head, the woven rush seat creaking in the silence of the night.

Melisende had done the best she was able with her supplies from the infirmary. The cell smelled of rosemary and if Cécile leaned close to old Benedicta, she inhaled the lightest fragrance of incense and balsam. Heavens knows if they had any incense left for their chapel but Cécile found she didn't care. She would be gone to Lyon after all, she thought bitterly, and then asked God to forgive her.

Around the room were pitchers of dried herbs – of

fennel, sage, lavender and more rosemary and she was glad of the largesse because Benedicta deserved the honouring and she and her friend in Christ had oft walked the gardens and orchard in summer, picking herbs and plants for drying.

She had shut the door, but the room became as cold as ice, and she leaned toward the sputtering, dancing flame of the candles that illuminated *Mère* Gisela's cross. The candles were tallow, always smoky and less than fragrant, but the priory could afford nothing better. Occasionally, the *Seigneur* de Drac would bestow a crate of beeswax candles, usually at Eastertide, but they were saved for the saints' days and they burned quickly and were gone even before they could be appreciated.

Melisende had washed Benedicta and dressed her in her habit, the wimple and veil surrounding the old nun's face which had settled into the smoothness of death. Folded at her feet was the shroud in which the nuns would swaddle her like an infant after birth. And then, after a funerary Mass, she would be buried in the little graveyard at the foot of the orchard where in summer speedwell grew and the bees worked to fill the skeps with honey.

She wondered if Benedicta had confessed to Melisende and whether Melisende had been able to shrive her. It should surely be the job of a priest, not the infirmarian. Would Benedicta go to Heaven? Or would she even now be wandering the maze of Purgatory, waiting…

Maybe if she, Cécile, prayed all night on Benedicta's behalf, her dear friend would be received into the heavenly halls.

So Cécile began. All night, through each of the lessons, and then again. Then she would finger her beads and offer prayers to Our Lady, and then tired, her knees screaming, she would lever herself up, walk around the body, and then collapse on the stool, the bony caps clicking as she subsided.

She could not mark the passing of the Horarium because

the priory's bell had long since cracked and been removed before it fell. But there was never a time when the nuns did not present to pray the Hours away. Over the years, one's rhythms became habituated and one would wake at the required times anyway. Except for the novices who would often receive a discreet knock at their doors by Melisende, Benedicta or Cécile.

Perhaps Gisela's Lyonnais cousin might like to purchase a new bell for the priory. It could sing across Esteil, making the convent more of living thing, rather than something almost past its prime. Cécile would suggest it. She might as well make her presence felt if she was to travel that far.

She guessed it was Matins as she heard feet moving along the further reaches of the cloister. The soft harmonies of the sisters, muffled by the chapel's thick doors, wafted on the nightcold air and she murmured with them, knowing her time with Benedicta was almost at an end and that her own journey was inching closer like some maleficent shadow. She pulled the stool to her friend's side and sat, laying her arm down on the edge of the cot and pressing her forehead onto it.

'Benedicta, watch over me. Please?'

'*Soeur* Cécile! Wake up! *Soeur* Cécile!'

Cécile woke with start as a hand shook her shoulder. As she inhaled, she smelled incense and something else not quite so pleasant, feeling the unnatural cold of a dead body beneath her arm.

Benedicta!

She sat up quickly, rubbing her eyes, her mouth tacky. '*Mère* Gisela,' she croaked. 'I'm so sorry. I…'

'Don't fret. It was a long night and you were tired. I will take over now 'til Sext. Wash yourself and perhaps sleep till you are required in chapel.'

Cécile stood, pushing the stool back, noting the candles had gutted and that watery light showed through the doorway. Rain pattered on the new-formed rosebuds and vine tendrils along the cloister. A dribble of water ran across the paving stones and the Prioress's clogs had stepped in it and imprinted the floor as she entered the cell.

'Cécile, the novices did an excellent job of the *dorter* and the merchants are due by Sext. I have left Sister Adela at the gate and she will take our guests to their chambers. I will call for you after you have rested, to meet those who will chaperone you. Thank you for your vigil – I am sure Benedicta is glad you were here.'

'*Mère* Gisela, did Benedicta have confession? Is she…'

'Melisende heard her confession, Cécile. And whilst it is unorthodox, you must accept that she died shriven. In addition, I declared that each prayer we make, each Mass we sing will be for this gentle soul until after her funeral. We will also sing a Mass for her each week for a month. Also, no doubt you prayed for her passage into the arms of Our Lord, did you not? So all will be well. Go, Cécile. Not to put too fine a point on it, but you are dead on your feet.'

Cécile took a last look at her old friend before turning out the door to walk to the *lavabo* near the kitchen, to scoop up the chill water onto her face. Again and again, not worrying about the icy drops on her robes or that her veil and wimple became wet. She wanted to wash away her sorrow and pain. She held her hands in the water, allowing the cold to penetrate through to her bones, noticing how white her fingers were and how her short nails had arcs of dirt under them. From what? she wondered, and then recalled she had cut the tallow candles before they were lit and that she had the awful wax beneath her nails. She scraped one under another to clean them, glad that the sisters were at their duties as she had no wish to acknowledge anyone.

In the kitchen there was clattering and the sound of chopping and she guessed the two lay sisters they employed were preparing the pottage that seemed to be their lot until someone gave them some meat – a piece of venison or part of an aged pig, some tough old hen. It depended on what prayers the giver wanted said. It should have been the reverse, that the convent gave out alms to those in need, but apart from the infirmarian being able to help the sick, they could never afford to give anything away, living on salted meats and root vegetables through the winter and praying that spring and summer would bring better sustenance.

It was why she had savoured the wheaten bread and she thought of it now, her stomach rumbling. She realised she hadn't eaten since after Sext the day before and so she walked into the kitchen, the lay workers acknowledging her with bowed heads. It was surely an advantage of being the Obedientiary. She noticed there was a platter of crusts left from the breaking of the fast after Matins and she took some, along with a wrinkled windfall apple left from last autumn's crop. She turned away silently, walking further round the cloister, past the scriptorium, and to another row of cells until she could push her door open and slide, exhausted, into the severe room. She sank onto her cot and chewed mindlessly at the bread and then ate the apple which despite its striped leathery skin, was fluffy and juicy inside. It served to wet her throat and she gratefully slipped off her sandals, rubbed her cold, aching feet and chafed knees before stretching upon the cot. She knew she should have offered up a prayer but she was tired and surely after her vigil last eve, she could be forgiven.

Her last thought was of Benedicta and her trusting smile. She held it to her heart.

She woke to the sound of Sext drifting from the chapel.

Domine Deus, venerunt ad auxilium.
Domine, ad adjuvandum me festina nobis.
Gloria Patri: Gloria Patri et Filio…

O God, come to our aid.
O Lord, make haste to help us.
Glory be to the Father and to the Son
and to the Holy Spirit, as it was in the beginning,
is now, and ever shall be, world without end.
Amen. Alleluia.

Persistent rain dripped through the climbing vines of the cloister as the nuns sang. The hymnal wafted in between the dulcet drips and she found a curious lethargy in her limbs. It was the first time she had missed any of the Horarium in twenty-five years and perhaps it was Benedicta's death, but she realised that she too, was old and that maybe her time approached almost as quickly as the time of her departure to Lyon. Maybe, in some obscure sense, they were one and the same.

She might die before returning to her spiritual home.

But then there was Benedicta's smile…

She would be doing something worthy, would she not? Finding a way to save the convent.

Because whilst she had been a good sister, a strong Obedientiary, what had her prayers really achieved? She would never know in this life. But perhaps the journey to Lyon offered her a chance to achieve something infinite for the Prieuré of Esteil. Without overestimating it, to perpetuate the convent.

So perhaps, she thought, it would become her way of

illuminating the life of God and His Family as the Latin wound its mellifluous way through her mind.

Deus Dominus, et fecit omnia, Creatio autem divinitus conservaretur.
Et omnis corruptiónem mutanda…

Lord God and Maker of all things,
Creation is upheld by you.
While all must change and know decay,
You are unchanging, always new.
You are man's solace and his shield,
His Rock secure on which to build.
You are the spirit's tranquil home,
in you alone is hope fulfilled.
To God the Father and the Son
And Holy Spirit render praise:
Blest Trinity, from age to age
The strength of all our living days.

She pushed off the rough blanket that she had drawn over her shoulders in her sleep, and stretched. Readjusted her wimple and straightened her veil because she had collapsed on the cot in her robes. She went to the pitcher on the floor and knelt with a grunt, her knees inhumanly sore, and once again washed her hands and face. Would she be allowed to wash her body before travelling to Lyon? Even though she had only bathed two days before? Cleanliness was a requirement in the convent. Melisende insisted that for their health and well-being, they bathed regularly. She would leave a bar of rough soap by the buckets of water in the barn and each nun went in, one at a time, stripped off their robes and shifts, ducked their heads as the cold water was poured by

Melisende, whereupon she ordered them to take the soap and scrub their bodies. She would pour another bucket then to rinse them off and hand them a square of coarse linen to rub their bodies dry. She would inspect their vestments, smelling them, checking for fleas and lice and if she decided they were suspect, she would hand out clean garments and pile the dirty clothes in a corner.

Later, the novices would take the clothes to the wash house where one of the lay women would help them to launder and then wring the robes out, every hand chafed. They would drape them over trees and bushes in the orchard or on the hemp line that hung between an apple and a pear tree. The clothes would then be folded and laid with herbs in a chest in Melisende's infirmary. No one owned their robes, or their veils, their shifts or wimples. It was all shared, a rough, worn poverty that underlined their rule. Poverty was a given in their lives and they learned to live with what they had and to confess to greed and want if they strayed from the path.

Poverty, chastity and obedience... Obedience...

There was quite simply no option if Cécile was to honour the Rule as she had for the last twenty-five years of her life. She must go to Lyon. It was the wish of the Prioress and therefore the wish of her Lord. She patted the folds of her robes and pulled open the door upon the grey and uncompromising day.

Soeur Adela was walking past, her clogs leaving a trail of mud upon the damp paving stones. Filth dragged her hemline down and her face was puckered into a frown, her hands tucked into her wide sleeves.

'Blessings to you, *Soeur* Adela.' Cécile resurrected her customary expression, the one of stern teacher, the Obedientiary who commanded respect but on whom the younger sisters could rely if they so needed. 'Are you not meant to be in the scriptorium after Sext?'

'It was my turn to remove the kitchen slops and now I am wet and dirty...'

'Indeed. And we must not have dirt or anything like it near the new psalter. Go to *Soeur* Melisende and tell her I have asked for you to have a dry robe, then please hurry to wash your hands and feet. I shall be in the scriptorium when you are ready.'

Soeur Adela nodded and clipped away, whilst Cécile beat a path to the prioress's small apartments. She knocked, heard a soft *'Intrare'* from within and pushed open the door.

The prioress sat at a table surrounded by parchment, wooden covered ledgers and some heavily bound texts. A small illuminated bible lay on a lectern. Cécile would like to have examined it as she could not recall it being from their own scriptorium and had not noticed it previously. She liked observing the work of others but it rarely came their way. The light in the chamber diffused through an oblong window filled with horn – the priory could not afford the stained glass of places like Fontevrault.

'Ah, Cécile. Do you feel refreshed?'

'I do, thanks be, my lady. I... I was grateful to spend time with...' her voice trembled faintly and she coughed it away. 'With Benedicta. She will be missed. I am also grateful that I was able to sleep and now feel I am ready for what may come my way.'

'You say that as if you think this journey will be dangerous...'

'Relics inspire many things, *Mère* Gisela, not all of which are good.'

'True.' Gisela placed the sheet of parchment she had been studying to one side. 'I've been examining the ledgers that you so carefully manage and which I must take over whilst you are absent, yet I am not sure I have your skill. I see we owe you for much, Cécile. I cannot believe how well you have managed to keep the convent alive with what little we have in our coffer. You have kept much of the problem to yourself. Why is that?'

'I… Your job is to manage the priory and keep Fontevrault believing in our efficacy, my lady. You were never excluded from the truth of the monies, but I shielded you from the worst.'

You are a saint, Cécile. But now I need to know…'

'You see it before you, my lady.' Cécile could no longer hide the penurious state of the convent. 'The ledger shows little of anything because there *is* nothing. But if you are judicious…

'With God's help.' Gisela's face drew down. 'And a mighty alaunt to scare away the canons. But I suspect we are lucky that we come into spring and summer. At least we shall have fruit and vegetables. How you took us through the winter, I shall never know. You are, as I said, a saint who has our Lady's ear.'

In truth, Cécile had made sure that root vegetables and autumn fruits were hoarded in the cellars. She had made sure what little meat they purchased was dried and salted. Herbs hung everywhere like a wood-wife's house and which gave the convent a heady odour of rosemary and lavender. It was more often better than smelling those sisters who had a problem with odour, that was a surety! They drank watered wine and wasted not a drop in the chapel. Their candles were tallow, their bread mostly dark ryebread, not fine wheat bread. And so must it continue. Except…

'I thank you, my lady, which makes this next quite hard. I saw Adela returning from taking the kitchen slops to the pigs and before she went to the scriptorium, I had to ask her to change out of her muddy robes and to wash. We cannot afford for anything to ruin what we are working on. Not now nor ever, it being our only source of income. The problem is that we have so few robes in the chest. So if this weather continues and the sisters have nothing to change into after working in the gardens or orchard, then quite simply, we must halt work on the psalter and on the cope. We cannot afford new robes…' she waved a hand at the paper-strewn table.

'I see…'

'I wonder if we can ask our lay sisters to do more of the menial tasks, just till the cope and psalter are finished. I will have returned with a relic and your cousin, and by the grace of God, the convent's circumstances may then change.'

'But we cannot pay the lay workers…'

'Then pay them with whatever you can. Even indulgences. We still have a little food stored in the cellars and already the vegetables are growing with spring warmth. Perhaps the sisters can go out in pairs and raid the hedgerows or search for fungi. We must protect what we are working on, *Mère* Gisela. This could be our finest work and we can expect a goodly payment for the consignment.'

'Then we must do as you say.'

'Prioress, I won't be here to supervise. It must be you and Melisende. Melisende is a good scribe with a very light hand. Indeed, it is why she is a good stitcher as well. Between the two of you, you must keep the solar and the scriptorium working smoothly…' But then Cécile's eyes widened and she clapped a hand to her mouth. 'My lady, I apologise…'

'You speak your mind, Cécile, and I value that. Melisende and I will do our best, you can be sure, and with Our Lady's grace, we shall manage somehow until you can return and take up your role again.'

'My thanks…' Cécile looked down, embarrassed and feeling her belly turn as the anxiety of leaving began to stir.

'Cécile, if I may say, you have the makings of a prioress.'

Cécile met her prioress's gaze, knowing that the woman could be right. With her experience, her knowledge of the Rule and the texts, her familiarity with true convent life. 'That's as may be, my lady, but I am low-born, and no prelate or canon would deal with such as I. Besides, I am content as an Obedientiary. My service to God and Our Lady is as strong. No offence to you, of course.'

'And none taken…' A knock sounded on the door. 'Ah…I think it is our merchant and his wife. The ones who will chaperone you to Lyon. *Intrare.*'

A man and woman entered. And it hit Cécile like a stone from on high. Suddenly it was not just something ambivalent but a truth that would happen on the morrow.

Chapter Four

Henri de Montbrison
Venezia

The sound of Biddy with her chickens woke him next morning.

'Here, my little darlings, chuck-a-chuck.' She rattled grain in a pail. 'Where are your eggs then? I have a house of hungry men to feed and you girlies must help me...'

Henri smiled, rubbing sleep from his eyes. Adam, master-at-arms, called her the Mother Superior and one rarely crossed her without having to deliver her version of Hail Marys on bended knees. She had learned to use unknown spices and to cook 'foreign' food. One day they might have English food at table, or Arab, or even French, often Jewish to suit Ariella and her father when they visited. Whatever the case it was irresistible to Henri who valued a full belly after the privations of the Holy Land.

Sometimes, when the words "crusade" or "Holy Land" wended unheralded into a conversation, he felt the pit of his belly empty into his bowels. Having no time to prepare himself, he'd suck in a deep breath and hold it, until the fear dissipated. He hated it – this horror from nowhere, because he prided himself on being light-hearted and a good fellow, as well as courageous and an adept swordsman. In short, a valued member of an army. It was all he had known from the day his lord, Renaud, Comte de Forez, had provided a levy for his liege, Philip Augustus of France, to swell the Capetian army for Jerusalem.

Perhaps Count Renaud sought to earn points with God, because he earned little respect from the men he sent as they died in numbers too many to count. In the beginning like the others, Henri, a man of twenty years, had been excited, eager, as all young men are in the face of war, filled with a battle lust, blood coursing thunderously round their bodies.

Until the first body landed at their feet…

Henri found Messina parched after the green forests of his homeland. Initially, the size of the massed numbers of English and French forces merging to invade the Holy Land was inspiring, fuelling that bloodlust, polishing the idea that "God's Will be done".

But Philip and Henry, in their royal chambers, were at counterpoint over Richard's breaking of his betrothal to Alys, Countess of Vexin, Philip's sister. Antipathy from the royal chambers spread quickly downward like a dirty tide, onward through the ranks without stopping. Tension between French and English mounted.

Henri left his companions this night, keeping to the shadows away from English and French alike. He wandered far along the seafront to sit on rocks, watching the water sparkle like damascened armour in the light of the moon, knowing that in a few days they would leave for Acre and battles proper would begin. What was it like to face the Saracen? He'd heard they were skilled fighters, as swift as lightning. His stomach flipped over and his hand felt for the haft of his sword. As his fingers prickled, he longed for the day when he could truly try his prowess and training. And then he wondered if he could kill a man.

Surely it was why he was a part of this gargantuan force. He crossed himself.

But then, was not the Saracen the enemy? Was it not for God and God alone that he would stand with his fellows in a shield wall?

He heard shouts behind him, exclamations and the crash of metal, and turned. Back along the foreshore outside a tavern, a drunken mêlée had broken out, French and English hurling insults like boulders from a trebuchet. It sparked of all that men felt in the inevitable waiting game they all played, tension releasing like taut ropes snapping apart. Within moments, poles and swords clashed and men yelled as haft hit blade.

Henri had no thoughts beyond protecting his French compatriots. They were his fellows, and how dare those patronising Englishmen with their sandy-haired, rough-edged king insult the French force. Ten thousand men who would fight under the Capetian standard with pride. As he ran, he slipped his sword free of its scabbard, broaching the outer edge of the mêlée, thumping two fists and a pommel on the head of an Englishman with Richard's lion emblazoned on his tunic and who had stumbled against him. The fight ebbed and flowed as buckets of water were thrown over the drunk men and Henri leaped back to avoid a soaking.

One bedraggled Welshman wearing a leather arm protector snarled, jumping toward the man on Henri's left, a sly dagger glistening in the flamelight. Henri recognised him, an archer given to bragging about his skill when drunk. Worse, welcoming a fight.

'Twelve arrows in a half breath, twenty-four for someone like me, and every arrow buried to its fletching in flesh! No one like a Welshman!'

The man at Henri's side shrieked as the dagger sank into his belly and at that moment, Henri knew rage. His face burning, body rigid with battle fervour, he screamed an insult, drawing the Welshman's attention toward him as another bucket of water arced over them. Henri shook the water from his eyes to focus on the man's bloodshot eyes, smelling the sour wine and rotten teeth upon the archer's breath, the taint of an unwashed body heavy in the damp air. Henri's companion had collapsed, his hands clutching his belly, moaning as a shining dark stain pooled on the cobbles. Henri lifted his sword and chopped it down toward the Welshman's arm, but the archer batted it away with his dagger, sneering.

A dagger, for God's sake!

Fury filled Henri, who was sober. His hands vibrated with the need to strike and he swung the killing edge of his sword with such speed that the Welshman's sneer stopped in a grunt, the dagger knocked to the ground, the man falling back like the drunk he was.

But not enough.

The sword had slashed his side, slicing through tawdry linen, entering flesh with force as Henri's wrath drove it on, pushing the man back against a wall. He flipped his wrist and the blade twisted in the man's guts and then Henri pulled it free, the Welshman falling to his knees crying, hands clutched over the wide wound, blood gushing. He crashed forward, his head jerking and then lay still.

The mêlée had ceased. Men groaned and staggered away into the dark, bystanders melting into the shadows. But Henri stood, his sword edge bloody, two dead drunks at his feet. As the rage drained away, he looked this way and that, craving assistance, guidance, but the street was empty, water and blood forming slick rivulets draining to the harbourside and then dripping into the sea. In the distance, he could hear the Watch – a threatening tramp as opened doors were quickly closed and barred, and torches were dowsed.

Henri knelt to turn the Welshman over, horrified at what he'd done. Perhaps the man lived. If he could get help…

But the man's wide eyes stared beyond Henri, glassy with death. His guts spewed from the sword-stroke and threatened to fall on Henri's feet and he laid him down quickly, moving to the man the Welshman had stabbed but he too had departed this life. Henri looked at his own hands, now slimy with blood and he staggered backward, grabbing his sword, rushing to the sea-edge to puke.

Each time he closed his eyes, he felt the sword enter flesh, heard the sharp intake of a last life-breath. Why had he twisted his blade? What prompted him to kill the man so cruelly?

Pungent yellow froth surged from his mouth again.

Thus was his innocence crushed.

Henri de Montbrison, Frenchman and liegeman of Renaud, Comte de Forez, had become a man of war.

'Get up, you lazy bastard!' Henri's blanket was ripped from his cot and thrown into the corner.

'God's toenails, Toby!' Henri sat up with the shock of the cool morning air.

'You lie about any longer and Gisborne will be kicking your time-wasting arse out the gates. He sent for you. He wishes to talk…'

'How long ago did he send for me?' Henri jumped from the bed, splashed water on his face and dug into the oak chest, searching for fresh hose and a tunic. Gisborne abhorred uncleanliness.

'Before we broke our fast.' Tobias took Henri's sword belt, running his thick, short fingers over the intricate tooling. 'Nice belt. Where did you get it?'

'Genova.' Henri grabbed it back and encircled his tunic, patting the sword sheath to lie by his thigh. 'How long, Toby?'

'A while? The bells were ringing for Tierce, I think.'

'Christ!' Henri ran his fingers through his hair, grabbing its length and slipping a leather tie around it, binding it away from his face and running through the door, leaving his usually neat chamber as if a rout had happened. He could almost feel the warmth of Tobias's grin on his back.

He ran across the forecourt of the villa, through the large wooden door and into the hall, tripping over William's dogs lying in a beam of sun. Amidst yelping, Gisborne leaned against the hall table, the lines from his long nose to his set mouth implying a less than patient demeanour.

'Montbrison!' His face split into a sardonic half smile. 'You honour me with your presence.'

The acidity of his tone was not lost on Henri. 'I apologise. Tobias has just woken me…'

'You had a late night.' A statement, not a question and filled with as much retribution as Henri could imagine.

'No, 'tis just that I slept too long.'

'Were you sick?'

I had a dream, but this one wasn't a nightmare...

'No…'

'Consult with Mehmet if you have a problem. Come to my chamber. I need to talk with you.'

Mehmet? What can he do about women, night-frights and alarm?

Gisborne spoke of the Arab doctor, another of the company, a man Henri liked. He had quarters within the villa and held the family together through all manner of ailments. They passed his rooms along a cloister, and turned into Gisborne's work chamber. The work table extended along one wall under a south-facing window. The room glowed with golden light from the east-facing entrance and birds chattered from the vines that grew along the Roman arches. It reeked of peace and harmony and a quiet prosperity. No one would know that chests of monies had been made by devious means and true. That secrets had been sold to Barbarossa, to the Russias, to Philip Augustus and Richard of England and even the Byzantines. Because the disguise was a thriving merchant business, goods the like of which western and northern countries craved. The finest silks from beyond the deserts, gems and mineral pigments, spices, wines, skins, artifacts…

Gisborne sat at the table and gestured for Henri to seat himself on a folding chair. It responded to Henri's weight and height, timber creaking as its legs spread a little further upon a dark skin rug. Gisborne opened a wood-covered ledger, standing an inkpot precariously to stop it snapping shut.

'This,' he said, acknowledging the book, 'is the inventory of our most recent shipment. In it, there are things – various hides, bales of cloth, pigments and a chest filled with artifacts.' He leaned forward and Henri had the feeling he was being taken into a confidence, something secretive. Political? 'The chest is … intriguing.'

'You say, sir? How so?'

Gisborne sat back and crossed a finely hosed leg on his opposite knee. He fingered his boots, the leather so supple it had fallen into soft folds around the ankle. 'We've never dealt in such artifacts before, Henri. We've bought and sold pottery, carved ivory caskets, inlaid chests, glassware even. This,' he gestured toward the inventory, 'is altogether different. Tobias stumbled across something that I think might be very valuable.'

'I am Comteintrigued, sir.'

'We appear to have relics, Henri.'

'Relics!' Henri laughed. 'How many dog bones do we have in our midst?'

Gisborne's mouth twisted. 'I may have said the same once, but these are not saintly bones. Nothing like it.'

'I swear you will have me twisting off my seat with anticipation.' Henri grinned, thinking Gisborne toyed with him.

'Tobias has sourced…' He frowned as if unsure how to describe the commodities. 'Artifacts, shall we say. From Jerusalem.'

'What sort of artifacts?' Henri was intrigued with Sir Guy's hesitancy. Here was a man who had made a living from being assured and confident and yet…

'Old plant trimmings. And silk…'

'Plant trimmings! By the saints!' Henri snorted. 'I mean no disrespect, sir,' he quickly added and then shrugged his shoulders, perplexed. 'But silk? We've had ells of silk through the house in my time with you…'

'Indeed. But this… this may be different.'

'I'm confused,' Henri sighed.

Gisborne got to his feet and strode to the door. 'Come with me to Saul's house. Fetch Tobias and meet me at the punt.'

As the bastard son of a loose-pizzled lesser Forez relative, a petty nobleman in so many ways, Henri had to fight for any sort of privilege. He had proved himself reliable, a trait he used time and again to set himself above penury and to earn his way. As a young man and because his peers did and because it was the right and proper thing and expected of every Christian of every age, he regularly attended Mass. He spoke occasionally with the priest who recognised a willing mind in the young man. Thus, Henri had learned basic letters, a valued commodity where more titled men could read nothing and write even less. He learned parts of the Bible, for the priest had nothing else with which to teach him, and it was this literacy, the affinity with Latin, his affable nature and his former war training that made him a suited Gisborne man. There was not one who could not read and write in the company – a decidedly rare skill, but it paid its dues handsomely and Gisborne returned the favour.

Henri sucked in a lungful of the lagoon air, the moist, heady mix of mud and salt, and feeling more clear-headed, he walked swiftly to his chamber to grab a cloak. As he re-entered the forecourt, he heard William shrieking with childish laughter, the dogs barking, and he knew that Tobias would be the root cause. He passed into the storage room where Biddy stored the dirty washing, and where Toby now sat, head wrapped turban-like with one of the infant Lucas's clean swaddling cloths. Looking like an Arab from Jaffa, he was, in story-telling fashion, a *djinn* filled with magic, one of the many legends he hoarded for his songs.

'Good morning, William,' Henri said, pushing the dogs down. 'Settle,' he growled and they fell away to sit at his feet, heads tilted and attentive. 'Toby, you're needed. Hurry!'

'By the saints, Henri, they adore you!' Tobias looked ridiculous, the swaddling precarious upon his head.

Henri scratched them behind the ears and they melted and lay prone. 'Gisborne wants us to attend him to Saul's. He's waiting at the jetty.'

William groaned and Tobias pulled off the swaddling, telling the boy he would return soon and they would continue the story. He flung his own small cloak around his shoulders and they hurried to the jetty where Gisborne waited, already seated in the stern of the small boat.

'Morning again, Sir Guy,' said Tobias. 'Good day for a bit of boating. Nice and calm.'

Gisborne grunted. 'Get in the boat, both of you. Toby at the bow, Henri, you row.'

Tobias jumped into the bow and sat, hands gripping the seat, knuckles bone white. Boats and water had never suited him although he pretended to a level of seamanship and in front of Gisborne, he assumed a doubtful nonchalance, so Henri untied the boat and flung the rope at him. Catching and coiling the rope would keep unseaworthy minds busy Henri reasoned, and then he stepped aboard and sat amidships, bending to the oarlocks and slipping the canvas-wrapped shafts of the oars down so the blades sat in the water.

With the three men aboard… well two and a half, thought Henri, there was little freeboard in the punt and he was glad of the satin surface of the *laguna*. He dug in his oars and rowed toward an islet closer to the centre of Venezia where flat wooden bridges joined marshy land to marshy land over flaccid canals.

The islets were edged in reeds and sedge and both estuarine and ocean birds piped and cried, skidding in over the surface or flapping away as the boat passed. On the wider water, other vessels skiffed here and there with purpose – some with just a person or two aboard, paddled and poled, others with a small triangular canvas flapping loosely in the breeze-lack. Many were loaded with goods – loaves of bread, bags of grain and flour, sides of bloody meat dripping into the water and swooped upon by seagulls eager for an easy meal. The standing boatsman would swing his punting pole at the birds and then dig into the water and mud without missing a beat. Landward, people led ass-pulled carts over the bridges, better dressed folk rode horses, and scattered all around on the low land of the islets was foot traffic, steps beating a muffled rhythm on the wooden crossovers. The odd litter, prosperous merchants draped in fine wools and damasks, notaries in their long black tunics, clerics in earth colours or faded ebony.

Busy, thought Henri. More so than Gisborne's pleasantly isolated islet.

He paddled toward Saul's house, a revived Roman villa, a prosperous building with moorings extending into the canal. Henri made for this, telling Tobias to jump ashore with the rope and make them firm. Tobias leaped with acrobatic grace, legacy of his Parisian training as a jongleur and minstrel, then moved along the jetty to a set of stone steps which led to the villa. The stones were worn with centuries of feet, slippery with the raising and lowering of tides, and the smell of weed, mud and humid airs filled Henri's nose as he followed the diminutive minstrel and the merchant into the Jewish merchant's house.

'Guy, you're earlier than I expected,' Saul pushed himself up from his work-desk. 'Come in, come in! Tobias, I thought you'd be knee-deep in child's play with William. And Henri, how good it is to see you again. I thought you were still in Genova.'

Saul's hair was almost white but he stood tall and unencumbered with the bone-bending of age. His face though, told a different story and there were many lines – laughter, sorrow, immense problem-solving. Like any Jew's, his was a troubled history. Whatever Henri had heard about the York Massacre and about Ariella's and Saul's peripatetic journeying toward Venezia, had come from Adam's lips. Quietly, over the trestle in the yard at the back of the Gisborne villa, when all their weapons and leathers lay in disarray as they cleaned them.

'They suffered, Henri. Ariella lost her mother and indeed thought she'd lost her father in York. Christ knows how they both got out alive when others were not so fortunate. In any case, they left England forthwith and Saul began his search for a safe place where he could live and trade. And by the Saints' nose hairs, he believes it's in this mouldy place. Thinks it has a great future. Love to know how he's scried that one from the mud and sedge. Christ's toenails, one could rot if one stayed amongst these moist bloody airs for too long!'

'And you think England is any better?' Henri asked as he ran lambswool down the fuller of his sword. Beautifully crafted, that gleaming, sweeping dip in the blade had made his sword a beauty to handle in the long days of the crusade. The sun glinted on the metal, satin-like with the oils left behind from the fleece.

'Well, maybe not London. Smelly and damp, I'll grant you. But you can get out into the countryside. Jesus, even climb a hill! Here, I always feel as if I'm halfway to drowning!'

Henri laughed. In truth he too found the flatness and forever-damp airs of Venezia trying, and was always glad when Gisborne sent him elsewhere. Except for leaving the lovely Ariella behind…

'Methinks, Henri, that you have an eye for her. All well and good, I agree she's a looker. But be warned. She broke into a thousand pieces after Messire Guillaume's death. It was only the journey to Constantinople and then the babe that lifted her from the mire. Tread lightly, my friend. She's loved by us all.' Adam thrust his sword into the scabbard and then began rubbing at buckles. 'Don't ripple the waters.'

'You have come to examine the cargo again? To show Henri what Tobias and Ahmed shipped back this voyage?' Saul spoke over his shoulder, busying himself with pouring wine for each of them – wine from Cyprus and smelling of the heat of summer days and with the flavour of oak wafting through. He passed the crafted glass goblets around and Henri imbibed, momentarily closing his eyes and remembering Cyprus as he had last seen it. Peaceful, sleeping in the sun, far removed from the blood-stained sands of Jerusalem.

'I thought it might be easier to show the goods to Henri, rather than try to explain…' Henri had rarely if ever seen Gisborne lost for words and watched the man run thumb and forefinger down either side of a patrician nose. Was the man reticent about this new cargo? Henri was beyond intrigued – excitement began to stir his blood, a spark lighting a dark corner made of shadowed memories.

'Then drink up and we shall head to the warehouse. I have the guards on duty day and night until we decide how we must handle this.'

Gisborne tossed his wine back and stood and he and Saul moved to the door. Toby and Henri placed their goblets on Saul's table and Henri muttered, 'Do *you* know what you found in Constantinople? What's the big secret?'

Tobias's lips tilted, not a smile exactly, as he replied, 'You'll see.'

They hurried after their superiors and caught up with them as they passed through Saul's richly tended garden, past doves and trickling fountains, through a thick wooden door set in heavy stone walls and where two men built like stone privies saluted Saul and stood aside. The guards piqued Henri's curiosity even more.

Light drifted in from high set windows that opened onto the garden, and the fragrance of chests and sacks of spices filled their nostrils. Cinnamon, cloves, frankincense, pepper, cumin, anise, carraway, mastic. Henri's senses swam.

He knew of men who indulged in the poppy, who sought a life of hazy dreams and heady experience. But he felt all one had to do was sit in this warehouse for a length of time and breathe deep, maybe suck on a good wine – the experience must surely be the same…

Stacked in even rows against the other wall were bales of cloth wrapped in coarse burlap. Henri had worked for the company long enough to know such bales contained silks – some heavy, some light-as-a-feather and sheer as a wisp of mist, embroidered and plain, but the commonality was their journey from beyond Khorasan where camels plied trails and had done for centuries. Sometimes, Henri would be breathless, thinking that if he had never joined Gisborne, he would have forever believed the world existed either in France or the Holy Land. In this warehouse, he had proof the world was larger, more exotic than he could ever have dreamed. It shook his soul to the core if he thought about it – shaking his beliefs like the last leaves from a winter tree and leaving him as vulnerable as the denuded branches.

Saul had moved to a chest and was unlocking it, slipping the heavy ironmongery from the latch. 'I *do* like the smell of sandalwood,' he said, apropos of nothing, laying the lock on the floor with a dull clatter and pushing up the lid of the chest. 'Things have travelled well within.'

'What things?' Henri blurted. 'What magic do you conceal in there?'

Saul looked up, his face in shadow. 'Something so rare, so filled with history, Henri, that even now I am speechless. Guy, I think you must unwrap it. I am a Jew, you are Christian. It seems right.'

Saul had spoken with a respectful reverence and through all of this, Tobias had remained quiet. Henri looked at him but he just shrugged as Gisborne reached into the chest and pulled out an ivory box, much carved and ornate.

He placed it down on a small trestle and the men gathered around him as he opened the casket. Inside, wrapped in dirty linen, were two small packets and he began to unroll the first gently, until the folds of linen fell away and an object lay on his palm. Henri tried to see round the broad sweep of Gisborne's shoulders and thought he glimpsed a shred of wood, a shard perhaps. Unremarkable.

Gisborne placed it on top of the linen and began to unroll the second package equally gently. Henri had never seen his lord and master behave in such a contained manner. Always matter-of-fact, almost dismissive. Volatile even. But this behaviour was as tender as a father with a newborn babe and the atmosphere in the room became so airless Henri expected an indrawn breath might suck the life out of the place.

Another decayed piece of … what?

Finally, the other packet was opened to reveal a flimsy piece of linen. Gisborne unfolded it carefully – a piece of worn and tawdry silk lay upon its surface, if it was indeed silk, the condition so aged.

Gisborne turned to his companions, leaning back against the table, one foot crossed over the other at the ankle. 'We are told that when Christ was taken down from the Cross, He had family members to see Him cared for and shrouded. One, Mary, His mother, washed Him with Her own veil…'

No…

'We seem to have a part of what is a very old veil. The

cloth is *byssus* from the Mediterranean and you all know of its inherent value as we've sold that type of cloth before. It's as rare as Biddy's hens' teeth. It's quite possible that the Blessed Mary may have purchased some for Her veil because the history of the weaving of the cloth does indeed go back to biblical times. Or perhaps someone honoured Her by giving Her a veil of rare fabric. We'll never know.'

'Are you saying,' Henri sputtered, 'that it's *Mary's* veil? That's impossible! How do you know?' Goosebumps lifted on his skin. He looked around the group, fastening his gaze on Tobias who stared back, impassive. 'My God,' Henri continued in the face of the profound silence. 'I feel as if I commit blasphemy even looking at it. How can you be so sure? And what will the Holy Church say?' A line learned from the old priest of his childhood filled his mind. From the Gospel of Saint John: '*Standing by the cross of Jesus were his mother and his mother's sister, Mary the wife of Clopas, and Mary Magdala…*'

He could not have been more stunned than if Gisborne and Saul, even Tobias, had smashed him across the head with a stave.

'This is why,' said Gisborne, turning back to the cloth to reveal the silk, fingering it with delicate care, laying the remnant across the table. 'It's only partial, but what can you see, Henri?'

Henri moved in closer.

The aged and stained fabric lay in a beam of light from the windows. Frayed edges and pulled thread added to the venerable impression. Henri sucked in his breath, his head light.

Across the centre was the imprint of a foot, man-sized, and through the centre of the foot a darker stain.

Henri looked around at his friends. He could not articulate what he saw and shook his head in disbelief. Tobias nudged him.

'Do *you* think it could be a man's foot?' the minstrel asked 'A man who has been crucified? A man whose foot was wiped or encased by a fold of this cloth?'

Henri stared at the fragment again. 'Perhaps,' he replied unwillingly. 'But the fabric could have been painted upon…'

Gisborne nodded. 'True. Except that *byssus* has properties that prevent such a thing. The fabric is always a golden-harvest shade. It never varies. Look you, even a thousand and more years later, this cloth is still palest gold.'

'I concede, my lord,' Henri said. 'But how do you know it's… the Blessed Mother's veil? What proof? That foot image could be that of any criminal.'

'Indeed. And we are unable to prove that it is what we say. Except why would a lowly criminal's foot be imprinted on high quality *byssus?* And then there are the other packets.' He waved his hand in the direction of the other two objects and Henri bent over them.

One was exactly a splintered shard of wood as he had thought, so old it barely held itself together.

The other?

Near Jerusalem, he had seen shrubby trees with thorns, the pricks growing in pairs. He had used a straight thorn himself to dig out a splinter from his sole as his boots wore to shreds and the harsh terrain made its presence felt. The Arabs called the tree *sidr*. Christians spoke of it with a distasteful reverence, calling it colloquially Crown of Thorns.

'I know it,' he said levelly. 'But it could…'

'Could be from any Crown of Thorns?' Gisborne asked. 'My thoughts as well. But then you have the splinter next to it. Part of the Cross, you think? They say it was made of cypress, pine and cedar. Smell it, even now it has that aroma. I think this might be a piece of the *suppedāneum* – the footrest on the Cross where our Lord's feet were nailed. Of course, I am only posing the possibility. But when you see the image on the veil, the thorns, *and* the splinter…' he was unable to finish the sentence and Henri thought that maybe the disenchanted knight of former times was more spiritual than he wanted the world to know.

But what about he, Henri? What did he think as he gazed at the three relics?

Relics? My God, we will have the Christian world seeking them out with murder and mayhem if they are real. The Holy church would want them in Rome. The Eastern Church? Surely, they would want them returned to Constantinople…

'How…'

'Did we secure them?' Gisborne continued. 'Tobias was wandering through a market, as he will tell you.'

'Can we sit, Saul?' Toby asked.

The old man indicated the bales of cloth. 'Of course. Make yourselves comfortable.'

Toby hefted himself onto a bale and sat forward, swinging his short muscular legs which were clad in dark hose. He clasped his hands together, the light from the windows catching on a gold ring with a dark green stone, and he began.

'It was my second last day in the city. We had a cargo-load of many beautiful things –the kind of goods with which we make our name. Ahmed was purchasing the last of our supplies and I was just wandering through one of the local markets in the Venetian Quarter, near the Church of Saint Akyntos where my brother is buried.

I came across a stall selling icons, very beautiful ones, and I bought some for the company. I told the stallholder that I need them wrapped safely for sailing across the seas and he took his time dealing with each one, I swear as if they were filled with the Divine. Folding this way and that with linen and then oiled cloth. But it was a calm day, warmish, his canopy was shady, and so I sat on a stool under the canvas and just gazed at all the faces staring back at me. They were mostly of the Virgin and Infant and the colours radiated purity. The blues, the golds…' He sighed. 'But I digress.'

'On the trestle at which I sat, there were a number of other things – prayer beads and crosses, gilded and gloriously rich. I almost purchased some of those. Maybe next time…' Tobias stopped for breath and looked at Gisborne who nodded. 'At my feet was an open moderately sized chest, sandalwood,' he indicated the one that Saul had first opened. 'And inside, another smaller casket, as you see.' He indicated the smaller casket the Jewish merchant had carefully prised open. 'As you can see, it's ivory with carved reliefs of early Byzantine warriors. It's quite lovely really and I asked the purveyor if it was for sale. I had a feeling it might fetch a good price back here. The man said yes, but that the lock was sealed shut, the key lost and thus it remained closed. I couldn't imagine that it would be a problem with the kind of lock-pickers we have amongst our crew and so I asked him the price, we haggled and along with the icons, I eventually had a casket to take back to the boat. I didn't think any more about it until we were well into the Sea of Marmara and Ahmed came to me with the thing in his hands. He said he believed there was something inside and that he could force the lock at which I said to do it with care as the carved ivory was valuable.'

Tobias was a superb teller of tales. It was not hard to imagine, the box, the ship and its captain – a warm day upon the waters past the Horn, Pera and Galata.

'He fiddled with a tiny piece of metal,' Tobias measured with his fingers. 'Like a woman's hairpin, and I left him to it, retiring to my sleeping roll and my songs as any sane man would. But in the middle of that night, he woke me to say he'd done it and that I might be interested in the contents. He had found a name carved into the inside of the lid, you will see it if you look – Xylinites. For some reason the name is familiar but I can't remember why. Anyway, inside…' his brows creased and he licked his lips. 'Well, we unfolded everything in the light of the flame and Ahmed commented on the *byssus*. But when he saw the imprint of the foot, he sat back and unusually for Ahmed, who has an opinion on everything, he said nothing, not a word. All *I* could manage was, "By the blood of Christ!" to which he finally responded in that bass voice of his, "Indeed". I'll be honest and say that from the very beginning I believed we had stumbled across something quite profound.'

Gisborne stirred, a black-clad presence who straightened from his seat. 'Let me stop you a moment. Do you think anyone observed you transferring the goods to the ship?'

Tobias' mouth twisted. 'I doubt it. We had loads of goods – bales, crates, sacks. Who would know? No, I am quite sure...'

'*Quite* sure?'

'I think so.' Toby visibly squirmed under Gisborne's interrogation. Henri raised his eyebrows and then looked at his own toes, wriggling them in his boots to take his mind off Toby's embarrassment.

'You *think*?' Gisborne's voice changed and Henri was reminded of the way a breeze strengthened.

'Alright!' Toby banged his fist against his thigh. 'You know something. Say and be done!'

This time Henri's eyebrows reached for the rafters. He'd never heard anyone raise their voice to Gisborne.

'Obviously,' Gisborne said as he leaned back against the silk bales, 'Ahmed did not tell you that another ship shadowed you all the way to Venezia. Even mooring close by.'

'No...'

'It is as well *one* of my men is alert then, isn't it? Instead of being lost in the romance of an artefact.'

'My lord...' Toby tried. 'Many ships followed us. We sailed on a common trading route. We weren't accosted and had a smooth voyage...'

'And yet, when that nondescript ship moored, one of its

crew stood close by where our goods were being unloaded and even more remarkably, two Templars left the ship. Did you not notice them?'

'I did. The white cloaks rather give them away,' Toby remarked, his face sullen. 'I have no love of the Templars,' he glanced at Gisborne, 'for very obvious reasons, *if you remember!* I was just glad to see them on their way.'

Henri recalled the Holy Land and the fierce fighting spirit of the Templars. He had every reason to hate them but would never tell, and tried to drag his mind from the desert sands. He broke into the conversation as he stared again at the three venerable remnants. Awed, shocked, disbelieving? All of those. 'Why Constantinople?'

Toby took a breath, glad of the change in timbre within the room. 'It's a veritable treasure trove of relics. Few of course are genuine, although how do we really know?' He looked at them all. 'Seriously, how *do* we really know? Saints were regularly dismembered on their deaths and bits sent everywhere. In any case, before we sailed, I visited my friend, Father Symeon of Sancta Sophia. We talked of many things and in the course of conversation, I asked him if there were relics within the basilica, or indeed inside any other basilica in the city. In the ensuing conversation, he told me about the greatest relic of all which had supposedly disappeared from the city many years before.'

Tobias sat back and quaffed some of the wine that Saul handed him and then, obviously aware he had an enraptured audience in the palms of his hands, he continued.

'Amongst many other legends of the cloth of Mary, is one that states that in the time of Charlemagne, the Byzantine empress, Irene, presented a veil, reputed to be Mary's, to Charlemagne...'

'I've heard this story,' Henri intervened. 'It was supposedly held in Chartres, was it not? And did not the cathedral burn in 1194? And they saved the relic and are building an even bigger and more bold church to house it?'

'Ah, but it *is* it truly The Veil?' Toby said. 'Many churches *claim* to hold it. Even in Rome, they say they have it hidden safely away. But exactly what do they have?' He waved his palm toward the relics. 'Its value is immeasurable. Spiritually and fiscally to the whole Christian world.'

'Yes,' said Henri. 'So *is* this fragment from Her veil? Or part of the holy shroud?'

'Ah,' said Tobias. 'Good point.'

Saul stirred, his long angular body casting a shadow between the door-light and themselves. He walked to a crate and picked up a block of frankincense resin – the odour reminded Henri of Mass in Montbrison and of his priestly teacher, the man who took the time to teach Latin to a youth who perhaps should have been at sword practice.

'It is a good point,' said Saul. 'Christ would have most likely been wrapped in a linen shroud. And the burial cloths should have been left within the burial cave because by our religious laws, they would have been considered impure. That said, someone could have taken them. Jesus was a loved prophet of the people, after all. But,' he placed the resin back in the crate, sniffed his palms and then wiped them on his robes, '*this* fragment is silk, not linen.'

Gisborne sighed. 'It pushes our beliefs to the limit,' he said. 'Why would Mary wear silk? We are given to believe that Christ's followers were plain living. Is it Mary's anyway, even if she wore a veil of silk? Or is it a veil belonging to a Christ follower who tenderly wiped His feet as He was taken from the cross…'

'That could well be the truth of it,' Henri supposed. 'Matthew says that Joseph of Arimathea, who asked Pontius Pilate if he could take down Christ's body from the Cross, was a rich man as well as being a disciple. Perhaps Joseph wore a silk robe and this is part of it, or at the very least, a long silk sash around his robe that he used to wipe Christ's feet.'

'And how do *you* know such things?' asked Gisborne.

'I was taught to read and write by a priest and much of the Gospels were copied in my lessons,' Henri replied with diffidence.

'So we can assume that Mary's veil *is* in Chartres? Or somewhere similar?' asked Gisborne. 'And this is from one of the disciples?'

Henri looked at the imprint of the foot, the faded brown outline and the shadow of the nail hole. 'To be honest, I don't know…'

Tobias jumped off his seat. 'It *is* Mary's! Perhaps Joseph of Arimathea gave her a veil of *byssus*. And perhaps She wiped Her son's feet. Think on it.'

Saul interrupted. 'But Toby, at the time, women only wore head-coverings in the synagogue, or if they needed weather protection.'

'But what if Mary needed *comfort*, such comfort that a head-covering would provide as Her son died before Her eyes? A Mother watching Her son pass away in dreadful circumstances…'

The other three men were silent, each deep in their thoughts, a profound quiet as the three not-so-innocent relics lay before them. Finally Gisborne shifted.

'What say you, Saul?'

Saul frowned, ill at ease with what he would say. 'I suspect it *could* be part of the veil with which Mary wiped Her son's feet… Especially when you see the thorns and the wooden splinter… yes, it could be…'

'Could?' asked Gisborne, rubbing the length of the hawk-like nose in frustration.

'Could,' Saul replied, crossing his arms.

'Henri?' Gisborne turned to the Frenchman.

'Oh Christ. I don't know. It *could* be. There is enough within religious texts to sow seeds. And I agree with Saul. The thorns and splinter are rather telling. But if you are selling it, can you convince the buyer, that's the thing.'

'Oh, we can convince anyone of anything, Henri. But there's a little more at stake here because of the fact that Ahmed's ship *was* followed right into Venezia. Tobias, I will ask you what you think although you've probably already indicated your thoughts. And in any case, you will err to the side of a romantic ballad, will you not?'

'I hardly think Christ's death was romantic, my lord. Dramatic? Infinitely sad? Honourable? All of that because He gave His Life for us, remember. Legendary? Yes, most definitely, as there are dozens of legends that have grown in one thousand years, and therein lies our problem. Any number of legends,' Toby repeated. 'For example, the idea that Mary covered a whole congregation at the Blachernae Basilica with her veil. Really? Hah! For myself,' he approached the relics and ran a finger as softly as a butterfly wing over the imprinted fragment, 'I believe a mother would wipe her son's bleeding feet if she could. I believe a mother would succour her dearest and most honoured dying son in *any* way if she could. I believe Mary wrapped Her son's feet in an end of Her veil and if we could see back to that awful day, I believe She would have placed a mother's kiss upon the feet that walked leagues to spread the word of love to all.' He turned and looked at each one, his eyes bright and then he shrugged and walked to the door to look out at the garden.

Henri felt winded with the emotion of Toby's words but he wondered at Gisborne's silence and cleared his throat. 'And you, my lord. What say you?'

Gisborne's strong mouth stretched in a flat line and the steely gaze he cast upon Henri would have made a lesser man step back. 'I think...' he replied. 'I think that this is a small piece of a veil that belonged to Our Mother. I believe She probably did exactly what Toby said. I believe that this is worth a king's ransom to the Holy Church here and in the east, and do you know? I almost don't want to sell it. It's so precious, so infinitely touching that it almost needs to be hidden, to be buried away where none will ever find it. Perhaps back in the cave in Jerusalem.'

Saul spoke into the stunned silence. 'An interesting thought. Are you saying you don't want us to make money with this?'

'I suppose I am. It seems ... wrong.' Gisborne appeared at odds with himself. Always in command, always with a searing comment or command flying from his lips. His gaze lay on the stones at his feet before travelling to Saul's eyes, searching for an agreement. 'Don't you think?'

'In fact, yes. I do. But returning it to Jerusalem is out of the question I believe.'

'It probably is. But there is another solution and it pleases me. If it pleases you, Saul. I say we keep the thorn fragments and the splinters. They may be useful at some point in the future. But in respect of the veil...'

Tobias had turned and now walked back to them. 'You intrigue me...'

'Be intrigued then. Because this is between Saul and myself,' Gisborne dismissed Toby in an instant. Lord and master.

Henri grimaced at the minstrel as if to say, *Ouch*.

'Saul, I have had word from Jehanne. Her mother is going into seclusion for a time at a convent where her cousin is prioress, not too far from Lyon. The convent is on hard times and Jehanne and Amée asked me to source them a relic that might entice the pilgrims. This,' said Gisborne, indicating the tired, aged fragments, 'could well be what they might like.'

'Might?' cried Tobias. 'Might? If they don't, they're touched with madness!'

'Indeed,' said Gisborne. 'Saul, what say you to gifting this to a Benedictine convent?'

Saul smiled gently. 'Look around us. We're surrounded by such wealth that men might not see in their lifetimes. I don't need more wealth. Neither, I think, do you. These little packets have been the greatest things that I could possibly see in *my* own lifetime and if they can provide succour to a convent and to Christian pilgrims, I'm at ease. You have my agreement.'

'Good! Then Henri, I am sending you to Lyon along with Adam and a shipment. I don't pretend it will be an easy journey. What say you?'

'To the danger or the journey? Either way, I will do your bidding, my lord.'

'Good man!' Gisborne slapped him on the back as Saul carefully wrapped the relics and replaced them in the small casket, then in the bigger one and fastened the lock.

'And me?' Tobias pulled on Gisborne's dark damask sleeve. A little child begging attention, only this one a man with a linked history to Gisborne. 'I fancy a trip to Lyon, my lord.'

'Argue it with William and my lady wife and if they unchain you, you can go,' said Gisborne. 'Now, I wish to sort business with Saul so you two are welcome to return to the villa but leave me the boat, will you?'

The day had cleared.

The mists so common to the lagoon had risen skyward to dissolve into pearly blue. The water glistened, here and there it sparkled, little discs of silver flipping this way and that as the lightest breeze skirled across.

'Pretty place,' said Toby. 'God's light.'

'Mm,' agreed Henri, thinking that really it was like any other lagoon in the sunlight, but assuming it was something to do with the always enthusiastic aesthete who walked at his side. 'Toby?' he asked quite carefully, not wanting to intrude or offend. 'Do you really believe it is Christ's footprint?'

Toby stopped, fixing Henri with a look. 'I do. Did I not say?'

Henri nodded. 'Of course.' They began walking again, skirting round a mule loaded with sacks of straw and a tired boy leading it. 'I apologise. But can I ask… what… um… do you believe in God?'

'Christ's toenails!' Tobias stopped again but Henri pushed him forward, so they could get ahead of the mule and its load. 'By the Saints, Henri! Tough question for this time of day.'

'I know. But what we saw back there … it makes me question many things. Christ's foot in God's name!'

'I know. When I saw it on the ship, I felt…' he shrugged his shoulders, 'shocked,' he finished lamely.

They turned down the side of one of the watery alleys that made up the centre of Venezia, looking for a food vendor. They found an inn, a substantial stone building buzzing with the noise of tradesmen grabbing food and drink between jobs. They asked for their costrels to be filled with wine, purchasing a pie each.

Toby swallowed a mouthful. 'Pork,' he muttered between flakes of pastry. 'Not bad although Biddy would have added salt and pepper, maybe sage. As to God?' He spread a hand and rocked it from side to side. 'I lost my love of Our Father when my brother…' He sighed and it rattled up from his chest, smelling faintly of roast pork and wine. 'When my brother died…'

Died? Executed in truth. Killed by the Byzantines after being unjustly framed for the theft of an icon, thought Henri. Adam had alluded to the event.

'But,' continued Tobias as they began to walk again, heading toward the first of the flat wooden bridges that would eventually lead them to Gisborne's villa. 'I spent time with two men, both monks. Father Symeon of Sancta Sophia and Father Giorgios from Myrina on Limnos. Both men had a way of showing me God's presence, that the infinite power of God's love is all around. It may perhaps be how I found my way back from the dark and into the light of Gisborne-ben Simon again.' They walked in silence as the soft light illuminated Venezia.

Toby, ever loquacious, had warmed to his theme. 'Faith's a funny thing. We need it in times of *extremis*, don't we? For the rest, perhaps it's a habit, I don't know. I go to Mass, I like the ritual. But I prefer the church of my eastern monks, Henri. For me, it's kinder and has a resonance.' He chewed on the last of his pie, wiped his fingers and tipped the costrel down his throat. Then, 'What about yourself?'

They had left the business district of Venezia and were walking along a slightly elevated track, it could hardly be called a road, their footsteps beating tattoos on the bridges, then muffled in the damp soil of the pathways. Always, the waterbirds sniped and piped around them and not far away, in a small punt, a lone fisherman was casting a net. It flew like a murmuration and then hovered to settle gracefully on the surface of the water and then sink. They had moved on before he began to draw it in.

'God left me the moment I killed a man,' said Henri with some distaste in his tone, 'when I was on my way to fight the Christian fight. He has not returned. Nor have I sought Him out. Tobias my friend, we are a strange company in Gisborne's employ. War and loss of belief in humankind does that to a man. Adam thinks the way I do. Leo? Well, he *is* a Muslim and like Ahmed, I have seen him observe the call to prayer. Perhaps it's only disaffected Christians…' He frowned and thought on his lack. 'And yet I find myself thinking the words of the Paternoster occasionally. I feel no guilt for my duplicity and yet Mother Church would condemn me.' He threw the crust of his pie to the water and a flotilla of wild fowl paddled rapidly toward it, honking in anticipation.

'Then what about the veil?' asked Toby.

'Ah,' Henri bit his lip. 'Extraordinary…'

'You believe in the existence of God's Son, then?'

Henri had to smile. Who would have conceived that such a gentle day stretching before them across the lagoon would cause, he, Henri, a man of the world and a mercenary one at that, to tread the path of theology in soft leather boots and with a handsome French sword sheathed in a fine Venetian leather scabbard and slung from a beautifully tooled Genovese belt at his waist.

'Yes,' he answered. 'And strange as it may seem, and despite my apparent heresy, I do believe the veil to be Our Mother's. It's just…'

'What?' asked Tobias. 'That Mary, Jesus *and* God have deserted you? My Byzantine friends would say that the Holy Family has not deserted any of us at all. They would say quite simply as Matthew says, *Seek and ye shall find.* Ooh, Christ's Blood but my foot is sore. I'd kill for a boat ride home.' He held onto Henri's arm whilst he massaged his sole with his other hand. 'I must have bruised it on a stone.'

Chapter Five

The man had a woollen cap squashed between hands which sat on the prosperous curve of his belly. Somewhere beneath the corpulence, there was a girdle which jingled as he walked and from which hung a dagger and leather purse – or at least what could be seen of same. His lady wife was almost as rotund as her husband and her breasts were like pillows and she reminded Cécile of any number of wet nurses. She had a soft face of indeterminate age, her head veiled in a white coif and wimple, her *bliaut* a shade of murrey and girdled below her breasts with a twisted silk cord. Her lips tilted into a smile which doubled the number of her chins.

'*Messire* Gervasius, *Madame* Geltidis, welcome to our convent. Are you comfortable?'

'Thanks be, my lady. Just so. The *dorter* is clean and the bedding fresh and aromatic. And we had a decent meal in Esteil. I have a purse from our group to pay for our lodgings within your priory...' He unclasped the clinking purse at his girdle and Cécile hoped to God there was gold coinage therein. Passing it over to the prioress, he glanced at Cécile. 'We leave at dawn tomorrow, my lady...'

'Yes indeed. And this is *Soeur* Cécile about whom I spoke. *Soeur* Cécile, these are your chaperones for your journey...'

Cécile bowed her head in acknowledgement, quiet, respectful.

'She will be ready to leave with you and will meet you at the gate at Prime. We thank you…'

'It is an honour, my lady. We shall see her safe, won't we, Gelis, my love?'

'Of course we will,' the engaging little woman agreed. 'You shall ride with me, *Soeur* Cécile, in the cart. And you can sleep with me in women's quarters at our stops. We can have a little chat about things, can't we? To wile away the time…'

She smiled but Cécile lowered her gaze. The two were larger than life itself and quite robust with their speech. She felt overwhelmed and she hadn't even left the convent.

The Prioress stood and guided the merchant and his wife to the door. 'Our sister will see you on the morn, kind friends, but I must ask you to excuse me and allow me to give our sister her last instructions.'

'Of course, of course,' Gervasius said as he unrolled his cap and shook it ready to place it upon his head. 'We shall see you anon then?' He leaned round the Prioress to ask this of Cécile. She nodded and then cast her gaze to the ground again, conscious that she had just given the impression of the village idiot to the merchant and his wife.

Living as a religieuse for half of her life had changed her. This she knew full well. Whilst she would on occasion, venture into Esteil with one or other of her sisters for supplies, her life was essentially enclosed and it was the very nature of the enclosure that had appealed to her when she entered the convent. To leave Esteil and those who knew her behind.

She never missed the village, nor friends, and definitely not her family, and when she did go to the village, there was something of respect in those eyes that met hers. Not the dismissive whispering about a deserted betrothed who was widowed before she had even married.

The convent life was quiet, rigorous to be sure, but spiritual comfort had a lot to recommend it. The stringency was a trial until her body and mind adjusted, but she took such great pleasure in knowing she was secure and that at the given times of the day, singing praise. The sound, the lyrical liturgy, the sense of rising up closer to her Lord, of having Our Lady by her side. In the darkest cold of winter when snow piled up on the edge of the cloister and slid from the tiled roof in muffled thumps, she would shiver along with the others. But she had no doubt that succour would be provided and by the time she tottered back to her cot and slid onto the mattress which had chilled within moments of her leaving for the chapel, she would feel a warmth from her soul and heart. Facile? She thought not.

But she was no fool, nor was she an angel or a sister treading the path to sainthood – there were times where she was so angry with slipshod and lazy novices. Those who wasted the precious silk and linen threads in the solar. Or those who would knock a small pot of ground lapis powder to the floor in the scriptorium. She had a temper then, would punish the recalcitrant with hard work. Hating herself but knowing of no other way to impress upon the inexperienced that such items were almost worth a king's ransom and that it was difficult if not impossible for the convent to pay for more.

She'd hear the novices as they dried their chafed hands after completing loads of washing with lye soap. 'I hate her!' 'You mustn't say that!' 'It's true. She's cruel. My knees are scabbed from forever scrubbing the refectory floor!'

But then, Cécile thought, you will not waste our precious supplies again, will you?

She asked God's forgiveness for her authoritarian way and would take her penance, often kneeling, even lying with her arms spread on the floor of the chapel for whole nights.

The novices thought she was mad at those times. And yet they deferred to her and when settled within the convent, began to see the kinder side of the Obedientiary, appreciating her wisdom and her skill.

As Gisela had said, she had the makings of a prioress.

If not for having to deal with the outside world.

The outside world. The open spaces closing in upon her. No stone walls or heavy latched gates, no Horarium, venal people. No protection. Fear…

'*Soeur* Cécile?' Gisela's voice broke into Cécile's anxious thoughts. 'You seem distracted.'

Cécile blinked and pulled her gaze from the door through which the merchant and his wife had departed. 'Am I? I apologise.'

'There is no need for apologies, but if there is anything you want to say…'

Cécile examined the face of her prioress. The woman smiled, a genuine tilt of the lips, inviting confidences, and she was so tempted to just speak, unload her insecurities and be done. But she feared the consequences – the loss of faith that the prioress might have in her. Worse, that her dear friend Benedicta would be looking down from the right hand of God and shaking her head, wondering why Cécile's love for the convent wasn't as strong as her own, "Cécile," she would be muttering, "This is your chosen path. I would have laid down my life to be chosen to save this precious priory…"

'I think I'm just rather overawed,' Cécile replied with as much calm as she could muster, 'by the loquacious merchant and his wife. It will be a…'

'Noisy journey? A lot of gabbling? Yes, I feel for you. Our convent life is illuminated by the silences, isn't it? Ah,' she added softly. 'I know our world has its strictures and harshness, but in truth it is nothing to the outside world and here am I, the Prioress, throwing you to the wolves. Don't think harshly of me, Cécile.'

'I do not, my lady. But I am afraid of what I will find on my journey, yes, and that I might let you down. That said, I'm also aware of the need for you to stay here. If you were to absent yourself, I am sure that Fontevrault would close us forthwith. You, at least, can keep the wheels turning. They listen to you.'

'I am glad you see this is the case. But I need you to comprehend two things. One is that I trust you implicitly to do what must be done. And secondly, I am glad you are under no illusions. Relics attract interest. Both Christian *and* venal. I will pray for you of course, but in any case, I ask you to beware.'

Cécile's heart beat once, hard, like a loud tocsin but she merely nodded and slipped shaking hands within her cuffs.

Thus the last day followed its rhythm. Sext, Compline. In between, she checked on the progress with the cope and visited Melisende who kept a watchful eye upon the scribes until the prioress could take over.

The psalter glowed and Cécile watched *Soeur* Adela as she deftly applied gold leaf, huffing on the gesso gently and laying the gilt shaving over, trimming, burnishing. There was something innately spiritual in the way gold leaf lifted the lettering to the Divine. What was more, Adela had a way with her pen, translating life as she saw it into the margins of the book, or lacing in and out of historiated initials.

'That is perfect, *Soeur* Adela. And your design around the initial is translating well. You chose spring flowers?'

'Yes, my lady. They are colourful and surely a sign that Our Lady smiles upon the world when they appear in the hedgerows and on the paths.'

'The parchment?'

'Oh, it is *such* good quality.' The sister rubbed a hand against her nose, leaving a tiny sliver of gold leaf to sparkle like a benediction. 'The best we have ever had! But we may not have enough to finish, my lady.'

'Then I shall request permission from the Prioress to purchase more in Lyon.'

Although only God knows how to pay for parchment, a bell and anything else the convent needs...

Adela brushed at the gilt on the work with soft strokes and then picked up her quill, a bird feather cleaned and dipped in warm sand and then cut and shaped to her needs. She began to fill in the body of a petal with a vibrant lapis blue and again Cécile's heart sank, because she knew that Melisende had very little of the ground powder in the infirmary.

'*Soeur* Cécile, may I ask who this psalter is for?' Adela spoke as she worked, bent over the page like a bird protecting a fledgling.

Cécile wondered at the propriety of telling one of the lesser sisters. Knowing it was for nobility would surely breed pride and pride was a sin. But she wanted Adela to believe in her artistry and to thank God for it.

'A merchant's wife, I believe. Although, they have reserved the right to renege if it is not to their liking. It is why I am pleased with your choice of flowers and seasons, *Soeur* Adela. A gift from God, to be sure. Carry on.'

Cécile took Melisende aside to discuss the dwindling supplies, trying to give them all heart that she would return with a cartload of goods.

God willing...

Matins. She lay back on her cot but could not sleep as she counted down the time until Prime and dawn and her departure, her fingers flicking back and forth over her prayer beads. She was glad she had been present for the Easter celebrations with the poesy of prayer and incense and good candles, but the gladness sank swiftly and she became distraught that she would miss Benedicta's funerary rites, a tear sliding from her eye and which she dashed away. You're an old lady, she thought, allowing tears to run. Benedicta would surely prefer a happier frame of mind. But as the night cold began to penetrate through her mattress and into her spine, she wondered on the warning from the Prioress. She'd expected there to be danger attached to a relic. She was not naïve. But how much? Would her own life be in danger? Would she and Gisela's cousin have an armed escort on their return? She sighed and shifted on the straw mattress, releasing the fragrance of sheafed hay. She had refilled her mattress not long since but she knew that after the *dorter* had been prepared for the merchants, there was little straw left until harvest. Always a struggle.

Cécile had a small sack with a change of linen, a clean wimple and a veil. Her cloak, one only and threadbare, lay on a stool with a sealed letter to her merchant cousin from the Prioress. Nothing more. Her sandals were worn but would see her to Lyon on a wing and a prayer. What need did she have of anything else? She was a nun, an elderly woman by any standards. God would see her safe…

After the prayers of Prime, and after the Prioress had blessed them all, she spoke quietly to the small group, intoning Matthew's words, her eyes passing from one to the other and finally settling on Cécile.

'Do not get any gold or silver or copper to take with you in your belts,

no bag for the journey or extra shirt or sandals or a staff, for the worker is worth his keep.

Whatever town or village you enter, search there for some worthy person and stay at their house until you leave.

As you enter the home, give it your greeting.

If the home is deserving, let your peace rest on it; if it is not, let your peace return to you.

If anyone will not welcome you or listen to your words, leave that home or town and shake the dust off your feet.'

'Amen,' answered the merchants and began to take their horses' reins and mount up with a creaking of saddles and a shifting of shod hooves.

Gisela took Cécile's hands in her own. She sketched a cross over the kneeling nun and then it was time.

'Come, *Soeur* Cécile,' the merchant's wife called, patting a pad of folded cloaks. 'Here now, you sit next to me and our good grey horse shall pull us comfortably. She's a strong girl is our Issy.'

Cécile climbed into the cart, the smell of horse's farts filling her nostrils as the mare shifted on heavy shod hooves. She subsided onto cloaks of good wool, dyed to shades of verdancy and as she touched them, she marvelled at the softness, the course wool of her own robes settling over them – tawdry, worn, embattled.

'*Deus venire vobiscum!*' Gisela called as the cart pulled away, the group waving back and Issy, the stalwart mare being led by a servant. The cart groaned and creaked, pebbles shooting sideways as the wheels turned on the rutted and muddied road.

Cécile lifted her hand but if she was honest, she would have preferred to leave it tucked in her other sleeve and to sit with her gaze downward, instead of observing the ever-receding view of the stone Prieuré d'Esteil. They trundled past the blacksmith's, the smoke from his fire twisting up in a knotted skein into the misty vapours of dawn. The communal oven, where a wife carted logs to the fire. The woman stared as the procession passed her, her eyes fixed on *Soeur* Cécile. Cécile looked back. She knew the woman, but too many years had passed for the woman to care because she showed no acknowledgement, good or bad.

They passed other hazy daub dwellings set back off the road where geese honked and hens chucked. A dog barked on the end of a chain, violent, as if they represented danger, and a couple of children ran to the door of a dwelling that had seen better days, its roof collapsing at one corner and the children grinning and waving – little rays of sunshine in a grim day.

'At least it's not raining,' said Geltidis, waving her hand at the budding trees and tender green pastures and further at the shadows of the Forez surrounding them.

Cécile's heart thumped fit to burst within her chest as the edge of the village passed them by, Issy's ponderous hooves dragging them further away.

Deus venire vobiscum…

The smell of cesspits wafted toward the cart as it lurched along the track, but they turned a corner and left the odour to tangle with the branches of blossoming fruit trees. Geltidis and Cécile had both lifted their hands to their noses and winced, dipping their heads down as they passed through the miasma.

'Small little place, isn't it?' said Geltidis finally, as she tucked a linen kerchief into the fine leather purse at her ample waist. 'And such a lovely convent. Such a well-constructed and well-appointed building. How came it to be in the middle of nowhere?'

The middle of nowhere, thought Cécile. Is it? Is anywhere else so much bigger? She knew Conques was and had gasped at the size of the abbey when confronted on that fateful journey, but in truth, whatever else did she have to compare from her experience?

She had explored the outer edges of the village and the close depths of the Forez, but all she needed and wanted was within the priory walls, so the world, what there might be of it, didn't matter. Except to provide the solar with its cloth and thread and the scriptorium with its fine parchments, pigments and gold leaf.

'It is,' she replied, 'an almost macabre story.' She rather hoped the merchant's wife would shrink from such a history and leave Cécile to her thoughts and prayers.

But no, the woman clapped her chubby be-ringed hands together and crowed. 'Macabre? Oh how wonderful! You must tell me!' Her smile was so wide that her chins doubled even more and hung over the wimple, confined only by the edges of a crisp linen veil.

They had progressed beyond Esteil and were heading easterly along a track toward the incline of the shadowy hills that would lead them to the first stop of Ambert.

'It will be a long day,' said Geltidis, 'and we can perhaps help by walking on the steeper sections. It gives blessed Issy a rest from our weight.'

Given that Cécile was like a meat shank, all sinew and bone from the poverty and asceticism of the convent, she took the comment in good spirit.

'But in the meantime, you must tell me the story.' Geltidis leaned forward and tapped her on the arm.

'I only know what the gossips say, my lady.'

'Nevertheless, I would know. Come, come!' Geltidis settled herself like a broody hen and waited.

God's faith! Cécile's whole life within the priory had been one of quiet space, of speaking when spoken to, of offering instruction when needed and of prayer. Gossip might be what the novices indulged in away from the control of the Obedientiary, but she had no part to play in that. The Benedictine Rule implored silence, indeed demanded it. For how else could one think on one's prayers or commune with God without silence to explore the way? And as to gossip...

'We absolutely condemn in all places any vulgarity and gossip and talk leading to laughter, and we do not permit a disciple to engage in words of that kind...'

There were things Cécile had left behind with profound gratitude when she had become a novice. Not the least had been being the butt of gossip when her betrothed had died and his family ignored her, moving on. Unfortunately, she was now back in the world of men, albeit temporarily, and despite ripples to the calm of her life she could not be rude to this merchant's wife. She was a kind woman after all…

'Back before my memory there was the *Seigneur* du Drac. They say he was a cruel man to the people of Esteil and beyond, wanton and bestial. Madame,' she quickly added. 'I am a nun and do not wish to think on what he might have done. I am sorry.' She looked at Geltidis and the question the excited woman had been going to ask died on her lips. Cécile continued. 'If anyone crossed the man, his mode of justice was to burn or kill. God was watching and judging, I think.' Cécile lurched as the wheels of the cart rolled into a rut and then out again. Grasping the side of the cart, she continued, 'For some reason, I know not what, he repented of his ways…'

'Oh! Do you think he had a visitation?'

'No one says so but mayhap he did. Mayhap Our Father appeared before him and dispensed wise words. But whatever the case, he decided to go on a pilgrimage. Leaving his wife and a son named Bertrand behind, he went to the Holy Land and was away for a long time. Life in our village apparently quietened and everyone was able to live without fear. This went on until le Seigneur returned to his chateau, absolutely unrecognisable, worn with the vicissitudes of the Holy Land and its privations, but alight with a holy dedication. He asked where was his son and was told he was in the forest with his pack of alaunts. I'm sure you know what alaunts are like.'

Geltidis nodded, her hands clasped at her lips, eyes wide.

'The Seigneur found his son and begged for alms, hoping to see that his son had not inherited his former wild and dangerous ways. He did not say who he himself was, looking like a pauper and roaming in the forest. Instead, he asked for charity. Bertrand laughed at the sight of this ragged man begging within Châteauneuf du Drac's demesnes and he argued that the man was breaking the law and as he stood in his father's stead dispensing justice, he could only assume the vagrant before him was a thief, a poacher, and bent on ill-gotten gains. The old *Seigneur* denied it emphatically but still, wanting to see some goodness in his son, he knelt and begged again, in God's name. Bertrand, in a fit of rage, ordered his dogs upon the man and he was torn apart.'

'Oh,' Geltidis's pudgy hands had flattened upon her cheeks and her eyes glistened. 'But that is appalling. To deny someone begging for alms in God's name…'

'Indeed. But Divine fate would play its part. On returning to the chateau, Bertrand was told that his father, travel-worn and tired, had gone to find him in the forest to be reunited with him. Of course, he realised then what he had done and would have ended his own life forthwith. But his mother, now an aged woman, begged him to make recompense with the Holy Father, in order to be forgiven.

'He built the convent?'

'Yes. In the year of Our Lord, eleven hundred and fifty one. Thus it is a very young convent. He also built *La Chapelle sur Ursson*.

'God above,' Geltidis sat musing on what had happened and then, 'So you were a young girl when he killed his father?'

Cécile nodded. She would not admit how little she cared about le Seigneur and how all her days were spent surviving her own difficult father. 'Our convent is essentially under the control of the Bishop of Clermont, Robert d'Auvergne,' she said, 'as it is on land they nominally own, but because it follows the Benedictine Rule it is administered by Fontevrault. It is a very convoluted arrangement and not at all to our benefit. We are not a wealthy convent, Madame. It is why I travel to Lyon on the convent's business.'

'But surely Fontevrault or the Bishop of Clermont support you, Sister?'

'To a very small point, Madame. Never forgetting that we

exist on a piece of the bishopric's nominal land. It is believed we waste good money and that we should be closed down. I beg to differ as our scribes and embroiderers are second to none. But what will be will be.'

'Bertrand de Drac does nothing to protect you? You are within his demesnes after all.'

'Ah, but since when did Church and State communicate with ease? *Le Seigneur* attends the occasional Mass when the Bishop sends us a priest and he delivers candles or grain for Holy days, but generally no. He has a private chapel at Châteauneuf du Drac near Peslières, and I believe a priest lives permanently within the chateau. I am not sure of our route but if we are travelling east we may see it. They say it sits on the edge of a ravine.'

'Husband', called Geltidis. 'Do we venture near Peslières?'

'Not directly, no,' said Gervasius, looking over the back of his solid-rumped rouncey.

Geltidis turned back to Cécile. 'Ah well, never mind. We can imagine it, can't we? I like imagining things. It's sometimes better than the reality. Now tell me, how came you to be a nun?'

Cécile's heart sank. She had hoped for peace, to be able to meditate on her mission and on the convent. But God played games with her. He seemed to have other plans than reticence on her part. Thus, she told the sorry story of her betrothal and the happier outcome of her time within the convent in two short statements. She smiled and pushed her hands within her cuffs, looking down to her prayer beads, hoping the woman would take the hint. For some swaying time, whilst the birds trilled around her and budding green began to envelope them all as the forest grew close to the path, silence filled the cart and she looked up to see Geltidis, her eyes closed, her head sagged over her chins and a vibration of soft snores emerging. Cécile heaved an enormous sigh. She thought it must be close to Tierce and began her prayers.

After, she sat watching Issy's swaying rump and half listening to the talk between the merchants floating back in a dulcet rumble. Names of cloth – wool, silks of all weights, damask, silk velvet, dyes, and the names of merchants – Gigni, de Clochard. At that, her ears pricked up and she shifted a little, keeping her gaze lowered.

'Although if one wants to be correct, it is no longer de Clochard, but rather Gisborne-ben Simon. But to me, it will always be de Clochard as they've always served me well. They have a new shipment arriving from Constantinople,' Gervasius of Mons commented. 'Their cloth is to be vied for.'

'Yes, I heard that a new shipment is on its way. But we are tied to the Gigni and have never been let down.'

'Alexandrus Gigni is an honourable man,' Gervasius replied. 'I can't imagine you would ever be disappointed.'

'Indeed, and as we are only after cloth, it's always a safe bet that we will be well served. Think you to stay with cloth?'

'I believe so. Although, if de Clochard had something that took my fancy, I would not be averse to diversifying. But then it would have to fit with what we sell in Mons – trims and such. We are known as sellers of cloth after all.'

'As are we in Toulouse.'

The talk drifted onward then to the affairs of men – money, wine, the weather and Cécile found the swaying of the cart and rhythmic clip clop of Issy's wide feet to be soporific. She tried to keep her eyes open but God forgive her, it was hard. Glad that the subject of relics had not risen, she dozed…

Chapter Six

Henri de Montbrison
Between Genova and Notre Dame du Ratis

Henri liked sailing.

Unlike Toby, who had subsided to lie against the thwarts with wan face and limp body.

'How do you sail the seas for Gisborne and stay sane, Toby? Are you sick every time?'

'Yes and no. The first day or two kill me, but then I rise from the dead, so to speak. With sea legs and a feeling that I yet may live. I'm almost there, in case you wonder.'

'Thank Christ the seas are calm then.'

'Yes.' Toby belched and swallowed. 'God be praised. Henri, I like you a lot, I really do, but be a good fellow and just leave me alone for a few hours. Can you do that for me? I just need to... not talk.'

He belched again and smelling the foetid air rise up to his nose, Henri sketched a bow and moved away, smiling to himself. Tobias Celho was such a likeable and cocky little man, no one could take offence. And by the Saints was he loved by the Gisborne-ben Simon house! Henri considered luck smiled upon him that they were companions on this journey. A triumvirate of excellent men really...

'Ho, Henri!'

Henri turned around. Adam of London, Gisborne's master at arms was lacing between the cargo on the ship until he reached Henri's side.

'Still ill?'

'Just a little. Swears he'll be up and about in a matter of moments.'

Adam grinned, his fierce red hair blowing round his face in the seabreeze. 'He will, you know. He's a tough little bugger. I'd have him at my back any time.'

Henri nodded. He and Adam had become friends from the time long since when they had almost been killed outside Lyon. When Guillaume de Guisbourne had been hunted by a man who purported to be his friend. Henri and Adam had been wounded that day but the man who sought to kill them had died and his uncle, Alexandrus Gigni, the most successful merchant in Lyon, had taken the tidings philosophically under the circumstances. He claimed he knew his nephew was a wastrel and that the man's life would end in misfortune. A tragic story that bound the three, Adam, Henri and Tobias, together – the triumvirate. Companionship on the crusade was a force of circumstance and those who were left headed to their home hearths and Henri was no different. But Montbrison held nothing and serendipity threw him in amongst this brotherhood. It felt good. Reassuring.

'How is she?' he asked Adam, nodding toward the sterncastle.

'Settled. She sails well and apparently so does the babe.'

'I'm surprised a mother with a young babe should choose to make this journey when she can live in comfort. Even more, I am surprised that Saul allowed her. And then, even *more* so that she chooses to return to where the child's father was killed.'

'Indeed, but then you don't know her as well as we do. She is a force to be reckoned with, and courageous. Even if she wished to return as far as England with a babe, she would set her mind and do it. Besides, Saul will give her anything her heart desires after her tragic loss. Anything to keep her happy. And you must remember that she'll lead this company together with Gisborne when her father dies. She has a vested interest in Venezia, Lyon and Constantinople. She is on as equal a footing with her father and Gisborne as it is possible to be.'

'Adam, I grant you all that. But revisiting tragic memories will have the opposite effect, surely.'

Adam shrugged. 'None of us know how we'll react in certain circumstances, Henri. Would I ever return to England? Would you ever return to Montbrison? We all have different motivations and I would never pretend to know hers.'

'Yes, but…'

'Henri, I told you once before that it was unhealthy to become obsessed with Ariella. Listen to my words. Leave her be. We have more important things to discuss. The vessel behind us for a start.'

Henri leaned over the wale to look stern-ward.

High in the water and with a welter of sails for' and aft, a ship was far closer than the horizon. The moist and choppy wind pushed their own heavy cargo vessel through the water so that bow waves broke like surf and the ship's wake streamed in windrows behind them. But perversely, it almost lifted the lighter ship atop the wave.

'She's flying,' whispered Henri in awe.

'Indeed,' growled Adam.

'She bodes ill?'

Adam sniffed. 'Who knows on the high seas? Can you make out a pennant? A coat of arms?'

Henri blinked, the breeze blurring his vision. He blinked again and cupped hands round his eyes, the better to see. The sail bosomed and billowed and he would swear there was an emblem. There! A symbol!

Bold. Undeniable.

'Christ God!' he said and turned to Adam.

'The bloody Templars!' Adam slammed his fists on the wale.

'It might be innocent.'

'Maybe.'

Henri turned back to scrutinise the ship as it closed the distance between them. 'I didn't see the Templars in Genova. Did you?'

'No, but that means nothing.' Adam's face darkened with anger and Henri's belly began to writhe. The kind of nervousness that plied itself before a battle began in the Holy Land, when men pissed themselves and worse.

'Do you think they mean to board us?' he asked.

'On what grounds? They have no reason to. No, I just despise them. They have caused Gisborne sore problems in his life and mud sticks.'

'Adam, if they know of the relics and they want them, they have every reason.'

'True, but not even the shipmaster knows what we carry, so how would the Templars?' Adam turned away. 'I will talk with the Genovese.' He slapped the wale again and then wound his way between the bales and *barils*.

The journey from Venezia to Genova had been smooth. A short bout of heavy rain which kept them inn-bound for a day but in truth, Henri thought, the layby did Ariella and the babe much good. Lucas was a contented infant. He fed, slept, smiled and had begun to mouth odd sounds that had meaning only for he and his mother. The movement of the horse lulled him and if there had been any sign of distress, they would have used a cart, but Ariella maintained she liked him slung in front of her and if he was hungry, she could readily feed him. As far as Genova, the child had caused no problems and at sea, even less. Only once had

Henri heard a mewling cry and it lasted but a moment. He admired Ariella's mothering skills – as much as he knew about such things.

After the rains, grey glowering skies hung down with mist and denser fogs lying in the valley folds and an occasional cold breeze to remind them that spring might be there in the trees, the grasses and wildflowers, but that winter rested in the slopes of the mountains and still had words to say. Even so, it was not bitter and a cloak wrapped a little tighter sufficed. At other times, the sky had been as blue as a gift from God, the air still and smelling sweetly of new beginnings. If they were not within a group of merchants, tradesmen or pilgrims and whilst they rested the horses by the road, it was quiet enough that one could almost hear the hedgerows growing, the grasses thrusting forth, bees excited at burgeoning blossoms and birds chirruping, flitting and flirting and finally nesting.

Life was good.

They had decided early on that with the value of their cargo, they would as often as possible travel with groups, for in such numbers there was safety. They liked the merchants, found the pilgrims heavy going, and the tradesmen to drink and become argumentative at inns. The three had a story – Ariella was travelling home to her husband's family in Lyon. A truth, unarguable. And she *was* a representative of her father's merchant house. Also unarguable. Tobias was her minstrel and companion, not far from the truth, and Henri and Adam were her bodyguards. Also truthful in so far as it went. The fact that in the babe's small pack of vestments, there was a linen-swaddled scrap of veil was neither here nor there.

The men bantered as they rode, mocking and teasing each other. Tobias sang and whether they travelled alone or with a group, all listened, for his voice was exceptional and he had an unerring knack for choosing melodies and words that always charmed his audience, whether they were love songs or drinking songs, or a beautiful chant for the pilgrims who, if they didn't know the words, would join in with the melody of a haunting refrain.

But for the most part, Tobias recounted the eternal story of love – a *pastorela*. Looking sideways at Ariella, she would become his target and she would smile at him, blow him a kiss and the enlarged company would whistle and cheer. A story would emerge – a delicious nymph-like shepherdess, a lonely traveller. Tobias would single out a man, a comely young soul and sing as if from the man's own thoughts. If the young man was sensitive, a flush of rose would creep across his face and he would lower his head. Tobias would continue with the story – how the traveller used everything contained in his bag; tiny pieces of gold leaf, silver wire, perhaps a small stone that looked as if it might be semi-precious. All in an effort to seduce her. The young shepherdess, however, earthy and wise to the ways of the world, would let him down gently and the traveller would be sent on his way, chaste, his bag of goods empty and singing of the woman's charms, but wishing, always wishing.

'So despite that they say '*Vincit amor omnia, I regit amore omnia...*' Tobias would say, '*Love conquers all*, be wise my fellow travellers – it's not necessarily true.' Invariably, when the melody of his voice had wafted to the trees and the lyrics had been scooped up on the breeze to dissolve into forest verdancy, the travellers, pilgrims, merchants or tradesmen would be silent, and then a cheer would burst forth with requests for more of the same.

Tobias, reins in one tight hand would wave an acknowledging but precarious palm to his admirers, more often than not throwing a saucy wink Ariella's way.

Tobias on a horse was a sight. Not a natural rider and with the difficulties inherent with his size, he paid hard coin to acquire the easiest, smallest and narrowest mount in any livery. It was evident that at the end of any day on horseback, it was not easy for him. But there was never a complaint. *'Tough little bugger...'*

He always needed a leg-up and swore mightily if Henri thrust him too hard.

'Keep it clean, men,' Adam chided.

Ariella laughed, brightness like sun on snow. 'You think I've not heard worse, Adam?' Lucas would gurgle from within the wrap around her shoulder and neck, settling to the sway of Ariella's horse, a mare with the placid demeanour of a fat matron and Henri would think how beautiful she was, by the stars!

They were harmonious days and if the group had been shadowed, if there was knowledge beyond them that they carried the greatest relic in Christendom, then they were unaware of it. Perhaps it was naivety, Henri thought, that they seemed secure and beyond harm.

Right now, he wished they were back on shore. Able to take cover somewhere, for here on the ocean there was nothing. No dense sea-fog in which they could sail a singular and muffled way. They were as exposed as a wart on a crone's chin. No other ship in sight between here and Marseille.

Just the heaving bow of a Templar ship cutting through the wave toward them.

Adam hurried back and crouched down, dragging on Henri's tunic, pulling him to squat on the deck, hidden by the bales of cloth.

'The Genovese thinks they will sail past. They have not signalled for us to heave to and if they're given no clue that the boat carries more than just merchandise, then...' his fists were clenched and his face ruddy in the breeze.

'But if you say you saw no Templars in Genova, then what is the problem?'

'I'm a naturally cautious person, Henri. And the Templars have no love of Gisborne. I'll tell you the story one day.'

'When William was taken hostage and Lady Ysabel went searching for him?'

'You know?'

Henri eased his backside on the planks, thrusting a few folds of his cloak underneath. 'William told me in his childish way and Tobias finished the story. Christ! Tobias! He will have no love of the Templars nor they him. Does he know to stay below the wale?'

'Yes. I told him, and Ariella also. We can't be too careful.'

The men remained concealed, occasionally lifting an eye high enough to see the vessel's bowsprit was now level with their stern and that they passed within three boat-widths of the Genovese's starboard. The sounds of husky shouts and the creak of canvas and ropes reached their ears and their own ship listed larboard, starboard and back again as the fierce wash from the large Templar ship hit their sides and the massive billowing sails took their wind. Adam and Henri stayed down but could hear the Genovese yell in response to a question of their destination.

'Marseille! And you?'

'Also. God speed!' And then the crowded sounds of timber and sail, ropes and men were gone and their own ship wallowed moodily in the waves, before finding its rhythm and continuing on as the Templar ship hove away into the western distance.

Henri had seen no one. A mere medley of voices, perhaps English, maybe French, but his heart hammered even so. Hiding reminded him of the Holy Land. Of rocks and folds which provided dusty concealment whilst horses and men clashed in the distance and he lay, cut about and weak, the sun pounding at his closed eyelids.

'Fucking bastards!' Adam mumbled as he stood. 'Never trust a man who wears a white cloak and claims to be clean living. Bunch of shit, if you ask me.'

'Say it as you see it, Adam,' Henri said, standing up and leaning back against the bales. 'Just tell me, if Tobias found the relics locked in an unknown box without a key, apparently concealed for many a long time, how would the Templars, or anyone else for that matter, have found out about it? Even the stall seller wouldn't know.'

'Maybe the Templars haven't. Maybe I'm just suspicious every time I see one of 'em. I don't trust their motives. Ever. They're the richest bunch in Christendom, God's gift as fighters damn them to Hell, and they claim to be God's agents! *Beau Sant* indeed!'

'*Beauçéant*,' Henri instructed. 'White to their friends, black to their enemies. And they still consider Gisborne a thorn in their sides?'

'I believe so until it is proved otherwise. But I need to talk to the Genovese again. I believe we need to sail into Notre-Dame-de-Ratis instead of Marseille. It won't hurt us to be safe.'

'Then I hope you have money to pay him, because this,' Henri waved his hands at the bales, 'is his to deliver to merchants in Marseille.'

Adam reached for his purse and jingled it. 'I have gold *livres* and silver *sols*.'

He left Henri and in moments, a pale Tobias had woven his unsteady way to Henri's side.

'Well, that was interesting. Adam is suspicious, no?'

Henri nodded, mouth stretching into a flat line.

''Tis better to be safe.' Tobias tugged at his tunic, straightening the creases and smoothing back his tousled hair.

'You too, Toby?'

'I have reason to be. It was a nasty business, William's disappearance. And Gisborne took no prisoners. In the end it was a bloodbath and perhaps the Templars will one day seek to avenge the death of their own. It has always been in the back of my mind. If we are ever in their presence, don't ever antagonise them, because they believe that God is guiding their swordhand.'

'Don't we all though? Is it not the way every Christian is trained to think?'

'Oh pff!' Toby nudged Henri. 'Don't become philosophical. I have you pegged as an unbeliever and haven't the energy to change my view on this voyage. Wait until we're on the road again.'

'What is your plan?' asked the Genovese sea captain as the three companions with the babe, readied to disembark. Notre-Dame-de-Ratis smelled of fish and boats, seaweed and Roman seawalls, and seabirds shrieked as boats offloaded their catch to the marketplace.

It was little use prevaricating because the Genovese knew Ariella was returning to Lyon, to her husband's family.

'We will find horses and ride the right bank of the Rhône to Lyon, through Arles and Avignon,' Adam said, as he hiked his bag over his shoulder. 'A smooth ride we hope. We have the babe to consider.'

The sea captain nodded as two of his men carried luggage to a waiting cart. 'Makes sense. I hope the weather is kind to you. God wish you well.'

Adam handed over his purse. 'My lord and master will remember the service you have done him by delivering us out of your way. I will be sure to tell him that we have found a sea-captain we can trust out of Genova. Would you be interested? There is much cargo to transport this way through the summer.'

'Via Marseille or here?'

'I suspect here. It's more direct than crossing overland from Marseille. This way, and assuming the waters are running well, the cargo can travel by barge direct to the *traboules* in Lyon.'

The sea captain spat on his hand and shook Adam's own. 'Tell him. I will be back in Genova in a month, God willing.'

Henri tugged at his girdle and laid his sword-belt flat so that the scabbard hung against his thigh. They had no intention of travelling the east route of the Rhône. They would travel up the west side via Viviers. Nothing wrong with casting seeds of doubt behind them.

They bid the Genovese thanks and made their way across a wood and stone wharf which bestrode a sandy shore. The marshlands close by had spread a fine layer of silt across the sand as the winter rivers filled the marshes, but even so, the sand was soft and lined the shore lightly in the early afternoon. The carter led the way into the small town, bigger than a village, with timber, daub and stone buildings lining alleys and lanes and the pervasive smell of fish over everything. Where fish were cleaned, clouds of flies and seabirds hung about, the birds fighting over guts and heads, raucous and angry, and Ariella jammed her fingers over her nose.

They wended their way along cobbled and dirt paths and beneath the walls of the church as the bell rang for None.

'Do you think the church has a hospice?' Ariella asked.

'They might,' said Adam, 'But we'll secure beds at the inn our friend here mentioned.' He indicated the thin man pushing the cart and who spoke in a heavy Occitàn dialect which left all bar Tobias struggling to understand his meaning.

'This church has extreme notoriety,' Tobias said, running his fingers along the stone wall.

'How so?' asked Ariella.

'It is called *L'Eglise de les Trois Maries*. Legend has it that some forty years after Christ's ascension, three women close to Christ escaped persecution by setting sail from the other side of the Middle Sea. One was Mary Jacobé, who was reputedly Christ's aunt, one was Mary Salomé, mother of James and John. And one was Mary Magdalene. An illustrious company of women, you'll agree.'

'And you believe this… legend, Tobias?' Adam's voice was tinged with a note of incredulity. 'Pig shit that a boat with three women could make it this far. Even true sailors might not.'

'Adam, I absorb everything and it is fuel for my musical fires. You know this,' Tobias replied, grimacing at the master-at-arms. '*Anyway,* rumour has it that they spent the remainder of their lives here. The church was built over a hundred years ago to house their relics and the statues depicting their holy selves. One of them is a black statue… I'm not sure why.'

'Maybe too much tallow candle-smoke and dirt,' said Ariella.

'Maybe. In any case, the church was built as a defensive structure as well, see the *flechières*? And inside, there is a *donjon* and a *salle du corps*. An odd thing for a church but quite a history of attack from Northerners and the Saracens. The folk around here must sleep with eyes in the back of their heads.'

'Wonder the Templars haven't commandeered it!' Adam grumped.

They wound their way past stalls of bread-sellers, hardy women tanned walnut brown from the summer suns, past groups of men stitching fishing nets. Children played tag or threw scraps of leather moulded into balls at each other. No different to any other town, thought Henri, as they held their noses passing a tanner's small yard.

'But,' continued Tobias. 'Think on this. The man reputed to be on that voyage was Joseph of Arimathea, the same man who had been at Christ's feet and who paid to have Him removed from the Cross and who may have provided the winding cloths. And possibly sundry other things to those who mourned…'

'So this church houses relics of these people? All of them?' asked Henri. 'Even Mary Magdalene?'

Tobias shrugged his shoulders. 'I don't know.' He spoke in Occitàn to the carter who answered back. 'He says of course. Don't all pilgrims to Compostela stop here because of that? Believe him or not, it's up to you. For myself, I thought her bones were further east near Aics.'

'Then what of her v...' Henri went to say, but Adam knocked him hard and shook his head, frowning and cocking an eyebrow at the carter.

For a moment as they walked, all were silent and then Ariella said thoughtfully, '*More* relics. Everywhere, relics to celebrate the life of Christ and His family. Different to we Jews... we are... perhaps a more literary faith. We value our texts, our Torah, the law of our Faith. It is enough. Although there is the Arc of the Covenant, I suppose...'

Finally, the carter stopped, indicated a low stone building and a high thatched roof far from the sea-edge and away from the stink of dead fish.

'It's called the White Horse,' Tobias translated. 'To do with native horses hereabouts.'

Henri looked around. The building seemed to droop with the weight of thatch made from the native sedge. There were no windows and no sign of separate rooms for those who wished to stay. To the side was a wooden arch and by the smell of feed and horses, he guessed it was the livery.

Adam disappeared inside, and Ariella subsided onto a solid stone mounting block, Lucas fretted a little and she looked up at Henri. 'He is tired and needs bathing, a change of clothing and a feed. We all do...'

'Would you like me to hold him?' Henri wondered from where such a request had sprung because he was hardly a wetnurse.

Ariella grinned and said, 'And which end would you pick up first, Henri?'

Henri flushed, wishing she didn't disturb him so, Toby laughing at his discomfort and reaching for Lucas as Ariella stood and untied the sling, sighing and rubbing the back of her neck.

Henri almost defended himself, wanting to remind them that he had a soft side and could hold a babe if he had to. He'd held puppies and lambs, even baby chicks after all. Instead, whilst Ariella walked back and forth, arching her back and neck, he sat by Tobias and looked at the infant.

The infant gazed back.

Eyes that vacillated between hazel and blue opened wide and fixed upon Henri, blinking and then staring at him as if to stir a memory from somewhere and it was like warm embers in a sleeping fire. Toby loosened the swaddling around Lucas, the child stretching like the mother, and then returned to his scrutiny of Henri.

'He is learning your face,' Toby said sagely. 'Next time, he can go to your arms without fear.'

The babe's serious gaze was unnerving to Henri who had only ever been glanced upon and away by those within the household of his childhood. Later, as an adolescent, it was glazed by orders, obedience and military instruction. As time moved on, and whilst still in a framework of orders, there was the chilling scrutiny of an enemy. Always searching for a place to thrust a sword or knife. A quick glance, a swift summation and a lightning-fast movement. Kill or be killed.

If there had been a woman, the looks were softer, seductive – calculating, as the thought of monies for services entered the equation.

And try as he might to banish it, there was the terrified expression of a child in the Holy Land…

Which was why Lucas's inspection was so unsettling. Nothing to offer, nothing to gain. Pure innocence.

The little one's mouth opened, a pink tongue moved across lips and he yawned, but his eyes never left Henri's and Henri found himself attached, as if tied by leather strips that would not yield.

Lucas's mouth twitched at one end.

'Jesu, look at that,' Toby whispered.

The mouth stretched and the gaze softened.

'He likes you, you old bastard! Here…' Toby passed the baby over and Henri took him, eyes locked onto the baby by something indefinable. The smile stayed as he settled the child in his grasp and then he began to walk around the grubby square, talking as if Lucas were a friend of equal years. The infant gurgled and stretched within his swaddling but not once did his inspection of Henri cease.

'You take my son hostage?' Ariella's voice was like warm honey and he turned.

'On the contrary, Madame. I think he might be making a hostage of me.' He looked down at Ariella and briefly, her proximity set his loins afire and he might almost have blushed had he not felt something beneath his hands. A small explosion and then the infant's grin becoming ever larger.

Ariella laughed, a throaty burble as she reached to take Lucas from Henri's arms. 'I think that if he did not need a bath and fresh clothing before, he does now. Thank you, Henri. It's evident that my son likes and trusts you. It's good to know.' She began to move away as Adam approached, but then turned back to Henri. 'By the way,' her face was not serious, but the levity of before had dissolved. 'No more of Madame. I am Ariella. We are companions, not mistress and servant, and Lucas, I can see, shall be your friend.'

She walked toward Adam, and Henri watched her go. His soul, always a little empty and filled with longing for what he had only ever had by default, expanded. That such a little child could fill a gap and build a bridge with a smile and emptying its bowels was a wonder of the universe and he warmed by consequence.

'Henri, come!' Adam called and Henri hurried over. 'They have no rooms, but will allow us to use the stables to bed down there for a price. I'm happy with that because we can be away at dawn with no fuss. I would that we get some distance under our belts. It will be a long journey.'

'Food? A bath for Lucas?' Ariella asked.

'I've arranged for horses, supplies, warm water to bathe the babe and for us to wash. But comfort beyond that won't happen 'afore we reach Viviers, and we'll be sleeping rough until then. Make the most of this night.'

Toby groaned. 'Christ's blood, Adam. Did you ask if the church has a hospice?'

'There is none...'

'And no room at the inn. By my soul, we are living the scriptures. A babe, a Madonna...' Toby muttered as he took his and Ariella's bags from the cart. 'And how do we transport our baggage?'

'I have paid for a horse each and a pack-horse to carry the supplies. All is well.'

'But how big...'

'They are Camargue horses, Toby, small and sure-footed. You will manage.' Adam took up Lucas's little sack and his own and Henri reached for his. By the set of Adam's shoulders and mouth, there was to be no argument and Henri would bet his life on the fact that Adam was disgruntled.

He'd been awry since they left Venezia and the more Henri thought on it, the more he decided that apart from the intimation of Templar interference in their journey, it was because Ariella had inveigled her way with them. Surely she must have known how much she would slow them down. They could not trot or canter, let alone gallop with the babe as luggage and what happened if their lives depended on a swift getaway? Now, at a walk, they might add weeks, not days onto their journey. They couldn't even travel up the Rhône to Lyon because the river was quickening with the melt and if there was rain, it might flood. Gods and Saints above, what had prompted her?

The only bonus that Henri could see was the unequivocal disguise provided by a mother and babe. Perhaps Gisborne and Saul had known this when Ariella persuaded them to let her travel. Perhaps in their secret way, they had known that above and beyond travelling with a leper whose presence would keep the most avaricious away, this plainly dressed matron and her infant provided one of the best disguises they could wish for. Of course, they would attract interest wherever they went. A lone woman with a babe, a companion, and two men at arms indicated monies of sorts. They sought to dispel that by dressing plainly and by showing no overt wealth. Henri hoped against hope that such a ruse would work on the roads.

Travel was never easy.

Chapter Seven

Soeur Cécile
The road to Ambert

'Sister! Sister!' Geltidis shook Cécile's knee and she woke with a start. 'Sister, quickly! Something is awry and we must hide with the cart, my husband says!'

'What?' Cécile blinked. The men were helping Geltidis down from the cart and were beckoning.

'Quickly, Sister!' Gervasius waved his hand. 'Hurry now. We can see men down the hill and they are approaching with speed. We must hide the cart and ourselves!'

Cécile, never before experiencing a time of physical danger, felt the blood drain from her face and she moved to the cart edge and slid down, avoiding Gervasius's hand. She hurried into the forest behind Geltidis as her husband led Issy and the cart, and another pulled the horses out of sight. The servant tried to clear their tracks with a broken branch, whilst the remaining merchant swirled his horse in a muddy circle, prints overlaying prints, and then he galloped ahead and out of sight.

'He is experienced in travel, Sister,' Gervasius said. 'Have no fear, he will hide and double back.'

'God go with him,' murmured Cécile as they moved deeper into the forest, seeking concealment.

They found a small rock outcrop, more a tumble, and they moved behind it, sheltered by trees that grew between the crevices. They could hear nothing and Gervasius hurriedly placed a nosebag of feed upon Issy in the hope it would keep the mare quiet. The other horses grazed on the spring pick of the forest floor and expressed no concern. As the servant led his horse toward them, the horse breathing heavily, Cécile felt the ground thunder underneath her feet and a flock of birds flew up in alarm, all the animals snorting and laying back their ears, the merchants laying hands on their noses and murmuring, trying to settle them. But the sound of the horses on the road receded quickly and forest silence settled itself around them again.

No one spoke for some time.

Cécile listened for a cracked twig, an upstart of birds, anything to indicate men and horses, but there was nothing. Gervasius moved back the way they had hastened, signalling for the women and servant boy to stay and beckoning the remaining merchant with him. Cécile wondered at this. What did the young and weedy servant know of protecting two women? Did he have a weapon? Did Geltidis? Cécile didn't, that's for sure.

'*Madame*,' she whispered over her shoulder. 'How many rode past us?'

'I don't know,' the merchant-wife replied. 'It sounded like three or four. No more than that.'

'Who were they?'

'If they were cutthroats chasing us, I'm sure they would have stopped and sought us out. No, I suspect it was men of business in a hurry to get to Amb…'

She stopped of a sudden, her words dying in her throat with a choke and Cécile swung round. Geltidis was held tight by a tall man, his arm holding a long-bladed knife against her throat. She panted in fear, her eyes wide, whites shining in the forest shade, and her gaze imploring Cécile to do something. The servant boy lay in a pool of his own blood, his throat slit.

For a single heartbeat, Cécile knew the worst fear of her life. Her mouth dried, sweat ran beneath her armpits and her knees weakened. She could bare believe that the boy who had led Issy and who wanted to earn money to support his mother in Mons had his life stripped so easily. Not a sound. And now here was Geltidis. *God help us!* She crossed herself and took a step forward.

'Stay where y'are…' the thief's voice was as hard as a frost, cruel and needle-like and with an accent that could have placed him anywhere from Toulon to Paris. 'Or this fat slut will get 'er throat cut. Get yer money…'

'I am a nun. I have nothing…' Cécile answered, her voice stretched as thin as catgut.

'The cart. Get what's valuable and bring it 'ere.'

'I don't know what is valuable.'

The thief dug the knife into Geltidis's neck and a small bead of blood appeared. 'In the coffer,' she squeaked. 'Coin and a pearl necklace… the key is on my girdle.'

Cécile hurried over to Geltidis and reached below her stout belly for the chatelaine of keys hanging off the handsome wide girdle. 'Which?' she asked as she clambered onto the cart. Issy shifted with the iron taint of blood in the air, her ears laid back. She took a nervous step sideways and the cart jolted but Cécile said 'Whoa, girl, whoa', imploring God and the Saints to intercede.

'Which key, *Madame*?' she repeated sharply. 'Tell me!'

'The shining one – the brass one,' Geltidis's voice croaked and she began to weep.

Cécile found the key amongst others and with shaking hands she tried to fit it to the lock, missing the first time and taking a breath to calm herself, *begging* God to hold her hand steady. It slipped into the cavity and she turned it, heard a click, whereupon it fell to the boards of the cart and Issy shifted again.

Cécile flicked the catches on the coffer and heaved it open, rifling through folded clothes and cloaks. She found two purses at the bottom, the coins jingling as she lifted one. She found a small velvet roll which she presumed held the pearl necklace. Her fingers closed on a book, as well. She noticed an intaglio cover, a Book of Hours, but she slipped a cloak over it and the extra purse, shut the lid and slid back off the cart, to stand before the thief.

'There are women's cloaks and clothes, nothing else. Here. Monies, a necklace.' She let them fall to the thief's feet but still he kept the knife at Geltidis's throat.

'Get the purse off 'er girdle, get the nosebag and tip the feed out and put everything inside it.'

Cécile moved close to Geltidis again, looking into her eyes, seeing fear so deep that it shocked her to the core. She'd never seen someone so afraid, not in her village life and definitely not within the shelter of the priory walls. She could smell it, smell the woman who had wet herself and even now stood in the piss-soaked mosses. She kept her eyes upon Geltidis, willing God to give the woman courage, letting her see that she, Cécile, was an intermediary with Him on high who would succour them. She prayed as she undid the purse, took the nosebag, emptied the oaten grain onto the ground and slipped the other goods within. She handed the bag over and with one grimy hand that had filth-filled long fingernails as hard as horn, he slipped the hemp noose of the nosebag over his shoulder, pulling Geltidis backward toward a large fir where his rangy, brown horse stood, ears pricked and tail swishing with fretting nerves. The felon shoved Geltidis down and leaped aboard the mount to spur it hard. It snorted, stepped forward, tripping over Geltidis who cried out. Then it lifted over the top of the merchant woman to disappear like a shadow into the heart of the forest.

Geltidis grasped at her stomach, crying as Cécile ran to her. '*Madame, madame*! God be thanked, he did not hurt you,' she spoke loudly trying to break through the woman's hysteria, laying a hand on the other's, trying to calm her. 'He has not hurt you. You are whole and untouched. *Messire, messire!*' she shouted over her shoulder.

The men crashed back to the clearing and stared at the servant, nervous hands filled with knife and dagger as they looked around the glade. 'What happened?' shouted the one called Ambrosius. 'Who…' but his voice was drowned out by the loud cries from Geltidis, who lay on the ground still, clutching at her belly, whilst Cécile held her shoulder, unsure what to do.

Gervasius knelt by his wife. 'Gelis, where are you hurt? Tell me, my dearest woman…'

'God be praised, *messire*, the felon did not touch her,' Cécile tried to inject some calm into the moment, even though her heart pounded as if it would burst. She felt such a pressure within her chest – tears, to be sure. And that had not happened since her father told her she was to marry the old miller. Then she had thought she would choke from the pain and after she had run to the stream at the back of the village, only then had the tears come and the pressure released. She looked around. There was nowhere to run…

'But something ails her, what happened?' Gervasius turned upon Cécile, a black cloud, and she shrank away.

'*Messire,* he threatened her with a knife at her throat but see, there is only a pinprick mark…'

'But she holds her belly, did he wound her there?'

'No…'

'Husband!' Geltidis grasped Gervasius's hand and placed it on her belly and Cécile only then saw the mark upon the folds of her bliaut – a muddy half hoofprint.

'The horse,' she gasped. 'It stood on me.'

'God in heaven!' Gervasius's face had paled as he looked around at his companions. 'Help me lift her, please help me!' Then he saw his young servant and cried out. 'Look at what they have done, God rot their souls! He was a good young man…'

The men lifted Geltidis, staggering a little under her weight and with gentle care, laid her in the cart.

'Sister, you must help us…' his gaze flicked from his wife to his servant and back. Wretched fear showed in his wide eyes and in the shaking hands he clasped together. Cécile cursed that she had never worked alongside Melisende in the infirmary. 'I need you to examine her,' he begged. 'Make sure she is whole.'

'But *messire*, I assure you, she was not raped. She is justifiably terrified. She just needs *your* arms.…' Cécile climbed into the cart. 'I cannot touch her. I…'

'But you must,' he broke in, strung tight with nerves. 'My wife is injured and you must help us.'

Cécile frowned. 'But *messire*, there is not a mark. She needs to rest and be calm. Give her some wine if you have it.'

'*You*, Sister, must examine her!' He pushed his finger hard into Cécile's chest. 'The horse trod on her belly. You *must* check that all is well.'

'*Messire*!' Cécile leaned back, grasping at her prayer beads, afraid of this bulky man who verged on madness.

'Sister!' Gervasius roared, puce face filled with anger. 'My wife is with child!'

Cécile gasped. The swelling belly, how could she not have realised? She would have to do this, with God's hand to guide her own. She must be calm, get the others to do something else whilst she probed the delicacies of this woman. 'I apologise. I did not know…' She knotted her hands around her beads, praying for guidance. 'Then help your friends to bury the poor young man, *messire*.' She tried to sound authoritative, as if she knew what she must do. 'Meanwhile I will examine her.'

Examine her and look for what? She hadn't a clue. When had she ever known a woman with child in the last twenty-five years? What was she to do? The men meanwhile had begun to scoop a depression in the dirt and she turned away, offering up a supplication for the lad's soul. 'Geltidis,' she said, 'may I lift your gown?'

Gelis nodded, tears seeping from the corners of her eyes. 'Yes…' she whispered. 'Soeur Cécile, I have lost four babes. This may be my last chance. You are my hope.'

Cécile could have cried. She had only ever been responsible for guiding the novices, for seeing them to their tasks and to prayer in the chapel, for adding numbers in the priory ledgers and making sure the house was as solvent as it could be. How was a woman who had given a promise of chastity to God able to help a woman who had such earthly issues? She lifted the folds of Geltidis's stained gown of vert wool and then the flimsier lengths of the piss-soaked linen shift. Beneath, there were even wetter braies lying at her pubis beneath a huge white mound veined heavily with blue. What was child and what was fat, she wondered, aghast when she saw the ugly mauve and yellow bruising in the faint shape of a horseshoe.

'Sister…'

Cécile tried to think on pregnancy. 'How far along are you, Gelis? May I call you Gelis?'

She smoothed her hands over the woman's swollen belly cursing herself again for not realising the woman was with child. Cursing herself for being so caught up in her own web of concern.

'I believe I am due to give birth whilst we are in Lyon…'

'Soon then…' Cécile wondered why the woman had elected to travel hard roads so close to her time. Tried to remember back to young women in the village. Did they talk about quickening, that a babe moved within the mother? She smoothed her palms over Gelis's belly and then, where the mound curved in a perfect parabola, she let her hands rest.

'Is it still alive?' Gelis begged. 'Pray for me, Sister. Pray for my child.'

Cécile closed her eyes, asking God for the smallest sign, willing her palms to feel. Nothing, nothing for vast moments as the men stacked rocks on top of a dead boy's body and birds trilled a chorus in the trees.

Gelis moaned. 'It is dead. Oh Mary Mother, then let me die…'

'Quiet, *Madame*. Breathe gently.'

Something! There! Was it surely something? Or did the woman tremor like a crone as Cécile felt across her belly?

Beneath her fingers a faint movement flicked like a chick flapping tiny wings. And another. 'Oh!'

'Does it move? Does it, Sister?' Gelis grabbed at Cécile's hands, pulling at her, tears running freely. 'Oh, by the Virgin. What does it do?'

'I think it moves. See?' She placed Gelis's sweaty palms on her belly and even as she watched, the belly undulated and she sighed with wonder. 'God be praised!'

'Sister?' Gervasius called and she whipped around.

'The child lives, *messire*. All is well.'

Gervasius placed the last rock upon the mound, wiping at his wet cheeks, his companions smoothing his back as the bold, loud merchant collapsed to kneel on the ground.

'It is his first child, Sister,' said one of the merchants, the one named Robertus.

One child lives and another dies, Cécile thought as she looked at the rocky mound covering the servant boy. What was his name, she wondered, and called herself to account for not finding out. She was a poor companion. 'Perhaps we can pray for your young man's soul before we leave,' she said. 'And ask for God's blessing upon *Madame* Geltidis and *Messire* Gervasius.'

They agreed, and when she had tidied Gelis, given her a costrel of wine to sip from and made her comfortable, she slipped from the cart and joined the men at the grave. 'What was his name?' she asked.

'Chrestien,' said Gervasius. 'He is from my home of Mons. He was a good young lad...'

Cécile wondered at the irony – a good Christian name doomed to rot under a pile of stones far from home. She sketched a cross and began, 'Father of all, we pray to You for Chrestien and for all those whom we love but see no longer. Grant to him and to them eternal rest. Let light perpetual shine upon them. May Chrestien's soul and the souls of all the departed, through the mercy of our God, rest in peace. And may we ask that You care for our friends Gervasius and Geltidis of Mons in their hour of need, and we ask for Saint Margaret of Antioch to intercede on behalf of their unborn child who will enter their lives soon.' Did she say that correctly? Will they see her ignorance in the face of an oncoming child, her discomfort? She reached for her prayer beads and continued. '*In nomine Patris et Filii et Spiritus Sancti.*' She then began the Paternoster and they joined her and at the end, she crossed herself, and head down, turned away from the men and back to the cart to climb aboard and sit with Gelis, who smiled with tremulous lips.

'Sister, it was God's wish that you accompany us. I thank you for giving us hope, for asking for succour and for...' she sucked in an anguished breath, 'And for seeing young Chrestien on his way. He was such a good youth, uncomplaining. And his mother is our housekeeper. What shall we say to her?' She was about to weep again, but Cécile pressed the costrel to the woman's lips.

'Chrestien was a brave and loyal retainer and he will be seen kindly into Heaven. As to his mother, we shall pray for her when we reach Ambert and perhaps we may light candles to illuminate her dark and our own. When you return to Mons, you will tell his mother how brave he was in the face of the cruellest odds and that he was given a Christian burial and that his soul is blessed to sit with Our Father Almighty.' She tucked a cloak around the woman. 'Gelis, you must rest.

Think of your little babe and the shock it has had. There…
you see, your babe and yourself need to sleep now…'

Gervasius had taken Issy's reins and led her from his own
horse. When he turned back to check on his wife, his face
was grey with worry, but he nodded a thank you to the nun
and they moved on. It was obvious from the rigid strain in
the merchants' shoulders that they wished to reach Ambert
forthwith. *She* wished so from the depths of her soul, wondering what her prioress would say about the killing, about
the merchant wife, about everything.

They were well up into the hills and Gelis still slept. Cécile
sat and watched her and every now and then she would
close her eyes and try to pray but she would see knives and
throats, blood and a dead youth and her eyes would fly
open again. She determined to watch the forest passing as
she fingered her beads, mouthing a prayer to the Virgin and
trying to displace the horrors of earlier.

It was perhaps some time between Sext and Tierce, she
thought. Her belly rumbled and she wondered if they might
stop for food or whether they would push on in the hope
they could be behind the gates of Ambert before Compline.

The forest surrounded them, intensifying the rattle of
the cart, the ponderous rolling of the wheels, the clop of the
horses' hooves, the crack of a stick being trodden upon and
the creaking of the merchants' saddles. One or other of the
horses would snort perhaps, throwing up a head to jingle
the metal bits, but the merchants had quieted, sunk into
the events of earlier, although their heads swung from side
to side as they examined the shadows. There was frequent
bird call but not a sign of another traveller and Cécile was
glad. She had time to settle her own nerves and to thank
God for small mercies and in the pious peace of the forest,
Gelis could sleep, heal from her shock, and allow her babe

to settle. The woman swayed back and forth like a beached and bloated fish, her belly sitting high as her *bliaut* folds fell away from the bulge. But in such an older matron, it was a poignant sight to see how she cradled that bump, even in sleep.

Cécile rubbed her own stomach as it grumbled. Despite being used to asceticism in the priory, her body knew when it would be fed – albeit bread and flavourless wine or ale. Of course, there was their daily pottage, almost always seasoned with the herbs that grew in abundance in the provender garden and orchard. Plain yes, but it filled empty bellies and it would be nice to stop for food, Cécile reasoned, once Geltidis woke. If nothing else, the mother and budding babe needed nourishment and it was beyond the forty days of Lent after all.

The cart rolled into a deep rut and Gelis snorted, opened her eyes and stared straight at Cécile, fear beginning to widen her gaze.

'All is well, Gelis.' Cécile leaned forward to pat the woman's hand. 'All is well. You have slept long.'

'Have I?' the matron answered and pulled herself up to sit. 'Have we far to go? Husband,' she called, her voice almost querulous, 'how far are we from Ambert?'

The merchant let go of Issy's reins, the tired horse halting and the cart rolling to stop as he jumped from his horse. 'You are awake. Are you…? Is…?'

'I am hungry,' Gelis said with some of her forthrightness of earlier. 'And judging by the way our babe kicks, I would say it needs nourishment as well. What say you, Sister?'

Cécile smiled. 'I think it is important for a mother to feed a growing babe, *messire*, and they have had a long day.'

Gervasius turned back to Cécile. 'What time is it, do you think, Sister?'

'Closer to Tierce, *messire*, and *Madame* broke her fast before dawn and has had a trying day.'

'Robertus, it is close to Tierce. Shall we stop and rest the horses, eat perhaps?'

Robertus rode back to them. 'There is a widening of the road ahead. And a good view forward and back, perhaps we can stop there. There may be a stream.'

Gervasius looked to his wife for assent and she nodded, watching her husband pull his weight into the saddle, the heavyset rouncey taking a step sideways. He grabbed Issy's reins and clicked her on and the cart began to roll forward.

They halted in a leafy loop of the road, where they had shade, a view forwards and back as Robertus had said. A small stream trickled down the slope of the hill and the ground was damp and mossy with a tender green pick here and there for the horses. Gervasius unharnessed Issy and loosened the girth on his own mount. Each man led a horse to the stream and Gervasius clicked Issy and his own after them, the horses drinking, bits clinking and chomping as they slopped water from their mouths. When they were sated, the men tied them to fallen timber and set about pulling food from their saddlebags.

'Sister, I smell like a cesspit from when I…' Gelis stopped and a flicker of fear dashed across her eyes. 'I need to wash. Can you help me? There are clothes in the coffer.'

Cécile wondered how much of this journey would be spent as Gelis's servant and then closed her eyes and squeezed them. She was such an unworthy Bride of Christ. Being devoted and loyal within the walls of the priory was so easy by comparison…

'Yes, of course,' Cécile opened the coffer and withdrew soft linens and a grey gown, looking to Gelis for approval.

'A clean cloak?' Gelis asked, fingering her piss-stained covering.

Cécile grabbed a folded cloak and privately wondered at the luxury of owning more than one in a lifetime and then she helped Gelis from the cart, the matron informing the men that she and the good Sister would need privacy at the stream as she needed to wash and change.

Seeing another woman naked was nothing new, not when she and Melisende organised and supervised Benedictine cleanliness within the priory. But she was unprepared for the sight of a woman so close to birthing a child. The stretched belly, the tracery of blue lines, the swollen and veined legs, the massive breasts. She turned away as Gelis sponged herself. Cécile gathered up the smelly clothing and bundled it in the cloak.

'Do you want to have this laundered?' she asked.

'No,' Gelis had pulled a linen shift over her damp body and shivered with the cold of the water, the bottom edges of her veil a little wet. 'I never want to see them again. Leave them by the tree. Perhaps someone needy will find them. Can you help me pull on my clothes, *Soeur* Cécile? I feel quite weak.'

'You need some sustenance.' Cécile settled the matron's linens below the bulge, easing the grey woollen robe down over veil and wimple. She had retrieved Gelis's girdle and tied it round the woman's belly and Gelis grimaced.

'I'm well covered, I know. But the babe makes me twice as fat.'

'You seem well with it. Do you want to remove your veil and wimple?'

'But it's not seemly for a matron…'

'We are a group travelling alone. You have had a fright, you need to be comfortable.'

Gelis pulled at the pins that held her veil and then without a thought, dashed both wimple and veil to the ground. 'Leave them with the other things.' She shook her hair out and Cécile was taken aback by the abundance of shining conker brown glory. Gelis looked younger in an instant.

'Can you plait it for me and get it out of the way?' she asked.

Cécile wove the hair into a neat plait and pinned it to form a decorous loop and then the two women walked back to the roadside where the men sat chewing bread and dried meat and swallowing the last of the wine.

'We have left food and drink,' Gervasius carried an armload to them. 'And we still have dates…'

'A feast,' said Gelis. 'Sister, take your fill. I am indebted.'

And somehow, Cécile knew she spoke a truth. Gelis, wife of the merchant, Gervasius of Mons, would see her as a friend for life after this day. For the first time since Benedicta's death, Cécile warmed to her soul.

Chapter Eight

Henri de Montbrison
Viviers…

'Admirable view,' Tobias said from the steps of the Church of Saint-Vincent. He swung his gaze across the tops of the stone and timber houses of Viviers to the Rhône rushing past the town in post-winter haste. 'But the river flows so fast, I doubt the barges will work until later in the season.'

'More riding you mean, do you not?' Henri nudged Tobias and the little man nodded ruefully.

'I ache, Henri. In fact, I have no idea why I climbed to this tower at all. I should have found some grass by the riverbank and just laid down in the sun whilst Adam pursued his business.'

Henri indicated they sit and rest, although around them it was hardly quiet. Against the tower of the church, scaffolding was rigged in a fretwork of walkways for stonemasons and carpenters as the church continued its expansion back from the main tower, adding strong walls to the building.

'Tradesmen are astonishing. Just think what they have built and what they are building as we speak. Think of Sancta Sophia, think of Notre Dame in Paris and so many others, think of all the stone houses, *chastels* of the rich and noble, halls…'

'Indeed.' They watched a stonemason hitting a *cizel* with a heavy-topped mallet, shards of stone falling away in a pile beneath the block, the dull tap-tap creating a piece that would fit perfectly in the puzzle that was the wall of the church. 'The tower reminds me of Notre Dame du Ratis. Not in shape but in its purpose. I'm sure building up the slope isn't just for religious aesthetics. But I can't imagine it will be a large church. Do you want to go inside?'

The doors were open and an older woman in earthy-tinted *bliaut* and unbecoming veil walked out.

'I think not. I have nothing to say to God today…' Henri replied.

'Henri,' Tobias wagged his finger. 'I despair of you. You remind me of Guillaume, he used to speak so. I have decided it's a lifelong disease wrought of your crusade service. Am I right? What has turned you from God? I'm a good listener, you know.'

Henri stood. 'Come, it's too noisy here. Let's find a bread-seller and some wine and lie by the river.'

'You are evading my question.'

'I'm not, truly. Once we're by the river, perhaps I shall tell you.'

'Good.'

'Or perhaps I won't. We shall see.'

Ariella and the babe slept in a small hospice near the marketplace and Adam was negotiating the sale of their Camargue horses and the purchase of replacements. The pack horse had developed a lameness and after its hooves had been cleaned out and a stone removed, the horse remained footsore. Too much of a liability. Adam felt they needed horses more suited to the rocky ways of their journey.

They had bypassed other towns and villages as Adam had no wish to encounter any Templars who may know of the secret being carried in a babe's swaddling. It was only Ariella begging for Lucas's benefit that they finally stop for a rest that had persuaded Adam. One look at her drawn face and he saw sense. It was enough.

That and the footsore horse.

Viviers reeked of solidity. Each stone building melded to another in cobbled alleys – legacy of the Romans, Tobias said. Houses conjoined as if common walls would give them strength in their old age, leaning towards the two men and creating shadow and dark. As they walked, goods passed them on shoulders, in baskets and on poles – breads, river fish, cooked meats and tanned leather. The fragrance of fresh bread, of roast meat and ripe cheeses had the men hurrying to find a seller. The market thrived so close to the flood plains of the Rhône and to a point, the place reminded Henri of his home of Montbrison and he said so.

'You never think to return?' Toby asked as they carried their purchases to a sweep of grass near the river and from where they could hear the winter melt rushing past.

'I've told you, there is nothing there for me.'

'But family…'

'My mother is dead and I am a bastard son. No one cares and they probably don't even remember me. In any case, why are you not in Liguria? Leave it, Tobias, there's a good fellow.'

Toby chewed on a crust of dark-floured bread that still smelled of the oven. He cut a slab of soft cheese with his dagger and then sipped at his filled costrel. 'Then tell me why you won't visit with God.'

'Christ Jesus, Tobias! You are like a horsefly. What will it take to brush you off?' Henri spat out a sharp flake of crust that had lodged in his teeth and pushed his hair back from his face.

'An answer?' Toby replied with equanimity.

'Jesus Christ Almighty!'

'For someone who has no wish to engage with Our Lord, you use His name often enough,' Tobias said and stared right at Henri, steely, no turning away.

Henri sighed and took a great gulp of his wine and then let the corked costrel drop beside him. It lay there next to the sheathed sword which had saved his life more often than he cared to remember and which by association, had taken the lives of so many others.

Taking a deep breath, he began. 'It started in Cyprus,' he said. 'I killed a man and as I took his life, I felt nothing but a red rage. Afterward, I felt disgust with myself on such a level that I thought God would smite me down there and then. I had killed someone who was marching to the Holy Land with me. We belonged to this giant Christian army and instead of killing the enemy, I had killed one of our own. In many ways, the crusade was probably my punishment.'

Tobias sat against a washed-up log, one leg bent, his arms looped around it, saying nothing as Henri told of his experience in the Holy Land. Of men gutted and spitted, beheaded, of women raped and killed. Of the innocent children.

'By the time we had fought our way across the Holy Land, I was done. I had become devoid of anything. No soul. No heart.' As Henri spoke, his jaw tightened and he felt as if a dam across a river was breaking. The similarity with the fast-flowing torrent nearby, with backwash, whirlpools and undertows was not lost on him. 'Forever swinging my sword so that grain by *bloody* grain…' He stopped and closed his eyes. But then opened them quickly because he saw what was too horrendous. He felt for the hilt of his sword and grasped it, fist closing so tightly, he wondered how his bones didn't break. 'Grain by *bloody* grain so that we could advance across the sand. Bloody, Toby. So damned bloody! All in the name of God. Do you know that the very act of fighting in the Holy Land is meant to shrive us of any guilt, any sense of misdemeanour? And yet by lifting our weapons, we break the commandment, *Thou Shall Not Kill.* It is a hypocrisy!'

Tobias remained quiet and Henri thought that his friend was indeed a good listener. And for one very small moment and despite the ingrained self-disgust, he was glad. He told Tobias of his own wounds, of his lacerated and pulverised back and of the Arab doctor who had urged him to leave.

'But I couldn't. My countrymen were fighting for Phillip Augustus and then in his stead, for the Duke of Burgundy and the Count of Nevers. How could I run away?' He looked down at the hand clenched tight upon the sword hilt and let it go, rubbing the tension in his palm.

'Before each battle, the stink of fear amongst us was more powerful than you could imagine. Have you ever experienced that? Fear that makes you piss, and for shit to flow freely from you like an undammed river? Beside you, a fellow might suddenly vomit and your boots would become stained with the splash. The noise of the Saracen drums was enough to make us shake. And then they would scream their cries and come pounding upon us like whirling winds. In and away, in and away and every time, more and more men would fall with their guts looping across the sands.'

Henri gripped his hands tight again to prevent their obvious shaking as memories spewed forth.

'The last moment of my time in the Holy Land is etched in my mind like a stone carving and not even the winds of Time can erode it.' Henri stared across the spate of the Rhône and he just wanted to say this last and be done. 'We passed through a small village, a nondescript place with no name and no value to our lordly commanders. You could imagine it might have been one where Jesus or his disciples walked. Perhaps it was, which makes what happened all the more despicable. There was a Templar commander who was chivvying us, urging us on despite that Saladin and Richard Plantagenet had agreed to terms. I don't know who this man was, just that he rode a Saracen horse and perversely, he had a voice of gold. He had a heart of Greek Fire though, and if the Templars were good men of God, this man was the very devil. As we passed this village, he ordered us to wipe it from anyone's memory and he galloped in and began laying around him, yelling at us to follow if we wanted to see our homes again. We had thought we were marching to the coast, to boats, to sail away from years of brutal turmoil and yet this man, in the face of a treaty that had been agreed by Richard Plantagenet and Saladin, began to kill the old, the women and the children. Because there *were* only the old and women and children. All men of fighting age had long since departed.' The bread and wine in Henri's stomach began to roil. 'There was a child...'

'Henri...' Toby grabbed hold of Henri's crunched fist.

'No. Let me finish. I've never told a soul. There was a little child, William's age, perhaps younger and he was crying for his mother who lay dead at his feet. He had a tear,' Henri traced the path on his own cheek. 'And the Templar just rode at him, raised his sword and decapitated him.' Henri stopped and closed his eyes to prevent the tears that threatened. 'Why, Toby?'

Tobias squeezed Henri's arm but said nothing.

'My *confrères* were utterly silent. The Templar galloped on, God knows where, may he rot in Hell! A priest walked back and forth amongst us, carrying a cross and chanting the Paternoster as though it would cleanse us and I wanted to jump on him, beat him, grind his face into the dirt. I thought that day that God wasn't even within earshot. If He *had* been, then Saracen or no, He would never have allowed the massacre. For a little child to die like that? Or any other child? Suffer the little children...'

The silence around them was filled only with the roar that was the running river, and from somewhere nearby a cock crowed. It was like a clarion call for Henri, waking him from a night terror. He looked up, expecting to see sand and desert shrubs, a small village with biblical walls and goats milling around. Instead, the verdancy of a Viviers spring surrounded him and the deep grass and blue skies of a fine day cleared the fog from his eyes. He looked at Tobias.

'And that is why I no longer talk with God. Tobias, on your life, promise you will tell no one.'

Tobias scrutinised Henri and Henri felt as if his soul was laid bare. All the bloody brutality, the guilt, the confusion and desperation.

'On my life,' said Tobias, laying his palm flat against his heart.

For a while, they sat eating and drinking and deep within their own thoughts. Henri wondered why he had told Tobias anything at all. Did it make him feel easier in spirit? 'Toby, in case you wonder, I killed no one in that village…'

'I respect you, you know. For telling me,' Toby finally spoke up. 'When I met you at the Gigni hunt, I thought you were just another *routier*. A decent enough fellow, easy to get along with but with killing your only skill. I watched that broaden when you joined us within the trading house. Your evident literacy and your adaptability. You fitted into our strange group. It takes a certain type, you know.'

Henri huffed. 'I know…'

'We all have stories to tell, Henri. Adam – he has never told any of us about England or the Holy Land. He's a gruff bastard, but by the Saints I would vouch for him anywhere. Then Leo – he alludes to his time on the galleys but never goes into detail. And of course, you know a little of Ariella and Saul and perhaps even some of Gisborne and his lady and son. We are all scarred in one way or another.'

'And you, Tobias? You too?'

'Indubitably. I have scars from which I never ever thought I would heal. In truth they cast a pall of sadness occasionally. One thing I learned though is that as often as not, we are the masters of our own destiny, God notwithstanding. We have His word to live by and if we choose not to at any time, then we reap any consequence. My brother was a prime example. Headstrong and wilful, he broke my heart and yet, he did it for what he saw as the right reasons.'

'I would listen…' Henri said.

'Oh, Henri, *that* is a very long story. And I need time to tell you. Time when we are on our own because I believe I see Adam up there.' He gave an ear-piercing whistle, putting two fingers in his mouth and blowing hard. All of Viviers would have heard it, perhaps a call to arms.

'Would you not want Adam to hear your story?' Henri asked as they watched Adam wave and hurry down the stone steps to the grassy swathe.

'He knows quite a bit anyway. Probably from family hearsay, and he never asks. Ho there, Adam of London. Were you successful?'

One less wrinkle in Adam's frown showed that he had been. 'Yes. Four horses sold, four purchased and before you ask, Toby, I have a small mount the size of a Camargue horse for you, not too wide, eight years and sure-footed, very quiet. But not particularly appealing. In fact, none of our horses are the kind that would make an entrance anywhere. But it's their endurance we need.'

He sat. 'Can I finish the bread and cheese?' Without waiting, he took some and chewed. 'I'm starving. Any wine?'

Tobias passed over his costrel. 'And *Madame*?'

'She and the babe cleaned up and one of the nuns at the hospice said they were sleeping. All's good.'

'And yet,' ventured Henri, 'you are still perturbed.'

'I am and with due reason. The Templars are here.'

Toby sat back. 'You say?'

'I do. Are they informed of us and what we have?' He shrugged at his own question and broke some more bread. 'I have no clue. If they show an interest in us, then we've got the answer. But to be frank, I don't plan for us to wait and see. As soon as Ariella wakes, we're gone.'

'And travel on the roads *again*. In the night?' said Toby 'The mother and babe, Adam. Have a heart…'

'Jesus, Toby. You think I don't know,' Adam snapped. 'But in truth, if I had my way, she wouldn't be here at all. And we'd be making speed to Lyon, not this God-damned amble.'

There it was. Adam's opinion. Aligned perfectly with Henri's. She slowed them down and was a complete liability. And yet for Henri, she gave this journey an added dimension that he held close. Whilst Adam might *think* Henri was infatuated with the lady, Henri would never confirm to any but himself that he was. He dreaded that she and the babe were in any sort of danger.

'There is a way,' he said.

Adam finished the last of the wine in Toby's costrel. 'I'm listening.'

'We split up. Two and two. The goods leave now with two of us and Ariella travels with one of us tomorrow. No unseemly haste. Nothing to arouse interest.'

Adam nodded and Henri continued. '*Or*, the goods stay with Ariella, concealed as they are, along with one of us. And then Ariella leaves conspicuously and easily tomorrow as if nothing out of the ordinary. Two of us leave in apparent haste now, drawing attention. What say you?'

'It has merit,' said Tobias.

'I have only one concern,' Henri added. 'If the Templars know what we carry, I suspect they will cover both our parties if there are enough of them. How many, Adam?'

'I only saw one and his serjeant, but there may be more.'

'They could split up…'

'Stymied,' said Toby. 'Checkmate.'

Adam stood and walked back and forth. '*Either* way, we are at checkmate. But I think this plan is the best way forward. Well thought, Henri. We have to assume they know we carry something of extreme value and that their being here is not just a coincidence. With that in mind, I think a swift evacuation today as though we're concerned, is the way forward. Toby, you and I will leave as soon as we've saddled up. Henri, you'll stay with Ariella. Be obvious in what you do for the rest of the day. Likewise on the morn, when you leave. Make sure you look as if you have no care at all. Toby and I won't see Ariella until Lyon, so there's a lot of care riding on your shoulders. Hers and the babe's safety for one, *and* the delivery of the goods.'

'Lucky you,' Toby grumped. 'Meanwhile I just get a further pain in my arse.'

'Henri is a trained killer, Toby. And despite that we all know you can when you need to, I'd prefer you by my side as we leave.'

Snarky and with a gracious bow, Toby muttered, 'I'm so honoured.' And then, 'I suppose we must leave at a gallop?'

'Yes. Come on. Horses to sort out. Are you right with this, Henri? You'll have the packhorse as well.'

'Of course.' To Henri, it was orders and there was nothing like subterfuge. His blood rushed and tired muscles tightened.

'Then stay here for the moment. Look relaxed and without a care. See you in Lyon.'

Henri remained seated on the grass and waved a languid hand as the two men left him. Alone with Ariella and with the Holy Veil. The magnitude of his journey from this point onward left him breathless. He admitted surprise that Adam had thought to leave him with Ariella – the man assumed Henri lusted for her, after all. But then, perhaps he saw principles in Henri as well. Principles that he could trust.

In case of eyes watching, Henri lay back against the tree and closed his eyes, relaxed and carefree, but allowing his mind to race on possible eventualities.

Later, as the afternoon sun waned and a chill breeze chased a mist up the alleys from the river, Henri walked back toward the hospice, stopping at a fruit stall to choose some windfall apples from a woman with worn clogs on dirty feet and whose overdress was frayed at the hems. She grinned at Henri, flirting, revealing a mouth with quite good teeth but with breath that almost flattened him. But the apples were good despite their age and he wondered from whose cellar she had pilfered them. Dropping a coin into her chafed hand, he pocketed two of the apples for Ariella, found a trough in which to dip the remaining fruit, rubbing the red striped skin to bite into the soft flesh as he walked. The juice burst from the apple and he stopped to lean forward so that liquid dripped into the dirt beyond his boots. Two men pushed past, one sneering at his sudden stop, the one whose white Templar cloak grabbed at Henri's boot leather. The other man was dressed in the sombre colours of a Templar serjeant.

The Templar scrutinised Henri and he had the absurd notion on this fine and sun-filled afternoon that he was being pierced by ice shards, so cold were the man's eyes. The man's clean-shaven face had a polished-marble gleam and everything about him was hard edges. Not likely to be forgotten was a distinctive salting of steel grey through his black trimmed hair.

Henri stepped back against the walls of a house. 'My pardon, sir,' he said, holding up the remains of his juicy apple, 'I do not wish to impede you.'

The Templar said nothing, but his look swallowed Henri whole, almost as if he could see through every lie Henri had told and would ever tell. He grabbed the voluminous white folds of his cloak and swept on, trailing the shadowy malevolence of the serjeant in his wake.

Henri watched them disappear further toward the river and found that he couldn't breathe. He tried to get a breath down deep but it was a mere panting, like a dog in the sunshine. And then he vomited, bits of bread, apple, wine and froth.

He recognised the Templar.

He breathed, a deep life-giving suck of air. And another until his breath slowed. 'Angel of Hell!' he whispered after the vanished Templar.

As he followed their path, for the hospice was not far, he noticed a scrap of parchment and bent down.

Not such a scrap. A packet with a broken wax seal.

He looked after the Templar, as if he should hurry to catch him and return what was undoubtedly a communication. Huh, not a chance in Hell! He felt the smooth vellum. No expense spared in the salting, liming, scraping and buffing – a quality piece of workmanship.

He ran his fingers over the wax which was as black as oak gall ink, but flakes were missing and he could identify nothing of a seal and something inside of him whispered, the part that had been trained by Gisborne and Adam, by Ahmed and Leo. Secrets were valuable. Sometimes beyond value and so he thrust the packet in his purse and hurried to the hospice, to ring the bell for entry.

The nun who had opened the gate pointed to a small herb garden, not much bigger than a privy space, where Ariella sat with Lucas, illumined by the last of the sun before it sank behind the roof of the hospice. Henri watched for a moment as Ariella adjusted her shift and gown after feeding the babe, smiling at the infant all the while and murmuring to him. The sight could almost have been a church painting, so perfect was it in subject matter and framed by the stonework of a small arch. She looked up as his footsteps crunched from the gate toward her.

'Henri! Lucas and I have just slept and eaten and are feeling more human and less like a pair of transitory moths flitting from place to place.'

'Ah,' he replied ruefully.

'Oh, not immediately,' she gasped. 'Surely not!'

'Not immediately, no. But tomorrow at Prime. And at our leisure, so be heartened. We shall not be hurrying. May I sit?' He did not wait for her response, settling himself on a simple wooden bench opposite her, his knees almost touching hers and he couldn't deny that his heartbeat had hastened that much more. 'In fact, it is just you, Lucas and myself. Adam and Tobias have left.' He explained the reasoning and she sucked in a breath when he mentioned the Templar encounter.

'They are here?' Her eyes widened and she held Lucas closer as if Henri had just mentioned that Pontius Pilate was in Viviers.

He described his accidental meeting with the Templar and his serjeant and then went on to describe the packet the man had dropped. He looked out of their sanctuary and seeing no one, not even the quiet gatekeeping nun, he turned his body away from the entrance to the garden. The purse drawstrings opened easily, and he pulled the packet out, holding it to turn over and over.

'Have you opened it?' Ariella asked as Lucas heaved in a breath and snuggled deeper into her arms.

'No.'

'Will you?'

'My head says yes.'

'A Gisborne man to the core...'

'It's as if Lady Fortune has allowed a commodity of great value to fall into my hands.'

'More like the Templar's carelessness,' she replied. 'Well then?' she nodded toward the packet but he held it closed for a moment.

'Ariella, you and I are now travelling together without company and it will seem totally at odds to have a matron travelling alone with her guard. It is unseemly at best, questionable at worst and may draw the wrong kind of attention.'

She sat back and her eyebrows shot skyward. 'How is that a problem? I am a mother with a child.' Her mouth twisted and she huffed in exasperation, shaking her head slightly. 'Henri, I shall be what I am, a widow travelling with my child to my husband's family home in Lyon. It is the truth.'

It was Henri's turn to sit back. 'You don't mind the gossip? That you travel alone without a companion? A man?'

She laughed, a throaty sound from deep in her belly and Lucas stirred, eyes opening to stare at her and grin. 'See there, even Lucas thinks it is amusing. Come Henri, you should know me well enough by now to know I don't care a fig for gossip.' She leaned forward and slid a hand under his as he held the packet.

'Very well,' he said, his skin tingling at her feather touch and he thought how Tobias would have laughed out loud and how Adam would have frowned with complete disapproval. But he reminded himself that so much of his work in Gisborne-ben Simon was playacting. As Tobias had said numerous times. He must playact with Ariella, for her sake as much as his.

He turned the packet over and carefully unfolded it. One sheet folded into three. There were no names, nothing to indicate a sender or receiver and no blessings. Just information. Information as worthy and valuable as a king's hoard for those who carried a king's ransom wrapped in swaddling cloths.

He looked up at Ariella.

'They know.'

'It is not possible...'

'Nevertheless. This,' he lifted it off his lap and dropped it again. 'This indicates they have known of its existence and are searching for it.'

'Explain. Read it to me.'

He folded it out over his knee, showing her the parchment that was devoid of words beyond one carefully written name and a seal.

'Gilbert d'Hérail?' she said. 'He is the Grand Master, is he not? And that?'

'His seal – the four shields; *la croix pattée de gueules* – the Templar cross, and *la croix d'azur*, which is his family's own.'

'And so? A touch ambiguous, I think. One could draw many conclusions.'

'Perhaps. But I believe it's the Grand Master's seal of approval upon this hunt for the foremost relic of all time. D' Herail is sanctifying anything de Tremelay may see fit to do.'

Ariella sat back. '*Deus*! Murder, think you?'

Henri folded the parchment back up and slipped it into his purse, tightening the drawstrings with a snap. 'In fact, yes.'

Chapter Nine

'They say he's very important.' Gelis walked along the dirt road with Cécile to the only hospice which had spare beds. The town was busy, thrumming with excitement and many of the *dorters*, inns and taverns were full. They were returning to the *dorter* after prayers in the old church of Saint-Pierre. A small church, originally a chapel for the Forez nobility, they had been crammed cheek by jowl with the pious. Nevertheless, Cécile took comfort from the prayers and from the sonorous Latin.

But she had been glad to leave and was ruminating on the peace of Esteil's tiny chapel when Gelis bumped her. 'I'm sorry. Who is important?'

'Sister! The priest is called *Père* Urbain and he has been here for a long time as officiating priest for the church. I spoke to him as we left while you were busy lighting candles.' She laughed and waved her hand. 'Anyway, the archbishop he said, is very important! Monsignor Reynaud de Forez no less. He is passing through tomorrow on his way to his family's demesnes in the forests and will kindly perform a Mass whilst he is here.' Gelis rubbed her stomach and stretched up and back. She grunted. 'This babe is so heavy. Perhaps I can get him to bless our little one. What say you?'

'Perhaps. Do you wish to return to the church to ask the priest?' Privately, Cécile doubted the archbishop would do such a thing for someone whom he didn't know and who came from another region altogether. Let alone a merchant's wife. A nobleman's wife, maybe…

'Perhaps not. I need to lie down for a little. This baggage that I carry is making his mother very tired.'

They walked on without speaking, each thinking their own thoughts. Around them the life of the small town pulsated, the marketplace fertile and lusty with fragrance and noise. The smell of bread, raw meat, blood, horse-droppings, of tanned hides and woollen fleece, of timber barrels, wine, body odour and human waste was no different to Esteil but each town that Cécile passed through was now increasing in size by increments and it confronted her, agitating her so that she wanted to sink into the darkly quiet depths of any church she entered.

They had passed through Ambert, a quiet place resting on the edge of the Forez verdure where they stayed gratefully in the *dorter* of a nunnery, with the men at an inn. Gratefully because the high slopes of the road from Esteil to Ambert had stretched horses and men alike after the attack. Gelis had subsided onto her cot in the *dorter* with a shaking sigh and Cécile had asked for the infirmarian to examine her, to make sure she and the babe had sustained no grave injury from the event. The woman was proficient enough, giving Gelis arnica unguent to rub into her bruises and an infusion of rose, lavender and sage for her aching head and body. For her heart and soul though, Cécile suggested they must go to the chapel and pray. Light candles for poor young Chrestien who now lay in a forest grave, and to beseech the Lord for His continued protection.

They spent two days in Ambert before beginning the short journey to Montbrison, but even so and despite her cheery nature, Gelis had begun to tire swiftly, dark shadows forming beneath her eyes. When she removed her wimple and veil before retiring, Cécile noticed a pulse jumping in her neck and that her face was often flushed. It worried her, knowing the longest part of their journey, from Montbrison, southeast to Saint Etienne was next to come. And still the road to Givors. Then, by the grace of God, they might be able to travel on to Lyon by barge, so that Gelis could lie back and be comfortable. By the Saints, what possessed this little woman to travel so close to the birth of her child?

The journey from Ambert had been a trial. The horse-drawn cart bumped and jolted, slipped and slid on the rutted and uneven road. Rain and passing traffic had dug deep grooves into the mud and the horses stumbled and lurched as they trod on stones and found hoof-holds in deep then shallow ruts – nothing was smooth. Cécile who was thin and agile from her life within the priory, managed adequately although her bones ached. But Gelis rocked and rolled back and forth, and often moaned and grabbed at Cécile's hands. Those moments terrified Cécile who above and beyond anything, did not want to have to assist Gelis in childbirth.

But they had reached Montbrison unharmed and Gelis seemed to brighten, no doubt soaking up the excited atmosphere of the town. To have a member of the nobility visit was thrill enough, but for that member to be the Archbishop of Lyon was a miracle for the town and proof positive that the noble family still held Montbrison in the highest esteem as their family holding.

As they passed through the edges of the forest approaches to Montbrison, Gelis's eyes had brightened and she pointed out wild mauve crocus and bright blue speedwell. Cécile smiled, recalling with a tender sadness that she had spent time at Esteil picking speedwell for the infirmary in springs past. Sister Melisende would pulverise leaves for an infusion for the coughs and colds of winter, or make a poultice of the whole plant for itches brought on by all manner of things. Briefly she wondered if she should find herbs suitable for childbirth, just in case. But what herbs? Surely there was only belladonna for pain.

And what of birthing rituals? She knew vaguely of prayers. But her job within the priory had been the quiet creation of beauty in script and silk, not the dangerous process of delivering life into the world.

'Saint Margaret, I beg of you. Help me and help my friend.' Because Gelis *was* Cécile's friend now. The two women had bonded in extremis and although Cécile would never tell Gelis, she needed the little merchant wife's worldly manner to help her cope with the large confines of towns, the noise, the proliferation of men. *'Let us reach Lyon whole and in one piece, each of us.'*

'Well! If there is to be a Mass, I can't imagine how that little church will hold us all. There is surely a need for a larger church in this town. It is the main stronghold of the Forez family, after all, from which the Archbishop comes. But a pretty town, I think. Look how the stream runs right through.'

Pretty enough, thought Cécile, if the little river Vizézy wasn't tainted with cess and putrid remains from the butchers of the town. At least it was flowing swiftly with winter rains and run-off and was flushed more often. She thought what value there was in living within the small village of Esteil, where such putrescence was so much less. She could barely imagine what Lyon would be like. Each town they stopped in was so much the worse for its size. She had seen nothing to make her wish to leave the priory for other more well-appointed places and she hoped to God that the prioress was holding off the canons. At least until she could return with this so-called beneficence.

If one could call a relic such.

'So, Sister. Do you really think your journey will be

worthwhile? That you will find excellent commodities in Lyon?'

Cécile jumped as if stung. 'Pardon? What say you?' She wondered if she had talked of the relic in her sleep and that Geltidis may have heard her. Maybe others had as well…

'Your silks and parchments. Do you think you will find them?'

'Oh. I see. Yes, I hope so. But as you know, my main purpose is to escort the Prioress's cousin back to our priory for a period of seclusion. It would be an additional joy however, to purchase more pigment and gold-leaf as well parchment and silk. And how I would love a bell for our chapel. It is some time since we had a chapel bell. The old one cracked and rang off-key and we took it down, as it was a danger to any Sister who might be ringing it below. But in truth, Gelis, as I have said, we are a poor priory and I have little monies with which to do such things.'

'God works in such mysterious ways, Sister Cécile. After all, to think that we buy our goods from de Clochard and go to visit the house and the Lyon market, and that you travel to the house to collect Madame Amée. Does it not make you think this is a journey blessed?'

Cécile smiled, less convinced than her friend and surprised at how quickly the woman appeared to forget the events of earlier in their travels. 'Indeed,' she replied.

They turned the corner to the small Benedictine hospice where they had slept the previous night – a place not as sweet-smelling as Esteil's *dorter*. Cécile thought the mattresses may have fleas; she was sure she felt the itch. She must try and find some of the speedwell, rueful that because she had relied so much on Melisende to provide the correct unguents and potions, she had never really taken note of what the good sister used nor how she prepared medicaments.

Excluding the infirmary, she wondered how the priory ran without her. Was the Prioress managing to keep the ledger? How were the embroideries progressing and was the copying and illumination continuing without error? She wondered if the nuns of Montbrison had as nimble fingers as those within Esteil? Perhaps she should ask to see any work, if that was how they survived; just to compare and give her confidence.

But then, these foreign convents, because they were surely that despite following the Benedictine Rule – they existed within towns where money was forthcoming, not isolated and far from anything like Esteil. The provision of hospices alone would generate income. Unlike little Esteil with its miniscule component of women and in a poor region.

The bells rang for Matins and Cécile levered herself from the cot. Geltidis slept on, and the *dorter* vibrated with coughs, snores and farts from those travellers eager to attend a Mass officiated by the Archbishop of Lyon himself on the morrow. The room was filled with shadow but a strip of moonlight through a narrow horn window lit a path across the rushes to the door. Cécile carried her sandals, walking barefoot across the dried, prickling floor, hoping she woke no one as she moved.

She closed the door quietly and found her way to a long cloister where she slid in behind a line of nuns, some of whom were carrying the bobbing lights of tallow-candle lamps. As they wound their way to the choir, she found a niche at the rear of the chapel against a stone wall beneath a pious stone carving of the Virgin. The Holy Virgin looked down, Her hands spread and Cécile considered that She was as like to protect Her servant here as anywhere.

It was easy to settle into the rhythm of the prayers of Matins and as the nuns sang the Magnificat, Cécile's heart soared.

Magnificat anima mea Dominum
Et exsultavit spiritus meus in Deo salutari meo

For he hath regarded: the lowliness of his handmaiden:
For behold, from henceforth: all generations shall c
all me blessed...

How she had missed the sound of prayer. The devotion, the duty. How she missed the sorority of like minds.

Geltidis...

Cécile liked her, truly she did, but there could never be the closeness she shared with Benedicta.

Benedicta, blessed be thy name...

She and Benedicta were blossoms on a vine. They shared such love of the priory. And, let it be said, pride in the work that came from the hearts, souls and fingers of the Sisters within Esteil.

But that frequent dark thought stained her gentle memories.

Why do we need a relic?

With more supplies and three additional novices, more ecclesiastical robes could be stitched, so that even the Pope would pay for a silk cope from Esteil. Even foreign queens would pay to own a Book of Hours copied by the nimble and blessed fingers of Esteil's scribes.

A relic, for God's sake!

Whose thighbone? Whose teeth?

Like a cold river mist, anger seeped up into Cécile's chest. To think she'd been ripped from all she held dear by the ridiculous machinations of a prioress with ideas beyond her station. To think she'd been subjected to fear the like of which the prioress had probably never experienced in her own life.

Separation!

Murder!

She shifted on her knees and the cold stone bit into her bones as the nuns sang on.

Deposuit potentes de sede, et exaltavit humiles…

He hath put down the mighty from their seat: and hath exalted the humble and meek…

As she moved, white pain ground into her kneecap and she gasped, the Sisters turning to seek out the sound in the darkest reaches of the chapel. She rubbed her knee, sinking away from observation, knowing she suffered punishment for unkind thoughts.

Mea culpa, mea culpa, mea culpa.

Thanks to the night, none of the nuns looked her way as they filed out, concentrating on the flickering shadow of the foul-smelling tallow candles, their sandals a fading whisper.

All that was left was the sighing emptiness of the chapel, the creak of timbers as they chilled, the moan of a cool breeze around the walls outside, and the fingernail scratch of a tree whose branches grew too close to the thick horn windows.

She debated returning to the *dorter* until Lauds, but she knew she wouldn't sleep at all this night, being stretched as tight as a bowstring, and she had so much to think on, so much about which she must talk with God. The truth was that she had no belief in the efficacy of relics. She believed only in God's innate kindness. Surely it was…

Her head flicked toward the door as it squeaked open to reveal a tall figure illumined by a lamp. She shrank back as far as she could, trying not to breathe because the shape was a man's – broad-shouldered and with a determined gait as he moved along the nave, shadowed by a shorter man.

'My lord,' said the latter. 'I thank you for coming at the Archbishop's request…'

The tall man looked around and metal clinked as he settled against a bench, leaning with nothing less than insouciance. Even Cécile could determine that much in his silhouette.

'A good enough place to have a discussion in private, Brother Severus. What do you wish to discuss?'

A monk? Is he a Benedictine brother? From Montbrison?

The monk cleared his throat. 'Archbishop Reynaud has heard tell of a relic, my lord and that you have access to this relic. The Archbishop has a great interest in securing it for Lyon…' His voice was high-pitched, nasal, as if he pinched at his nostrils.

'And are *you* aware of the fact that the Templars may keep it as their own.'

A Templar knight?

His voice rolled deeply from his throat. A beautiful sound that almost charmed. But at the mention of the word *relic*, Cécile had stiffened, squeezing every muscle in her face so as not to gasp and betray her presence. Safety lay in silence.

'But my lord, the Archbishop will offer…'

'Others will offer as much, Brother Severus, if not more. Be under no illusions. Popes would go to war to own this relic and it is beholden upon our order to guard its safety. Why does Archbishop Reynaud covet it? Ah, for power perhaps. Has he an urge to seek the Pontiff's throne for himself?'

There was a degree of threat in the question and for a shred of a moment, Cécile wondered whether the Templars were the Pope's army. She had heard as much in idle priory gossip, but had also heard the Templars were richer than any monarch, spiritual or otherwise, and as such a law unto themselves.

The monk shook his head with haste. 'No, no, not at all. His Grace the Archbishop is a devoted servant of His Holiness. But he feels Lyon's cathedral would be a supreme holy home for a great relic. May I tell the Archbishop that at the very least, you will negotiate?' This last was halfway between a wheedle and a whine and every nerve in Cécile's body squirmed at the sound.

'You may tell him the relic is on its way to Lyon. Till then there is nothing more to say.'

'My lord,' the monk coughed, a desperate sound. 'I am required to ask for a firm agreement that the Templars will negotiate with the Archbishop's representative, that is,' he coughed again, 'myself over the purchase of this great thing.'

'And I reply that we will negotiate with whomsoever we please, *if* we please. Now, Brother Severus, is it not past your bedtime? I know it is past mine. I wish you well.'

He brushed past the monk and in a moment, not even the echoes of his glorious voice were left and Cécile knew she would remember the mellifluous tones till the day she died. The monk sighed and followed after the knight, his sandals tap-tapping to the door. The profound black silence of night settled, a heavy, muffling cloak, and Cécile's heart pounded loud enough to wake the dead.

The words *relic* and *Lyon* stunned her and she sucked in a lungful of air now that she and the chapel were alone. The coincidence was biblical in scope – the Templar's relic and her own *had* to be the same. But a relic that popes would go to war over?

She wished she could talk with someone but Prioress Gisela had been adamant. This was to be a secret until the relic was in the care of Esteil.

Something that could cause a war?

What price the lives then, of those who lived within the priory?

She fingered her prayer beads over and over, praying for guidance of some sort.

The Templar's voice had been beautiful. Never in her life had Cécile heard a voice that flowed like the choicest golden wine. As blasphemous as it might sound, it was how she expected God's voice to sound. Her own father's voice had been coarse, like rough river gravel. So too the man she might have married. The priest who performed the Mass and confession at the priory had sounded like the monk, Severus. As if his testes had been cut. And as that thought raced through her mind, she flushed and squeezed her eyes tight, begging for forgiveness.

Unkind thoughts always – she crossed herself. She realised that what she had heard and what her prioress had asked of her could never be revealed in the confessional.

It was by her assessment far too dangerous, and again she wondered why Gisela had entrusted this task to an elderly nun so inexperienced in the ways of the world. Her thoughts jumped and swirled until she was exhausted, eyelids growing heavy. She pulled her cloak tighter and shrank ever deeper into the stone shadow of the chapel, resting her eyes until she knew no more.

The bells for Lauds woke her and she watched the nuns from her chosen covert, too tired to assess them like the Obedientiary she was. She prayed along with them and they filed out again. She heard noise from further away, perhaps from the kitchens, and then slept again until Prime and this time, the chapel was filled with the nuns and those men and women from the *dorters*. She moved stiffly and surreptitiously next to Geltidis, pulling a smile from tired corners.

'Oh, Sister, I looked for you…'

'I rose a little earlier. Old habits. How do you fare?'

'Pff!' Geltidis wafted her hand. 'Fair but fat! I'm glad we have the cart. I shall ride like a queen today.' Geltidis spoke from behind a façade of gaiety but Cécile worried. Her friend's fingers and face were swollen…

After breaking their fast, they squeezed into the back row of Saint Pièrre's for the mass officiated over by the Archbishop of Lyon. Another man with a tiresome voice, thought Cécile, waiting for a thunderbolt from above to strike her down. But she admired his vestments, trimmed in rich golden thread which shimmered by the light of candles. The smoky air wafted to the buttresses and the smell of incense drifted from the swinging thurible. It was a sight, for sure. Filled with the largesse of golden plate and silken robes, and a crowd of monks hovering around the archbishop like worker bees around the queen. A choir chanted, the deep voices of the monks thrilling Cécile who loved prayer song, even if it was sung by men.

But Reynaud de Forez had no message of consequence and it seemed as if he sped through the prayers, barely waiting for the responses. Once, as everyone knelt, Cécile caught a glimpse of a monk close by the archbishop, noticeable for the dense black of his habit. His face was as long as a cloth-fold and what showed of his hair was dark and stringy on his cowl.

Rat-like.

Perhaps it was a common way with monks, she thought, and then vowed to God to be charitable and kind and not suspicious and cynical.

Later, blessed and mellow, the group left Montbrison with its twin streams and houses leaning precariously toward the shallows. The merchants wanted to reach Givors and the barges to Lyon as fast as they could safely travel. Gelis had rocked to sleep, for which Cécile was glad, hoping that rest would ease the poor wife's apparent discomfort.

They trundled along, as they had done before Montbrison, passing verdant forest and blooming speedwell, which Cécile hurried to gather in bunches. The hedgerow grasses blossomed, bees and wasps buzzed, butterflies flitted decadently and birds sang loudly in the fecund air. It was balm to her troubled soul.

The merchants discussed the trading they had observed in Montbrison and left the nun alone.

Huh, trade…
What did they know of relics, she wondered?
Especially relics that could begin wars.

Chapter Ten

Henri de Montbrison
Givors

The Gier river flowed into the Rhône with a fierce backwash. The winter thaw from high in the mountains and the heavier than normal spring rains had swollen the river, and a muddy stain flowed out into the Rhône with swirling currents and dirty logs.

Constant downpours had forced Henri, Ariella and Lucas beneath rocky overhangs and spreading trees and once beneath the ruined arch of an ancient and crumbling Roman bridge. Lucas had been remarkable, coping with the damp like one born to it.

But their horses were less so. At each stop, they flattened their ears and swung rumps toward the oncoming rain, caring not that they trod on feet or knocked women with babies. The horses' hooves were also softening in the muddy conditions and when they travelled uphill over a stony path, the animals picked across it as if it were thorns. Henri expected lameness, hoping they would last until they reached Givors and the barges.

When they eventually stood by the Rhône, he was concerned. The river snapped and pulled at the riverbanks so that here and there, morsels fell into the flow and disappeared swiftly downstream.

'It looks bad, Henri.' Ariella manoeuvred Lucas into a more comfortable position. 'I'm mostly stalwart but even I have had my fill of horses and of rain and yet I look at that flow and wonder how a barge might conceivably travel upstream. It is impossible.' A heavy log flicked up like a twig and was consumed by the white confluence.

The sky above them was soft blue, puffs of thistledown cloud floating where heavy grey had been earlier. It was hard to believe that rain had deluged for what seemed forty days and forty nights. In fact, it had only been two days but the wet had sunk into their bones and God knows how the child faired.

Henri had kept a guarded eye behind, to see if they were followed but with the downpours and then heavy mist, and the mud muffling any footfall, it was hard to tell. He assumed not, but castigated himself for assuming anything.

'I shall make enquiries whilst you and Lucas dry out.' He turned to see her nuzzling the top of Lucas's feathery head. The child had a wine-tint to his hair – Ariella's child without doubt. 'The river will settle, Ariella. And worst case, we will have to ride again. Better to do so than risk our cargo.' He smoothed a loving hand over Lucas's head. 'I mean Lucas, you understand.'

She smiled – a radiant beam of sunshine. 'Then let us find a roof under which we can sleep.'

He left her at a tavern. They had a small room above the stair, right under the damp eaves, but it was next to the side-hung chimney and the warmth off the stone filled the chamber with comfort even if the cots were barely more than a sack of straw on the floor. They could see through the cracks between the floorboards as well, men drinking and eating, the innkeeper, his wife and daughter constantly plying trencher and mug around the noisy space. But the food smelled good and warmth was desirable. Henri felt Ariella and the babe would be safe whilst he searched for a barge.

'Put the bar across the door whilst I'm gone, Ariella, just to be safe. Have you all you need?'

Ariella sat cross-legged on the floor, scooping bread and meat-juices from a wooden platter into her mouth, Lucas lying between her knees. 'Yes. We shall be safe, don't worry. Take care and come back soonest.'

He pulled the door shut behind, hurrying down the stair and outside in the direction of the barge wharf. The sky hung flagrant blue and softest peach, belying what had befallen in the days previous. A damp spring without doubt.

As he approached the wharf, he could see a group of raucous people surrounding a heavy-set man who had a tangle of harness hung over his shoulder.

'I don' care,' he was saying. 'You could offer me the Archbishop's gold staff and neither me, me men or me horses will tow barges to Lyon while the river's up.'

The voices rose in a hubbub again.

'I says no! Maybe it'll be a sennight a' more afore I dare put out on that river. An' you won' find any other who'll do it. We know that water and it ain't safe.' He pushed past the group and then on past Henri with a jingle of harness and bits.

'Excuse me, messire,' Henri grabbed the man's arm, feeling the solid muscle beneath his fingers. 'If you cannot transport folk, can you direct me to someone who has strong horses that will get me and my mistress to her family in Lyon? I would pay.'

The man's eyes narrowed. 'How much?'

'Whatever you say.'

'Where'you from?'

'Venezia.'

'Where's that then?'

Henri could hear a voice calling to the barge master and broke in, '*Messire*?'

'It won' be cheap…' the man replied as his eyes ran over the quality or not of Henri's clothes.

'I need to get to Lyon, this fellow has mounts?'

The man squinted at Henri and then spat sideways. 'Go to Laurenz, folk'll tell you where he is.'

He strode on and suddenly Henri was engulfed by the small crowd from the wharf.

'What did he say?'

'Has he changed his mind?'

'My wife needs to get to Lyon…'

This last was said by a rotund man, his expensive attire crumpled and dirty and whose beard was in need of a trim and whose cloak was sodden at the ends. Henri looked behind him and observed an equally rotund, short woman leaning heavily on the arm of a nun.

'He has not changed his mind and suggests we ride to Lyon if we are in a hurry.' Henri spoke kindly to the group – three men and two oddly assorted women – but he had a sudden flash of an idea. 'Perhaps we can ride together, safety in numbers.' He took a breath and dived into the lie. 'My mistress and her child need company…'

The men looked at each other. Bedraggled by road travel and indubitably strained, they shrugged. The round man spoke up.

'We have ridden for days from the west and since Esteil, have been dogged by some misfortune. This…' he nodded at the river, 'is surely the last straw.' He huffed and then cleared his throat. 'As you say, we could ride to Lyon in a bigger group for safety. My wife…' he indicated the round woman, '…my wife is due to give birth at any moment and we *must* be in Lyon before that happens. The good Sister travels with us. If we can get new horses…'

'How many?' Henri wondered how much might convince Laurenz to sell more horses. Then again, money was money.

'There are only five of us, so three riding horses and a cart horse? We have a cart.'

'Is your cart large enough to fit my mistress and her child? If so, I only need a horse for myself. Have you sound horses to trade?'

'Yes. Good ones from Montbrison but tired and sore.'

Something like the point of dagger pricked between Henri's shoulder blades as his birthplace was mentioned. 'I shall render the exchange, if you trust me, *messire*. Four saddle horses and one cart horse. I suspect he will drive a tough bargain. Are you ready for that?'

The men nodded. 'If it gets us to Lyon,' the fat man said.

'Then we must introduce ourselves. I am Henri from Venezia …' Henri bowed his head, 'whom do I have the pleasure of addressing?'

'We leave at dawn.' Henri watched Ariella's face crease with dismay. 'I'm so sorry for you and Lucas but I can see no other way. Staying in Givors for a sennight may be dangerous. We need to keep moving calmly, but always forward.'

'You sound as if you are speaking to footsoldiers, Henri.'

'I'm sorry, I did not mean to patronise.'

'Patronise? Of course you're not. You are just being sensible. My late…' she stopped and frowned. 'Guillaume was the same. As if you both must protect the world.'

'To a point, yes.' Henri took Lucas from her arms and carried him about the chamber, rocking him gently. 'This is your world, this fine little son, and I am happy to protect him. And to protect you.' He didn't look at her and thought to himself he must step back a pace. 'It is my job, after all.'

She folded swaddling cloths and slipped them into the sack that was Lucas's. 'It is that,' she answered.

They ate, she gave Lucas some broth and wetly mashed vegetables which he sucked from a crust and then whilst she fed him from her breast, seated on their uncomfortable beds, Henri descended to the inn to purchase a jug of wine, pay for their stay and inform the innkeeper they would be leaving at dawn.

'The barge men do not sail though,' the innkeeper said as he poured wine into a jug.

'No, but we changed horses and we leave with a group of merchants to travel onward.'

'You changed horses with Laurenz?' the innkeeper grinned.

'Indeed,' Henri replied. 'And he almost emptied my mistress's purse. She told me to give you the rest for bread, cheese and wine to sustain she and her child to Lyon.' He tipped up the purse and there was the chink of silver *sols* onto the trestle. He shook the small leather sack to show that it was empty and then hung it from his belt. 'I'll give you the lot for good supplies.'

The innkeeper's bloodshot eyes widened. 'Yes,' he said slowly. 'But then what will you have for Lyon? You must pay an entry tax…'

'My mistress has family there. We will get word to them and they will come to the city gates.'

'Alright then. I shall provide you with a loaf and a wheel of cheese and if you have costrels, I will fill them. For all of that.' He indicated the silver with a twist of his thumb.

Henri knew that what he was offered by the innkeeper was worth far less than what he had laid out but they needed food. It was money well-spent.

'You travel with merchants you say?' the innkeeper asked.

'Yes, from Mons and Toulon I believe. There is also a woman due to give birth at any time and a nun.'

'Ho, a nun! Then she can pray for your souls that you all reach Lyon safely.'

'A blessing, I suppose,' said Henri, recalling the angular face of the older religieuse and how she passed a severe gaze over him when he spoke with *Messire* Gervasius from Mons.

'I open the inn to the public when the bells ring for Lauds. Your supplies will be ready then.'

Henri thanked him and climbed the steep stair. Ariella lay sleeping near the chimney, a cloak over she and the infant. Her gentle breath huffed in and out and Lucas stretched without waking and then snuggled into his mother's shape again. Henri lay down, musing that this must be what a marriage is like and thinking thus, recalled his friends. Toby would have laughed himself into apoplexy, pointing a finger and winking. It made him smile. He preferred not to think of Adam.

He felt sleep pulling at him but heard the murmur of a deep voice beneath and then the reply of the innkeeper, and being what he was, he leaned over and peered down through one of the cracks. Wide shoulders were swathed in a white cloak.

'No barges? For how long?' The voice was deep, well-modulated and articulate and it set Henri's guts rolling, instant fear trickling beneath his armpits.

'Maybe a sennight, they say. Depends on the weather. The barges'll be delayed on and off for this whole season. So much rain.'

'A sennight, God curse it!'

'You can ride. I know of a group from hereabouts, leaving at dawn. Same as you, they wanted to get to Lyon by barge and have no other way…'

'Who is in this group?'

'Well now, I'm not sure. Some merchants, I think…'

'And that is all?'

The man, a Templar knight, *the* Templar knight, stood over the innkeeper and the innkeeper turned his back and reached for a wine flagon. 'I sell wine and vittles, *messire*. I'm not a barge man. Nor do I care who comes and goes, except to take their money for my goods. Do you wish for some wine?'

'I thank you,' the Templar began to turn, 'but no.' His cloak flurried and folded as he reached for the door which he pulled open and then slammed shut. Then the innkeeper trudged across the room and a bar was heaved into place over the door.

Henri lay back, trembling.

That voice…

He would never forget it – the voice that called for a massacre of the innocents. Gilbert de Tremelay. A name branded on Henri's heart and soul from the past and which dogged him like a shade.

He looked at Lucas in the protective circle of his mother's arms. He was right to move on. He and Ariella must play their parts like seasoned performers. Their *'truthful'* story must pass examination and he thought on that until his eyelids became heavy, but sleep was unwelcome as he knew he would dream and may scream. It was something he would not allow Ariella or the innkeeper to hear.

'We come from Venezia,' he said early in the morning as Ariella fed her babe. 'And we go to stay with your family in Lyon as we decided.' He made a business of strapping on his sword and dagger, as she pulled folds back over her breasts.

'Why?' she asked.

'Why what?'

'Why do we go to Lyon?'

'If we are pushed, then we say the truth, that your husband died and Michael is offering you a home within the business.'

'But what if these merchants know of de Clochard? It's not a small business in Lyon. Most will have heard of it.'

'Then we will exclaim on the joy of coincidence and say we are all smiled upon by the Saints. Happy and light, as little depth as we can manage. Can you do it?'

'Henri, why the truth?'

'Less untruth to trip over.'

She pulled at a loose thread on Lucas's swaddling before settling him in a sling to carry him. Truly he was God's gift, never crying, always calm or smiling. 'I am uneasy.' Ariella was on edge, he could see it as she withdrew from him like an ebbing tide.

'I'm sorry,' he said. 'I know you are tired and that you relished the idea of the barge instead of horses. But at least we have a cart...'

'Yes,' she answered with a degree of sarcasm. 'At least we have that.'

For one brief moment he was angry and wanted to remonstrate. It was her choice to journey to Lyon after all and no one, least of all her father who granted her every wish, gainsaid her. He brushed past her to the door. 'Then we must join our companions. Are you done?'

'I am done,' she replied and he ground his teeth at her tone.

The two merchants, Robertus and Erembrouc of Toulon, had elongated faces and shoulder length lank hair, reminding Henri of Byzantine icons. The remaining one, the fat one, the fellow called Gervasius, hovered around his wife like a horsefly.

She in turn, was like a child's ball – curved everywhere; face, hands and belly. Granted she was with child, but when she was assisted onto the cart, it creaked as if its back was broken, and two more women and an infant yet to climb in. Henri hoped to God the timbers were stout and that the cart horse he had acquired strong enough.

The woman, Geltidis, was accompanied by a nun in worn dark robes and a less than clean wimple and veil. She was as thin as a whiplash and her face was all angles with thin lips, and yet, Henri noticed that when she spoke to the merchant's wife, her voice was considerate and mellow.

He wondered what the group thought of he and his mistress and her child, and so he joined them with a cheery greeting, effecting geniality. Ariella passed Lucas to him and used his arm to climb into the cart. Lucas gazed around, dark eyes alight, settling on Henri with a smile that revealed little toothbuds. Henri grinned back and then kissed the child's forehead. No act there – his heart warmed every time he held the child. Ariella sat against sacks and reached for her child.

'Thank you, Henri,' she said without looking at him, settling the child and introducing herself to Geltidis.

Henri turned to the nun. 'Sister, may I help you?'

'I thank you, sir, but I will walk for a little. It is pleasantly cool and I will stretch my legs.'

'You are sure? I can walk and you may ride my horse if you prefer.'

'Thank you, no. I will manage.' Her tone had hardened just a little, as if she wasn't used to being challenged.

'I am Henri, Sister,' he replied, in an effort to charm the frostiness from her. 'From Venezia. My mistress is called Ariella and her son is named Lucas.'

'I am *Soeur* Cécile from the priory of Esteil, *messire*. Ah, we begin...' She struck off, dismissing him, intent on her own company and Henri mounted his horse, settling himself in the saddle and leaving his reins loose as the beast ambled behind the cart. The purchased cart horse pulled with ease, its shoulders rolling softly and its hind legs placed wide and with a surefootedness that pleased Henri. It snorted with a kind of muted pleasure, breathing in the moist air of the riverbank, and his own horse snorted back.

Geltidis chatted to Ariella quite gaily, although Henri would bet she wasn't well, with shadows beneath eyes that were set in a pasty face. He marvelled at Ariella's calm composure as she answered her companion back.

'Well then, *madame*,' said the matron. 'You have a

beautiful babe.' She rubbed her bulge. 'And I will soon join you. Although I would that it waited until Lyon.' There was a degree of querulousness in her voice, perhaps fear, as there had been no mention of other children.

The conversation became women's talk and Henri twitched his horse's reins to leave the cart, jogging to Gervasius's side. '*Messire*, a fine day for travelling,' he said.

'A change from rain to be sure,' Gervasius agreed. 'Our journey has been plagued with it. I shall be pleased if we make Lyon by nightfall without a drop more on our heads. It has been a wet spring.'

'Indeed. The rivers are swollen and my wife so hoped to journey to Lyon by barge. With the child and such.' The men swayed in their creaking saddles, the horses blowing down their noses, clinking their harnesses, shaking their heads and settling into the rhythmic ground-covering walk that was the sign of good livery. Henri was glad he had been able to repurchase his earlier horses. They were good travelling beasts and he would bet his right thumb they'd be in Lyon by the time the gates closed.

The road was well-travelled, rutted and muddy but there was a smooth swathe to the forest edge and he and Gervasius guided the cart horse so that the women would be more comfortable. The nun, Henri saw, had already found the swathe and was striding along, hands folded into sleeves, head bowed and lips moving. He was impressed with her stoicism – he didn't want to be, for he found those who retired to the cloister to be less than remarkable, even escapist. Tobias would have reached up and smacked him about the ear, telling him not to be so patronising.

'My wife is due to give birth any moment,' Gervasius was saying. 'And this has been such a difficult and tiring journey. I would we were settled before she begins her labour.'

So all the hovering around his wife like a nervous cat with a kitten had been for a reason, Henri thought. 'She is a strong woman to travel in such a condition.'

'Strong? Ha! Will of iron! Women!' He laughed and it was a pleasant sound, honest, jovial. Henri warmed to him. 'Are you faring well, my love?' the merchant called back to the cart.

'Of course!' Geltidis answered. 'And in good company.'

'And you, my good Sister?' Gervasius called to the nun, breaking into her meditations. She raised her arm and her sleeve fell back to reveal pale, blue-veined skin. She had graceful hands with long fingers and Henri bet that she didn't clean out the piggery or work in the gardens at Esteil.

'A determined religieuse, no?' he asked of Gervasius.

'Indeed. And to be respected, *messire*.' He told Henri of the attack upon them after they had left Esteil and *Soeur* Cécile's role in the aftermath. 'She is such a calming presence for my wife. Gelis has not been successful in birthing babes and is nervous and to have the sister as a companion on our journey is a blessing from God.'

'The sister travels with you for that reason?'

'No, not at all. She travels to Lyon to select some merchandise for her priory and to escort her prioress's cousin back for a retreat. It just happened that we could chaperone her, it is more seemly for her according to her prioress, and as I say, for my wife it is a blessing.' Gervasius slid his fingers along his reins and shifted in the saddle. 'I tell you. I am as nervous as my wife for the outcome.'

'She did not think to stay behind?'

'*Messire* Henri, let me ask you. Is your employer so biddable?'

Henri burst out laughing as he thought of Ariella and the babe having travelled by ship to France and now this. 'It seems you and I are the unlucky ones, *messire*. *Madame* Ariella plays the game of being an amenable widow in society, but behind the gates, she yells at me and consigns me to a far corner!' Henri looked at Ariella as she lifted Lucas up to look at the world.

'But she looks a kind woman.' Gervasius pulled off his cap and was about to rub his fingers through his hair when a shout from behind caused all four men to start and look back, Gelis grabbing at Ariella's arm and the nun moving swiftly to the cart to face whomever approached. Henri liked her for that and began to reassess her. One could never tell from appearances alone…

Two horses approached at an easy canter, the rider on one with a billowing white cloak. Henri could feel the blood draining from his face, his heart thumping against his breastbone like a hammer on an anvil. Ariella looked around at him but he avoided her eyes, instead drawing in the reins as his horse began to sidle.

'Good day to you, sirs and ladies,' said the Templar knight whose voice was like the Archangel Gabriel's. 'Sister, blessings upon you.'

Soeur Cécile dropped her head but she drew her hands together within her cuffs and her shoulders had stiffened like a spear shaft.

'Good people, I was told you are travelling to Lyon. Perhaps we might accompany you.'

Robertus spoke up. 'My good sir,' the relief in his voice was tangible. 'With pleasure. We were attacked further back on our journey and to have the support of an honoured Templar is a blessing.'

Henri could have choked on the idiot merchant's words and instead, examined the weaponry hanging from the knight's belt. Sword and knife – yes, he knew about those, had seen them in action and pushed at the memory of a child's tender neck. He squeezed his shaking hands on the reins.

Why did the knight and his serjeant want to travel with this motley group? Why did they not just continue on?

'My serjeant and I need to rest our horses as it has been a long journey thus far. This slower passage will please them. I would not damage their legs and feet in these wet conditions.'

The words made sense as the mounts were good-looking, well-bred beasts. Not something the knight and his man would want to get rid of quickly, but the animals had barely raised a sweat since Givors and Henri would bet they could have continued at a steady pace until Lyon. He doubted the knight had any interest in social discourse and his own unease began to climb as he wondered at the Templar's purpose.

Templars had dogged their steps every inch of this journey and he shuddered to think of what might happen if they knew that next to them, concealed in a babe's swaddling, lay a relic the like of which they might kill for.

'A journey from where, *messire*?' Gervasius asked.

'From the Sainte-Eulalie-de-Cernon Commandery.'

'The hospital near Montpellier? Ha. I know it!' Gervasius laughed, slapping his horse's neck so that the animal threw up his head and snorted.

'Indeed. I am Gilbert de Tremelay and my serjeant is called Jean de Laon.'

Gervasius introduced everyone, men and women, and Robertus suggested they move on if they wished to make Lyon by curfew.

Henri said nothing at all, allowing the three merchants to converse. He had watched the nun with interest. She turned to climb into the cart with the other women and her face was ashen, her tight mouth sucked in and bitten so that she had no lips at all.

Henri would bet his life on the fact that something had rattled the ramrod spine belonging to the Bride of Christ.

Tu quoque, soror Cécile.

You too...

As for him – he knew that voice. It had haunted his

dreams since Outremer. The voice was the Devil's and he could have killed the man without a thought if his hands weren't shaking and his head had not been filled with a fog.

'*Messire*?'

Gervasius reached over and tapped his arm.

He started and turned to the merchant. 'I'm sorry?'

'Our knightly friend was speaking to you.'

Never had Henri worked as hard to smooth his face to a naïve flatness. '*Messire*, my apologies. My employer's babe kept us awake in the night – growing his teeth they say – and I am dead asleep on my feet.' He smiled at the Templar, marvelling at how easy it was to playact when one wanted.

'You come from Venezia, I believe?'

'Indeed, my lord.'

'You are a long way from home.'

'As you say.'

'Why?'

Christ, what business is it of the Templar's? Henri's hands sweated on his reins and it was all he could do not to draw his blade in a fit of panic.

'My mistress has recently been widowed and she has been offered a place in her late husband's family home.'

'And yet she chooses to leave family behind in Venezia?'

'Yes. I believe her husband held a financial interest in the company. She is thinking of her young son, I dare say.'

'Did you travel from Marseille?'

'In fact, yes.' Henri lied. 'How did you know?'

Had this Templar seen Henri, Adam and Tobias as they crouched amongst the cargo on the ship to Notre de Dame de Ratis? All the play-acting would be for nought if he had.

The Templar's face remained passive; like some carved stone block before he replied. 'Your mistress doesn't mind the cart?'

'She would have preferred the barge,' Henri said rue-fully. 'Wouldn't we all? But…' He shrugged and pointed at the filthy brown river that sped by in evil whirls and where forest detritus punctuated the flow.

The knight looked to the river, raised his dark eyebrows and rode on in silence.

Henri held his horse back until the cart was level. 'How do you fare, *madame?*' he asked.

'Well enough, Henri,' Ariella answered archly, her eyes cool. Feeling the trembles leaving his hands, Henri spoke to the pregnant matron. 'And you, *Madame*? Are you comfortable?'

Gelis frowned, snapping at his obvious lack. 'Whilst carrying an oliphant, no, I am not.' She sighed and pushed against her bulge. 'But thank you for your concern.'

'And you, Sister?'

The nun looked at Henri as if he needed an exorcism, her face drawn tighter than a tabor skin. 'I am where God intended me to be,' she replied in a strained voice. 'Therefore, I am comfortable.'

'Good, good,' Henri nodded. 'Now all of you, tell me if you are not. Your comfort and safety are paramount.'

He let the cart roll on and waited whilst Gervasius joined him in the rear guard. The Templar knight and his serjeant rode with the other merchants and Henri had no doubt the men of trade believed they had received a gift from on high when the knight had ridden into their midst. After all, the Knights Templar had been formed to provide safe passage for pilgrims to the Holy Land. Lyon may not be the Holy Land but the merchants were indeed on a pilgrimage. Their talk had the reverential about it. The knight and his serjeant were therefore just fulfilling their charter.

But if only the merchants had seen what Henri had seen in the Holy Land. The way that knight had ridden down old men, women and children, ending their lives with one swing of a sword blade. Henri felt his face drawing in, tightening with the familiar tension, hardening to something that went beyond hatred.

There would be an end to this man's life, he swore, as he flipped his horse's mane back and forth across the wither. Swift and clean. As a Templar he supposed the man deserved that much. But as a servant of his fellow man, he deserved a disembowelling.

Chapter Eleven

Soeur Cécile
Lyon…

Cécile sat frozen.

The Templar's voice was indisputable – the voice of an angel but the manner of the Devil, surely.

But then what manner? What had the knight really done? Nothing by her knowledge, except bargain with that dungheap-rat of a monk from Lyon.

But she had only to look at the Templar's face – marble cold and with harsh angles, to know that he was maleficent. She ran her fingers over her prayer beads, her simply carved Paternosters, mouthing the Lord's Prayer beneath her breath.

Pater noster, qui es in caelis…

…et ne nos inducas in tentationem: sed libera nos a malo.

… deliver us from evil…

She let the beads fall to hang from her girdle and tucked her trembling fingers deep into her sleeves, swallowing and breathing deep before gazing around her. The knight and his serjeant had ridden ahead with the other merchants, but Gervasius rode behind the cart with the young matron's guard, Henri.

She felt ashamed of her dismissiveness when Henri had enquired of her wellbeing. He seemed a pleasant enough man – caring of his mistress and her child and with a happy spirit, but what would she know? She had known him for a heartbeat.

He was carved ruggedly – a square chin and clear eyes, salt and pepper stubble that made him appear older than his mistress, Ariella. His hair lay on his shoulder in wheatsheaf and nutmeg streaks and she noted the breadth of his shoulder – indication of a practiced swordsman, perhaps.

Gelis had nodded off, a faint sheen on her brow which disturbed Cécile. As for the young mother called Ariella, she sat with her babe, looking down at him as she ran a tender finger from temple to cheek. When she looked up, her eyes met Cécile's and her mouth set in a line as she leaned forward to whisper.

'Sister, our friend is not well.'

'She is with child,' snapped Cécile. 'And near her time.'

'Indeed, and I think she may not be very long from birthing,' Ariella replied calmly. 'And perhaps as well…'

Cécile's hands fell from her sleeves and she grasped the rattling side of the cart. 'But we must reach Lyon before it happens!'

'We must hope that is the case,' Ariella answered. 'For once it begins, we cannot halt it. It must follow its natural course.'

'*Deus!*' Cécile muttered and then a little louder. 'I know nothing of birthing.' She wanted to hand Gelis to a midwife or an infirmarian, and then leave them so that she could go to the Cathedral to pray, to invoke the Holy Mother and Saint Margaret of Antioch, begging them to intercede for Gelis. 'What must we do if she begins?' She had affection for rotund little Gelis from Mons – her kind jollity, her belief that this time she would give her husband the child he craved. She had never once betrayed anxiety that perhaps she, the infant or both could die in childbirth.

'She may be anxious and we must keep her calm,' Ariella said. 'Have you any medicinals at all?'

'Only speedwell that I fresh-picked…' Cécile wished she had packed a medicinal supply from the priory's infirmary but she had been too lost in her own disquiet, never thinking she might need to help others. How disappointed the Holy Mother and the Holy Father must be in her constant self-interest. 'Good for fleas, I think, but for childbirth?'

'I see…' Ariella replied. 'Well, if a healer or midwife had been called, she would have some amber, or ivory or coral, rose oil, vinegar, butter and perhaps a linen roll with prayers upon it and which could be laid on her belly. A crucifix as an intercession with the Holy Family. And even poppy for pain relief although that might slow her birthing. At the very least we should have valerian to calm her. At least you have prayers, Sister. And a crucifix perhaps?'

'Yes, I have a small crucifix, but what of the other?' Cécile replied.

'I don't know.' Ariella stopped and licked her lips. 'I am what they call a good breeder. My waters broke, my pains were no worse than bad back ache and…' she looked down at her baby who had woken and was playing with his fingers. 'And Lucas just slipped out. So quickly I barely knew it had happened. Mayhap Gelis will be the same.'

But Cécile knew she wouldn't. Her pallor, the sweaty sheen on her forehead, her size, her swollen face, hands and feet. No, it would not be easy and it might be fatal – that much she could tell just by looking at her companion.

She tried hard to concentrate on *Madame* Ariella's conversation. It made it easier to avoid thoughts of the Templar, if nothing else.

'Sister, have you business in Lyon?' Ariella was saying.

'Mm? Yes. Yes, I do.'

'You seek goods perhaps?'

Cécile could feel the blood draining from her face as surely as if a knife had wounded her. 'Goods?' she asked, sounding like some sort of fool.

'For your priory.'

'Oh. I see.' She twitched her mouth into what she hoped might pass for a smile, although since she departed Esteil she thought she may have forgotten how. 'Yes. My priory has a reputation for faultless work in the scriptorium. I shall try to source good parchments, pigments and gold leaf. Esteil also has had success with embroidery for vestments – so I will try to find some silken thread, mayhap some good cloth.'

And a relic. But neither you nor that golden-voiced, archangel knight shall know…

Young Lucas began to mewl and Ariella unwrapped him. 'He is wet,' she said and reached into a sack beside her for clean cloths. 'And he grows his teeth. It is such a wonderful time, isn't it, my little man?' She tickled the fatty bracelets of his thighs and he chortled.

She let him kick, the child's nether regions bared to the sun whilst she smoothed cream around his groin, the odour of the unguent reaching Cécile.

'What is that?'

'A cream made by an Arab doctor who admires the works of Hildegarde von Bingen. Do you know of her?'

'Of course! Our own infirmarian uses her works as her guide.'

'This is calendula and pork fat mixed with the liquid of crushed oats and some essence of violet to give it a more pleasant odour.' Ariella lifted it to her own nose and sniffed. 'It is almost time to be rid of it but I trust it to last until Lyon. His little buttocks and groin are rash-prone and this helps.'

Lucas had become quiet, staring at Cécile and she flushed with the innocence with which he viewed her. He reminded her of the Holy Infant and she was humbled.

His mother wrapped a cloth around his bottom and then dipped a hard crust of bread into a costrel. 'Goats' milk,' she said. 'He likes to mouth the crust on his tender gums. It's like the Circle of Life, isn't it? We start as a toothless infant and end as a toothless ancient.' She sat him up. 'Can you mind him, *Soeur* Cécile? I need to relieve myself.'

She passed Lucas over without waiting for a reply, jumping nimbly from the cart and hastening to the forested edge. Henri looked after her, shrugged and then moved on, leaving her to do what she must.

Cécile held the child in unfamiliar hands and presently, his gaze moved to settle on the prayer beads. They were simple golden wood, broken up with deep brown seeds polished to a subtle glow and with a small wooden crucifix hanging from them. Something hummed within her – warmth, some instinct to nurture, and she handed him the beads, unthreading them from her girdle and watching as his tiny fingers clutched them to raise them to his mouth.

She thought that in his own way, in this infantile act, he was communing with the Holy Family and mayhap They might see Their way to protect this strange company.

But protect them from who, she wondered as she sought the broad-shouldered figure of the Templar knight ahead.

A piercing scream, 'Henri!' split the air. 'Henri! Boar!'

The cart horse's ears laid back and it snorted. Gervasius tightened his grasp on the lead-rein and the guard, Henri, spun his horse around, leaped to the ground, drew his sword and disappeared into the trees at a run. His horse shook its head wildly, backing until its rump hit the cart. Cécile had laid Lucas in a pile of sacks next to Gelis who worriedly slept on, and so she reached a calming hand to the horse, speaking, moving forward until she could slide off the cart and hold the animal, trying to gentle it. All the horses were throwing their heads high, ears back, sniffing the air as it split with the rabid shriek of a wild boar.

Christe eleison, she breathed. Where was the Templar?

She could only imagine the carnage – an unarmed woman and a man with a sword. He needed a boar-spear, for Christ's sake…

Another shriek, animal this time.

Please protect this babe, Lord, and his parents…

Cécile glanced back but Lucas lay calm, staring at her as if he knew things she could never understand. The horse pulled hard on its reins and she held on for dear life, knowing they needed all the mounts to be able to reach Lyon in time.

A groan and snort behind and Gelis's eyes opened. She tried to sit up but winced. 'What goes?' she asked, thick words running together. 'Why have we stopped? Where's the child's mother?'

'Be calm, Gelis. All is well,' Cécile offered.

But it wasn't. Gelis's voice rambled on, a distressed murmur as she shifted, hauling herself to sit up, the cart rocking with her weight. 'Sister, I need to piss. Help me…'

'No! You must stay where you are! Just for a moment…'

'But…'

'No, Gelis! There is a boar! Stay still!' Gervasius ordered. 'You must wait! Do as you are asked, I beg of you!'

Another ear-splitting squeal, long, cutting the air as if with a cleaver and Lucas's mouth dropped, his bottom lip quivering.

'Cosset him, Gelis!' Cécile ordered. 'Stop him crying. You must.'

Gelis stared at the nun, her mouth ajar but she leaned as best she could to the child, rubbing his hands and cooing, her voice shaking. His eyes had filled with tears but he gave her a small smile. Another shriek, animal again.

And then the man from Venezia emerged with his arm supporting his mistress. His sword was stained and Ariella's veil had gone, revealing a disarrayed wine-coloured glory. Behind them, sword more than stained, rode the Templar and strangely, his gaze met Cécile's.

Was it triumphant? She thought so.

Henri de Montbrison helped his mistress back into the

cart where she sat gingerly, taking Lucas into her arms and holding him close, her face slowly assuming its normal colour.

'Thank you, Sister,' Henri reached for his horse's reins, having wiped his blade on the grass. He mounted and Cécile felt some of his vapid bluster had gone. That he had become serious in a moment.

The Templar had dismounted and wiped his own sword on the damp riverside grasses. Gathering the assembled group in a superior glance as he sheathed the weapon, he mounted his horse, clicked through his teeth and went on to catch the others further upstream.

'Gelis,' asked Cécile. 'Do you still need to relieve yourself?'

Gelis looked down and then up again, horror-struck. 'No… but it won't stop…' A damp stain had begun to spread across her gown folds. 'Oh, I am so sorry, Ariella. There is so much of it…'

Ariella laid Lucas, now sleeping, back against the luggage. 'Gelis,' she took the woman's hands in her own. 'Gelis, you do not wet yourself. Your waters are breaking.'

Gelis's face crumbled, folding in on itself, paling from red to ash. 'No… no, no, no…'

'Gelis, stop!' Ariella ordered. 'It is normal.'

'But we are not in Lyon!'

'We will be. Now let us dress you in dry clothing, and perhaps you should have some wine. Messire Gervasius, as soon as we are done, we must make haste. No stops if you please.'

Cécile helped Gelis from the cart, asking the men to turn away, helping the woman out of her sodden bliaut and tunic. Her veil slipped off with the clothing, revealing the brown hair streaked with wheaten highlights which instantly made her appear more youthful and Cécile felt a rush of fear for the woman, praying from her heart that the Blessed Mother should protect her and allow her the joy of a child. Surely women had paid enough for Eve's sin in the Garden of Eden and if they had not, wouldn't Gelis's own labour be tax enough?

She reached into a small coffer and pulled a tightly folded crimson wool gown out, trying hard not to think of blood as she eased it over Gelis's taut, swollen belly. Ariella had plaited Gelis's hair more tightly out of the way and as she tied the plait up on the woman's head, Gelis groaned like an old cow and bent over her belly.

'It is good,' Ariella said. 'Your first pain, and see, it has gone already.' She passed Gelis the costrel of wine. 'Drink up now. It is unwatered and will help to loosen your muscles and nerves and make it easier. Let this wine be your friend. And here,' she passed over a circle of ivory. 'If it helps, bite on Lucas's teething ring.' She grabbed an empty costrel. '*Messire* Gervasius, fill this with good clean water at the first stream we find. Not from the Rhône just now – it is not clean enough.'

Cécile marvelled at the authoritative tone of the young widow as she ordered them all and she found she didn't mind because apart from prayer, what did an elderly nun know about anything?

'Henri,' Ariella continued. 'Let the others know what has happened and that we make haste onward. Ask if they could ride on with speed and advise the Lyonnais gate that we are coming? Mayhap they could even ride to rue Ducanivet so that when we arrive a midwife or infirmarian will be waiting? What think you?'

Henri nodded and touched his heels to his horse so that wet clods of mud flew up in its wake.

Ariella and Cécile settled Gelis back against the soft luggage in the cart whilst Lucas slept on. Ariella instructed Gelis to drink more wine whereupon the Mons merchant's wife sucked a mammoth swill and then burped prodigiously. 'Pray for me, Sister. Pray to Saint Margaret, to Saint Ursus of

Aosta, to Saint Anne the Blessed Grandmother, but mostly
intercede with the Holy Mother. I…' she grabbed at Cécile's
hand. 'I am so glad you are with me, and you, Ariella.'

The young woman from Venezia had not bothered to
replace her veil but had re-plaited the rich abundance and it
dangled down her back so that Cécile could see the colour-
ing inherited by Lucas. As she positioned herself with her
babe, the light caught on her long-fingered hands and on
the marriage band. On the fingers of her right hand were
two dark spots like the nuns in the scriptorium might collect after a day's hard work. Something about those spots
removed the last of Cécile's suspicions.

'You have been writing with oak gall ink,' she commented.
'It stains.'

Ariella looked down. 'Yes. I had many papers to sign. I
am not proficient with a pen and ink and am messy.'

'And what business did you say your husband was
involved with?'

'I don't think I did,' Ariella answered smoothly and Lucas
woke then, demanding food and thus Cécile's mild conversation was diverted. The cart rocked into a rut and out again,
and they both looked at dozing Gelis. Her face glimmered
and there was something about it that was almost febrile.

'She is not well, is she?' Cécile whispered. She had so
many questions in her head. How did this woman from
Venezia know of rue Ducanivet and the Lyonnais merchant
house for one?

Ariella mouthed the word 'no' in case Gelis should hear
but added, 'Her pains are far apart which is a good thing and
mercifully I have seen the babe kick. If we keep on and the
rivers and streams haven't covered the road, I think we will
reach Lyon in time.'

'I am praying, *Madame.*'

'And your prayers are what she needs, Sister. You are a
great support to her.'

Something softened inside Cécile and she bent her head in thanks. That she should lurch from one crisis to another so rapidly after spending a life in organised devotion within the cloister of Esteil was almost too much for her to comprehend and she found she needed her prayers far more now than then. Simply, the words gave her the strength to continue on. 'Tell me of the boar, Madame,' she said to change the subject.

Ariella eased Lucas from her breast, the infant sleeping again, and she modestly drew the clothing about her. She laid him on his make-do bedding and grasped her bliaut folds, showing a ragged rip from hip to hem. 'This,' she said, 'almost killed me.'

'The boar did that?' Cécile sucked in a breath.

'Yes. As he rushed at me, I sidestepped and his tusk caught my gown and pulled me down. His impetus took him to the other side of the clearing and I had time to jump up and run to a fallen bough, but in trying to climb over it, the shreds of my gown caught on the branches and I was trapped.'

'*Deus…*'

'I had my back to the brute which was when I screamed to Henri. I could smell the beast's hateful odour and when I turned, its eyes were fixed on me, small malevolent little black beads filled with hate. If it had been human, I swear it would have cursed me. I screamed again…' The widow shook her head, closing her eyes as she recalled, but then she fixed Cécile with an intense gaze. 'Henri ran into the clearing with a vast branch and an unsheathed sword. He threw the branch and it hit the boar enough to distract it and it changed direction, but Sister, my heart was in my throat as I swear that boar was old enough to know all the tricks. I expected Henri to be picked up by the tusks and disembowelled before my eyes. But he… Henri… swiftly stepped sideways and brought his sword edge down on the brute's rump in a fierce blood-letting swing, giving him time. He ran to me, grabbing me, tearing my bliaut even more as he ripped me away from the fallen bough, shoving me behind him. But then the beast was turning, screaming...'

'We heard it...'

Ariella took a breath. 'Out of nowhere, the Templar galloped into the clearing, white cloak waving like a warning and the boar slowed in his charge when he smelled the horse. The Templar rode upon him and brought his great sword down on the animal's neck, half severing it. God knows how, but his horse danced clear of the tusks and the Templar leaped off and bought his sword two-handed onto the animal's neck again and this time, the animal just fell to its knees, pumping horrid black blood everywhere. *Soeur* Cécile, I ... we... Henri and I owe the man our lives and do you know, his white cloak had not one mark upon it.'

Cécile felt enormous sadness for the widow and her servant that they should owe the Templar anything. But she reached forward, staggered at her own temerity and squeezed Ariella's hand.

'He said nothing,' the woman continued. 'Just rode out to join you. He seemed to... No! I must not be uncharitable.'

'Seemed to what?' encouraged Cécile gently. She wanted to endorse her own feelings about the man. To think nothing good of him.

'To enjoy the slaying, if I am honest.' Ariella sat for a moment, frowning. 'But then every man enjoys the hunt, does he not?'

But there is hunting and then there is hunting, Cécile thought, recalling the smugness that flashed across his eyes, the satisfaction as he had dismounted and taken his sword tenderly to the riverside and wiped it on the damp grasses. As though like a demon, the gore had excited him.

Cécile!

In an instant, she could hear *Soeur* Benedicta admonishing. After all, the knight had saved two good people and should be owed respect. But then Ariella and her servant had not heard him as she had. Respect was earned and he had failed that day in the church.

She would not forget.

Part Two

The Finding

*'In dangers, in doubts, in difficulties, think of Mary,
call upon Mary. Let not her name depart from your lips,
never suffer it to leave your heart.'*
Saint Bernard of Clairvaux…

Chapter Twelve

Henri and Cécile
Lyon

Henri pounded along the road, winding past the swollen river and splashing through mud and pools of silted water, water droplets flying up like wings at his sides. As he rounded a bend, the horses ahead sensed him and began to swing their rumps, ears flat, heads throwing up so that their riders had to pull the reins hard.

Henri drew up with a muddy slither, noting that drops of filthy water flicked up satisfyingly onto the Templar's cloak but he ignored the man, ignored his status and his evident authority as the knight sat the half rears of his horse with ease.

'Robertus,' Henri puffed, shortening his reins as his own excited horse sidled and spun in circles. '*Madame* Geltidis is beginning to birth her child. *Messire* Gervasius asks if you can make haste to Lyon and inform the Watch that we come with a sick woman so that they will allow us entry. *I* ask if you can go to Michael Sarapion at Clochard, in rue Ducanivet to inform them also. I believe *Messire* Gervasius is their client? My mistress feels they will get help – a midwife…'

If Robertus was surprised that Henri mentioned rue Ducanivet with such familiarity or that Michael Sarapion's name dropped from his lips as if he was a close friend of the man, then there was no sign. As for the Templar, nothing crossed his face.

'Of course,' Robertus agreed, worry creasing the elongated expression and dragging it down further. 'Poor *Madame*. Tell *Messire* Gervasius that we pray for his wife and for his imminent child's safety.' He dug in his heels and with a sharp 'Hyar!' he led the group as they galloped forward, Henri turning his own mount away from the inevitable flying wet clods, to return along the road.

Even above the suck and grumble of his horse's cantering hooves, as he drew near to the cart and the labouring woman, he could hear her screams and his heart plummeted. He slid to a stop and jumped off, leading the steaming mount to Gervasius who almost wept.

'What happens?' Henri asked.

'I don't know. I fear for her…' Gervasius looked like a man between Purgatory and Hell. 'I fear she…'

Henri looked to Ariella who bent over the woman. '*Madame*?'

She didn't look up, wiping Gelis's face with a damp cloth as the woman shook, her arms and legs trembling, a faint spittle appearing in the corners of her mouth. The cart moved forward all the time, the nun walking and carrying Lucas who was wide awake and looking at his surroundings. 'I am not sure,' Ariella whispered as she wiped again and again. 'She began another pain and screamed, there is nothing wrong with that, it's what women do, but then she began to tremble. And now? Now, she has fainted and I am… I don't know.' Ariella met Henri's gaze and it was obvious to him that she was confused, not in her habitual control, maybe even a wisp of fear flicking across her eyes. 'How long to Lyon?' she asked, desperation tightening her words.

'Sister, what hour do you think it is?' He knew *Soeur* Cécile breathed the Hours, that they ran through her body and soul like lifeblood, telling her exactly what time of the day it was. He had watched her taking up her Paternoster beads, presumably at Tierce today and mouthing the prayer.

The nun hitched Lucas onto her bony hip and infant fingers reached for her coif and then her veil. 'It is past Sext and on the way to None.'

'Then we will be close to Lyon by Compline. Can she last do you think, Madame?'

'I hope so. I would prefer she was not seized by these fainting fits…'

'God forbid!' the nun muttered. 'She is possessed! We must pray! You must stop the cart and we must invoke…'

'Nonsense!' Ariella snapped. 'The physician, Avicenna, said that these moments can be treated and in any case, it may just be fright. She has already lost babes at such a time. We must get her to Lyon and soonest but by all means pray for her, Sister. She needs all our assistance at the moment, but not, I might add, an exorcism!'

Gervasius's face was white as he crossed himself, the ruddiness draining from him like an ebb-tide and Henri sought to bridge any gaps, believing now was the time when solidarity was required. 'Then what can we do?' he asked of Ariella.

'*Messire*,' she asked the pale merchant. 'Do you have any medicines in your luggage? Poppy? Valerian?'

'Um, I…' Gervasius's brow creased. 'I am unsure. Gelis packed…'

'Is it likely?'

'Perhaps. She was suffering from bad head pains.'

'May we look through your luggage?' Ariella had covered Gelis with a cloak, but there was no disguising the odour that permeated the air with each rock and roll of the cart. The woman had soiled herself in the midst of her faint and would have to be cleaned as they moved onward.

'Of course…'

'And perhaps you might lead the cart horse at a swifter pace. We seem to be slowing. But mind you, not too roughly!'

Gervasius grabbed the carthorse's reins and clicked the beast on, the cart moving forward with more determination.

'Henri,' Ariella whispered. 'We must keep *Messire* Gervasius busy, away from us. Can we send him to refill the costrels? I have used much water to sponge Gelis and I will have to clean her again. It won't be a pretty sight and I don't want him to see.'

Henri forbore to ask the obvious question – which of the two would survive? Mother or babe? He thought he knew and grabbed the costrels.

Cécile shuddered. She was in the presence of heathens, surely. Could they not see that the woman was possessed by the Devil and in need of spiritual cleansing? *Deus!*

Lucas murmured and gave the softest chortle and she turned her troubled gaze from Gelis and from the young widow who now searched through the casket and sacks. She hadn't liked this woman's rudeness – the way she snapped and made Cécile feel like a superstitious peasant. But the truth was a Falling Sickness *was* a possession and that was surely what beset *Madame* Gelis. In the Gospel of Mark, Christ healed a boy of the Falling Sickness. Surely therefore, praying to Christ and asking for intercession would help. That woman! *She* was surely not a Christian or she would have known.

That woman was now peeling back Gelis's cloak and grasping a dagger.

'*Madame!*' Cécile gasped. 'Holy Mother, what do you do?'

'Sister,' Ariella whispered. 'Keep your voice low and do not excite *Messire* Gervasius or upset my son. We need peace for Gelis so that she might rest between her pains.' She lifted the dagger, a finely crafted weapon Cécile thought, but then what would she know? It was also one that could make quick work of Gelis's swollen belly. Cécile could imagine the terrible slash and Ariella pulling a babe forth. Instead, however, she slit the cloth of Gelis's bliaut gently, not skin and tendon after all, but stained wool that was now putrid with excrescence. Very carefully, she kept slicing until all the filth had been cut away. Then with a clean cloth, she washed Gelis's nether regions as gently as if she tended her own son. When she was done, she rolled Gelis first one way and then another, the woman as limp as a wet rag, so that eventually she lay on the cloak with another covering her.

'You are very gentle,' Cécile grudgingly acknowledged as Ariella bundled the dirty fragments of cloth into a ball and threw them to the side of the road. She poured wine over her hands to wash them, and then some water and then, sniffing cautiously, she wiped them on the edge of the cloak on which Gelis lay.

'She is a sweet lady, Sister, and I do not want to see her suffer. I have found some poppy and will make a concoction and when she wakes, I shall give her some...'

'You know about these things?'

'No... not completely. The poppy at least may slow her pains. When I lived in my father's house, we had a Saracen friend, a physician, a kindly and informative man and he told me that the poppy is miraculous for easing pain...'

Cécile truly felt as if she now supped with the Devil. This woman who would not allow an exorcism and who consorted with Saracens. God-fearing? Unlikely. If Cécile had not been holding that angelic son, she would have crossed herself, begging for any or all of the Holy Trinity to protect her. As she thought, she looked down at Lucas and he smiled at her, his infant's hands touching her face with such gentleness, the fingers opening like stars. She smiled back at him and found cause to wonder how a heathen could birth a child that was surely one of the cherubim.

'Henri!' Ariella called softly. 'Do you think we can proceed at a trot? The cart harness and shafts are well fitting and we perhaps might not jostle *Madame* too much. We need to cover more ground and I believe the trot won't tire the carthorse unduly.'

'As you say, *Madame*,' Henri replied.

Cécile grabbed the shaft before they began to pick up speed. '*Madame*, you had best take your son. If we are to move faster, I cannot jog carrying him.'

'Of course. He needs a feed in any case and the movement of the cart will lull him. Thank you, Sister. I can see he is comfortable with you. I wish we could all fit on the cart but I fear Madame needs space…'

Cécile was about to reply when Henri interrupted. 'Sister, if we are all to keep together and make haste, I urge you to sit behind me on my horse.'

'I…' Cécile couldn't imagine sitting behind a man, let alone on a horse.

'Sister, I must be forthright and I apologise, but you must see that *Madame* Geltidis is in extremis and for her sake and that of her babe and for *Messire* Gervasius, we must pick up the pace. Please…' He held out a hand and Cécile grunted, seeing the truth of his words, reaching out her own palm to place her sandalled foot upon his leather shod one as he hoisted her astride his horse. She tried to settle her robes below her knees but could not prevent stringy legs bared. A flush surged over her face, prickling beneath her wimple but she realised that none of her companions cared as they got about their duties – Henri to reach for the carthorse's reins and click it to a trot, *Messire* Gervasius in the distance, looking for fresh water. All oblivious to Cécile's aged legs and to the quicker passage of the trees and of the swollen river at their sides.

Cécile tried to balance but kept sliding and grabbing for the guard's gambeson until he said over his shoulder, 'Relax yourself, Sister. Loosen your spine and sink into the horse's rhythm. You will find it is much easier.'

God save me and damn *you*, she thought. She had *never* ridden a horse in her long life and would admit to terror as the ground sped beneath the animal's trotting hooves and she began to pray, grasping at pieces of Saint Augustine of Hippo's words:

'*Holy Mary ... help the fainthearted, comfort the sorrowful... intercede for all women consecrated to God; may all who keep thy holy commemoration feel now thy help and protection. Be thou ever ready to assist us when we pray, and bring back to us the answers to our prayers. Make it thy continual care to pray for the people of God, thou who, blessed by God, didst merit to bear the Redeemer of the world, who liveth and reigneth, world without end. Amen.*'

As she prayed, she softened and in truth Henri was right; as she sat more comfortably, her tight grasp upon him eased and she found a rhythm. If the situation was not so dire, she might almost have smiled.

Henri's mind ran way ahead of him, turning back to laugh at the shock and horror upon his face. He had never attended a birth, had no wish to watch a woman and unborn babe die. And now he rode a horse with a nun grasping onto him from behind like some message from on high. And as for Ariella – she had distanced herself from him and joined a sorority of women who lived with life and death every time they were with child. It was a terrifying thing, this birthing business. He had never given it much thought. What man would?

And as he wondered, so another moan began behind him, climbing rapidly to a scream.

'Henri, stop the cart. Stop!' Ariella called out. 'Gelis, Gelis! That's it, just breathe. You are having your birthing pains, that is all.'

Henri had stopped the cart and he and the nun turned back to see Gelis with her legs drawn up, her face blood red and contorted.

'God is taking my child. He is killing me…' she cried out, thrashing her head from side to side.

'Gelis! Enough! God is not taking your child. This is normal. If you just breathe carefully, the pain will ease. That's it. See? It is like a wave coming and going. Has it gone? Good. Now lie back and drink this. It will help.'

There was no frenzied shaking this time, as Gelis lay back after drinking the draught straight down. Her hair curled around her face, tendrils dragging in the sweat but her face was madder-stained and she looked as if she would burst.

'Gelis, as the babe moves down, your body moves to assist it. Like a ripple, yes? The pains are far apart just now, but they will come closer together and you must be calm and just breathe. Thousands of women do this every day, so you are just one other. It is natural.'

'It hurts,' Gelis's voice trailed off miserably and a sob followed.

'Of course it does. You don't carry a tiny little pupkin, you carry a fully-formed babe. But I will help you and in no time, we will be in Lyon with a midwife and you will be a mother.'

But Gelis's eyes had drifted down with exhaustion, with the poppy and with something else. That woman is ill, thought Henri, and he would bet his life that neither she nor the babe would survive. Poor *Messire* Gervasius…

Henri swore as the would-be father of the moment hammered back along to the road to re-join them, costrels banging against his mount's neck, the pale face of earlier now patterned with two hectic red dots upon his cheeks.

Before Henri could open his mouth, *Soeur* Cécile leaned

around Henri's back. '*Messire* Gervasius, she is dozing and doing well, do not be alarmed. Ariella is caring for her.'

Henri revised his view of the nun again. Despite her pepperish attitude toward he and Ariella, there was no denying she cared for the merchant and his wife. Her hands held on to his gambeson and for one brief moment, he could imagine Tobias' eyes lighting up and some humorous lyrics about old nuns and young knights filling the air.

But by the Saints, this was not a humorous moment.

Gervasius almost wept, poor man, and despite the obvious loss that would no doubt occur, Henri almost envied him the love he held for his wife. And despite himself, Henri muttered a small prayer to Saint Margaret of Antioch for Gelis.

'*Madame, madame*,' Gervasius asked of Ariella, his voice trembling, 'Why is she so lifeless? Should she not be awake and helping our child along the way?'

'*Messire*,' Ariella said as she took the costrels from him and stowed them beside Lucas who slept. 'She sleeps between the pains. It is quite normal. Mothers get very tired, you know…'

Henri felt pride in Ariella's calm demeanour; it could not have been easy. As many doubts as ran through his own head must be running through hers. She was no midwife and had only birthed one child herself and by all accounts, that had been as swift as a running stream; like some kind of earth mother born to rear babes.

'But the baby. Will it not die if it stays within for too long?' Gervasius twisted the leather reins upon themselves.

'*Messire*, some women take a day or more to give birth. We should be glad that Gelis sleeps because she conserves her energy.'

'Should we?' muttered the nun behind Henri. Henri turned to look back at Ariella who flicked her eyes at Gervasius. *Send him on another errand,* she seemed to be saying.

Henri went to speak but the nun called out to the merchant before he had a chance.

'*Messire* Gervasius, can you ride forth and find a village that will sell us bread, maybe a little honey and some wine if they are prepared to part with it? We all need some sustenance on the move, especially Gelis when she wakes.'

Gervasius looked to Ariella for guidance and she nodded. ''Tis a good idea. Have no fear, I shall tend her.'

Gervasius sat silent for a moment, staring at Gelis as if she might disappear while he was gone. Then, 'We are in your debt, *Madame* Ariella. Thank you.' He nodded to all and set off at a wet canter, his mount's hooves sinking almost fetlock deep into the muddy track.

Henri clicked the cart horse into a stronger trot and they lurched on, four disparate people alone with their thoughts, nothing but the sucking sound of hooves in the sludge, the jingle of harness and the occasional snort as a horse blew down its nose. As the cavalcade passed, waterbirds honked and with a clatter of wings, lifted themselves above the reeds and flowing water, to scoop across the shore to less noisome shorelines.

Henri wondered if there were any villages close to the river. Surely it was a flood risk, evidenced by this spring. But then the fertile river flats must be a significant fact of life in this valley. He looked to the sky, noting the pale azure of earlier had become mottled with grey cloud and that a moist breeze had sprung up, enough to ruffle the manes and forelocks of the horses. It smelled like a breeze that promised rain and he only hoped they could reach Lyon before the weather set in.

They rounded a bend in the road, leaving the river further over their right shoulders than before. The trees hung heavy, boughs sagging with the damp growth of a new season. He pulled the cart-horse's reins and clicked it on to the less boggy verges. He was pleased that the horses had not broken a sweat yet and he hoped they would continue calmly as Lyon edged nearer.

Far in the north-eastern sky, he thought there might be wisps of smoke, grey ribbons against the greyer firmament – the kind of fret that would hang over a city of some size.

Please let it be close…

'You seem to be praying, *messire*.' The nun's voice was low and he appreciated her quiet discretion.

'As one does, Sister.'

'You do not strike me as a spiritual man, though.'

He had no idea how to respond and was glad that the cart horse stumbled so as he could concentrate. 'Hold tight, Sister. It is a little uneven here.'

'Uneven,' the nun rocked, but using his gambeson, with a grunt she pulled herself straight again and then in a tart voice, continued, 'Or is it more that you are unwilling to reply on the matter of your soul.'

There came a moan from the cart and Ariella called out, 'Be prepared to halt, Henri.'

'There is your answer, Sister. Now is not the time. Whoa, ladies, whoa,' he pulled the handful of reins gently, both the cart horse and his own responding to his voice.

Thus the journey came in waves like Geltidis's labour pains. A series of starts, rolling forward at some speed, and then a halt – punctuations that drove Henri to distraction. He just wanted to reach Lyon and deliver this splayed and screaming woman to someone who could help her. He would scoop Ariella and Lucas up, arriving at rue Ducanivet with their secret cargo. Then they could begin as they meant to go on – collect their breaths, rest and rely on the hospitality of the trading house before commencing a return journey.

He felt a needle-like splatter upon his face and then another and looked at the grey-as-grief sky. 'God help us,' he muttered.

'God helps those who helps themselves,' the nun answered tartly from behind.

'And where in the scriptures does it say so?' Henri could almost taste the acid on his tongue.

'It doesn't. But God would always help willingly if He saw His flock making an effort.'

'Jesu!' Henri replied. 'Tell me, *Soeur* Cécile – how does a leper help himself, or a blind man? How does poor *Madame* Geltidis help *her*self? And how can we stop it raining?'

'Pray, *messire*,' said the nun in a tone that condescended from the heavens. 'If you know how. And besides, it will not rain; the clouds are not yet full enough. The drops you feel are but sprinkles from the trees.'

Henri bit his tongue.

'You seem to stutter when you acknowledge your mistress,' the nun said as he harried the horses to a trot.

He looked up at the heavy sky and then round at Ariella and at Gelis who lay with her eyes closed, her legs splayed in such an undignified manner. He sighed before he answered.

'Sister, show me any servant who is not intimidated by his lady mistress and I will acknowledge a Divine miracle. Hold on tightly please, we are going to move apace.'

Bloody old cow, he thought. He hated been patronised.

Perversely, he had loved the priest who had taken him under his wing when he was young. The monk had been generous and kind, bestowing upon him the sort of knowledge that none of the young nobles with whom he lived were privileged to have. In his naïve youth, he had thanked God in those days. He was under no illusions – his belief in the Holy Father and Divine Goodness had only died on the crusade.

Henri's father might have turned the youth into a priest to get rid of him. The Forez noble, an extremely lesser one with ideas far beyond his station, had abnegated any and all responsibility for Henri's servant-mother once she was with child. It was all to do with swiving. And then she had become ill, a fever, and no one but the priest could help as she sank to death. Henri's father would barely have known that his bastard was now an orphan and he banished the child to a forgotten corner.

But the young sons of the nobility of the Montbrison demesnes liked Henri. He was the kind to have standing at one's back and they fostered friendship, giving him their old clothes, inviting him to table and encouraging him to join them in learning knightly skills. He was like a lamb with no mother, bent on survival, taking what sustenance and comfort he could from whatever source and always with good spirit.

None forbade him, least of all his father who stared right through him if they crossed paths. He never took his father's Forez name, why would he, and if any should ask, he always told them he was merely Henri of Montbrison and none questioned it.

The priest, *Père* Adémar, had buried Henri's mother with the sacraments without asking for payment because he saw the intelligence and potential in the youth. For Henri, *Père* Adémar was the anchoring figure in his life, one who taught him not just literacy and numbers but common sense.

His friends at the table would mock him lightly about the priest, gutter comments about men's unholy desires. But Henri never rose to the bait. Mostly he believed in men's goodness. It wasn't until Cyprus that he discovered he even possessed a dark vein that could kill a man in one blow.

The priest might have wanted Henri to take orders, to become a scribe within the Holy Church. But Henri gently disabused him. He liked the feel of a sword haft in his hand, a horse between his legs, the surge of blood round his body when he participated in challenges in the yards or out hunting boar and deer. He was good with weapons and he knew it and welcomed the chance to serve those who wanted him and when came the time to form a crusading army for Phillip Caput, he went more than willingly.

Père Adémar blessed him, telling him that by offering his soul to God in this wondrous crusade against unbelievers, he was assuring himself a place in Heaven. He said he would pray for him twice a day and say Mass for him each week.

Mass, Henri now thought. What good is Mass when men die a thousand times and a thousand times more so that one can do nothing but walk through blood and entrails?

'Henri? Are you listening?' The nun's hand hit the side of his gambeson, a mere moth's wing-beat against a window-pane. But enough to draw him away from his black self, the one he hated. 'Your mistress calls to you,' Cécile said.

My mistress?

He turned back and looked over his shoulder at the cart.

'Do we see Lyon yet?' called Ariella.

'Almost!'

Chapter Thirteen

They rounded a drooping hornbeam tree and Cécile was reminded of her childhood when she would grasp the feathery pendules, smelling the powdery dust of late spring. As they cleared its grasping wet growth, the Rhône lay spread before them, a broad muddy sweep. Cécile was sure she could see a bridge a misty league away, maybe less or more. Maybe two bridges and an islet between, and she could smell smoke on the air, that much she did know.

'Ha!' called Henri back over his shoulder. 'Lyon! See?' He clicked the horses on, the pace steady and ground-covering.

Wretched man, thought Cécile. She couldn't pinpoint why she felt as she did. Maybe it was just that he led them to a destination of which she was afraid. And that he seemed to have an answer for everything and if not an answer, an order. Glancing round his back, she spied Lyon again and decided it was too big.

Her heart began to flap in her chest like a trapped bird. Here, there, faint then strong and she wondered if she was too old for it to beat as it did. Of its own volition, her hand crept to the rough wool of her robe, and forming a fist, she pushed hard against the erratic beats. Slipping a fraction, she grabbed at Henri and then righted herself.

'Sister? All is well?' he asked above the jingle of horse metal and the creak of the cart.

'Perfectly,' she snapped.

A groan punctuated the slip-slop of the horses' steps, rising along a scale until it became a screech.

'Henri,' shouted Ariella. 'Halt, halt!'

Henri pulled on the reins and muttered under his breath as Cécile slid off Henri's horse, her bare legs splattered with mud. She grabbed for Henri's stirrup to keep a footing and then hurried to the cart, holding her robe folds as high as she dared.

'Gelis, it is I, *Soeur* Cécile, hold my hand.'

Gelis's eyes opened, bloodshot and exhausted, a sheen of sweat glossing her face on this sunless day. 'I hurt,' she cried. 'It won't come! I need the cloth with the prayers, the one the church has. Else my babe and I will die!'

Cécile glanced at Ariella. 'What cloth? I have not heard of this?'

'The midwives often have a strip of linen that might have prayer scribed upon it. It is meant to assist in the birth if it is laid across the woman's stomach. Sometimes, if the church has a relic of some saintly cloth, they will make it available for a price.'

'A relic…' Cécile said breathlessly.

A groan of deep and inexorable pain began behind the two women. 'Help me, I am dying…' Gelis's voice wailed like some Dame Blanche, the cry of a ghostly woman presaging death.

'You are *not!*' Ariella climbed back onto the cart and grabbed Gelis's hand and shook it. 'You are birthing a babe. It is big and it hurts. I too birthed a child, remember, and I survived,' her voice softened. 'And so can you if you un-knot a little and help the child by breathing when the pains come. If you stiffen, you will hurt more. Now sit up as the wave breaks,' she hauled Gelis under the armpits into a sitting position and spread the woman's legs, as *Messire* Gervasius came pelting along the riverbank toward them.

'I have food and wine,' he called, 'and we haven't far to

go! Oh *Deus*, is she… has she…' He began to dismount even before his horse had stopped.

'*Messire*!' Ariella called out. 'Stay there, if you please. When a woman is birthing her child, she must not have men close by.'

Cécile knew this much was true and she nodded. 'The Church forbids it, *Messire* Gervasius. Even when we reach Lyon, you must allow that Gelis be assisted by women…'

'I think,' broke in Ariella, 'the best you can do for your wife is perhaps hurry to Lyon and make sure the others have organised a midwife and a birthing chamber. We will be hard on your heels and everything must be ready. Could you do that, please?'

Gervasius's mouth opened and closed like a landed fish and his eyes filled. 'Of course, if you think…'

'Bless you, *messire*,' Cécile said, walking to him, reaching up to take the bundle of food and a small costrel of wine. 'It is quite the right thing. We will make sure she reaches you as soon as possible. Now go.'

Gervasius turned his horse and with one last, almost defeated look, he cantered off, more clods of muddy sludge splattering in his wake.

Gelis had collapsed back, eyes closed and Ariella slid from the cart to help Cécile once again mount behind Henri. 'That was kind of you, Sister, thank you,' she said.

'You don't wish for *me* to leave then?' Henri asked of his mistress as the nun settled herself on the rump of his horse.

Ariella looked up. 'No, Henri. But we must rely on your discretion and your skill with horses.'

'*Madame*,' Cécile said, 'Would it help to lay my paternoster beads across Gelis's belly? I don't have linen on which we could write a prayer but my beads have been worn smooth by years of invocation.'

Something passed between the widow and her servant, but Cécile was hard put to determine what it was. A glance, a frown, the flicker of an eyelash.

Ariella spoke first. 'Sister, in truth I'm not sure anything will help until the babe has been turned.'

Henri and Cécile gasped together.

'No...' Cécile had seen enough goats and sheep birthing around Esteil to know that the wrong way most often meant death.

'Yes, and I am not sure I know enough to remedy the situation.' Ariella hastened back to the cart and Lucas, who had begun to mewl. 'Henri, speed, but with care.'

Lyon! A hateful place.

From the moment they broached the city gates and began to cross a river that joined a little further downstream with the Rhône – the Saône they said –and she hated that, too.

As they approached the city walls, Cécile had been overcome by the size of the place, by the river that rushed through the spans of the bridges, by the smells that drifted their way. Mostly food, but rot, ordure and damp. She felt cowed, belittled, and shrank behind Henri's back as the guards at the gate waved them through.

Mercifully, Gelis was between pains. But nevertheless, inside the walls of the city, they were met by a number of men and women. One must have been the midwife, because she immediately clambered in beside Gelis and then urged haste upon any who would listen. She was a stringy woman of later years from whom the smell of herbs drifted, reminding Cécile of the chest of communal robes at Esteil. She had a lined face and hairs sprouting from a brown wart on her chin, making her look like some wild thing from the forests, certainly not God-fearing. Cécile would have liked to examine her eyes and hands closely. One could tell a lot about folk from that – it was how she knew which of her novices would be God's handmaidens and which would be the Devil's. But light was limpid, the torchères along the bridge struggling against the river mists and spray that were drifting upward as the late spring dusk settled.

Ariella had taken Lucas in her arms as she slid from the cart. A lady not much older than the young mother hurried up to her and kissed her on either cheek as if they knew each other well, and suddenly the disorganised rabble became a cavalcade which followed the cart over bridges that terrified Cécile. How could the spans withstand the force of all that water?

And the Templar knight, so lately of their company and not missed, had been waiting at the gates. When they moved off, he followed as a rear guard and Cécile felt the Devil's claw at her neck.

Who *were* all these people? It seemed to the nun that between the gates and the place they called Presqu'île, she had seen as many folk as lived in the entire village of Esteil. In the distance she heard church bells ringing and the clear unambiguous call was like God's hands reaching out and saying, 'Fear not, Sister, all will be well.'

But Father, something is not right…

She changed her grip on Henri's gambeson as they journeyed over the Pont de Saône and then turned left along the riverbank and journeyed between tall houses that pressed in upon them.

Amongst the sound of horses' hooves and men's and women's footsteps. 'Praise God,' murmured Henri. 'Rue Ducanivet.'

But how do you know?

Had he not said he had never been to Lyon?

And people, more people, God help us!

Folk crowded out of double wooden gates between two tall houses and vaguely she had the sense that a huge tree grew in the middle of the courtyard…

'Henri!' A little man, a grotesque she thought, bounced up and laid his hands upon Henri's reins. 'You took long enough!'

'It took an age, Toby. Long story.' Henri stretched his back. 'Can you help *Soeur* Cécile down, if you please?'

'Dearest girl!' A shrill voice sounded across the flickering light and shade of the forecourt and Ariella was crushed against the substantially well-draped bosom of a small matron. Despite herself, Cécile was intrigued at the familiarity between everyone in Lyon.

'Sister? May I assist you?'

Cécile looked down to see the grotesque close by her leg, bowing his head. 'I am Tobias Celho, minstrel to the house of Gisborne ben Simon and to various royal houses across our lands.' He held up a small chubby hand and grinned. 'I am at your service.'

She shook her head and dismissed the little man. 'I am quite able.'

He frowned and stepped back, glancing at Henri, and then replying in the most perfect well-modulated tones. 'As you wish, *Soeur* Cécile…' Bowing again, he walked toward the house, his head high, acknowledging everyone as if he were a potentate. The curious thing, thought Cécile, was that they all acknowledged him with affection.

'You will find, Sister, that Tobias is a good and kind man,' Henri said and she felt as if she had been slapped across the cheek and by a common guard at that, but she said nothing in reply.

And how do you know this little… minstrel?

Light from the house fell across the forecourt like tabards of amber and it might have been beautiful if one could not hear the cries from Gelis from within. Cécile gritted her teeth and knew that she needed to be with the little wife as she tried to birth her child against the odds.

But she longed for the peace of the cloister, to be where she was in command of her situation, where a mere twenty women existed together, mostly in Benedictine silence. Instead, she was in command of nothing and was drowning in noise, from the cries from within the house, to horses nickering, their hooves clattering on the cobbled stones, of people shouting and laughing and of dogs barking and running between folks' legs. She slid off the horse and as before, reached for Henri's stirrup to steady herself and then, slipping into a shadow, she felt for her Paternoster beads, her fingers scrabbling urgently when they were not to be found.

Her comfort, her contact with the spiritual soul of her priory and her God had disappeared. Somewhere along that muddy highway, lay her worn, precious beads and she could have wept. 'I've lost my beads,' she said to no one and turned as a soft hand reached to the crook of her arm.

Henri dismounted, glancing toward the loud matron who was making her way across the yard to the old nun. He led his horse to the stables, passing it to one of the house grooms to deal with, giving it a pat on the rump as it followed the lad into a stall.

'Good to see you at last.' Adam's gruff voice caused him to stand straighter and he prepared himself for an inquisition.

'And good to see you too, Adam of London. You must have flown over the ground like a lightning strike to be here and settled already.'

Adam grinned, his red hair flaming under the light of a torchère. 'Aye. We set a scorching pace. Not hard to do when we had company hot on our heels. But enough said. Come to our chamber and you can refresh and we can talk privately. Is all well?'

Henri knew he referred to the relic and he answered confidently. 'Yes, all is well. Except for *Madame* Geltidis who decided to begin her childbirth whilst we were on the road.'

Adam scowled, 'Not just tardy, but Templars and childbirth as well. By the Saints, Henri, this was supposed to be an unremarkable journey.' He crossed the forecourt, walking into a busy hall with a star-spangled ceiling painted Virgin blue, and then to a passage, before turning into a chamber with four cots and no room for a fly on the wall.

'Plenty of space then?' Henri said, looking at bare white-washed walls and the tiny horn-covered window.

'We can get rid of a cot and I'm sure it will suffice.' Adam threw Henri's bag onto a bed. 'Besides, Toby doesn't take much room.'

'What don't I take?' The door opened and Toby slid in, hoisting himself onto the one cot shrouded in an elegant cloak of finest black wool.

'Space, you little man,' said Henri reaching to grasp his arm. 'By God, it's good to see you both at last!'

'At last, indeed,' said Toby. 'What happened to you?'

'In a few words, we joined with merchants for safety. The wife of one began childbirth which slowed our journey. You can hear her cries even now. And we were joined by a Templar knight and his serjeant which rather concerned Ariella and myself.' He pulled open his bag. 'God, I just want to bathe and pull on clean clothes…'

'A bowl of water and a top and tail here in the room will have to suffice till the morning,' Adam replied. 'Why did you feel concerned with your Templar?'

'Christ's toenails, Adam!' Henri said. 'Weren't *you*? Also, *we* carried the relic, remember. Besides…' he looked around. 'Is there any wine?'

'No. *Madame* doesn't like wine in the chambers. It's hall, yard, or nothing. Besides what?' Adam's eyebrows beetled forward over eyes the colour of a summer sky. His demeanour was flushed, ruddy, giving him the look of someone always on the verge of temper, but Henri knew the man, knew his steadiness and liked him, owed him comradeship.

'Henri?' Adam's tone was muffled to Henri's ears as he pulled clothing off. His heart had begun that awful beat that presaged memories he wanted to bury so very deep and leave there. 'Besides what?'

Can I tell him?

He threw the clothing onto the cot and began to strip his filthy hose.

'Christ Jesus, Henri,' Toby flicked dried clods of mud from his black cloak, clicking his tongue against his teeth. 'This chamber was clean…'

'Jesus, man!' Adam growled. 'Besides *what?*'

Near naked, Henri found the bowl of water in the corner and a linen square and began washing. 'I know the Templar,' he said, rubbing furiously at his face and neck and then his chest and armpits as if all the scrubbing might wash away the bloody memories.

'I see,' Adam replied. 'Go on…'

'In the Holy Land. He… was less than knightly,' Henri finished.

Toby slid to the end of his cot and faced Adam. 'Murder, pillage. A nasty story.'

'A long one…' Henri looked at his friends and then began to wipe his groin, his legs and his muddied feet.

'Tell him, Henri. You have nothing to lose.'

This last was said kindly and Henri was grateful. He dragged on a clean linen chemise and a fine scarlet wool tunic, and as he began to pull on his braies, he told the story of the Holy Land, his hands shaking as he then tried to slip on hose and fasten them. He dared not look at either man and just kept trying to knot the ties. 'Jesus!' he finally swore in exasperation.

Toby jumped off the cot and began to tie the hose for Henri. 'You're sweating,' he said. 'Stay here and I'll fetch some wine, *Madame* be damned.'

He left in a swirl of purpose and Henri subsided onto the cot.

'It disturbs you,' Adam said.

Henri said nothing, just wishing he didn't feel as if he would choke. And then, 'Does your time in the Holy Land not disturb *you*, Adam? If it does not then I would that you tell me how you manage it.' He sighed.

Adam chewed at his cheek for a moment and then, 'Yes, it disturbs me, but then no deaths are pleasant and it seems to me that we've chosen a life where death is ever-present so we have to accept what emerges from the ends of our swords. You are a mercenary in the pay of Gisborne and you can't let your past dictate to you.'

'Easier said than done.'

'Henri, when I met you at the Gigni Hunt, you seemed like a man who had your life well in check. Nothing's changed…'

'It's easy to hide one's fallibilities if one has to and I did. Until that seed of the Devil, the Templar, rode back into my life.' Henri found a wooden comb in his bag and sat on the bed, pulling at the days' old knots of his hair. The rhythm seemed to calm him and he noticed that Adam said nothing, just allowed him to settle. He was a good man, Adam of London, a solid leader.

'Somehow, the Templars know we carry the relic,' Henri said finally as he slicked his hair smoothly back from his forehead. 'And by God I would love to know how they found out.' He pulled the parchment from his purse and passed it over.

Adam unfolded it and ran his thumbs over both the exterior and interior seals. He folded it again and sequestered it in his own purse. 'Indeed.' The Master at Arms stood and smoothed his tunic beneath the sword belt and girdle, settling his sword by his side, fingers restless against the haft. 'But I can tell you this. The Templar won't get the relic because I've promised my lord Gisborne it will stay safe and that's an end to it.'

'And how will we do that, Adam?' A wave of exhaustion rolled over Henri and he wished he could lie down and sleep till morning. It was the way of it whenever he had to confront the dark.

'Kill every last one of 'em!' Adam smiled beatifically as Tobias sidled in with a costrel.

'Not very grand,' the minstrel said as he passed the wine to Henri first. 'But we can share. You look as if you need it.'

Henri tipped back his head and drank deep and then passed the costrel to Adam. 'That I do, Toby. Between Ariella's autocratic manner, the merchant's wife with her pains and the sour old nun, it was a trying journey, even without the Templar and his serjeant.'

'Well, the merchant's wife is yelling like a stuck pig, I can tell you. It will rather put a dampener on dinner in the hall but I know Madame has created somewhat of a welcome feast, so we need to be brave. And you won't be happy, but I heard that we are two extra at the table. The Templar and his man will be joining us.'

'Christ Above!' Henri threw himself back on his cot. 'I plead exhaustion. It's not an untruth…'

Neither Adam nor Toby took notice as Toby added, 'I have to sing for my supper it seems. Loudly I presume, to drown the sounds of the merchant's wife. Mayhap if I sing a religious song, it will charm a smile from the sour old nun.'

'Sour, yes, but despite her manner I'm glad she was with us because she kept Madame Geltidis as calm as she could and in the strangest way, I think she acted as some sort of buffer between the Templar and us. Which also meant the Templar and the relic. She fades with no one. Stands chest to chest and I tell you, if she had a sword, my bet is that she would not shrink from using it. Don't judge her. I did and I think I was too harsh."

Adam passed the costrel to Toby and he shook it. 'Hah! Thank you for leaving *something*. No one likes to be penalised for their size, despite the good Sister's best intentions, and I too need this.'

Henri lay back on his cot and closed his eyes the better to forget, but Toby's voice followed him, saying quietly, 'I think I know…'

'You know what?' Henri muttered from the heaviness of almost-sleep and opened his eyes.

'How they found us, or more particularly found me and then of course, the relic was simple after that.'

'Go on,' Adam took his dagger and leaned forward, beginning to clean his nails. The candlelight of the chamber reflected on the blade of the weapon and shot back a reflective spark on the walls.

'Remember I told you the story of the veil in Constantinople. Did I mention that Emperor Tiberius was supposedly healed of all his ailments on viewing the cloth? Did I also mention that the cloth was copied and used as a banner to encourage the Byzantines to protect Constantinople in various skirmishes? No? Did I mention that it disappeared from the court perhaps four hundred years ago? There is a legend that Germano I, the Patriarch of Constantinople was so afraid for the safety of the cloth during the early Iconoclasts, that he threw it into the sea and it was never seen again. Some will tell you that it floated across the sea all the way to Ostia and Rome, but seriously, whilst the Holy Church might like their flock to believe that story, I for one do not. I believe that *it*, or parts of it, were sent here and there. The part we have was placed in the ivory casket and sent somewhere safe. A place called Xylinites which I actually know. A small church in the far country-side outside of Constantinople.' Toby sank into the flow of his story, as was his want. 'Was the casket stolen then, or mislaid? Who knows? Maybe it arrived in the hands of our marketplace trader legitimately because many of those tiny churches scattered around the countryside are so very poor. Lack of interest by the Imperial Court seems to imply that it was forgotten about as time passed and their own problems became manifold. So much water has passed under Byzantine bridges since then.' Toby stopped and upended the costrel, draining the last drops away.

Henri, despite himself and his antipathy to the Holy Church felt that Toby's telling plausible and he looked at Adam. The man's eyes were slitted as if he were thinking hard.

'Whatever the case,' Toby continued, whetted and energised, 'the Templars knew of the veil, knew its provenance. They research well, I think, and with … gentle pressure shall we say… they can secure answers to their investigations. You have to admire their persistence because methinks such investigation would have taken a hellish long time – a century or more. They presumably tracked down the cloth, or some of the parts thereof and the casket, the most recent trader and me. Being unique in appearance, it wouldn't have taken much to trace me to the docks and thereafter…'

Adam who toyed with his dagger muttered 'Mmm.' And then louder as he sheathed the dagger. 'Your story has veracity. Did you tell Gisborne any of this?'

'The man doesn't give one time to open up, let's be honest.'

'Right!' Adam slapped his thighs and stood. 'Either way, we have a valued relic under our care and the Templars do not, and they ain't going to have it. So, heads up my friends, and keep your guard. We have the enemy not just at the gates, but right in our midst. Shall we to table? I'm starving!'

Chapter Fourteen

Cécile's prayer beads had been her solace since she had entered the priory and it was as though she had lost a lifeline but she remembered her robes – the priory's robes. They at least would be comfort.

She hurried to the cart and found the serjeant tossing the baggage around and she simmered. 'Do you look for something?'

He swung to her with hooded eyes. 'My lord requested I see you all settled and then join him.'

'You say,' she responded crisply. Why did he disturb her, apart from the fact he was obviously lying? Was it his rude arrogance or the fact he took her for an old fool? She began to reach for her bag. 'I can take my own…'

'Leave all that!' called *Madame* de Clochard. It seemed as if she parted the seas between Cécile and the man, separating them and diluting the atmosphere. 'My men will carry it in, Sister, so come to your chamber and refresh. You sir, can go to the stables, where you will find water to clean yourself.' She stood with her hands on her hips so that the serjeant could do little but walk away.

If Madame de Clochard had noticed anything awry, she made no comment, instead taking Cécile's arm and leading her inside to a heaving hall where preparations were being made for a meal at a long trestle table. Cécile gazed up at the beautiful blue ceiling where stars glittered in a heavenly firmament and not for the last time wondered at how wealthy this merchant house was.

'Sister, I think you are Cécile, yes? My cousin sent me a letter to say you would be coming this month. You look tired. I suspect it was an uncomfortable journey, as is always the case when the barges are unable to move freely.' She talked on and Cécile let the words slide over her as she gazed at the folk in the hall, smelled the roast meats that sizzled in the kitchens and watched large trenchers of bread being laid along the length of the table. The walls were whitewashed but hung with glowing ruby rugs, the like of which Cécile had never seen and at the hearth, a fire was being tended and it crackled warmly. The place wasn't sumptuous, but it bore more finesse than Cécile had seen in her whole life.

'Here, Sister, up the stair. Careful now. I have given you a chamber on the first floor. It's only small but it is quiet and overlooks the river. I thought you might appreciate the peace…'

A scream followed hard on the matron's words and Cécile went to free her arm and run back down the stair. 'Gelis!' she cried. 'Where is she?'

'We cleared our business chamber for her and she is even now being assisted by Lyon's best midwife. Come, Sister. As soon as you are clean, you can attend her. You are covered in mud and I have had warm water placed in your chamber for your use.'

Cécile tried to pull away but the matron held tight, placating her. 'Sister, she is well-tended, I assure you. As soon as I have settled you, I will go to her and indeed Ariella will join her when she too is clean.'

Ariella? Why is she *such a part of this house?*

'And what of *Messire* Gervasius?' Cécile asked. She felt as if she were in a fast-racing tide and that whatever control she might possess disappeared as the flood pulled her in its wake.

'He is cared for by the men, as is the tradition. They will make sure he is comfortable.'

The matron was older than Cécile thought, wrinkles fanning out from her eyes over soft creamy skin, lines drifting from her nose to her chin. Her chin, whilst not as many folds as Gelis's, was… endowed, thought Cécile as kindly as she could. Palest grey hair had escaped the woman's veil and wafted between rosy cheeks and snowy linen; everything about her radiated modest success. 'Come now,' she chided. 'Here is your room, you can clean up and we can go and help… what did you call her?'

'Gelis.'

'That's it, Gelis. Now, I have lit a lamp and closed the window. If you are cold you must say. You and I are old bones, Sister, and we feel the cold.'

Cécile begged God to take the talkative matron away so that she could find peace and calm. 'Thank you, *Madame*, for your consideration. I am obliged…'

Before she could finish her request for a moment's solitude, a knock on the heavy door broke their attention. Pulling the door ajar, *Madame* found the Templar serjeant standing with a bag in his arms.

'Yes?'

'The Sister's luggage, *Madame*. My lord asked that I make myself useful in return for the invitation for us to dine.' His voice was like a rasping chain across stone.

'To dine?' *Madame* Clochard's tone had become coolly autumnal and Cécile was impressed, conscious that it could and no doubt would slide to winter if the woman was pushed.

'*Messire* Michael Sarapion invited us in gratitude to my lord for saving *Madame* de Guisborne and her guard from the boar.' The serjeant's grey eyes glinted and Cécile disliked him even more.

'The boar?'

Cécile cut through the interminable discussion by

grabbing her bag. 'Then we won't keep you. God's blessings upon you.' She closed the door in his face and turned to the matron. '*Madame*, I am beyond grateful for your care, but I need privacy to pray and ask for Saint Margaret's intercession for Gelis.' She opened the door again and stood to bid Madame adieu.

Madame de Clochard flushed. 'Oh,' she gathered her folds around her ample legs, 'of course you do. How remiss of me. Until later then…' she smiled brightly and left the chamber and Cécile closed the door, leaned against it and sighed, closing her eyes.

But the birthing cries penetrated, even through the heavy wood, and Cécile hurried to the bowl of tepid water, dragging off her veil, her wimple and her robes. She took a square of linen and began to wash, the first time since she left the confines of the priory and tears stung her eyes as she remembered. She knew she should be strong and rely on God to keep her safe, but she felt tossed about and adrift and sat on the cot as she sank her feet into the bowl, watching the clouds of muddy filth eddy around the sides of the pewterware. She marvelled at the thickness of the mattress beneath her bones and at the feel of the softly woven woollen blanket against her nether skin. At the fur draped over the end of the cot. It all seemed far too indulgent for a nun in the service of the Lord, she thought, and resolved to fold the excess and leave it outside her door.

The cool evening air dried the moisture on her body and she took her bag, undoing the gathered neck and reaching inside, scrabbling amongst its contents. 'What is this? Where are my things?' She stood up and shook the contents out, aghast to see a trail of infant's linens, a tiny chemise, swaddling cloths and a small woollen blanket.

'My robes!'

She grabbed at her old robe and flung it on, tying it with the dirty knotted girdle, eyeing the soft creamy-coloured linens and then frowned as she noticed a golden cloth, worn and tired, frayed with life's vicissitudes. Certainly not baby's wear…

She ran her fingers across the weave, noticing that her hands at least were clean, the pale papery skin alive with a web of blue blood-vessels. The fibre of the cloth was as soft as spider's filament under her touch and she carefully took it and unfolded it across her cot, aware of her heart pattering with guilt that she should touch something that belonged to the infant Lucas, and his family.

The cloth was longer rather than wide and frayed heavily at the edges but the golden colour was like palest molten metal, not faded at all. She tried to imagine the age of the piece and why it was with Lucas's things but she was tired and had almost refolded it before she noticed that she had not opened it to its fullest extent. One more fold and she found there were dark stains. She squinted, aware that her eyes were tired.

Is that not the imprint of a foot? Two feet?

And what is that? A darker stain on the arch of each foot.

She bent down and traced the feet with a finger.

They look like ancient bloodstains. As if nails had been…

She dropped the cloth and it floated to the cot as her hands jammed against her mouth.

No…

She refused to countenance the image.

Impossible…

She folded the cloth quickly and it caught on the rough, travelworn skin of her hands. She pressed her palms on either side to flatten it and like silk, it was cool to the touch but warmed swiftly and her heart unwillingly warmed in tandem.

You never desert your people, Lord,
never abandon your chosen.
Right and justice will return,
bringing peace to the honest.

She scrabbled at her shorn grey head, pulling on the grubby linen wimple, fastening it beneath her chin and tucking the excess into the neck of her robe. She folded the travel-stained scapular neatly but left it on the floor, and then draped her veil over her head, assuming once again the demeanour of a Bride of Christ. Carefully, she packed all the baby's goods back into the sack and slipped the knotted rope over her shoulder. Reaching for the silken pad, she held it tenderly to her chest, aware that she may hold a rarity in her palms.

She stood for a moment at her open door. Some innate caution made her open the bag and place the cloth inside and she was glad, as when she moved down, the first folk she encountered were the Templar and his man. Leaning against the wall, speaking quietly and watching everything, examining, nothing was beyond their gaze. She had to squeeze past and the Templar nodded and said 'Peace be with you, Sister.'

She murmured, 'And also with you…' and hurried onward toward the howls emerging from a passage opposite. There was a door that sealed the passage off and so she pulled it shut behind her, breathing out with blessed relief that she had halted the Templar momentarily.

She knew they searched for something. Why else would the serjeant have been sifting through the bags in the cart? But she couldn't be convinced that what she had held this evening had any significance to anyone. Especially a Templar. An old piece of frayed silk?

And what role would silk have ever played in the cruci…

She found she couldn't even think the word. It was blasphemy, so wrong.

The chamber was warm, a fire burning, and what window spaces there might have been had been covered with weavings. Groans and murmurs drifted to the ceiling where a miasma of sweat, smoke, oils and lavender hung like a cloud. Cécile felt as if the weight of everything might drop upon her and drown her, so thick was the atmosphere.

Madame de Clochard turned around. 'Oh, Sister, you have come when we need you most. Our midwife has managed to turn the babe and it is close. Gelis is in need of you, I think. Ariella, move now and let the Sister take your place.'

This woman that the matron lovingly called Ariella, made no comment as she shuffled out of the way.

The midwife looked up from where she sat on a small, three-legged stool as if she were about to milk a cow. 'Sister, Gelis and her babe are exhausted. You must pray to all the Saints for this next to go smoothly. Ah,' she sighed, her hand on Gelis's moon-like belly as the poor thing whimpered and moaned. 'Here it comes! If only we had a prayer belt…'

Gelis's face was pasty with sweat. Her eyes, wide with fear, bloodshot and feverish, cut through Cécile's heart and so she retrieved the silk from the bag and held it out, ignoring the gasp from Ariella. 'Perhaps like this?'

She unfolded the pale golden cloth and laid it over Gelis's belly as the woman's groan pitched higher and higher until she was screaming. Her face flushed the colour of a pomegranate and her hair hung in damp ringlets as she strained to birth her child.

The baby slithered into the world in a rush of fluids. Cécile had seen all manner of common farm animals in the village, but never anything like this – a child. A real child! So much blood, water, a waxy substance and above it all, the sight of a perfect small creature, despite its puffy face. Surely Saint Margaret had been listening.

This…. this wonderful thing, thought Cécile, unable to stop her eyes from filling, is the reward for Eve's pain.

The midwife grabbed the child, sliced at the cord in two places, wrapping a hempen string around the small stump. She then grasped the child firmly and rubbed at the waxy blue body which seemed to flop this way and that, lifeless in her arms. There was a tiny intake of breath and a trembling whimper as the midwife rubbed harder and then slapped the little bottom whereupon the baby sucked in a bigger breath and cried loudly. Gelis sobbed as the child was laid upon her.

Cécile had never dealt with babes at all apart from young Lucas. She had never missed motherhood and yet when she saw this life delivered to the world and the perfection of the hands and feet, of the little mouth and startled eyes, she experienced such a pang – a longing that slid from her soul into the pit of her stomach and then into her heart. She smiled at Gelis. 'God be with you both, my child. A beautiful baby...'

Tears slid from the corners of Gelis's eyes and her voice was barely a thread of a whisper. 'Have I a son or daughter?' She ran a trembling hand over the infantile head, birth grease and a smear of blood coming away.

'Oh...' Cécile had no idea and didn't care because the infant was alive and perfect.

'A girl, *Madame*,' said the midwife. 'And she has all she needs – fingers, toes, eyes and ears and can cry with the best of them. Ah, there we go...' She caught a bloody lump in a bowl as it slithered between Gelis's legs and then pressed a cloth into Gelis's groin, before picking up the bowl, adding the infant's cord to the mess and handing it to *Madame* de Clochard. 'Have this buried with respect, and more linen if you please, and some marrowbone broth. And you, Sister, pray. Our mother is in need of intercession.'

Cécile's heart contracted and she began to mouth her prayer, aware that Ariella was standing at Gelis's side, smoothing her sodden hair from her face – a kind and gentle action from one mother to another. From the hall came a muted cheer and then the sound of mugs being banged upon the trestles and even the nun could not stop a smile softening the tension in her face.

My Lord and my God! I offer up to You my petition in union with the bitter passion and death of Jesus Christ Your Son, the Blessed Mother, and of all the Saints, particularly with those of the Holy Helper, St. Margaret, in whose honour I make this novena. Look down upon me, merciful Lord! Grant me Your Grace and Your Love, and graciously hear my prayer and my request for Your blessing upon the life of this child and its mother, Your servant Gelis. Grant them both the gift of a long and healthy life. I ask this as an intercession in the name of Saint Margaret. Amen.

She crossed herself and moved to catch the frayed silk which had begun to slip toward the rush-covered floor. Some deep intuition, even a tingling in her fingertips, made her lay it again down low upon that swollen belly and to then begin the Paternoster through trembling lips. The midwife continued to wad linens against Gelis's groin but the floor around the birthing chair on which the new mother lay was covered in a slick of blood and stained linens with more dripping obscenely.

'I need you women to pull her up,' said the midwife, wadding moss hard against Gelis's groin. 'Sister, the birthing belt, keep it on her stomach if you will.'

Cécile repositioned the soft folds, yet again aware of the cool of the silk and the tingling warmth in her fingertips. She helped Ariella to lift Gelis by the shoulders and the midwife raised a dull pewter mug of dark red wine to the exhausted woman's lips.

'Drink, *Madame*. It will nurture your womb after its energies. Are you in pain?'

Gelis's eyes were glazed and Cécile reached for the infant before she slid from her tired mother's hands. 'No… Tired… My husband…'

'*Madame* de Clochard has gone to tell him,' Ariella replied as the merchant matron left the room with her grisly bowl. 'Gelis, what shall you name your daughter?'

Gelis had closed her eyes and Cécile wondered if she had fallen asleep or become unconscious, but then, 'Cecilia… after the good Sister…' Her voice trailed away and Cécile gazed at her almost-namesake, heartstrings stretching over and under, binding her to the child.

'Perhaps I can wash little Cecilia,' Ariella said. 'And wrap her…' She reached for the little one and Cécile rendered the child up, feeling a tug on her soul.

'A good idea,' said the midwife. 'Swaddle it well for I have work to do and Sister, so do you.' The look she gave Cécile was meaningful and serious, her face set in a frown, as she replaced one bloody handful of moss with another. Cécile wondered if she would be paid if Gelis or the babe died. Certainly, her reputation might suffer and suddenly Cécile felt such a pang across her chest. Not unlike the pain she felt when *Soeur* Benedicta had passed away before she left Esteil. Something also spoke of the intercessory strength of that ancient cloth and so she knelt on the uncomfortable and bloodied rushes with her aching and travel-weary knees and began to pray again to Saint Margaret of Antioch.

Chapter Fifteen

Cécile's prayers finished with a soft Amen and then she whispered to the midwife, 'Tell me…'

'She bleeds so heavily…'

'But she won't die?' Women birthed babes all the time. Some died. But Gelis?

'She may. Sister, there is nothing left but prayer now. This is in God's hands. I have truly done all I can do.'

Cécile's mouth was as dry as sand, and she felt a huge sob welling in her chest. She knew she was tired, hungry, even thirsty, God help her, but this pain – the pain of seeing a new infant born against such odds and whose mother had been so brave – Mary Mother but it hurt. She moved in close to Gelis and laid one hand on the large, soft belly, her other on the cloth at the woman's bulge. Did she commit a blasphemy if this was indeed a cloth from the Virgin? If this was indeed the blood of Christ in the murky brown stains?

Her face chilled as if the Holy Ghost stood in front of her and a strange dizziness roared in her ears threatening to fold her at her knees. But no, it was surely only lack of sleep. She could cope with that. Gelis's needs were far greater.

'*My Lord and my God,*' she began again. '*I offer up to You my petition in union with the bitter passion and death of Jesus Christ Your Son, the Blessed Mother, and of all the Saints, particularly with those of the Holy Helper, St. Margaret, in whose honour I make this novena…*'

'Gelis,' Ariella had returned with the baby. 'Hold your child. Gelis, wake up!' She shook the bleached and ill woman. 'Gelis! Wake now! Your child needs you! Here…'

Gelis awoke from wherever she had retreated but she was as pale as a shroud and with blue stains beneath her eyes that spoke of finality and long sleeps.

'See,' Ariella spoke with tender firmness, 'she is very beautiful.'

Cécile looked at the puffy little face as she continued to speak her own prayer, her hands remaining on Gelis's belly and on the cloth. The infant was clean, its hair a cloudy wisp of nutbrown down. The little pink lips opened and a tiny tongue moved in a circle as if searching for something.

'*Look down upon me, merciful Lord!*' begged Cécile. '*Grant me Your Grace and Your Love, and graciously hear my prayer and my request for Your blessing upon this child and its mother, Your servant Gelis. Grant them both the gift of a long and healthy life. I ask this as an intercession in the name of Saint Margaret. Amen.*'

There was nothing then but the sound of the women breathing, of the midwife as she wadded linen pad after linen pad against Gelis and of the babe, finding a nipple and latching on with animal ease.

'Thank God,' the midwife sat back on her heels. 'Look you, it slows…'

Deus…

A tear ran down Cécile's cheek and Ariella bent to her. 'Sister, God's heart has been touched, I think. All will be well now, I am sure.' She took the infant from Gelis who had fallen into a doze and laid the child in an old crib that stood in the corner of the chamber. The door opened and *Madame* returned with a tray on which lay a bowl of earthy marrow-bone broth, a carafe of wine and a set of glass goblets. The burble of men's happy voices drifted in from the hall and then someone singing some bawdy song.

Cécile breathed in a sour breath, disturbed at the lack of propriety outside and then she saw the goblets on the tray.

Glass!

She had only ever seen glass within church windows and this wonder before her was just another to add to her fund of experience from this journey. Madame laid the tray down and a darkly-robed man stepped from behind her.

A priest?

Hastily, Cécile whipped away the soft gold cloth, jamming it up her sleeve and pulling Gelis's gown down to a seemly level, grabbing a blanket that lay folded on a stool and laying it over the woman's full, deeply veined breasts. She knelt on the floor and began to help the midwife wipe up the blood, so much blood, with what was left of the linen. They threw the bloody cloths in the smouldering fire of the side-hung chimney whilst Madame woke Gelis.

'My dear, this is Frère Thiou. We asked for him to visit you.'

Asked?

Cécile wondered at what point Madame had given up on Gelis. At what point she believed the woman would need to be shriven. 'But *Madame*,' she said. 'Our new mother is hale. She has fed her babe and is now resting…'

Frère Thiou raised his eyes to examine Cécile and she felt a rising tide … of what? Inferiority? Anger? She met his scrutiny with a steeled gaze of her own.

'And you are?' he asked, not unkindly which surprised her. Her own experience of the monks from Fontevrault had always been less than pleasant.

He was a well-tended man, Cécile decided. His skin shone, his robes were clean, a lot cleaner than her own, and he smelled of frankincense. He was neither fat nor thin and his greying hair was cut in a tonsure. He had remarkably clear blue eyes and laughter lines and Cécile decided he was less threatening than the Templar who no doubt sat in the hall without, as an extraordinary drama had unfolded within this chamber.

'*Soeur* Cécile, Obedientiary of the Prieuré d'Esteil. I have travelled with *Madame* Geltidis.'

'And what have you done here?' he asked. His tone was curious, his voice low and melodious, as if he could almost break into *plainchant* at any moment.

'Prayed,' Cécile answered shortly. 'It is what I do.'

'Then Our Father was listening and I commend you, *Soeur* Cécile. *Madame* Amée, I think there is nothing for me to do here beyond blessing the mother and child. May I ask that you come to a Thanksgiving mass…'

'Of course, of course, as soon as we are able, *Frère* Thiou.'

'Now, the child… ah, she *is* lovely. Bless you, my little lamb.' He sketched a cross on the child's downy forehead with his thumb, blessed the mother and left, leaving a beneficent smile trailing in his perfumed wake.

'A nice man and a trusted priest,' said Amée de Clochard, as if she too had experience of those who were not trustworthy. 'Now, shall we clean up our new mother? There are buckets of warm water outside the door.'

In time, Gelis had been washed and then robed in a clean shift and blue *bliaut*. Cécile had cause to think it was the same blue as the Virgin's robes in altar triptychs and that must surely be a good thing. Ariella plaited Gelis's hair and then wound it off her neck onto her crown and they left her unveiled because she was leeched of energy and looked as if she might collapse if they did not let her alone.

Amée stood, hands on hips with Cécile, as the last of the marrowbone broth was spooned into the new mother's mouth by Ariella. 'A miracle…' she murmured.

The midwife agreed. 'As you say, *Madame* de Clochard. A complete miracle.' The woman crossed herself. 'She lost the most blood of any mother I have attended. You had only to see her face to see that Death was taking her by the hand. But I have never seen blood stop flowing so swiftly. *Soeur* Cécile, your prayers…'

'I said nothing more than would anyone else in the circumstances.' Cécile squirmed. She wanted to be in her chamber, on her knees, thanking God with every bit of energy left in her body.

'Then the birthing belt,' the midwife persisted. 'It must be that. Where did you get it?'

'It is from our priory,' Cécile said with the ease of the most polished liar. 'It is nothing special.'

'What prayers are written upon it?'

'None. It is part of a veil that belonged to our first prioress…'

God forgive me for lying. For making little of a cloth with Your Son's lifeblood…

'And there has never before been a miracle?'

'Not at all. I think what you witnessed today was the blessed Holy Trinity helping a mother in need…'

'Then I am more than grateful.'

Perhaps *Madame* de Clochard sensed Cécile's unease, because she passed a clinking bag to the midwife and then pulled out two silver sols. 'The bag is from the father with undying gratitude. The coins are from me as added thanks for your skill. Two of de Clochard's guards will see you to your house. I would not want you robbed in the dark of night.' She put her hand under the midwife's elbow and guided the woman to the door. 'We are all in need of rest as I am sure you understand.'

'Indeed, *Madame*.' She took up her baskets. 'The new mother should improve now, but if you need me just send. And by the by, I would use a wet nurse. Gelis is too weak…'

'I have one waiting in the kitchens.'

'Then I bid you *adieu*.'

She closed the door quietly and in the growing peace of the room, where only the fire crackled and glowing ruby sparks flicked upward into the darkened chimney space, Ariella spoke.

'My son will need me and I for one am done. Sister, you must be deathly exhausted.'

'Not deathly…' Cécile demurred.

But not far from it.

Her legs trembled to hold her and she held the cloth deep in her sleeve, wondering why it had been in Lucas's bag.

'Then to your chambers, ladies.' Amée ordered kindly. 'Here is the father and the wetnurse, so you can rest easily.'

Cécile did not often give credit, but something about the matron reminded her of the strength and efficiency of *Mère* Gisela and at that very moment, faded cloths and babies notwithstanding, she almost felt as if she had come full circle, but decided she just needed to sleep.

After the long and painfilled wail, the cry of the new birthed baby was like a cork pulled from a costrel. The hall erupted into cheers and Gervasius was nearly knocked down by thumps on his back.

'Thank Christ it's over,' muttered Henri.

'Indeed,' agreed Tobias. 'It has been a long haul, has it not?'

'I don't know how women manage it, Toby. It makes the children they birth so precious.' He reached for the flagon of wine and refilled his mug. 'Look at Gervasius. So proud…'

Henri felt the pressure of someone walking behind and then a detested voice. 'Did I hear you thank God that the woman is done, *Messire* Henri? Do you not like children? And yet you care for the Jewess's as if it is your own?'

The Templar's expression was smooth but a muscle jumped in the man's cheek as he had emphasised the word, *Messire*.

The layers of threat in that one statement made Henri swallow on bile. The man knew Henri was no servant, and he also hated Jews and had marked Ariella…

Before he could respond, Toby had grabbed his *vielle* and slid off his seat to push past the Templar. He confronted the man – puffed up, brave and perhaps mildly drunk. 'I would hazard a guess and say that perhaps *Messire* Henri likes children more than you yourself. Excuse me, I must sing a song of congratulation for our new father.'

It was as effective as if he had jammed his fist into the Templar's mouth as the man's expression closed down to nothing. But Henri knew his demeanour. Knew that he would have marked Toby and that it was only a matter of time before he sought to avenge the slight.

'Ah well, that's like fat in the fire,' mused Adam over his wine as the Templar walked away. 'Not that we didn't already have to deal with that bloody man anyway. God's teeth but Toby's tail can have a sting!'

The little scorpion sat on a dais near the fire, singing of joy and happiness, and people's faces were marked with memories of families and friends, of children and mothers and everyone clapped when he had finished. Michael Sarapion stood and proposed a toast to Gervasius and his wife and all sank another mouthful of wine, banging their mugs on the table as *Madame* de Clochard emerged from the passage door, passing a bowl to her housekeeper.

'Gentlemen! And daughter,' she acknowledged Jehanne who sat at the head of the long trestle with Michael Sarapion. 'I thank you for your support of our new family but must ask you to be a little quieter. The new mother is exhausted and needs her rest.' She walked to Gervasius and kissed him on either cheek. '*Messire*, you have a little daughter and if I may say, she is very beautiful.'

There was the smallest whisper around the hall at the word 'daughter'. A son would surely have been preferred by most. But Henri saw nothing but gratitude and relief on Gervasius's face and knew the man was glad that both his wife and his child were alive. Anything else would have been greedy.

Madame de Clochard spoke briefly with Jehanne and then disappeared into the kitchen. She reappeared not long after with a tray filled with glassware, a flagon and a bowl of steaming broth. The passage door shut once again behind her and Toby began another song – a robust song with a beat that he marked on the bowl of the vielle. He obviously had no fancy to be quiet at that moment.

'D…dronken –
Dronken, dronken, y-dronken
…dronken is Henri attë wyne…'

'A good song from home and in my tongue,' laughed Adam clapping his hands as the verse and rhythm continued. 'By Christ he can sing.'

Tobias pulled the audience in close, lyric by lyric and they sat enthralled. Did they know that they sat in front of someone who had sung for the monarchs and nobles of Europe, who could speak four or five languages, who counted the infamous Blondel as a friend? And who could spy with élan and who had a nose for the very best that marketplaces had to offer?

None of it mattered though, as the Templar stared at Henri's musical friend. There was nothing inscrutable there. His eyes were filled with fury. This night had obviously not been a good one for the Soldier of God. Toby had belittled him, albeit only in front of a couple of men but for an individual who suffered no one's importance but his own, it was a burning taper. Not least because Tobias would be seen as a misshapen imp born from the loins of the damned.

'Henri, did you see his man sorting the bags on the cart?' Adam murmured as Toby began to sing something to wind the company down, a soft and gentle song inducing pillows and sleep. 'Seems he was looking for something.'

'Yes. But then he would never find anything, would he.' A statement. They had worked hard to sequester the relic in the best way and it seemed to work, judging by the thunderous clouds that rolled across the knight's face.

'This is not an end to it though,' Adam warned. 'That man knows we carry something of great value. I could see it in his face and with the way he taunted you. He will unwrap the subterfuge in short order, I think. By Christ we'll have to be on our guard.'

'The fires of Hell will burn brightly then, won't they?' said Henri. His face had warmed with the wine and a spicy poultry dish and it served to ease the perennial disquiet with which he lived and which the Templar had inflamed. He was tired and longed for his cot, needing time to pull his trailing thoughts together. He had no fears for Ariella, Toby, or even himself within this house, but beyond de Clochard's walls it might be another thing.

The midwife emerged from the passage and passed swiftly to the kitchens. An unknown woman dressed in serviceable wool and linen came to the table and fetched Gervasius and the man stood, happily inebriated and dancing on his toes like a young man in love. The two went through to the birthing chamber amidst a trail of well wishes and finally Ariella and the nun emerged with *Madame* de Clochard.

The whole table stood as the three women entered. It was reassuring to see the respect offered to them, Henri thought as he searched the room for the Templar. The man remained. sitting, eyes slitted and rolling a goblet back and forth across thin lips.

Madame bade Ariella and the nun a good evening, watching the women begin to climb the stair as if they had the burdens of the world upon them. Complete exhaustion radiated whereas *Madame* de Clochard managed to stay fresh, to look as if she could do the same again.

She murmured something to Jehanne and Michael and then followed the others up the stair and Michael stood.

'Men,' for apart from Jehanne Sarapion, it was only men who sat at the table. '*Madame* has asked me to wish you all a good night. It has been a momentous evening for all and given that our visitors have not even had time to sleep since their arrival, Madame suggests we finish our wine and return to our quarters. She thanks you for your assistance at the gates and will see you in the morning. My lord,' Michael bowed to the Templar. 'I thank you for your company this evening and publicly thank you for protecting our comrades from boars. No doubt we will meet often whilst you are in Lyon.' He lifted his goblet in a smooth toast to the Templar. The man nodded back, and as all around the table began to make their way to their billets, he too stood, beckoning to his man who sat at the far end of the table. Michael escorted them to the yard to fetch their horses.

'Where do you think they are staying?' asked Henri.

'I had thought in the country. To my knowledge there are no Lyonnais commanderies. I may be wrong. But I thought I heard mention that the Gigni have invited the knight to stay.'

'Alexandrus? Surely not…'

'It is nothing but a rumour. Michael will know.'

Henri yawned. 'Then it is one you must quash on your own. I'm done, my friend. Will you forgive me?'

'Go. I can't afford to have you or Toby at less than your best. I want you reporting to me tomorrow alert and armed, so sleep well, my friend.'

Henri sat on his cot, peeling off top and bottom layers of clothes until he sat in his braies. Lowering himself onto the soft mattress, he dragged his cloak and a woollen rug across his body. It had been a long few weeks since a cot had felt so luxurious. He missed Venezia, he realised. He had left with the eagerness of one who wants a new challenge, never thinking that the challenge would be couched within the body of the Devil's kin. But he pushed at that thought and his chest rose and then fell. As the warmth of the bed seeped into tired riding muscles, he stopped thinking anything and drifted along the windrows of a sea-deep sleep.

God knows, he thought later, how he didn't hear Adam and Toby take to their own cots, or even more, how he didn't hear them rise at sparrow's fart to break their fast. He woke to the sound of poultry clamouring for food and a bucket rattling as it was placed on the ground. The patter of grain hitting the paving stones and the excited burble of the chickens as they pecked for their share woke him a little more and he stretched. Realisation that it was *not* Bridget and her chickens in Venezia and that he was in fact in Lyon with a woman and her child, a nun and a relic to guard, had him throwing off his covers, dashing cold water into his eyes and pulling on last night's clothing. He pulled his hair back and fastened it at the nape with a strip of leather and then buckled on his sword. Hauling the door open and wincing at the light streaming in through an outer door, he hurried in the direction of the stables.

'Where is Adam?' he asked a young fellow who was brushing a plain, heavy legged gelding.

'He went to the church, *messire*. He and *Messire* Tobias with *Madame* de Clochard and *Madame* Sarapion.'

'And *Madame* de Guisbourne? Where is she?'

'She left with them…'

Henri saluted the groom and walked with purpose into rue Ducanivet, sidestepping two men with a barrow loaded with sacks of grain. He noticed how intrinsically the next-door property was now a part of Gisborne be Simon with walls knocked between the houses and people busy between one property and the other. He looked through the gates of the second house, curious to see how the trading business was expanding, wondering how the Gigni now perceived Gisborne ben Simon. The Gigni owned a whole street after all. But for Gisborne ben Simon to have two riverfront properties with access to the *traboules* and the river. It was, in many ways, money in the coffers.

Ah yes, things had changed since his time in Lyon a year ago. That fateful time when he had first met Ariella ben Simon, lover and then 'wife' of another man. From that moment she had dominated Henri's thoughts. There had been other women, but they were for fornicating. Ariella stood on a pedestal.

Huh! If nothing else, it gave him something to think about when the demons rode roughshod.

As he inspected the second address, the heavy *traboule* doors were pushed aside and a giant of a man backed out. His shoulders were wider than a staff, his height dwarfing those around him and he had a flaxen plait lacing down his back. He carried a thick bale of cloth over his shoulder as if it were as light as gossamer.

The bells for Tierce began to ring from the cathedral, sonorous sounds that chastened Henri for being idle and slow-witted and he began to run up the shallow gradient of La Grande Rive. The day was a lapis blue, a summer blue he thought, with mare's tail clouds flicking across the sky. Looking back, he noticed the ubiquitous river birds, especially the cranes, circling above the Saône, and that the river was quieter, smoother. Perhaps the barges might begin again and then Lyon would be as if lifeblood flowed into its very soul.

Excitement filled the air when the first barges of the season began to arrive. The merchants dressed prosperously, as though they attended a fair. To show the populace that they made money, that their goods would be the stuff of dreams. As each shipment was carried up from the *traboules*, it would be marked on a wax ledger, to be added to a parchment inventory later by notaries and such. For the Gigni and for Gisborne ben Simon, Lyon was just one more stage from where they would syphon off the extraordinary and exotic and redirect it to Paris, the Holy Roman Empire, and even as far north as the Russias.

Henri liked the return of those who had traded with the Russias. Inevitably, dense furs with sleek pelts would arrive, golden amber like frozen honey, intricately carved horn-handled knives, beeswax, sealskins, even *barels* of salted herring – goods that appealed to the southern marketplace.

On their way south, the traders would travel through Lübeck and Cologne, perhaps collecting precious metals from the mines, and then onto Bruges from where there would be a direct route south via Troyes. Henri was well aware that Gisborne ben Simon had an agent both in Lübeck and Troyes and as he walked along, he wondered idly if there were plans to build a larger company presence with bigger warehouses, a residence, more staff. The net that the company cast, rather like fishermen, would settle across all the seas from Europe to the Black Sea and even to the end of the world past Constantinople.

It took one's breath away.

As he strode through the Saint Estienne Porte into the cathedral grounds, the bells had ceased their carillon, but he had no wish to enter and so sat on the steps to watch the Lyonnais go about their day. Artisans mostly – bakers, cobblers, butchers and more, along with two-wheeled carts pulled by asses and filled with bags of flour, fruit and vegetables, animal skins. Meat dripped bloody runnels across the paving stones as butchers hurried to deliver ordered haunches.

'You do not go to Mass?'

Henri jumped up as Ariella's contralto voice sent a ripple along his spine. In moments, she had folded beside him, her gown draping grey shadows around her feet.

So today, she is still the Widow de Guisborne…

Very occasionally, she wore a rich wine colour or a verdant green and he could believe then that grief had loosened its hold upon her, but today was not the day. Today she had a snowy wimple and veil covering her hair and from her crown to her toes, she could have been a nun.

'Mass holds nothing for me, Ariella. God and I talk elsewhere if we talk at all.'

She gave a small laugh, hollowed out and sad. Touching his forearm, she said, 'You remind me of Guillaume.'

Henri was unsure if it was a compliment and asked, 'How so?'

'He was not a believer. He lost his love of God when his parents were cruelly slain and it only compounded when he fought in the Holy Land.'

'There is an irony,' Henri replied. 'He and I share something because Faith was tried in the Holy Land and found severely wanting.'

'Henri! Ssh!' She looked around but there was no one close by.

'Nevertheless, 'tis true, Ariella. Tell me, are you alone? Should you not have a chaperone?'

'I did. But I sent her home with my purchases and decided to wait for Amée and Jehanne. One surely could not be safer than on the steps of the cathedral.'

'Safer perhaps, but mayhap the centre of gossip.'

'I care little for the loose tongues of Lyon. I am here but a short while and they will lose interest…'

She looked across the square which had become busier as folk left Mass and vendors clamoured to sell food and wine. For a moment it was a busy *melée* and then it was cleaved down the middle by a man and his offsider. The white cloak billowed and then set like the sail of a trading galley, bows moving ever closer. Henri's fists clenched.

The Templar halted. '*Messire* Henri.' He bowed his head in something approaching etiquette. 'I bid you good morning.' He turned a cool face toward Ariella. 'And to you, *Madame*.' He emphasised her title as if it were poison on his tongue so that it insulted rather than charmed. 'There is every reason why you, *Madame*, do not attend our masses. But *Messire* Henri, should you not be giving thanks? For any number of things.'

Henri sprang to his feet, but Ariella reached a hand to his ankle and squeezed hard so that he took a breath. 'It is *our* business, my lord.'

'Oh,' De Tremelay looked down his nose as if he had stepped on dung. '*Your* business. Is it not *Gisborne*'s business to which you attend? And I wonder how much of that is consorting with a Jewess?'

The blood roared in Henri's ears. The kind of roar that had caused a sword to be drawn and plunged into soft flesh in the past. But Ariella squeezed again and he desisted.

'It puzzles me as to why the old Jew ben Simon would allow his daughter to travel so far with a babe. Is it something like subterfuge? What in God's name have you all got to hide?'

He turned away, and as his cloak swept behind him, he called, 'Till next time.' The serjeant hurried in his wake, barely looking at Henri, and Ariella even less so.

'Spawn of Satan,' she muttered.

'Who?'

'De Tremelay! His serjeant too, but I suspect if you asked either of them, they would say my father and myself represent Satan's offspring, not them.'

'Ariella...' Henri squatted down, taking her hand carefully from his ankle.

'Henri, I am used to it. It is after all why my father and myself became nomads after the York Massacre. We were searching for somewhere kind, safe and welcoming. Venezia seemed to offer what we needed and we have been happy and because it is some time since I have experienced blatant disrespect, it comes as a shock today. But two breaths, a glance at the blue sky and the knowledge that my little boy awaits, that rue Ducanivet is my second home and that my father is safe in Venezia, and I am again at peace.' Henri helped her stand as she continued, 'Do you think de Tremelay knows? Could he?'

'I think he suspects.'

Ariella kept his hand in hers and allowed him to lead her down the steps to the cathedral square. 'Henri, *Madame* Amée was almost bursting with the idea that a miracle might have happened to Geltidis and she is naturally loquacious. If she begins to gossip…'

'Then we must have Adam speak with her. Explain the dangers. What of *Soeur* Cécile?'

'She spoke to me yesternight as we went to our rooms.'

'And?'

'She asked me why a Jewess would carry a birthing cloth hidden in Lucas's bag. She doesn't prevaricate. When she wants to know something, she comes right out with it. It seems Lucas's luggage and hers were mixed and when she emptied what she thought was her bag, that's when she found it. It was she who brought it to the birthing chamber and she who laid it on Gelis's belly. She saw the imprints upon it and I think she put two and two together. We all watched what happened, Henri. The midwife, Amée, the sister and myself. One moment Gelis was bleeding to death. Really bleeding as though she had been cleaved apart, and then after a prayer of invocation from the sister as she laid the cloth over, the bleeding stopped,' she clicked her fingers. 'Just like that.'

'What do you believe?'

For a long moment Ariella just looked over the square, her eyes distant, lost in a birthing room where a woman had received her rites and where a babe was deemed to be losing his mother. Then, 'Christ was a Jew, Henri. Beloved of many. He was the son of God, they say, and many miracles have been attributed to him. I watched a woman whose belly was wrapped in the Virgin's veil and with Christ's footmarks upon it and she didn't die when she should have. How can I not call that a miracle? And me a Jew…' She turned to Henri, her eyebrows raised.

He could offer no alternate reason for what had happened. He knew that every woman who bled so badly at birth is known to die. A life for a life as a little babe lay there and a mother's lifeforce dripped remorselessly onto the ground. He shrugged his shoulders in return as something cold slid down his backbone. He didn't want to believe in miracles from God's hands. Why would he?

Chapter Sixteen

A voice hailed them from the top of the steps as people left the church. Amée led, a potentate surely, with Jehanne at her side and Tobias and Adam following like pages doomed to gather her skirts and train, and carry them wherever she wished to go.

'There you are! Henri, I am disappointed that you did not see fit to join us…'

Henri looked at Toby but the minstrel just tipped his head and raised his eyebrows.

'I apologise, *Madame*. I slept in.'

'Slept in! Anyone would think you had drunk the night away. Ah well. Let's hope in the final judgement that God will look kindly upon you. Now listen to me – I need you and Adam to go to Presqu'Ile and collect our good sister from the convent. She decided to pray with her Benedictine sisters – somewhere more suited, I gather. I do feel for her. She has no experience of a place the size of Lyon. It must be quite daunting.' She waved to a group of well-dressed folk who walked past. 'I want you to bring her home safe to us.'

'Of course, *Madame*.' Adam replied. 'But I need to ask a favour of yourself and *Madame* Jehanne. In fact I need to ask it of the whole house.' He lowered his voice and gathered everyone in close. 'I need you not to engage in any way about what you saw last night as *Madame* Geltidis gave birth.'

'But…' *Madame* Amée drew in her many chins.

'*Madame*,' Adam butted in. 'Heed us. It is a matter of great import and puts the lives of any who know at stake.'

'God's heart, Adam, you frighten me.'

'Good,' he replied. 'At the risk of alarming you, it is vital.'

Ariella spoke then, offering a further ripple into troubled waters. 'The midwife…'

'God damn!' Adam muttered and then looked at the women. 'Begging your pardon, ladies, But we must track her down and do whatever it takes to make sure she keeps last night's secrets.'

Amée's face had paled and Jehanne held her mother's arm as she said, 'Adam, we know that we can trust you implicitly. If you feel this is necessary, then we will do as you say. Won't me, *Maman*?'

Amée looked at Adam as she replied breathlessly. '*This* is why I need to go into retreat for a time. My nerves…'

'*Maman*…' Jehanne slipped her hand over Amée's own.

'If you think it is necessary,' *Madame* de Clochard sighed.

'I do.' Adam almost growled. At the mention of the midwife, his face had flushed, a sure sign he was perturbed.

'Then can you hurry to fetch *Soeur* Cécile?' Amée asked. 'I want us all behind the locked gates of Ducanivet until you explain.'

They parted company at *rue* Trammasal where the house of the merchant, Alexandrus Gigni dominated the street. The Gigni crest was embroidered discretely onto tunics, and staff passed purposefully under the arched gateway. Most of the houses in Trammasal were owned by Gigni, evidence of his success in the carved crests on each door.

'Huh,' said Adam. 'He *is* competition. And with strong familial connections with Firenze, Pisa and Genova. The Gigni could be such a threat to Gisborne…'

'Hard to demean Alexandrus, though,' said Henri as he

stepped round a well-dressed man and his wife leaving from the main doorway and being farewelled by a demurely clad notary. The black-clad notary saw them and called and they halted in their tracks.

'Adam, Henri! How good it is to see you!' The cheerful official hurried toward them, evident delight in his buoyant step. '*Messire* Alexandrus will be pleased that you are returned to Lyon.'

They both bowed their heads and Adam said, 'It is good to see you also, Odo. It has been a long time. You are well?'

'Indeed. Busy – *Messire* Alexandrus runs me off my feet but I must not complain. He is a kind and generous master.'

'The business does well?'

'Oh yes. We are diversifying into monies now. *Messire* Alexandrus believes there is a great future. Do you visit socially?'

'Another time, Odo. We are carrying out business for *Madame* Amée. But while we have your ear, is it true that one of our travelling companions is staying here? A Templar knight by the name of...'

'Ah, the lordly Gilbert de Tremelay.' The faintest frown etched across Odo's brow. 'He was invited, but in a note delivered to *Messire* Alexandrus, said he must decline the invitation and that he would be staying in a Templar establishment. It surprised me, as I was not aware of a *commanderie* in Lyon.'

'You don't like him, do you?' Adam grinned at Odo.

'Adam, I have never met him but his man, Jean, who delivered the note, is a sullen brute and the letter itself was phrased rather inelegantly. But then,' he sighed. 'I am speaking out of turn and you must excuse me.'

'Odo,' Adam replied. 'Henri has just travelled for leagues with both men and I think...'

'He means I don't like him either,' said Henri. 'Despite that he saved *Madame* de Guisbourne's and my lives.'

'God help us! He did?'

'From a wild boar, so we owe him that, if nothing else.' Adam explained. 'Odo, we must be about our business. You know what *Madame* is like. I tell you, she can be more terrifying than the Templar!'

Odo laughed. 'It does me good to see you both. Take care and make sure you visit *Messire* Alexandrus before you leave.'

They both walked on, turning to wave to Odo, whom they both liked. Adam said, 'It's a good community here. More friendly, less cut-throat than Venezia.'

They had reached the *Pont* de Saône and were squeezing amongst folk moving to and from Presqu'Ile and the further city gates. The bridge seethed and Adam swore.

'Is aught wrong?'

'So many people. Anything could have happened to the sister and who'd know? I hate crowds.'

They hurried onto the islet that was Presqu'Ile. Less houses, more green space, but like the other side, warehouses and alleyways. The convent dominated the landscape, stone and timber buildings surrounding large grounds and a heavy gate and impressive grille preventing ingress. By the side of the grille hung a plain iron bell and Adam rang it impatiently. Henri sucked in a discrete breath, aware that Adam was tense. It did not bode well.

The grille slid back and a heavy face gazed at them. Adam explained their presence and the face continued looking at them dumbly.

'Do you understand?' he asked, rubbing his hand against his neck.

'Um, *òc*,' said the nun.

'Well?' Adam did little to hide his frustration.

'I will get the Abbess…' the grille squeaked shut and Adam turned away.

'*Jesu*! And while they're at it, why don't they grease the

grille!' His neck was red and wisps of his fiery hair waved in the freshening breeze. The strands writhed around his head like angry vipers.

'Calm down, Adam. You are worrying unnecessarily.'

'I never worry unnecessarily, Henri. I have a gut feeling and I usually act upon it. It's why I'm a Master at Arms.'

'You think something is awry?'

'In fact, yes…'

The sound of a bolt sliding, of a bar being raised and the heavy old gate was swung wide. Standing in the opening was a woman, no doubt the abbess because she had an air of authority about her and the common-faced gatekeeper stood behind her, looking up at the men from under low beetled brows. The abbess slipped her hands up her wide sleeves and tilted her head a little to one side.

'*Messires*, you have come to collect *Soeur* Cécile, I am told.'

'Yes, Mother Abbess.' Adam deferred quite nicely when he wanted something, thought Henri.

'Then you have missed her…'

'God…' began Adam and Henri aimed a small kick at his calf.

'We have?' Adam changed tack.

'She arrived just before Lauds and partook of the prayer with us and then we allowed her to rest in a spare cell we have for visiting nuns. She was to join us for Matins but before we filed into the chapel, she received a note that had been delivered to our gatekeeper. It seems a dear friend was in dire straits following the birth of a child at which *Soeur* Cécile had assisted. She had been summoned to sit by the woman on her deathbed. Cécile left us as we rang the bells for Matins.'

'I see. Then we are too late.' Adam's colour was rising like a floodtide. 'Mother Abbess, can you tell me who came to collect *Soeur* Cécile?'

'Indeed. A Templar, Gilbert de Tremelay and his man. It was my duty to have one of our sisters accompany *Soeur* Cécile, but it seems that the knight sent her back at the gates and *Soeur* Cécile didn't demur and travelled alone. Now, *messires*, I must leave you as I have a meeting with the Archbishop's men. Go with God.' She turned away and the gatekeeper pushed her shoulder against the large gate, shutting out the view of the cloistered gardens and a plain stone fountain whose water caught the morning light and sent flashes across the paths.

'Christ all bloody mighty!' Adam slammed his palm against the convent wall. 'How to find her before she gives the secret of the cloth away.'

Henri looked around. Suddenly each house, each building, each alley was alive with deceit. They walked quickly to the bridge and surveyed every building between themselves and *rue* Ducanivet on the other side of the river. 'Damn it to Hell and back...'

'Hell indeed. I'm now *convinced* that bastard de Tremelay knows what we have in our possession. If torture is needed to find it, his man would do it – a nun notwithstanding. And in any case, if she doesn't give them the knowledge they seek out of fear for herself, she will surely give up the facts out of fear for others. Henri, we have to find her.'

Peace.

The gate slammed shut behind her and there was nothing but the quiet of a Benedictine convent, flame lit and mellow in the hour before dawn. The gatekeeper nun began to lead her to an antechamber across the shadowy gardens, saying she would inform the abbess of Cécile's presence. Cécile asked the nun not to disturb the Reverend Mother and that she would be happy to sit quietly in a corner of the chapel until Lauds but the gatekeeper said she must follow rules so that presently, Cécile sat alone in a small whitewashed room with a dark oak settle and a carved crucifix on the wall. She leaned her head back against the wall, wishing her prayer beads lay in her hands as the silence wrapped around her.

Dear God, Our Father, but how she had missed this. The way one could always find a quiet corner in which to retreat. Where one's thought could centre on the Holy Family, and prayer became a living connection. Since she had left Esteil, it seemed she had been surrounded by noise. No one took time for reflection and prayer and the very self-indulgence of those who surrounded her made her uneasy. If this was the outside world, then she was happy to return to the cloister post haste.

On the other hand, she had made a friend in Gelis, had helped birth a babe and had stumbled in her naïve and unsophisticated manner, upon one of the greatest secrets in Christendom. She crossed herself and clasped her hands in prayer for a moment.

Oh, she knew of its value, thanks to the Templar. If she hadn't heard him bartering with Archbishop Renaud's man, she would have remained oblivious but as the fragment of veil unrolled before her eyes, it took a bare heartbeat to recognise what she held.

How? Did the realisation flash across her mind like a shooting star?

No, but it held the radiance of something truly holy. It was infinitely soft, as if the Virgin touched her. And when she saw the footprints, it was obvious they were Christ's. How could anyone deny it? For one thing, the nail holes – marks of a painful torture.

But then, logic said they could have been anyone's – anyone the Romans chose to crucify. Why, even the Gospel of Luke talks of a *Penitent Thief* who hung beside Christ.

Seeds of doubt rose like thorny vines. Perhaps she was wrong. Perhaps it was just an old piece of cloth passing itself off as a relic.

Perhaps…

But something had caused her heartstrings to vibrate and her fingertips to tingle when she held the fragment. It was like a Divine melody, and something as tenuous as intuition bound her to what she believed she had found.

There was no doubt.

So. Ariella the Jewish widow had concealed one of the greatest relics of Christendom. A priceless fragment that men would kill to own. Even archbishops and Templar knights, it seemed.

The door opened and her thoughts quickly packed themselves away. A plain woman with bright eyes as sharp as a fox's entered and motioned Cécile to stay seated.

'Sister, you are welcome. You are from Esteil, my gate-keeper says. A long way from home.'

'Yes, my lady. I have come to accompany the Widow de Clochard back to our convent for a period of retreat.'

'Amée? She goes to Esteil? I did not know.'

'Her cousin is our prioress, my lady.'

'I see. I was unaware she had a relative in the Church. How interesting. And you, *Soeur* Cécile, what position do *you* hold?'

'I am Esteil's obedientiary with ten novices currently in my care. I am also in charge of the scriptorium, our embroidery output and I manage the ledger for *Mère* Gisela.' She wished her voice didn't betray a degree of pride but there was no hiding it and so she tucked her hands into rough woollen sleeves, grasping the fists tightly to settle herself down.

God Above but she was tired.

'By the Virgin, *Soeur* Cécile, you are worth your weight to Esteil! I hope your prioress realises this.'

'She treats me fairly, my lady, and we share as much of the mundane running of the priory as we can. But it is she who has the hardest job. Senior clerics wish to close

Esteil because it is so small and we are not financial. Even though our work is considered exemplary, they want us to join another convent. It is only that we are in Fontevrault's purview that we are surviving, and *Mère* Gisela is hoping for a miracle.'

'And *Madame* Amèe is part of this miracle?' the Abbess asked with more perspicacity than Cécile liked.

But the woman continued swiftly, barely pausing for a reply. 'Miracles come for many reasons, *Soeur* Cécile. Perhaps if you would like to join us for Lauds, we can pray for one such to occur.'

'It is my heart's wish to observe the Hours within a community, Mother, and I appreciate your kindness. I had hoped for some peace to observe the Hours when I reached Lyon…' Never had Cécile wanted something so badly. Other than returning to Esteil as soon as was possible. She, who had never had to ask for anything at her convent but had rather ordered things to occur, now found herself in the role of supplicant. Even beggar.

The senior nun's eyes softened and she laughed. 'I do love your expression. De Clochard is a prosperous and noisy environment. I know it well. I know *Madame* Amée too and she is not the quietest person. Generous to a fault but rarely quiet.'

'Lyon is noisy, my lady. My convent is so very small and the hamlet in which it stands not much bigger. I have felt buffeted by things out of my experience on my journey here. God willing, if it is at all possible, I wondered if I might stay within this convent for a few days and follow the Hours with the community. *Madame* Amée will make sure you are compensated…'

She had no idea if Amée would do such a thing and just trusted to Fate and the Saints that this was so.

The Abbess scrutinised Cécile. 'We do have space as it happens and I would be happy for you to stay with us.

Benedictines are renowned for their hospitality as you know. Come with me now. I dare say Lauds is not far off and I will show you the way to our chapel. After Lauds, I will take you to a cell where you may sleep until we break our fast.'

The Abbess carried a lamp and the light swung to and fro in front of them as they walked along the cloister. Their feet beat a slight tattoo, leather on stone and the cool dawn air slid under Cécile's robes, slipping over her sandalled toes and up her bare legs. Briefly she closed her eyes, grateful beyond belief to her Lord and Saviour that she could leave *rue* Ducanivet and revive herself within this convent. A bell cut short her thoughts and began its loud carillon.

'Ah, Lauds, *Soeur* Cécile. Come, here is the door to the chapel. Please, I am happy to include you with us. You may join us in the choir if you so choose, or you may prefer to sit in the chapel proper. I leave that to you. We do open our doors at Lauds so that the people may pray before they begin work, but then I am sure you know this. We never have a full complement of the local folk – people drift in and out.'

The sisters had begun to file into the choir, heads bowed, hands folded within sleeves. Tall and short, fat and thin, old and young, pretty and not, there were many more nuns than Esteil. The bench seats creaked as women sat and prayer beads rattled, sandals scuffed the floor and the heady odour of women began to fill the space. An intimate smell of women who worked hard and bathed only once weekly. It was something Cécile was used to. She looked around her, noticing the beautifully carved screen separating the nuns from the common folk. The altar with highly enamelled silver chalices and a large silver cross. A tiny unchristian part of her noticed the cloth on the altar was plain linen and sparingly embroidered with a scarcity of goldwork and she prided Esteil on their miraculously nimble fingers.

A few people had filed in to sit on the chapel trestles but she couldn't see them clearly and it was only as a male voice offered a prayer that she realised a priest stood at the altar.

'*Almighty God, give us wisdom to perceive you...*' he began but running footsteps along the nave and interested whispers from the small number of folk caused Cécile to break off from the Benedictine prayer she knew by heart. The nuns all looked at each other but none spoke as a dour-faced obedientiary threw a glance over the community. The beeswax candles dipped and dived and Cécile could see the curiosity on everyone's faces. The Abbess stood up from her seat and edged around the screen where there were further whispers, and then she returned, bending to Cécile and saying quietly,

'Sister, methinks you must come. There has been a message for you from a *Messire* Gervasius. Ah, I see you know the name. His wife needs you urgently. She has taken a turn and has not long to live. The message was delivered by a Templar knight and his serjeant. The knight has had to depart as he has business beyond Lyon, but he bid his man to deliver you safely to the house. I will send one of my sisters to accompany you...'

At the mention of Gelis's illness, Cécile's heart plummeted to her cold toes.

Surely the cloth would have made her well into perpetuity, not just for the birth of her little daughter. Was it perhaps just an old scrap after all? She felt defeated of a sudden. Desperately tired and overcome.

'I will leave immediately, Mother. Thank you for your kindness, but I assure you, Jean the Templar serjeant and I know each other well. I travelled from Montbrison to Lyon in a group of which he was part. Do not take a sister from her prayer, I beg you. *Adieu* and peace be with you...'

She hurried down the nave, past curious faces built of planes and shadows in the flickering light, the prayer following her to the doors:

'*Almighty God, give us wisdom to perceive you, intelligence to understand you, diligence to seek you...*'

But then the door slammed behind her and she broached the weak light of early morning where a pearly river mist had cloaked all in soft wisps of what might have been gossamer silk from Constantinople and beyond.

A man in the brown mantle of the Templar serjeants turned as the door closed. Beneath the cloak, he wore a black-as-night tunic embroidered with a blood red cross.

She shivered. The damp river chill seeped into her bones. 'Jean,' she said. 'God's blessings upon you at this early hour. They say you are the bearer of bad tidings...'

'Yes, sister.' He was a man of few words and his voice grated as if his throat were perpetually sore. He held out his hand to help her mount. 'Come...'

She loathed the idea of sitting behind him, even less holding on to his cloak once he had mounted in front of her and settled himself. He kicked the horse on and they left the monastery smartly.

He kept up a steady trot and she tried to relax into it the way Henri had instructed her, but she was tense and afraid for Gelis and could not soften her seat. She slipped one way and then the other but managed to stay on as the sound of the horse's hooves caused the early foot traffic to slip off the road and watch as they rode by. They reached the *Pont* de Saône along which folk headed into the town and Cécile kept her head turned to the river on her right shoulder, allowing her legs to dangle as loosely as she dared. She tried not to hold hard to the serjeant and he said nothing to calm her as he urged his horse off the bridge on the city side.

Then with a noise as sharp as a cracking branch, something terrified the horse and it baulked before rearing high, legs flailing. Cécile slipped back off the horse's rump, crashing to the hard cobbles. The air rushed from her as her back hit the roadway and she barely had time to lift her head to see Jean astride the back of the maddened horse as it bolted, before a thump on her temple and the most sickening flash of light in her eyes sent her spiralling down into blackness.

Nausea woke her, her mouth filling, and she turned on her side as best she could, retching until she was empty. There wasn't much – she had eaten very little since arriving in Lyon but the bright yellow froth smelled rotten and her insides stretched painfully with the effort. Exhausted, she wriggled away from the putrescence and then collapsed, closing her eyes against the awful pain that hammered in her temple. She knew nothing again until a soft rhythmic sound, a gentle thump-thump, eased into her consciousness. Watery sounds thrashed occasionally, by which she assumed she was riverside – perhaps near a millwheel. Mary Mother her head hurt. She lifted a hand to her wimple and winced as she probed a bruise. More than a bruise, as her hand came away bloodied. She eased her veil away and then pulled the wimple off, wadding it against her temple, then examining it in the gloom, trying to see how much she bled.

She knew it hadn't happened when she fell. Of that she was positive. In quick succession, she knew also that some-one, some devil-seed had hit her. She turned her head, a movement that made the very air swim and found she lay on the dirt in a decrepit room. It smelled of damp and mould and was shadowed, apart from striped light which slanted in through slats.

She wanted to curse those who had hurt her, but thinking and moving made her feel ill and so she lay still, listening to the thump and rush of water. She would close her eyes and lapse and then wake with a jerk and then drift again until finally bells woke her and she listened.

Prime! She had been drifting, hidden in this place, from Lauds through to Prime! What was she to do? Someone somewhere must be missing her, surely. She felt old and unsure and tears crept from her eyes. As she wiped them away and ran shaking hands through the stubble of her hair, a door opened, letting in a beam of light which hurt her eyes and made her head pound.

A cloaked shape with a hood dragged over his head stood at the door whilst another dressed similarly walked over to her and grabbed her by the arm, pulling her to stand.

'Where is it?' said the one at the door. It wasn't a voice she recognised. Gravelly and common, thick with something, as if his mouth was filled with food.

'What?' she asked, not quite so innocently.

The fellow holding her arm shook her hard and she cried out, earning a backhand across the mouth. Her teeth bit down hard into her bottom lip.

'The cloth, you raven.'

She took a breath. 'What cloth?'

Another belting the other way and she thought her neck might break, so hard was the impact. She prayed to God to help her, as her lips split further.

'The one that saved the woman's life.'

'There was no cloth. I don't know what you talk of...'

Another strike and she fell to her bony knees, her ears ringing. She worried that she was old and might not sustain much more, her heart beating so fast she thought it would burst. She was on all fours and knew that the next attack would be to her body from booted feet and she knew also, that like the women they treated within the priory of Esteil, some things could be fatal.

'*Pater noster, qui es in caelis, sanctificetur nomen tuum. Adveniat regnum tuum...*'

'Sister, we know.' Was it Jean de Laon's voice? She wished it was the Templar's. She *needed* it to be the Templar. She could then commit de Tremelay's name to Hell as she died. 'The cloth that performed a miracle, yesternight. Where is it?'

She thought of God's grace and the Virgin's hands in the miracle of that cloth. She had always assumed a kind of danger would be omnipresent for a nun coming from the country to a city she had only heard of, but this? What would *Mére* Gisela say? She braced herself for a bashing. *'Fiat voluntas tua, sicut in caelo, et in terra. Panem nostrum quotidianum da nobis hodie, et dimitte nobis debita nostr...*

Chapter Seventeen

'Sister!' A hand eased under her head and a cool cloth wiped her temple and her lips. 'Sister, wake now.' The voice had a curious lilting tone, not Gallic at all, and ineffably deep, probably from the bowels of the earth for all she knew.

She opened her eyes and met the troubled gaze of the biggest man she had ever seen.

'Better,' the man said. 'Can you sit up? Petrus would like you to sit if you can. The floor is not for the likes of nuns.' He smiled to lighten his tone and she allowed him to help her. His huge hands held her respectfully and he propped something behind her – an old bag of grain? Its smell brought to mind ducks, chickens and Esteil and she almost wept.

'Here. Drink.' He held a leather costrel to her lips and she let a small drop of wine lie on her tongue. Then she swallowed, grabbing at his hand and trying to take more.

'A little, Sister or you will be ill. Do you know those who did this?'

She closed her eyes to indicate no. She couldn't shake her head for fear it would rattle her brain and neither could she speak.

'Hmm,' the giant frowned, enormous lines stretching from nose to mouth. The man's hair lay like a frozen waterfall down his back – glistening and white and twisted into a plait with pieces escaping round his face. 'Petrus thought he recognised someone because Petrus has a sharp mind and even better recall. There, good. Is the wine helping?'

She blinked slowly. Yes. It flowed through her empty stomach and through every blood vessel, loosening her tired, bruised body. She felt tears leaking again and grimaced at her frailty but even that hurt.

'Poor Sister. Petrus will make attackers pay. He is angry at anyone who attacks women.'

His bass voice was so soft and kind that she gave in to her weakness, allowing tears to seep like a shower of spring rain. Relief – definitely relief.

'Sister, Petrus must leave you to find help. I will be moments only.'

She grabbed his hands, those huge paws that had been so gentle and her damp eyes opened wide. 'Please,' she croaked. 'Don't leave me. Help me up. I will walk with you…'

'Sister, you are very weak and Petrus always comes back. On his life he promises you will not be hurt again.' His big hands folded hers back upon themselves and he took off his cloak and covered her. 'I will be back forthwith, Sister.'

He left, the door closing and she wept again, trawling through her brain for prayers of supplication. Fear did strange things as she dragged a word from here and there. She trembled, but as the warmth of Petrus's heavy cloak cossetted her, she finally found prayers, and thanked the Lord for sending Petrus and for his kindness. She tried not to think that he may not return.

There was something about his raw honesty, his brute size, that gave her a measure of confidence and her bruised spine began to stiffen. She was an obedientiary after all. Again she thought, what would *Mère* Gisela say? She was positive the prioress would never have thought Cécile's journey would indeed risk life and limb. What made it worse was that Cécile knew her current state *was* the work of the Templar knight, de Tremelay. A Soldier of God and that he should do this to a Bride of Christ!

How was she so sure?

She had an intuition. As strong as the intuition that the cloth that lay in Lucas's bag *was* a fragment of the Holy veil. That and the horror to which she had just been subjected confirmed de Tremelay's guilt.

The massive cloak continued to warm her and her eyelids finally shuttered despite her headache. But her last thought was a prayer that God would make de Tremelay pay. Without remorse, she fell into an exhausted sleep.

'Ho! Adam of London!' a volcano voice rumbled behind Henri and Adam as they stepped off the *Pont* de Saône.

They turned and Henri recognised the bulwark mass of the man he'd seen in de Clochard's second yard.

'Petrus!' Adam reached out a fist and punched the massive fellow's upper arm. But he moved on, calling back over his shoulder. 'De Clochard? I will see you there later! We have urgent business.'

But the giant took one step and hooked Adam's shoulder. 'Petrus thinks you look for someone.'

Adam frowned and Henri saw that he trusted this brute of a man whose white hair shone like moonlight despite the grey misty day. 'Yes?'

Petrus tipped his head to the side of the bridge and they moved out of the way of traffic. 'A nun?'

Henri sucked in a breath. 'You have seen her? Where?'

Petrus's gaze slid to Henri and Adam said, 'Henri de Montbrison. A Gisborne man, a good fellow. Trust him, Petrus. He has been travelling with the nun all the way from Givors.'

Petrus examined Henri head to toe and then nodded. 'Follow me.'

He walked through the crowds, people splitting apart from them like the Red Sea from Moses. Obviously a man used to getting his own way, thought Henri.

They hurried behind him as he turned right past the crumbling dwellings and warehouses south along the Saône. The water lapped at doors, even low windowsills, but the river was less frenetic, speedy but not angry.

Petrus turned between a decrepit warehouse and an old mill house with a broken wheel that slapped and creaked as the water turned it. 'Quiet. Do not frighten her…' He eased the lean-to door open and ventured into a mouldy interior with Henri and Adam close on his heels.

The room was empty.

A sack of grain lay on the floor with the indent of something, but of the nun there was no sign.

Petrus cursed.

'She was here?' Henri asked.

His massive companion turned to look at Henri, his eyes glacial. 'I will kill him…' He said it quite calmly and Henri believed him.

'Who?' he asked the big man.

'That brown-cloaked arsehole.' No prevarication.

A sound came from above and the smallest shower of dust fell down between the planks. Petrus looked up. 'Sister?'

Soft footsteps occasioned further dust and Henri hurried up the broken stair, marvelling that the old nun would climb such a thing. When he saw her, saw her face and lips and how she angled her arm across her middle and with a huge cloak over her shoulders, his admiration for her courage knew no bounds.

'*Jesu*, *Soeur* Cécile, what have they done to you?'

'Ah, *Messire* Henri,' she managed. 'I am fair but it does hurt a little when I breathe. Do you think you can get me to *rue* Ducanivet?'

'Of course. Here, let us…'

But Petrus pushed them away and scooped her into his arms as if she were nothing but thistledown. She allowed the big man and he negotiated the steps without any words from her. Henri and Adam followed and they emerged into the pewter daylight of Lyon, tracing their way back to the bridge and then along the road, skirting puddles, to *rue* Ducanivet. Petrus made nothing of the journey and the nun was disinclined to talk, even letting her head drop to his broad shoulder. Henri and Adam looked at each other and then dogged Petrus's large footsteps until they passed through the gates into de Clochard's yard.

'Inside,' said Adam, opening the main door to the house. 'Hey, you there,' he called to a groom brushing a horse. 'Fetch the physician from Gigni. Tell him we will pay double his rates if he comes immediately.'

They entered the hall and *Madame* Amée swung away from the table at the noise, screeching when she saw the nun in Petrus' arms.

'*Soeur* Cécile! Petrus, bring her to her chamber, quickly!'

'*Madame* Amée,' countered the nun. 'Do not fuss. I am alive and God willing will stay so. This young man has been most kind. He found me and has delivered me safe to your house.'

'Young man!' muttered Adam. And then, '*Madame*, I have sent for a physician…'

'Not just *a* physician, Adam! *The* physician! Lyon has many who claim to know the workings of the body but only one who knows anything at all and he is beholden to Gigni. Jehanne!' this last was yelled from the top of the stair. 'Wine, warm water and a change of clothing for our sister, if you please!'

Henri glanced at *Soeur* Cécile. Noticing a wry expression creeping through her swollen bruises, he grinned. For once, he and the nun seemed to agree on something – that noise is less than pleasant when one feels awry.

Her stoicism was intriguing. He would bet his life that she had never been beaten before and yet she carried her injuries with a stalwart courage that truly impressed him.

When he had said she was not to be underestimated, he had meant it.

Petrus laid her carefully on the simple cot and she immediately sat up, nursing her middle. 'Thank you, Petrus. I am in your debt. I hope we can talk later.'

'As you wish, Sister.' He crossed his hand over his heart and backed from the room and Henri could barely hold his amazement. A bear who had become a lapdog in a moment.

'Out, Henri!' *Madame* de Clochard pushed him toward the door, gathering Adam who leaned against the door frame. 'You too, Adam. Make yourself useful elsewhere. We are able to help our sister-friend now. Thank you.' She shut the door in their faces after allowing Jehanne and a servant to enter with a tray of wine and fragrant bread, a bowl of steaming water and an armload of clothes and linens.

Henri blinked, a bucketload of questions on his mind and then said, 'I'm hungry.'

Adam ran past him down the stair. 'Meet you in the yard. I want to catch Petrus.'

By the time Henri had passed through the kitchen, grabbing a chunk of sweet-smelling bread, Adam had caught Tobias in his slipstream and both stood with Petrus. All were serious.

'Let's get food and go somewhere quiet away from here,' Adam said.

'The *traboule*. I have a key.' Petrus tapped the effeminate purse that hung from his leather girdle.

'I'll fetch food,' Toby added, noticing Henri chewing. 'If our friend here has left anything.'

'Well?' Adam chafed.

Petrus sat himself on a step and looked up at Adam who stood above him. He radiated such an obscure calm, thought Henri. Frightening, like the mesmerising swing of a counterpoise trebuchet before boulders leave the sling, or that inexplicable mid-flight beauty of a firestorm of arrows before they meet their mark.

'It was the serjeant,' his voice rumbled from deep in his chest.

The *traboule* echoed and re-echoed with his quiet words and Henri looked around to make sure no one would hear, but of course they had locked the upper door behind them and were in sight of the river entrance. A *torchère* lit the gloom and the walls seeped with centuries of damp, a soft green ooze that crept from the crevices. Ahead were the last few steps before the river, but so wet had been the early spring that water lapped at the lowest landing.

'How so?' Adam asked.

'Petrus saw them,' said the big man as he delicately folded a crust over a piece of cheese. 'Petrus was at Presqu'Ile when the serjeant rode out of the monastery with the nun seated behind him. She looked afraid, so I followed.'

Henri sat up sharply. 'The sister sat behind him? Why would she do that?'

Petrus pushed the food into his mouth and proceeded to chew.

'In your own time, Petrus,' Adam remarked with sarcasm and Henri waited for the fellow to bite back, but he merely swallowed and grinned.

'Still impatient, Adam of London. Time has not mellowed you.'

'Has it mellowed *you*, Big Man? I would bet my life that the right circumstances would have you bouncing men off walls.'

'Maybe. But Petrus senses that in this instance there is much at stake, so your manner is forgiven and Petrus will continue. If it may please you.'

'Ooh,' whispered Toby to Henri, 'I love this counter-sarcasm. It makes for good entertainment.'

'At the end of the bridge,' said Petrus, 'someone or something scared the horse and it shied. But then Petrus saw serjeant use his spurs and the horse reared. Sister toppled off and landed on her back on the road. The serjeant spurred again, and his horse seemed to bolt. Petrus knew something was badly wrong and tried to push the crowds apart to get to the nun, but a cart forestalled him and by the time he could get past, all he saw was a man disappearing to the right of the bridge by the tumbled warehouses, with the nun thrown over his shoulder. Petrus was shocked that no one seemed to care and so he followed, close enough to see where they went but not close enough to make a difference.'

'Why didn't you come immediately to get us?' asked Tobias.

'There speaks minstrel and not mercenary,' said Petrus. 'Because, Little Man, sister may have been killed whilst he was gone and Petrus could not allow that.'

'You are so sure,' Adam said.

'Petrus is always sure. It is why Gisborne employs him. You know this, Adam. You and I have known each other a long while...'

''Tis true, Adam,' Tobias rejoined. 'Don't doubt the man.' He then sat back and to Henri's chagrin, assumed a small half smile, as if this would make the most excellent ballad.

'How do you know then, sir?' said Henri. 'Tell us, for pity's sake. This isn't some game of chat over a wine in the tavern.' He just wanted plain speak.

Petrus's cool gaze swung over Henri and there was a moment when Henri wondered if this was what Christians felt in the lions' den.

'Henri of Montbrison,' Petrus said. 'Think what it is about the serjeant that you noticed. Something that sticks in your mind.'

Henri recalled the godawful journey from Givors and then shrugged his shoulders. 'Nothing. A bog ordinary man of looks and manner who said little…' but then his head flew up and he threw his gaze around the group. Suddenly he knew. 'Except, when we reached the gates of Lyon, I heard him speaking. It's his voice! It's guttural and thick, as if he's swung from the gibbet or been slashed across the throat…'

Petrus sat back, satisfied. 'Petrus examined all the buildings until he found one with a waterwheel. It seemed likely because its door-latch was newly crafted. And then Petrus had to hide as two men arrived, hooded and cloaked, and it was then that the evidence was too strong to ignore.'

He threw back a mouthful of watered wine from a costrel before continuing. 'Yes, Henri. It was the voice. Petrus heard it at de Clochard, when the ostlers were grabbing the luggage to carry inside. He became terse, even rude with them. As you say, the voice is hard to forget.'

'Good enough,' said Adam, slapping his thigh. 'Do you agree, Henri? Tobias?'

'I've accused men with less evidence, Adam. And besides, that chap hardly had the voice of angels.'

'Go on, Petrus…' Adam indicated with a wave of his hand.

'Petrus climbed into the water on the opposite side to the wheel so he could hear. The serjeant asked the whereabouts of a cloth, but the sister offered nothing and so they hit her twice. They asked her again, she began to pray and then there were two muffled thumps. Petrus hunkered down because the door flew open and the two men came out. *"Leave her,"* said the serjeant. *"If she dies, then so be it. But if she is still alive when we return, she will give us more. I will make sure."* They locked the door but for Petrus it was like breaking a stalk of straw.'

Without caution, Henri waded in. 'Why did you not enter earlier to save *Soeur* Cécile the bashing? You could have easily helped her with your bulk.'

But Petrus replied calmly. '*Messire* Henri, Petrus did not

know how they were armed. They may well have had knives to her throat and slit it without a thought before Petrus had broken the door down. Petrus would not want a nun to die. Or any innocent woman.'

It was a plausible response and Henri could say nothing more but by the Holy Spirit his blood was beginning to boil. A kind of seething that precipitated battle lust; a feeling he didn't want to remember at all.

'Besides,' the blond man continued. 'Petrus will kill him soon. It is a pledge made when the first hit landed upon the old woman.' He brushed crumbs from his hands and stood. 'Adam of London is happy now?'

Adam sucked in a deep breath and his lips frowned sideways. 'To a point. But before you go off seeking revenge, I would that we planned. But I do thank you, Petrus, for rescuing *Soeur* Cécile. Be under no illusions.'

The flame of the *torchère* fluttered as a breeze blew up from the river, smelling of all things damp and muddy. Henri had sunk into thought and despite anything that Adam might say, as the blood surged around his body, he knew he would kill de Tremelay as surely as Petrus might kill the serjeant.

'We will leave Ariella and Lucas here and collect her after we have been to Esteil. Petrus, I would like you to join us in escorting *Madame* Amée and *Soeur* Cécile. It will be a dangerous journey as we will have the relic and we will have two elderly women to see safe. Settled?'

'A pilgrimage,' said Toby. He brushed food from his green woollen tunic. 'Sometimes,' he continued, 'I long for the excitement of Byzantium.'

Adam clapped Toby's shoulders. 'You think the journey to Esteil will be dull? Don't underestimate it. We will be watching our backs all the way, I assure you. De Tremelay will cover every likely outcome. What about you, my friends?' he looked at both Henri and Petrus.

'I will come,' said Petrus.

For Henri, it was a plan he liked. He vaguely knew of Esteil and something about *Soeur* Cécile made the journey an intriguing one. And he *would* kill de Tremelay, of that there was no doubt. He swore a pact with himself, then and there.

If he had any regrets, it was that Ariella would not accompany them and he wondered if Adam had made the decision deliberately. As to working with Petrus, in truth he liked the man. An enigma if ever. This would be an interesting task at the very least.

The big man mused. 'Petrus thinks he will achieve his ends on this journey.'

'Might de Tremelay decide *not* to follow us, Petrus?' Henri asked.

'No. Why else would he have got his man to attack the nun?' Petrus had removed a dagger from a scabbard at his belt and was using the tip of the blade to clean his nails. The handle was horn, intricately carved with the looping runes of the far north and its pommel and guard were softly burnished brass. The blade itself glimmered in the flamelight, the damascening receding and flowing like an ocean wave – a beautiful weapon.

''Tis true,' Adam agreed. 'And why you must have your wits about you.'

'Are we done?' Petrus asked, wiping the blade on his tunic and slipping it into the scabbard. 'Petrus would be elsewhere.'

'Where?' asked Toby, moving toward the steps.

'Nowhere that would interest *you*, Little One.' Petrus clapped a mighty hand on Toby's back and Henri winced, expecting Toby to fly forward, then realising that this giant had a full measure of his own strengths and delivered accordingly.

He went ahead of them, the *torchère* in his hand and unlocked the *traboule* door into the yard. Henri blinked at the light, although in truth it was still pearly and grey as Petrus disappeared through the gates without a farewell.

'Huh,' said Toby. 'Little One indeed! A good man but a strange one…'

Adam headed over to the stables, saying over his shoulder. 'No stranger than anyone else in Gisborne's pay.'

It was true. Henri knew every man had a story to tell, every one of them could hold an audience to attention if they wanted. But Tobias was the only entertainer amongst them and he made sure his ballads were hedged and pruned to exclude the personal and incriminating.

The yard seemed quieter than he expected for a working day and he and Toby went into the hall to see if the physician had attended the nun.

The fire was heaped but unlit, and a few candle trees alleviated the gloom of the day. The sparse flames lit upon the gilded stars of the blue ceiling and the walls pressed close with warmth from the discreet hangings. *Madame* Amée sat at the table on one side of Ariella who rested her head on her arm. Jehanne nursed Lucas who studied the starry heavens with intensity.

Amée's hand rubbed Ariella's back gently back and forth and Henri was struck by the obscure silence within the hall. Any chamber that housed *Madame* would surely be ringing with sound.

'There, my sweeting, there…' she said and began to rub Ariella's back again.

'Is ought wrong?' he asked. 'Ariella?'

She looked up, her face wretched.

'Ariella?' His throat tightened and he sat on a trestle on the other side of the table as Toby eased himself in beside her, taking her taut hand.

'This…' she said allowing Tobias to remove a piece of

parchment crunched within her palm. He smoothed it, read it, sucked in an audible breath and passed it to Henri.

Henri turned it around and in the light of the candles, read the spidery writings contained therein.

To Ariella de Guisborne from your brother in law, Guy of Gisborne, greetings.

It is my sad duty to inform you that your father and my esteemed business partner Saul ben Simon died today.

He was attacked as he entered our warehouse and despite the best attentions of Mehmet Al Din, died in our care.

Be assured he did not die in pain and he was able to speak with us to the very end. His last words were for you, Ariella, that you should remember him with love as he remembers you.

Come as soon as you are able. Ahmed will wait at Arles.

It was signed by Gisborne, and the now flaked black wax had been impressed with the three-arrow insignia that was Gisborne's own. Henri's own breath sucked in, aghast at the monumental loss so baldly announced in oak gall ink.

'If this came by mounted messenger overland from Arles,' Toby said, 'then even at a full gallop and changing horses frequently and assuming it arrived swiftly in Arles by ship, this awful thing happened moments after we left Venezia.' He gently rubbed Ariella's hand.

'I would say so,' agreed Jehanne as she switched Lucas to her other shoulder.

Ariella had been looking at the opposite wall, her face tear-stained, lost in a piteous revery. Then she spoke and her words crashed to the floor. 'He was murdered,' she said, 'because his murderer wanted something he had. He was killed because he would not give in to them.' She stood and walked back and forth, her gown folds slamming against the furniture legs, first one way and then another, her hands fisted. 'It was the Templar, he wanted the cloth! My father died, not just because he was Jewish, but because the Templars want that relic and they knew my father had concealed it within the warehouse. What they were unaware of was that we had just left. *Curse* them!' She slammed a fist down on the table and a candle tree jumped, one candle falling so that Toby grabbed it and snuffed the agitated flame.

Amée guided her grief-stricken guest up the stair whilst the others remained at the table. An air of shock hung round and for a while none said anything as they tried to absorb the momentous nature of what had happened. Jehanne continued to nurse Lucas who had fallen asleep on her shoulder.

'This explains the speed of the Templar vessel behind us on our way here,' Henri said. 'They surmised the relic had left Venezia...'

'But to kill Saul,' Henri said. 'Where are their godforsaken morals?'

Toby scoffed. 'Morals? My experience with the Templars is that morals and ethics are shaped very much to their own needs. They dance to their own tune and then claim that what they do is done in God's name. Curse them to Hell and back!'

'Poor Ariella,' murmured Jehanne. 'She and her father have been through so much.'

'Indeed,' Henri added. 'And he was a gentle man. A fine friend to all who knew him...'

There was a grinding noise as the door opened and then slammed shut. Damp river air wafted in with Adam and Michael, the candle flames bending away from the entry, Lucas stirring.

'I can see it is true then,' said Michael, looking around. 'Christ on the cross!'

'Ariella?' Adam's face was pinched and ruddy. Whether the red skin was sadness or fury was hard to determine. Either way, it was emotion and right then, Henri decided it would be highly dangerous to bait the bear. No telling how he would react.

Toby shook his head, biting his lip till it went white, handing him the note to read.

'My lord Gisborne will be shattered,' Adam said as he folded the parchment after reading it. 'Saul and he had a unique and equal partnership built on the purest trust. By the Saints' nose hairs, someone'll pay mightily for this.'

'Who?' asked Michael as he poured Burgundian wine from a pitcher.

'The Templars, of course,' Adam replied.

'You are so sure?'

'We have no reason to think otherwise, Michael. Ask Soeur Cécile or Petrus. They will confirm it. In any case, this rather changes things. Toby and I will take Ariella and Lucas back to Venezia. We will leave at first light tomorrow, if we can find a barge to take us downstream. Henri, you and Petrus must guard the nun and *Madame* Amée and their cargo to Esteil. Like I said before – that is the most dangerous job. Toby's and my job is difficult for other reasons entirely. I would that you left the day after us, despite that neither Ariella nor *Soeur* Cécile may be strong enough. We can only afford to give them that one day to rest.' He saluted them, no smile cutting through the ruddiness. 'I must find Petrus and a barge immediately.'

'Adam,' Henri called after him. 'Find a barge for us. We would travel as far as Givors on the river if possible.'

Adam saluted and the door was pulled shut leaving shock and grief behind.

Henri thought that Adam consistently under-rated the nun and he had no doubt that in her own way, she would be a strength to be noted. He excused himself and went to his chamber, sitting on the cot with a wax tablet and making a note of what his party might need. Everything had changed in the blink of an eye. Life and death. Here and gone.

Something began to fester inside, a feeling he hadn't experienced for an age and he threw the wax tablet on his cot and wound his way along the corridor, passing through a framed doorway into the second building.

The whitewash was almost fresh and light came from a horn window at the end of the passage. He wondered which door was Ariella's and laid his head against one, hearing nothing. Further along, he listened again. He heard the scuffle of a foot against the timber floor and so dropping a prayer into the air, he knocked.

'*Intrare…*'

Good. It was the nun. Henri pushed at the door.

'Greetings, Sister. Do I disturb you? How do you fare?'

The nun's face had begun the fierce change to violent yellow and blue and her normally gaunt features were puffy, more pronounced by the snowy wimple binding her face. Her head was covered in an undyed but fine linen veil and she had on a simple grey robe in handsome wool, belted at the waist with a plaited hemp cord. He knew instantly that the clothing had been provided by de Clochard, because nothing about *Soeur* Cécile had indicated she would have such quality robes from her convent.

'Better, praise the Lord,' she replied. 'And I see you eyeing my robes. They belong to *Madame* Amée and not what a nun would wear, but one can't be ungrateful.' And in a rare moment of wistfulness she added, 'Would that we could provide such garments for our convent but we are a poor house…'

The words hung in the air because both knew the value of the relic that would soon grace the altar of Esteil.

'Then I am heartened that you improve so swiftly, Sister. Indeed, I must say that you have the strength of a soldier.'

'A soldier?' she huffed what could almost have been a chuckle and then more seriously, 'No. Never a soldier, *messire*. Isn't that what the Templars are? Soldiers fighting in God's name?'

He had no doubt that if she could, she would have spat after the comment. Her backbone of iron became more obvious with each word she uttered.

'Sister, may we both sit?' he asked.

She frowned, the creases disappearing into the bruises and swelling. Her lips sat in a straight line which was as well, Henri thought, because the split in her lower lip was a deep one and he wouldn't want it to bleed.

'You have something serious to say, *messire*.' She indicated a stool near the door and she sat on her cot, her grey robes falling in fluid folds about her. Her feet appeared beneath the cloth and clad in nearly-new soft chamois boots. That would be a first for those calloused and humble feet, he would bet his life upon it. But before he could speak, she raised a hand as if forestalling him.

'Why did you pretend to be a guard to Ariella?'

'Ah.' He scratched his neck. 'I didn't pretend, Sister. I am a guard and as you are aware, we carry a priceless relic. A relic that is to be taken to your convent with as much secrecy as we can manage. For Ariella, she travelled as what she was, a widow on a journey to see her family in Lyon.'

'A Jewish widow…'

'Does that matter, Sister? In the scheme of things?'

'I suppose not, except a lie is still a lie, even by omission. And what of her family? This is not her family. Friends perhaps, but not family.'

'But she is, Sister. She is the daughter of one of the joint owners of the company and the father of her child, Guy of Gisborne's step-brother, managed de Clochard until his death. One needs to understand the Gisborne-ben Simon company to know that is more than just a group of friends. All of us in the company, from *Madame* Amée to me, to Tobias, Ariella, Michael Sarapion, and hosts of others, even the ostlers and the guards. We are all part of the family. And we grieve just now. Ariella's father, a kind and gentle man, has been murdered and we believe it was for the relic that he gave his life.'

She said nothing, but Henri would bet her sharp mind digested everything. As he mentioned Saul's death, she gasped and crossed herself. 'We must leave at dawn two days hence, Sister.'

'Mary Mother, so soon?' Her hand flew to her chest and it was the first sign Henri had ever seen that the woman was feeling her age. But he thrust away any compassion and pushed on.

'Too soon for everyone, *Soeur* Cécile, but things have changed with Saul's passing…'

'Changed,' she intoned and her hands moved to the girdle where hung a small circle of onyx prayer beads with a tiny wooden crucifix hanging off them. A gift, he thought, because he had heard her declaiming the loss of her own. 'Changed…'

He told her the detail of the murder, of how close father and daughter had been, of Ariella's terrible grief. He told her of the need for Ariella and Lucas to leave as soon as a barge had been found and how Adam and Tobias would accompany them back to Venezia. And finally, he impressed on her of the urgent need to spirit the relic to Esteil and how dangerous the journey would be.

'Does *Madame* still plan to travel?' Cécile asked.

'Yes. You will be guarded by Petrus and myself.'

'Ah,' she replied. 'The gentle giant. My saviour, led to me by God's hands…'

Henri thought it had less to do with God's hands than Petrus's sharp wits but he said nothing.

'*Messire* Henri, you say it is a secret, this relic. And yet the midwife has seen it, exclaimed upon it as it performed its miracle. I looked at that woman's mouth and whilst she fulfilled her purpose here with Gelis, she smiled the smile of a fox with small sharp teeth. And I do not trust that smile nor the mouth that formed it. She will gossip, *messire*, because it enhances her status. And she will talk if money is her end-purpose. She is fox-witted and you must know what that means.'

'Indeed, Sister and I suspect that Petrus is paying her a visit. We must hope he is not too late.'

'Then if the giant is visiting her, I shall pray for her soul.'

Yes, thought Henri. This Bride of Christ is sharp. There's no doubt.

'Well then, it is as it must be, *messire*.' *Soeur* Cécile stood. 'I thank you for telling me personally and I would pray now, for Ariella and her father. God would make no distinction, I am sure. After all, His own son was a Jew.' As she spoke, she had been shepherding Henri to the door and he left with the feeling that he had been dismissed by someone with a far greater authority than his own, although he chose not to think on it.

Instead, he thought on Saul, whom he had so respected and liked. He thought on Ariella, whom he would love if she would but show interest. And finally, and with thanks to leave the sadness behind, he thought on de Tremelay and the festering inside him began to change.

Hotter, stronger. Like a cauldron of boiling oil on a rampart.

Anger that he hadn't felt since when?

The Holy Land?

No. Outremer was fear incarnate, not anger. He had no time for anger as he deflected sword thrusts and dagger cuts. There was only the fear-driven need to survive – nothing more.

There were times when the piss and shit ran freely even from his own body. But the fear was inevitably replaced by a numb state of being. Half the time he barely knew where he was or who he was fighting, just so long as his blade was wielded and he was still alive.

But there had been that one time in the Holy Land when anger, a seething blinding anger had risen above him to flap its mighty wings like some avenging angel. When de Tremelay had beheaded the child, he had thought he might fly down upon the knight with a flaming apocalyptic sword. But he was a mere man on the ground whilst de Tremelay was on fleet horseback and impossible to catch as he rode down young and old alike.

It was then that Henri's anger shrank to lie in a cesspool in his soul, just waiting.

And now…

Chapter Eighteen

Cécile sat back on her heels, allowing the prayer beads to drop from her hands.

Dear God but she felt so old and tired. That young man, Henri, had added too many rocks to the heavy bucket she carried. A lesser person might have cursed *Mère* Gisela to perdition for what she had put her obedientiary through. But Cécile wasn't a lesser person.

Or was she?

Had she not just blindly accepted that the midwife might have to die for the sake of the relic and for the convent? Did she condone violence in order for Esteil to take possession of the relic? *Deus!* How many had died over the centuries in the search for the veil?

At least one, obviously – one of the family with whom she stayed; the father of that extraordinary woman with whom she had spent hours in a cart from Givors.

She had prayed until her worn knees ached, begging the Father and the Virgin Mother to care for Ariella. She had no idea if Jews were invited into Heaven. She thought not, but she asked God anyway, so that Ariella's father would not face some sort of terrible Purgatory. She also asked God for some sort of sign about de Tremelay.

She knew without doubt that de Tremelay had caused Saul's murder, that the man had caused her own injuries. That he was prompted by a belief that the greatest relic in Christendom belonged unequivocally to his Order.

'Dear Father, how can such a man be allowed to continue to wreak such havoc?'

But no holy signs appeared and she wondered if God recognised some sort of secret desire for revenge in her pleas.

Huh! As if the Holy Trinity would countenance that!

She grasped the side of the cot and levered herself up, rubbing her knees where the sickening pain lay bone-deep. Worse than the bruises and splits upon her face.

Nevertheless, pain or no pain, she must visit Ariella. The Jewess was a good woman, a loving mother and so capable with Gelis as she helped the woman through her birth throes. Cécile owed her that much – the hand of kindness in the woman's worst hour.

But there *was* another time in poor Ariella's life. Now she thought on it, she remembered what Jehanne had quietly imparted as she helped the nun from the warm tub, drying her and slipping these soft robes over her battered head. Jehanne had spoken in a hushed voice, saying that dear little Lucas's father had died from an attack such as that upon Cécile, before the infant was even born. It was said that Guillaume de Guisbourne was the love of Ariella's life and that since his death, she had kept up a peripatetic existence with little Lucas upon her back, as if she and the infant perennially looked for something.

Cécile walked swiftly along to Ariella's chamber at the far end of the passage. As she raised her hand to knock at the partially opened door, she heard a ripping sound and then another, along with a rhythmic invocation.

She pushed against the smooth wood and entered but Ariella's appearance pulled her up short. The Jewish woman's tawny hair was in disarray, her face mottled and florid from weeping. She was holding shreds of a fine woollen shawl in her hands and barely noticed Cécile at all.

'Ariella,' Cécile said gently.

The Jewess lifted her head.

'I am sorry, my child.' Cécile moved forward and in a movement at odds with her withdrawn nature during the journey from Givors, she reached for Ariella's hands and held them. The fingers were cold and stiff with tension and long, knotted, woollen threads were caught in them, so that Cécile smoothed the hands out.

'Don't take the *tzitzit*,' Ariella begged.

'The what?' Cécile led Ariella to sit.

'The fringing, the knots. It is a prayer shawl of Father's, a *tallit*. Oh…' She began to keen, a low-pitched moan as she swayed back and forth. 'I need to sit *shiva* and I can't because I am not in my father's house. I need to perform *keriah*, and this, this prayer shawl is all I have of Father's from which to tear a piece to wear and now I have damaged that which is him…'

'I see,' Cécile said, although she didn't. She had not known this woman long but she had never seen her so unravelled, so emotional. Always controlled and in command of herself and those around her. Poor young woman. 'Then you must have the torn shreds, Ariella, and wear them by your Church's law. Of what is left, could you not carry it to comfort you on your journey? When you reach Venezia, there will surely be another *tallit*, the one worn most lately by your father and then you can have something of him close…'

'No. They will wrap him in his *tallit* to bury him…'

'Then there will be another cloak, something which you can lay over yourself every night and feel your father's love.'

Ariella looked up for the first time and met Cécile's gaze. 'Yes. You are right…' She sat very still then and wound the *tzitzit* round her fingers. 'Do you want something, Sister?'

So forthright, thought Cécile. 'No, not at all. I heard of your loss and I wished to comfort you if I could. I owe you that for what you did for Gelis.'

'But I'm a Jewess, Sister. Surely not your most favoured person.' Ariella spoke harshly, daring Cécile to answer.

Cécile frowned and tossed her head. 'But tragedy makes friends of us all, Ariella. And a loss is a loss in any family. You have been hit by a terrible tragedy and I thought you might like me to sit with you. We can… what did you say? Sit *shiva*?' She had no idea what sitting *shiva* meant but guessed it spoke of solidarity and prayer in the face of loss. As she did for Benedicta before she left Esteil. Honouring the dead.

'But I will say Kaddish and *you* won't understand.'

'But perhaps if you say it slowly, I can follow…'

Ariella looked down at the twisted *tzitzit* and then took a breath. '*Yitgadal v'yitkadash sh'mei raba b'alma di-v'ra…*'

It was a long prayer and when they had both said 'Amen', Cécile asked, 'What did we say? Can you tell me?'

Ariella continued to wind the cords and knots through her fingers, back and forth, straightening them, laying them flat and then winding them again.

'Glorified and sanctified be God's great name throughout the world

which He has created according to His will.

May He establish His kingdom in your lifetime and during your days,

and within the life of the entire House of Israel, speedily and soon;

and say, Amen…'

And so it went on and when she was done, Cécile crossed herself again, winded by the strength and similarity of the words to her own Christian prayers. 'It is not so different, Ariella. I thank you.'

'No, Sister, it is I who must thank you for your kindness. I am distraught with my loss and have never felt so alone, not even when Lucas's father passed away. I adored my father and now I am all that remains of the ben Simon name…'

'Not so, my child. You have Lucas. He is his grandfather's child, is he not?'

Ariella closed her eyes and a tear crept forth. 'Yes,' she whispered.

'Then have strength, Ariella. For his sake and in your father's memory. You leave tomorrow. Did you know?'

Ariella shook her head. 'No. But I hoped that was the case.'

'Adam of London and the little man…' Cécile continued. 'Toby.'

'They are to attend you and you will be in Venezia swiftly.'

Ariella gave the smallest smile but one that barely broached the shores of her grief. 'I am so selfish, *Soeur* Cécile. Your face – you've been hurt. Is this all for the sake of the relic?' She shook her head. 'That someone would hurt *you*. I despair. What will you do when we are gone?'

'*Madame* Amée and I will have Henri and Petrus to guard us to Esteil.'

'With the remnants of the accursed veil.' Ariella's anger cut through the air in the chamber like a sharpened blade, and why shouldn't it, thought Cécile? Why should the Jewess care about scrap of fabric that had been the cause of her father's passing?

'Apparently.'

'Then beware, Sister. There are enemies.'

'I would disagree.'

The Jewess frowned and went to speak but Cécile interrupted, continuing, 'Not enemies, but rather just one. Singular. He is a Soldier of God, a Templar. They call him de Tremelay.'

Ariella's eyes deadened to muddy winter frost, all hazel light gone, her fingers winding the *tzitzit* so tightly round her fingers that the ends turned blue. 'He murdered my father.'

'And I believe he was responsible for this,' Cécile gestured to her face. 'He will receive God's punishment, Ariella.' Never had Cécile been so sure of anything and something surged through her body. She preferred to think it was just the blood of an aged zealot than anything more violent because Mary Mother, she would hate God to be listening.

Because there was a part of her that hoped de Tremelay would die.

An eye for an eye…

Later, sitting on her cot and rolling the little prayer beads back and forth through her hands, she thought about the time back in the forest when de Tremelay could have killed Henri and easily taken Ariella hostage to secure the veil. Why save her from the boar and allow her to continue on to Lyon?

The prayer beads rolled smoothly, becoming warm under her touch as she realised he would never take such an obvious action. For what would that do to the saintly reputation of Templars everywhere? Word would spread rapidly about the rogue knight and many might say other Templars were as badly stained.

No. De Tremelay was careful if nothing else. And she, *Soeur* Cécile must be equally so. But a line from the Benedictine Rule whispered as the beads slid back and forth: *'Observe my rule, and all misfortunes will for you be turned into successes; your enemies will be transformed into friends…'*

Deus! Cécile had no wish to befriend the Templar. She had no wish to understand Templar society. This whole journey had been revelatory in the extreme. She, who had lived by prayer for the love of God, interspersed with stitch and thread, with the occasional quill and ink of the scriptorium and with the heaviness of a day of numbers within the ledger, had been forced to confront venality and brutality of the worst kind. She sank to her knees, clasping the beads in her prayerful hands.

'O Lord, I place myself in your hands and dedicate myself to you. I pledge myself to do your will in all things: To love the Lord God with all my heart, all my soul, all my strength…'

She travelled on through the prayer, gaining strength.

'Not to kill. Not to steal…To help in trouble. To console the sorrowing. To hold myself aloof from worldly ways. To prefer nothing to the love of Christ…'

Did that not then ameliorate her visceral desire for justice for de Tremelay?

'Not to give way to anger. Not to foster a desire for revenge… Not to return evil for evil. To do no injury: yea, even to bear patiently any injury done to me. To love my enemies. Not to curse those who curse me, but rather to bless them. To bear persecution for justice's sake.'

So there, there it was! I cannot see him punished, she thought. I must bear what he has done to others and to me with humility and grace! I must accept the terrible crime he has committed, the pain he has caused!

God help me!

'To keep constant watch over my actions. To remember that God sees me everywhere. To call upon Christ for defence against evil thoughts that arise in my heart…'

The tears began to flow as she realised that this was her greatest trial. De Tremelay had forced her to her knees in the face of the Rule.

'To ask forgiveness daily for my sins, and to seek ways to amend my life…To pray for my enemies. Never to despair of Your mercy, O God of Mercy. Amen.'

Ah, she was weak.

This she knew and no amount of kneeling on the hard floor, castigating herself in front of the Holy Trinity would alter the fact that she shivered in fear of de Tremelay, felt anger at him and wanted him dead.

Her anguished heart beat like a trapped butterfly and she knew she must calm herself. She pulled herself to the cot and sank into its softness, thinking of the little priory, of the rosebuds and vines that would be gracing the cloister by now and of the psalter and the chasubles that would be emerging from the sisters' hands.

And then she remembered *Soeur* Benedicta's words to her in her dream before she left on this dreadful journey.

'*You have been chosen to approve this relic that will be the saving grace of our priory. Without you, our home might cease to function. Go with joy, my sister, and trust in the Lord.*'

Trust in the Lord…

The simplicity of Benedicta's words was the comfort she needed and she held them to her wild heart, anchoring herself in the whirlwind that beat around her.

Trust in the Lord…

Henri watched the woman walk to the gates, still open in the soft dusk that had begun to seep over Lyon. The sky promised a better day on the morrow. The cloud had peeled back revealing a pale shade the colour of the wild lavender that grew in the hills behind Montbrison. Folding through the delicate colour was the peach of dusk and it reminded him of the peaches of Cyprus. Rounded, luscious, with a velvet skin…

Ariella…

She had veiled herself and her lithe body was swathed in a cloak the colour of lichen and made of fine wool. She walked slowly to the side of the road and stood at the stone wall, gazing out upon the river. The surface of the Saône was like marble, promising a barge the next morning and Henri's mouth set in a line.

He pushed away from the stable wall, walking through the gates, nodding to Raol. 'I will fetch her. I know you want to shut the gates.'

'As you wish, Henri. Madame needs time, I think.'

He was a good man, Raol. All Henri's *confrères* were men to be trusted. He spoke Ariella's name as he came up behind her, not wishing to startle her.

She turned. Jesu but she was wretched. Her beautiful

face was blotched and drawn as tight as a drum and her eyes were red. 'Henri...' her throaty voice was deeper, scratched and worn.

'I am so sorry,' he said. 'Saul was kind and welcoming toward me when I arrived in Venezia. He didn't treat me like a common *routier*, but as a member of the family returning to the fold.'

She studied her hands, clasped tight in front of her. 'He was never patronising, Henri. It wasn't in his nature. I think we... he... had been discriminated against for so long that he made it his mission never to do the same to others.' She looked up and her eyes sparkled with unshed tears. 'And he liked you. He found your intellect challenging. He always looked forward to talking with you, dissecting the human race and its philosophies. He often said that in another life, you may have been a monk or a philosopher...' she sucked in a short breath, stifling a sob. 'That is what I shall miss. Apart from his overarching love for me, I shall miss such talking.' A tear crept forth and she went to wipe it away and he noticed the threads wrapped round her fingers. He recognised them immediately – *tzitzit*. He had seen her father with his *tallit*, the strings at each corner knotted and swaying as he walked.

'*Keriah*?' Henri asked.

'How did you know?' Her eyes opened wide, the tears held at bay.

'Your father. I was interested to learn of your Faith. I have none of my own and can be a sponge.'

'He *taught* you?'

'To a point. But he may have thought I was a lost cause. Gisborne sent me hither and yon. We never had time to build anything.'

'Time enough though.' She studied him with a new intensity. Something he had not seen before.

'You say?'

She smoothed the remnants of the *tallit* and said, 'Father

must have felt you warranted his time and attention and I find that… I find…' she didn't finish but Henri had the strangest feeling that they had found a bridge and crossed it together.

'I don't know how I will manage without his strength, Henri…' another tear ran down her cheek.

He wondered what he could say that would have any meaning and began cautiously. 'Ariella, it was obvious to all of the households both here and in Venezia, that Saul believed you had a core of iron. Else he would never have let you travel as far as you have done – across the Middle Sea to Lyon, to Constantinople.' He reached for her hands and held them firmly to make his point. His heart skipped at the touch of her flesh and he took a breath before continuing. 'Not just a core of iron but a deep understanding of the business of trade. He knew you would *be* ben Simon one day and he groomed you for that day. That *inevitable* day. If I may say and I beg your forgiveness for being forthright, that day is here and he would expect you to carry on as you have done already for the company. And besides, you will have Sir Guy, Lady Ysabel, William, Tobias, Mehmet, Ahmed, Adam… so many of us to support you. A whole family.'

She began to weep softly and he pulled her toward him and held her and she wept into his tunic.

'Ariella, I would do all I can to leaven your loss but I am to travel to Esteil with *Soeur* Cécile and *Madame* Amée so you must lean on Toby and Adam. They will see you safe back home – you and little Lucas. Toby will be like your brother…' Her head fitted neatly under his chin and he kissed the veil on her head. He wondered if she felt the feather-light touch and hoped to God he hadn't overstepped the mark, before looking up and seeing Adam and Tobias standing in the yard watching. It was too dusky to see their expressions and for that one moment he didn't care. And then he stepped back, gave her his arm and said, 'Come. Raol must bar the gates and you must eat. You are a mother who needs strength to sustain her little son.'

Her hand rested in the crook of his elbow until they reached the door to the hall, the gates to *rue* Ducanivet slamming behind them and the bar sliding into place. As he handed her in the door to the hall, she turned. Her weeping had ebbed and she looked up at him and something passed between the two of them.

'Thank you, Henri. I am grateful.' She smiled – a poignant expression but a smile nevertheless. She moved inside and he watched her go – the slender shoulders straightening, the head a little less bowed. And then he went to meet his comrades, bracing himself for the worst.

'I see,' said Toby.

'Do you?' asked Henri.

'Christ, Henri,' snarked Adam. 'What have I said to you?'

'Adam, I did nothing but act as a friend should in a time of great need. Shove your manner where the sun doesn't shine. You too, Tobias!' He stalked past them to the well to wash his face and hands before heading to Amée's table.

The meal was an all-male event.

The women ate in the solar, providing moral support to Ariella it seemed, and Henri was glad. Less so, however with the look on Adam's face and the all-knowing grin on Toby's.

'Look,' he said to them both as the board was laden with a roasted meats and steaming bread, with root vegetables, cheeses and platters of fruit. 'Just accept that Ariella needed someone at that moment and that I was the person. There is nothing else. No more no less. I would have thought we have much else to discuss than the rights and wrongs of succour to a friend.'

'A friend is acceptable,' said Adam. 'But don't get ideas. It's a sure way to be booted from the company.'

'Fuck you!' hissed Henri, swallowing some of the smooth Burgundian wine and then some more as that deep-seated anger began to rise like vomit. 'Get your mind out of the gutter and lead us, Adam. Like the Master at Arms you are *supposed* to be.'

Tobias snorted, pushing himself back a little from the table as if anticipating something.

Adam's eyebrows shot for the blue-starred ceiling and a fierce ruddy wash spread up his neck to his cheeks. He slammed his pewter mug on the table causing the others at table to lift their heads and watch with interest.

Unclenching his fists, he looked at his knuckles and murmured, 'Oh yes. I shall lead and you shall do as you're ordered. Ah Michael, well met,' he added, as Michael Sarapion eased himself onto the trestle seat. Adam's greeting was louder than the low volcanic comment of a moment before. 'I have found a bargeman willing to take us south, leaving at dawn. I've also found a barge to transport *Madame* Amée and the nun the day after.'

'Good,' Michael replied, piercing some pork with his dagger. 'I'm glad the barges are on the river again. For trade and for your swift return to the coast. Are you concerned the Templar will follow you?'

'I doubt he will; I suspect his attentions will be on Henri's party. Theirs is the more dangerous journey.'

He glanced at Henri and his expression dared him to speak to him again in such an insubordinate manner but Henri merely filled his mug and continued drinking. Tobias said nothing, whistling under his breath.

Henri spoke not one word to either men when they retired and he lay staring at the ceiling as each fell into sleep with heavy breathing and then snoring. In his stomach, snakes writhed and the familiar panic began to fizz along his limbs, up to his throat which felt as if it was closing. His scalp tightened and he slid from the cot, grabbing a cloak and his boots and easing through the door. He knew it was pointless trying for sleep. He would tremble and if he fell into sleep, would thrash with dreams and it was something he allowed none to observe. The stable beckoned, as did any space away from others, where he could nurse his black thoughts and wait.

Amée's little dun rouncey, an elderly and thick-set mare, nickered as Henri slid into her stall. She was a gentle beast, the kind that would plod gamely for leagues with nary a shy or balk. Henri settled in the corner, wrapping his cloak against the cold, despite the sweat that had gathered on his brow and his armpits. He gritted his teeth and shuddered and the mare reached out a velvet muzzle and sniffed him gently, before settling on his forehead and licking the sweat away. Her rough tongue relished the saltiness and her rhythmic licking calmed him as nothing other than poppy might have done.

He wondered if ever the night-stalking sweats would stop. He could go for months and there would be nothing and he would barely remember and then out of the dark, the devils would ride upon him in vivid, blood-soaked colour. Such a weakness, he thought, one he hated admitting to. As for Adam and Toby – he had shared the moment but he suspected, nay hoped, they would honour the confidence. And so he, Henri, must get on with the business of living the best he could. A play act – as he had thought so often. To all who knew him it was a convivial performance and he played it well.

Ah, he thought, his eyes becoming gritty. Secrets *are* best kept and he must bury them deep because he had business to finish.

He thought of Ariella and how well they fitted together. She in his arms and beneath his chin. He would move heaven and earth to keep her safe, but instead, he had been given the job of guarding two old women, and one a nun in Heaven's name!

As for the relic – he tried hard to refute its origins and ignore its significance but it was pointless. How could he? It was an ancient veil with the imprint of two nailed feet upon it. It was *byssus* and he knew the properties of *byssus*. He guessed it was old, but how old? When did they stop crucifying men?

Such thoughts wound through his mind, becoming fainter and more haphazard as the old mare's breathing warmed him. He allowed sleep to claim him, stretching his length along the side of the stall and sinking down deep into the heady straw.

He woke to the feel of his hair being pulled as the rouncey mouthed his scalp. She nickered and despite that it was still dark, he could see the bounce and roll of *torchère* light in the yard and knew the mare wanted to be fed. He heard buckets being filled from the grain store and pushed himself to stand, brushing off the straw, leaning forward and scrabbling at his hair to remove the night's detritus. He palmed a handful of cold water from the mare's almost empty bucket and scrubbed at his face, wiping the cloak over and then swinging it round his shoulders and sliding into the yard before he was noticed.

The air was cool and crisp and he breathed deep, sucking it in like a man who might drown, a long cleansing breath that wiped the cobwebs of a bad night away. The *traboule* door was open and goods were being taken downward to the waiting barge. Overhead, the night sky had softened to a pearl glimmer with the gilt of sunrise in the light to the west. He walked down the damp steps, water drip-dripping and the flame shadows like a gyre upon the walls. An ostler, Johannes, he thought the man's name was, climbed up toward him and he asked who was on the shore.

'Adam of London, *Messire* Henri. And young Tobias, along with the bargemaster and his men.'

Henri decided to turn back. He would like one word with Ariella without the scrutiny of his friends and as he stepped through the entrance into the yard, Jehanne appeared nursing Lucas and everyone else stood at the door to the house, farewelling Ariella. Even the nun was there, but he had decided she never slept anyway, living on the airs of prayer.

Jehanne stepped into the *traboule* and Henri smiled at her. 'She's coming,' *Madame* Sarapion said. 'I shall go ahead with the babe. He's well asleep.'

Ariella began to make her way across the yard and as before, Henri offered his hand. She took it, her eyes downcast. He knew he must speak before they reached the bend in the steps, because for sure Tobias and Adam would be watching for her.

'Ariella, please travel safe. Lean on Adam and Toby as much as you need because grief is a heavy thing,' he managed.

'I will, Henri, I swear. I cannot thank you enough for last evening. I will not forget your kindness. And if I may say…' She stopped descending and he halted with her. Her eyes found his and whilst the flames showed him little of the warm hazel or her magnificent ivory skin, he *felt* her beauty. They say one can smell anger and fear. He could smell something altogether different in the close confines of the stony tunnel, something intimate and precious. 'I won't forget *you*,' she said. 'Come back safe to Venezia, Henri. My father would insist upon it, I think.'

They rounded the bend and below they could see the high water, the barge lying close by the landing, two men holding it against the shore. Adam and Tobias stood waiting to hand Ariella aboard and quickly she whispered one shocking thing. 'Kill him for my father, Henri.'

Henri passed her hand to Tobias as if he hadn't just heard the ice-cold words, locking the plea deep inside. Whilst the minstrel settled her aboard and Jehanne passed Lucas to her, Adam gave his last orders.

'Do whatever you must to keep the relic and the women safe, Henri. Saul's life is one too many and so there is a debt to be paid out. I leave it with you and Petrus. Your barge will be here later. The bargemaster is a friend of Petrus. Go safe now and go well.'

They grasped each other's forearm, hostilities forgotten and then Tobias hopped ashore again and grabbed Henri's fist as if they were to arm-wrestle. 'Your palm is sweaty, Henri!' He smiled and winked. 'Go safe, my friend. *Adieu.*' He squeezed Henri's hand and pulled him down so that he could whisper. 'We will care for her, I swear. She could do worse than you, you know. We shall get her home safely so that she may wait for you.'

Henri said nothing, just saluted them as the barge began to move into the current and drift away. The bargemaster stood in the stern, a massive stern oar guiding them as the crew began to pull their own oars, keeping their course straight and true. The water swirled lazily, leaving a message of vengeance and retribution in its wash as Henri unlocked Ariella's plea from his soul. It was like having a fragment of the *tallit* and he swore under his breath that he would do her bidding for her father's sake.

Saul deserved nothing less…

Chapter Eighteen

'She says they have no bell at the convent,' said *Madame* de Clochard.

'I see…' Henri replied. One was always cautious with *Madame*. He had been warned.

'Then we must find one…'

'*Madame,*' Henri swallowed a sigh. 'It is enough that we transport the sister, yourself and the relic, without carrying a cast-iron bell as well.'

'Not just cast-iron, Henri. It must be coated with copper to be as musical as our cathedral's own. This is my cousin's convent after all.' She tapped him on the arm. 'We must find one today and arrange for it to be transported separately. In addition, she needs to buy linens for their church embroideries and supplies for the scriptorium. We can supply perfect linens but we have nothing left of our pigments and parchments so you must go to the Gigni and see what they have.'

It was easier to agree and in truth, Henri relished getting out of the house. Madame was flitting around like a butterfly in search of blooms. Here, there, and back to here again. He wondered if she truly had any idea just how valuable the relic was or that their lives would be forfeited by any who wanted to lay claim to the veil. Better that she did not, perhaps.

He walked toward the Gigni house set a little higher on the slope behind *rue* Ducanivet. The day smelled of all that late spring could offer – blossom, pollen, grasses, bread cooking, meats roasting, the dyer's stinking of piss and pigments. The singe of the blacksmith's where a man bent over the off-hind hoof of a long-legged and solid black gelding. The passing odour of men and women who needed to bathe, the more pleasurable fragrance of those who did not. The smell of ordure that the city fathers had not resolved and over which Henri had to jump as he turned a corner into La Grande Rue. Above everything was the smell of the Saône – of mud and water. It was fortuitous that the town sat above the high-water mark because spring had been a time of floods and could have destroyed so much as the river rose above the line of slime that edged the banks. The birds pipped, piped and honked – geese, ducks, mallards, grebes, mergansers and here and there swans dipping in and out of the rushes that bent under the withdrawing levels of the water.

Henri liked Lyon with the wide sweep of that mercantile river, the *traboules* and trade running in and out of the town. The Romans had recognised its potential and its boatsmen were legendary and so Henri took comfort in the thought that they would be in good hands on the morrow. At least until they reached Givors.

'Henri!'

The rolling boulder sound of the voice pulled him from his thoughts and he turned. 'Petrus! We missed you! Adam and Tobias have already left with *Madame* de Guisborne and her son…'

'Petrus had things to do. They did not need him to say farewell.' The huge man looked fresh and clean, smelling of neither wine, food nor anything worse.

'A friend of yours is to be our bargemaster, Adam says…' Henri began.

'Petrus knows.'

Of course you do, thought Henri, you probably organised it. 'Where have you been?'

'Here and there,' Petrus answered.

Henri could feel the blood rising and, taking a breath to cool the simmering frustration, he said, 'Petrus, we must work with each other to get these women safely to Esteil. We need to trust each other, and part of working together means we must communicate.'

'Of course.' Petrus's face had set like a piece of carved stone. 'Petrus trusts Henri but perhaps Henri does not trust Petrus.'

'I do,' Henri said swiftly.

'Then perhaps Henri should accept that what Petrus does is almost always for Gisborne ben Simon, never for himself. Henri needs to stay calm. A long journey lies ahead and jumping about like men with bee stings is not in our interests.'

A point to Petrus, Henri decided. 'Agreed. But answer me this then, my friend. Was it essential business that you carried out?'

Petrus's eyes closed to slits as he stood over Henri. Christ he was tall. 'Trust, you say.' He bent down and whispered in Henri's ear. 'Petrus saw to the midwife.'

Henri sucked in a breath.

'She will not speak about the cloth anytime soon.'

'Petrus, is she…'

'She lives, but a long way upriver. Without monies.'

'You are easily identified.'

'You think Petrus did this? Not at all. Petrus has friends.'

Henri let his breath go and shook his head. The man was unbelievable. No wonder Gisborne employed him; finally the man's determination and self-direction made Henri feel calmer about what was to come.

'Then come to the Gigni with me. If I can purchase what we need, some help to carry the goods to the yard would not go astray.'

'Petrus will come,' the big man replied and fell into step beside Henri.

They entered the yard through the handsome gates on *rue* Trammasal and right on the tail of a highly bred brown gelding with fine saddlery and a well-groomed rider astride. The man wore grey wool trimmed with velvet and a vestige of silky hair hung from an almost bald head. His cloak draped over the horse's rump and down its flanks and Odo, the Gigni's notary stood waiting for him at the door.

But he spotted Henri and Petrus, they were not hard to miss, and with a quick word to the man who had now dismounted, begged him to wait if he pleased, until Odo had shown the other gentlemen to their appointment with *Messire* Alexandrus. He would return as soon as he could.

As they hurried with Odo into the house, Henri said, 'But Odo, we have no appointment with *Messire* Alexandrus…'

'Oh,' said the ascetic notary waving his hand in the air, 'I am aware of that, but that man is a bore and Alexandrus would do anything to delay the visit. All is well.'

They walked along a passage and stopped in front of another handsome door where Odo knocked, before leading them into the chamber. '*Messire*, I have two men who have business with you…'

Gigni turned from the table at which he had been working. He was a tall handsome man and his hair was still the magical silver it had been when Henri had attended the Gigni hunt a year before. Gigni's face lit up.

'Henri and Petrus! I swore by God above that Odo was bringing that awful man into the room…'

'*Messire*, he waits,' Odo said. 'I will ply him with wine, but I thought you may like to talk with Henri and Petrus and delay your business as long as is seemly.'

Gigni laughed as Odo left. 'My God, Odo knows more

about me than my left hand knows of my right hand. He's worth his weight in gold! A goblet of wine, perhaps?'

Henri thanked him and whilst Gigni filled three goblets, they sat on heavy oaken chairs.

'It's a beautiful wine that I purchased from Cyprus. Liquid sunshine, I swear. See what you think?'

They toasted him and the wine slid down their throats. Like the smoothest honey, Henri thought, with an after-taste of oak and peaches and as Gigni had said, sunshine.

'Fine wine, *messire*,' said Petrus.

'It is, Petrus. As you say.' Gigni eyed off the huge man who threatened to break the seat with his weight. 'But I imagine you didn't come to sample my wine, did you? What can I do for you? There must be something, I'm sure. When the Gisborne ben Simon house visits, it is most often business.'

'Indeed. We have a nun with us from Esteil. She is to escort *Madame* Amée back to the convent for a retreat. It seems the prioress is *Madame* Amée's very distant relative by marriage.'

'*Deus!*' Gigni laughed, a pleasant sound that gurgled from deep in his belly. 'Does the convent have any idea of what Madame will be like behind their walls?'

Henri smiled. 'I think not. They will possibly never be the same again. But the nun is also here on business. The convent has run out of parchment and pigments – it seems they have a fine scriptorium and we have none left. We're waiting for a new shipment to arrive. We wondered if you have anything...'

'In fact, yes. I have a small supply of *velluri* from a rather good parchmenter we now have in Lyon. Sadly he is a small business and his output is slow. Nevertheless, I would be happy to sell you some. It's very fine – quite thin and thus can be folded or rolled for storage. As to the pigments, we haven't much left. The floods have precluded the arrival of stores from our men in Firenze. I have some turnsole and madder, galls for the ink and I believe there may even be some goldleaf tucked away. No chalk or pumice for parchment preparation though. Our stocks of minerals are low and I confess to being glad the bargemen are returning to the river again.'

'Indeed,' rumbled Petrus. 'I spoke to a bargemaster yesterday, *messire*. They are keen to be back on the water.'

'Good!' Gigni slapped a hand on the table. 'I shall have one of my men deliver the *goods* to *rue* Ducanivet if you like. I might even bring it myself. I would enjoy speaking with *Madame* de Guisborne again.'

'Ah…' Henri said. 'Madame left at dawn to return to Venezia.'

'So soon?' Gigni put down his goblet. 'She hasn't been here a day and night.'

Henri then told Gigni of Saul's death, of the need for Ariella to return to take up her father's mantle.

'Murdered! Do the authorities know by whom?'

'It is doubtful,' Petrus said.

'I… I am speechless.' Gigni's face had folded. That he liked Ariella and had come to know her well when she lived in Lyon was obvious. He picked up a piece of wax and rolled it back and forth across the desk. 'Was it mere happenstance, think you, or was it trade-related?'

Henri sighed. This next was delicate. 'We believe it was trade-related, *messire*.'

'God's teeth!' Gigni threw the wax into a corner. 'I am not naïve enough to think we can conduct trade without jealousies, but this…'

Henri tossed back the rest of his wine, noting that Petrus had barely touched his. '*Messire*, may I ask if Gilbert de Tremelay still stays with you? We travelled from Givors together and in fact, Madame Ariella and I owe him our lives. He saved us from a boar.'

Gigni's mood had flattened and he answered distractedly.

'The Templar? He did not stay with us at all. He thanked us for the offer but said he must make haste to his preceptory in the west.'

'Oh. Do you know where?'

'Saint Christoph's in Toulon? Or maybe not,' Gigni shook his head, swiping a silver lock of hair from his forehead. 'I am not sure. He was a very monosyllabic man. I confess I didn't like him and thanked God for small mercies when we received a message to say he was leaving Lyon forthwith. No thanks for offering hospitality, nothing. I wouldn't have offered if my arm had not been twisted by the Archbishop.'

'And what of his serjeant?' Petrus asked. 'Petrus has business with him.'

Gigni's lips turned down. 'I have no idea. I assume he would go with de Tremelay, would he not? Now, let us fetch the *velluri*...'

Henri stood, placing his empty goblet on a pewter tray. '*Messire*, Petrus and I will convey the goods to *rue* Ducanivet. We do not want to trouble you and besides, we leave for Esteil in the morning.'

'So soon for you as well! Then I am glad I was able to speak with you – even though you deliver such heavy tidings.'

They followed him along the passage as he called for Odo, his robes swishing around his elegant height. Odo appeared and was apprised of their order and then Gigni begged them to excuse him so he could deal with his tedious client. He clasped both their arms with much affection, it was plain to see. As plain as the pain which dragged at his face, making new lines of old. 'Tell *Madame* Amée that she will be missed whilst she is in retreat and tell her to travel safe. As to *Madame* Ariella, I shall send a personal letter. Saul was a good and honest trading friend and will not be forgotten.'

They thanked him for his hospitality and presently, as the bells rang for Sext, they returned to Ducanivet with a package of parchment and a jute covered crate of remnant pigments.

'Ah Henri, there you are,' busy *Madame* bustled into the yard from the door to the hall. 'You too, Petrus. I've been to an armourer who is willing to make a bell to our specifications. Michael will send it on when it is ready. What have you there?'

'Scriptorium supplies, *Madame*, as you requested. Have you begun your packing? I would like to load the barge this evening and be gone as the sun rises on the morrow...'

'*Soeur* Cécile says she is packed, but then she travels like a bee – whirring wings with nothing on her back and a sting in her tail. So, I have taken the liberty of packing extra cloaks and robes for her. One never knows.' Amée vibrated with nervous energy and it was impossible not to like the woman.

'*Madame*, may I suggest you take a small medicine chest?'

'*Deus!*' And then she frowned, perhaps remembering Gelis. 'Indeed. If you and Petrus promise to pack weapons.' As she walked inside, she called over her shoulder, 'Gelis and Gervasius are with *Soeur* Cécile in the birthing chamber should you wish to visit.'

Henri grinned. She was no fool and he had no doubt she would carry her own knife.

'*Madame* will be a force on this journey, Henri,' Petrus laughed. The sound reverberated around his cavernous chest and filled the yard. 'The nun as well. Henri and Petrus must buckle up.'

Henri paid his respects to his former fellow travellers and wished them well. They said they owed him much and promised to pay for a Mass to safeguard the passage to Esteil. As he leaned over Cecilia's crib and watched the infant sleeping, he reflected on the difference between the innocence of the newborn, as near to death as it had been, and the tragedy of Saul.

He could see it in his mind's eye. Saul walking to one of the waterside warehouses, comfortable in his solitude, for Venezia had never been unkind to he or his daughter. He was a member of the small Jewish colony but he also mixed with Christians just as readily. Muslims too, let it be said.

And then someone might have surprised him, held a knife to his throat and demanded the location of the veil. He, being conscious of the safety of his daughter and grandson who transported the relic, would say nothing. Not even as the killer pricked a threat to his throat so that a small amount of blood ran over his *tallit*. They may have pricked him again elsewhere to frighten him, but this man had been through much anti-Semite hurt in his life and was unafraid. Finally, as he bled from many goads, his silence would light his attacker's fuse. A temper would explode like Greek fire and he would plunge a dagger deeply into Saul's chest.

The river had slowed further overnight and their barge slid along with the current. They moved into the confluence of the Saône and the Rhône with only a small backwash and a few eddies beneath the Pont de Saône. The bargemen's four oars squeaked in the tholes and the bargemaster's long stern oar kept the vessel true. They had been joined by two other barges intent on reaching the coast to collect cargo from the exotic traders who had arrived from across the Middle Sea. One flew a Gigni pennant at its bow, but the other was a barge contracted by de Clochard to collect anything from whomever had been waiting in Arles for Ariella.

The sky threatened once more – flat grey cloud, metallic and unsavoury, and the air still and heavy. The trees lining the river bowed their heads, sick of the threat of more rain and longing for their leaves to open widely and glisten, and for insects to fly amongst the growth; indeed, longing for summer with its warmth and promise of a good season. At that moment, it looked as if the many crops sown through last autumn would rot or drown in the Rhône valley and then heaven help the people who must be fed.

Petrus and Henri watched the banks glide by. The women sat together further for'ard and Henri could pick up the occasional sound of *Madame*. Of *Soeur* Cécile, there was nothing.

'You prefer working for Gisborne to joining your king in his battle against Richard?' Petrus asked.

'No,' Henri replied. 'The King has successfully won Aumale with those of his retainers who fight under his banner. He doesn't need me. I'm done with war.'

'Petrus thinks you might be done with one kind of war but not another.'

For one moment, Henri recalled the Occitan Mercadier, the infamous *routier* and his Brabantine force who were lauded by Richard Lionheart for their ruthlessness and who fought tooth and nail for Richard, Coeur de Lion. By the stars above, Mercadier and de Tremelay could have been womb brothers.

'Perhaps. But I fight for better reasons and with better *confrères*. Don't you think?'

Petrus shrugged.

'And you, Petrus. You must surely have a home which calls you.'

'Petrus is at home wherever he places his head.'

'Even Constantinople?'

Henri referred to Petrus's rumoured service as part of the Varangian Guard in that city. It was a brave man, they said, who broached the history.

'Petrus does not speak of it. Be wise and do not refer to it again.'

Henri shrugged in return, passed over a costrel with watered wine and pushed himself up to walk to the stern where the bargemaster looked behind at the straight line of wash disappearing in the muddy water.

Henri despaired of having any real relationship with his travelling comrade and wondered again at the pairing of he and the big man. Surely he and Adam would have been better. And then he grinned to himself at the image of small Tobias, good-humoured dwarf and entertainer, paired with the taciturn giant.

Perhaps Adam was right…

'*Soeur* Cécile,' said Amée. 'Are we not fortunate to be on the barge instead of riding? Lord! I love my mare but days in the saddle chafe me and there will be time enough for being saddle-bound after Givors.'

Cécile once again wished her travelling companion had taken a vow of silence before she left Lyon. The constant buzz of her voice raised Cécile's hackles.

'I'm glad I have you to converse with now, Sister, because I suppose after I have spoken with Gisela on our arrival, I will be vowed to silence, won't I? Lord, this will be a penance. If nothing else rights my wrongs with God, it will be the rebuttal of conversation. Pity it's not Lent – giving up the freedom to converse would be my offering.'

'*Madame,* the Benedictine Rule won't be as strict for you in retreat as it is for we Benedictines who live within the priory. We are sworn to it. You will be allowed some lenience. However, as Obedientiary in charge of inexperienced novices, I do ask that you refrain from engaging with them unless it is essential. It is hard for them to adjust at the best of times.'

It was the longest speech Cécile had made to Amée and the matron was rather taken aback and sat in silence for a little.

Then, 'Sister, we are in danger, are we not?'

Cécile blinked at the question. She had not been expecting that and she thought very carefully before she replied. 'Perhaps. I pray for God's protection. You must as well.'

'Oh, I do. I have. I even paid for a Mass to be said at the cathedral. I was very careful to make sure it was only for our protection as travellers and nothing else. The relic…'

'The relic must be kept safe, *Madame*. The Holy Mother deserves nothing less. Indeed, Christ deserves nothing less.'

The matron's eyes softened. 'I have to pinch myself sometimes when I think about the provenance of the veil. And the miracle. When I asked Gisborne to find a relic, I confess this was as far from my mind as you could conceive.'

Cécile gave a half smile. It was easier now to relax the taut muscles on her face, despite the bruising. When she had left the priory, she was as contained as if she were in a prison, but so much had happened and people, she found, were by and large quite kind. She fingered the grey robe she wore, the gift from Madame – the malleability of the wool and the evenness of the weave. It was almost as if the softness permeated far inward, rubbing away at the crisp edges of her soul. *Mère* Gisela would surely find it amusing.

She levered herself to her feet, her knees clicking, the pain rising – some things obviously didn't change. '*Madame*, excuse me, I need to stretch my legs whilst the going is smooth.'

Amée nodded and waved her away with a little flick of her hand and the usual smile playing with the pads of flesh upon her cheeks. Cécile marvelled at the whiteness of the woman's wimple and veil and thought that travel would soon change that.

Cécile first walked between the four oarsmen, trying to keep clear of their broad shoulders. She kept upright by grabbing onto the luggage, what there was of it, that was stacked amidships, walking up the larboard side, breathing deep at the bow and then walking down the starboard side to where Henri stood leaning against a sealed water *barel*. He nodded and made room for her and she hoped to God he would allow her some silence to pray.

She would never admit it but she *was* afraid. After she had been beaten, her heart had wavered without stop in her chest and it was then she realised she was old, God help her, even frail. She just needed the strength to return home with the relic. Her lips moved.

'*In dangers, in doubts, in difficulties, think of Mary, call upon Mary. Let not Her name depart from your lips, never suffer it to leave your heart...*'

'Pardon, Sister? You spoke?'

She started and found her hands were gripping the prayer beads and that she might have murmured the prayer. 'I... I was praying for our ongoing safety.' She released the prayer beads and they swung back on their thin silk cord against her body.

Henri stood quietly as the riverbanks drifted by and the oyster-coloured light of another grey day dropped around them. Finally he shifted and turned to her.

'And did God listen, think you?'

'I spoke to Mary, not God. My prayer was written by the founder of my order, Benedict of Nursia.'

'You have great faith, don't you?'

She picked up her beads again and ran them back and forth through her hands. 'I do. God has been kind to me and He came to me when I most needed Him – but then, you don't need to know my story. What about you, *messire*? God is *your* sustenance, surely.'

Her companion cleared his throat. She had thought he was an exceptionally grounded man, one who ordered his world securely, and for that he must surely rely on the wisdom of God and the Holy Book.

His reply shocked her.

'Sister, you are aware I fought with King Philip Augustus in the Holy Land?'

She nodded. Amée had told her.

'Then, please understand what I say is without malice to

you or your order or to anyone else who follows God. I once did the same.'

'But you don't now?'

'No.'

'That is a shame…' What else could she say? She wasn't given to the words of the confessional, especially with men outside of holy orders.

'Sister, in my view, God left us alone in the Holy Land. The fight was obscene and I won't offend by describing what we Christians went through. Be assured that the Saracens went through their form of Hell as well. If there had been a God, then such inhuman brutality would never have occurred.'

'*Messire*! You speak heresy!' Cécile closed her fist hard around her beads until she could feel pain. This man, this *guard* of theirs; he had no piety and she was to rely on him? *Deus!*

'Perhaps I do, but I left the Holy Land as gutted as those who had been slit from neck to knee. They supposedly died for God's honour. The only difference between them and myself is that I live to tell the tale.'

Anger welled right through to Cécile's fingertips. 'Huh,' she replied sarcastically. 'Then if you are so against violence, why did you join a trading house that is so prone to violence? Since I have known you, violence has been implicit, I have been assaulted and Ariella's father has been killed. Is this normal in your life?'

He was taken aback with her rebuke but he obviously had respect for women, and nuns in particular, because he took a breath and quieted himself before replying. 'How would you suggest I live then, Sister? I am the bastard son of a very petty nobleman. I have no inheritance and thus I learned skills on which I can rely, taking charge of my own life.'

'But you read and write. Ariella said so.' Cécile recalled Ariella speaking about Henri with a softness in her voice and she wondered if the two had forged a friendship. A Jew and a Christian…

'Ah…' he replied with a sheepish grin. 'You have skewered me, Sister. I was taught to read and write by a priest.'

Cécile gave a dry laugh and again let her beads fall against her legs. 'A point to monks and nuns then, *messire*.'

'What would you have had me do?' Henri asked. 'Become a monk? I think you would find I am not at all monkish. Or perhaps you think I could have become a notary – trained at one of the great universities. Paris or Bologna perhaps.' They both watched a crane lift from the riverbank and fly back upstream toward Lyon. 'I would be bored in an instant,' he continued. 'With Gisborne ben Simon I am a part of trade across our world. It offers me a likeminded brotherhood and, Sister, for someone *with* no family, it offers me a family life. Perhaps you might thank God for that.'

She wasn't sure if he was being sarcastic but then how could one dispute him?

'*Soeur* Cécile, I apologise if I offend you, but I thought an honest reply was best.'

She nodded. 'Thank you. I too am straight forward…'

'This I know, Sister.' He grinned. 'Then you will accept that I have chosen my path? Just as you have chosen yours?'

'Indeed,' she replied. 'But I fear for those who anger you, my dear. And I fear for you. I will pray for your soul.'

She cursed her glib reply. If only she could step down from her role as Obedientiary, but it was all she had known for so long. Instead, she made lofty pronunciations that sounded like a crusty and patronising old priest.

Henri pushed himself away from the *barel*. 'Thank you. But have no fear for me, Sister. Instead pray for those who cannot protect themselves. Perhaps pray for your fellow sisters. Now, I must talk with Petrus. Givors will be upon us with speed and we must plan.'

And just like that, this even-mannered exchange was over. She must be mellowing, she decided, that she was able to converse with lay folk more readily. Dare she admit that her hours and years behind the priory walls, whilst giving her security, might have stunted her a little? But hadn't she always been a retiring person? She tried to think back to her youth but realised that from the moment she passed through the priory gates, life before Orders had almost been erased and at the time she cared little. Did she care now? She thought of the extraordinary joy that the priory had given her and knew she would be forever grateful to God and the Holy Family.

But right now she needed that Holy Trinity to stand beside her and protect she and her companions, indeed the whole priory, until the relic was safely ensconced in the chancel.

Chapter Nineteen

'It will never be safe. That is the reality,' Henri said as they watched the small town of Givors emerge out of the misty distance.

'But Petrus thinks that once the relic is handed over, then that is our business done.' Petrus had laid out a dagger, a sword and an axe on the deck and sat with a wad of lamb-swool, greasing the blades back and forth – a rhythmic motion.

'True. But one can't help wondering what is the point.' Henri picked up a small piece of the wool that had come free of the wad and smoothed it so that the rough crimp in the fibre became obvious.

'The point is that Henri does his job.'

'Petrus, don't you ever think beyond the task? Of people's future and their safety?'

'Petrus is not a priest, so no. In that way lies madness. Petrus does his job and moves on. It is better for Petrus that way.'

Petrus was right and Henri had done exactly that ever since the Holy Land. Pushing on with the job and pushing down the guilt. Not that the guilt didn't surface at the most inopportune times. But he wondered how the string-thin old nun could have got under his skin so much. Why did he really care about her? Was it her stoicism? Her blind Faith?

'Henri…' Petrus continued. 'Do not let the nun's fire

disturb you. The truth is that she and her sisters have Christendom in their favour. Petrus believes they will survive.'

Henri blinked at the man's soul-deep words. 'Are *you* a Christian?'

Petrus slipped his thumb along the edge of his dagger, sequestered the blade in its scabbard at his belt and then continued to oil the axe with the lambswool. 'Petrus has his own beliefs.'

'Christian?'

Petrus sighed, almost world-weary as he tucked the axe into the top of his luggage – a large canvas sack with a draw-string. 'The Greek Church.'

Henri sat back. So many questions now revealed them-selves. Petrus *must* have been a member of the Varangian Guard because they were required to follow the Greek Church in their service to the Byzantine emperor. To Henri's knowledge, limited as it was, there were even translations of the Greek liturgy into Northern tongues exactly for those early Varangians.

But the look in his companion's eyes, an empty and ice-filled wasteland, forbade further interrogation.

'This barge journey has been a welcome reprieve,' he said to fill the gap. 'I don't fancy the journey after Givors.'

Petrus pushed his sack over to the other cargo. 'Eyes will be needed all around and weapons within reach. The Templar will not let the relic go easily.'

'Then our plan is to get moving and swiftly.'

'Petrus agrees. Get horses. Good ones.'

The sight of Givors was like any other riverside town. A small place compared to Lyon, it was inundated with muddy river-flats which the birds filled with flapping wing and honking note. Rushes and sedge grew in abundance along the edge of the river, leaning in the downstream direction of the floods that had swept through. The rough stone walls that lined the moorings had been scoured by tumultuous water and logs lay in black tangles along the flats.

Fishermen cast nets from the banks, hauling in zander, perch and trout and other men looped chains about the windfall logs to haul them onto dry land where they could, perhaps next autumn when they had dried, feed the cooking fires of Givors – even floods provided bounty. Thickly verdant forests graced the hills and in this dour light, Henri liked the look of the place. Pity it had sour memories.

Smoke moved in finger-thin skeins of *gris*, upward to the uncompromising sky. Chopping sounded as villagers sought to build a log pile before the next downpour.

Sniffing the air, Henri thought that he and Petrus should keep the women safe and dry in Givors overnight, because for sure the rain would come. There was an earthy smell along with the crisp note of likely fresh rain and the leaves and shrubs were brightly green – anyone could recognise the signs. He chafed at their delay but knew that wet elderly women and wetter horses were hardly a recipe for a swift journey.

'Henri knows this place?' Petrus looked around as the crewmen tied off thick mooring ropes.

'This is where Ariella and I met *Messire* Gervasius and *Madame* Geltidis.' He wished then that he'd been able to scry the future to see what would happen – the inveiglement of de Tremelay into their midst, the drama of the birthing…

'You can secure good horses?'

'I believe so. There's a man, Laurenz, with whom I secured a previous deal. Maybe he is ready for another.'

'Then Petrus will take the women to the inn while you buy horses, yes?'

Henri jumped ashore and began to walk to the livery where he had previously sold their own tired horses and where he had secured new ones for an entire party.

'Ho, Laurenz,' he called, as he entered a low wooden barn with stalls and where the warmth of horses and the sweet smell of hay wrapped around him. He always felt secure in a stable and smoothed the rump of a heavy grey gelding as Laurenz emerged from a stall.

'I wonder if you remember me,' Henri began.

'You are returned,' Laurenz said. 'So soon?'

'I delivered my mistress to her family in Lyon and now I escort another member of their family to a retreat in Esteil. She is accompanied by a nun.'

'So, you need three horses strong enough to carry you to Esteil over that bloody wet ground.' Laurenz had pulled a thick stalk from a sheaf of grass hay and used it to clean his teeth of which there were still a few in his mouth.

'Five, and one needs to be tall and strong enough to carry a big man.'

'Like the grey you lean against, perhaps? As to the others, I still have your exchange mounts. For a small price you can have those back.'

'You mean more than you gave me for them?'

Laurenz wobbled his head from side to side and gave a sly grin. 'I sell horses, *messire*. Coin will get me halfway into Paradise, and then I can barter with God when I get there.'

'How much more?'

They began to haggle and finally settled on an exorbitant figure which included the grey and a pack horse and which might just blow *Madame* Amée's wimple from her head. Henri tipped up his purse and poured *Madame's* silver sols into Laurenz's hand. 'We will be here at dawn. For that price, I hope they will all be harnessed and ready.'

Laurenz spat into his palm and shook Henri's hand.

The four travelling companions spent the night at the inn. The innkeeper, like Laurenz, was surprised Henri was back so soon but gave the squashed chamber above to Madame and the nun and agreed to Henri and Petrus lying near the fire after closing. The four sat at a rough-hewn table spooning a fish broth into their mouths. It tasted fresh, with flavourings of wild dillweed and it filled the empty space in their bellies, along with barley-bread that was heavy and a little stale.

'Nothing that won't soften by being dunked,' said *Madame* cheerfully, quaffing an ale to wash things down.

Soeur Cécile said nothing, working her way through a crust of the bread and half a bowl of the broth.

Petrus cocked his eyebrow. 'You don't want more, Sister?'

'No, thank you. I have had sufficient. You may finish it if you like.'

As he reached for the earthenware bowl, the door latch rattled and opened, allowing a waft of river air to enter and fan the flames in the hearth. Bile rose into Henri's throat at the flash of white falling from wide shoulders. The stranger was followed by three other similarly garbed men and Henri dare not look at Petrus. Instead, he focused on the nun who looked up, took in the new arrivals and straightened to pike-handle stiffness, her hand reaching for her prayer-beads, her face paling to the colour of her wimple and he feared she would faint. Her glance slid to Henri and he smiled at her, willing her to have confidence.

'*Messires, Madame*, Sister…' said the Templar who had entered ahead of the group. 'Is the innkeeper here?'

The innkeeper stepped from the back storeroom. 'That'd be me,' he said, ruddy and ruffled with a surfeit of wine. 'Can I help you?'

'Good even' to you, sir. We look for shelter this night. Have you a chamber?' He spoke with a Poitevin accent and looked as if he had seen thirty summers. All bar one of his fellow knights were a similar age, well-muscled as they thrust their white folds out of the way.

'Can't help you,' said the innkeeper. 'I only have one chamber and the ladies got here afore you.'

The spokesman turned to the others, looking at the older man who nodded his head. 'Another inn you would recommend?' asked the younger knight.

'Nope. There's only me.'

'Can we get food then?'

'There's enough left of the fish broth and I have a crust or two of bread…'

'We have been riding all day with nothing, sir. Your food and some wine or ale would suit us. I thank you. May we join you at the table, good folk?'

Henri nodded but *Madame* stood. 'You may sit here, my lord. The good Sister and I shall retire. We are elderly and therefore tired after our journey. God's grace to you.'

Amée sailed away like a ship in a fair breeze, *Soeur* Cécile in her wake and Henri was glad because the nun's demeanour had tightened like wet leather left in the sun.

The four Templars squeezed around the table and Henri shuffled to allow them in. Petrus sat firmly and no one dared ask him to move. His hand had drifted to the top of his dagger and sat casually on the pommel as if he just passed the time of day.

'We have just come from Saint Christoph's Commanderie near Toulon,' said the self-assured younger Templar, 'and we are heading to La Couvertoirade. And yourselves?'

Tell the truth, thought Henri. Don't obfuscate…

'We are escorting *Madame* from Lyon to a retreat at the Prieré D'Esteil. The nun is the Obedientiary there and is her travelling companion.'

The knight looked around at his *confrères* and then back at Henri. 'Esteil is near Conques, is it not?'

'I believe so,' said Henri, 'Esteil is very small and comes under the aegis of Fontevrault. It is said that Queen Eleanor has a soft spot for it although I wouldn't know why.'

'I see. Fontevrault, you say. Then it must be quite a secure priory. So many these days falter and die.'

Henri raised his eyebrows. 'Do they? I am unaware, *messire*. I and my friend are just *routiers*, muscle for hire.'

'*Routiers*. You have fought?

'I have – for the King in the Holy Land. Indeed we both have, but we don't talk of it. Tell me, sir. We met a knight in Lyon – a Templar, Gilbert de Tremelay. His serjeant said they were travelling to Toulon. Have you met them on the road?'

The innkeeper laid broth in front of the men and then returned swiftly with bread cut into chunks and a full pitcher of ale.

'De Tremelay you say? Not at all. Saint Christoph's is our home, so we would know if he was expected. I think you may be mistaken.'

For a little, there was nothing but the slurp and drip of hungry men who finished the broth and chewed on dunked crusts.

'But I know *of* him,' the Templar continued. 'A firebrand in war and deeply committed to our Order.'

Henri kept his guard. 'I see,' he said. Was this knight dissembling?

'When do you continue on your journey?' the knight asked.

'At dawn, my lord.' Henri wondered if the other knights had taken a vow of silence for this fellow to be doing all the talking. Did Templars do such a thing? He thought not.

'As do we. I wonder if we could sleep on the floor. If it wouldn't disturb you, of course. I assume it is where you will sleep?'

He was an affable man and it was hard to find any edge against which they could push. It annoyed Henri that he couldn't colour the whole brotherhood with the evil that was de Tremelay.

Henri and Petrus excused themselves to walk. Fresh air, they said. The smell of fish broth clung to the rafters and daub walls of the inn and permeated the weave of their cloaks.

'Anon, sirs.' Henri bowed slightly and he and Petrus took their leave. 'We hope we won't disturb you on our return.' They didn't speak until they were almost at the quay.

'Henri believes him?' asked Petrus.

'It has a ring of truth and the knight was naturally forward – but very smooth with it. What I did find odd was that he was the only spokesman. What do you think?'

Petrus clicked his tongue. 'Christ knows. Petrus will be forewarned. He has never trusted knights who wear white into war. Petrus needs to relieve himself, Henri.'

Both men stood at the edge of the river, easing their bladders. '*Soeur* Cécile was uneasy,' Petrus mused.

Henri turned to look over his shoulder in case the deepening gloom of night had ears. 'No more than one would expect. She is a nun and uncomfortable in the presence of earthy men, knights of God or no and she has reason to squirm. She carries a great weight.'

Petrus tucked himself away. 'Responsibility comes easy to some and not others. Petrus thinks she will be happy back in her cloister. In between times, we must put up with she and her breviary.'

Henri knew he meant no hurt to the nun; Petrus and Cécile seemed to have a bond of sorts after the man had rescued her. 'We must hope that she remains safe,' he said.

Petrus grunted and they turned back to the inn. When they entered, they found the knights stretched out against the walls, with cloaks wrapped around for warmth and with a saddle cloth each for a headrest. There was a single candle burning on the trestle table and almost down to the wick, the shadow of the flame jumping across the supine bodies. None seemed awake, but anyone could feign sleep if they wanted.

He and Petrus lay down, wrapped in their cloaks, cushioning their heads on an arm and back-to-back. Henri never slept heavily – even a spider scurrying across a web could wake him.

The inn creaked and groaned and an owl's call cut through the night. Behind him, Henri could hear rats scuttling across the outer edges of the chamber, but then rats were common and didn't concern him. Not like those who might be seeking a piece of old cloth with rusty marks in the weave.

The chamber was completely dark when Henri sensed something. His eyes flew open and his hand slipped to his knife. He felt rather than heard a change in Petrus's breathing against his back.

They kept still, eyes piercing the gloom.

Someone moved in the obscure space, stepping around the sleeping room with care. Henri slipped the knife from its scabbard, desperate to roll onto his back. Petrus lay stiff and ready, and around them, men grunted, snored and farted.

Then, a whisper…

'*Messire* Henri…'

The innkeeper stood above Henri, arms loaded with kindling.

'*Messire*, it is almost dawn.'

Henri's breath gushed out and he sheathed his knife, rolling onto his back and turning to Petrus. The big man rose with the sinuous ease of a great cat and both moved across the room as the innkeeper began to stir the still-glowing coals of the fire, laying fresh kindling on top and encouraging a flame. The smell of charcoal, ash and smoke had filled the room overnight and a fug lay at the top of the stair as Henri went to wake the women. Petrus waited at the foot of the steps – an impassable bulwark.

When Henri tapped on the door, a bar slid back and the door was pulled open by *Soeur* Cécile, cloaked and ready to travel, her old canvas sack hitched over her shoulder.

'We're ready, Henri.' He could barely make out her face in the light of the candle lamp she carried. The smell of tallow laced into the smell of fire and of sweaty men and he would bet his life that the nun had never slept so close to those who might threaten her chastity. 'I have been awake since Lauds,' she said. '*Madame* Amée is just pulling on her cloak and we can be away...'

'Do you not wish to break your fast?'

'*Madame* made sure to pack cheeses and smoked meats in Lyon and she tells me there are almond cakes and dates. We can eat as we ride.' There was no mistaking her haste as she chivvied Amée.

Looking down at the stirring Templars, Henri agreed with her urgency.

They were well away from Givors and the sky had lightened to the interminable grey that had plagued Henri's journey. A light mist drifted over them to begin with, lying on the wool of their cloaks in beady veils, not unlike the transparent silks the company bought in Constantinople – cloth that had travelled from somewhere beyond Henri's imaginings. But the mist changed to a persistent drip and Henri cursed this bloody awful spring that had visited such weather upon them. All he wanted was sun ... Venetian sun, blue skies and clouds like pillows of goose-down. Instead, he and his companions hooded themselves like monks, riding with their heads down. The horses swished their tails in disgust but stamped on, perhaps sensing that a warm stable and good feed awaited at Montbrison. He on the other hand, being of Montbrison stock and related in a far distant way to the Forez family, had no wish to go anywhere near the place.

Sometimes he cursed his mother, a serving woman, for opening her legs at all. Sometimes he cursed his father who couldn't keep his cock in his braies. Either way though, he existed, and by and large the good outweighed the bad. But like last time, he had no wish to run into anyone who might recognise him and he supposed that in that respect, the weather had done him a favour. For who would know four monk-like travellers amongst all the other damp hooded characters riding into and out of the town?

Cécile could not hide her disquiet from Amée. Once they had reached their room last evening, Amée had remarked on Cécile's tense pallor.

'You are frightened,' she said without restraint.

Cécile shrugged her shoulders. 'I trust no one right now, Amée. Least of all the men in white. And you forget...' She tapped her chest, a flattened bony chest beneath the dark grey gown that Amée had given her and which was belted in plain plaited hemp. Cécile's spiky grey hair was hidden beneath an undyed linen wimple and veil and her prayer-beads hung from her girdle. Her feet were still encased in the soft chamois boots Amée had given her and God help her – she crossed herself – it was the one thing Cécile didn't want to return. It was true comfort to have her calloused old feet warm and dry for the first time in twenty or more years. 'You forget what is near to my heart.'

Strapped under fine linen wound round Cécile's chest like a bandage, lay the relic.

As they rode along next day, her hand moved from the reins of her horse to her chest. Was it right to say that she felt pain there? And why? Surely she should feel the warmth of love everlasting. But no, it *was* pain and she decided it was the heavy responsibility of bearing such a great thing to Esteil.

She knew that de Tremelay craved it, that the Archbishop of Lyon desired it, and God knows how many others might wish to own it. She felt the need to constantly look over her shoulder to see who might be following and she gasped when she saw in the distance, one white cloak flapping as a horse cantered along the track behind them.

'Henri!' she called urgently. 'Petrus! We are followed!'

The men hauled on their reins and Henri ordered the women into the deep verdure on the side of the road. He followed them, a block between Petrus, the women and the relic. Petrus meanwhile turned his large grey horse around and with a sword drawn, stood ready. The horse's ears pointed, alert to the approach of the other horse and it skipped sideways and then back again. Petrus growled at it and the ears flicked back and forth.

Cécile's heart pounded in time with the approaching hoofbeats and she held her reins so tightly the leather dug into her hands.

'Ho there!' The Templar of last night pulled at his reins and trotted up to Petrus, smiling as if all was right with the day. 'Where are your compan…'

Henri rode out from the trees but left the women concealed. 'One can never be too careful, my lord,' he said and Cécile marvelled at the calm manner in which Henri and Petrus stood guard. Even she could see that they would kill the Templar if they had to.

'Of course. I have no wish to frighten anyone,' the Templar apologised. 'I did not introduce myself yesterday. I am Amoury de Poitous of the Commanderie Saint Christoph. I was supposed to be riding with my brothers south to La Couvertoirade as I mentioned last evening, but one of our number is my superior and has requested that I deliver a message to the Forez family in Montbrison. I had hoped to catch you before this and ride with you, but my horse cast a shoe and the Givors blacksmith took his time. Do you have any objection to my travelling with you?'

Ah, thought Cécile, listening to the knight deliver his plausible words. So glib and familiar. Had they not been through this exact thing with de Tremelay?

She wished she could indicate to Petrus or Henri not to agree to his request, but what reason could they give? That their company was two elderly women not given to the presence of men, especially the one who was a nun? He might understand the women's discomfort but is not charity on the road expected amongst travellers? And how odd it would look for a nun to be so uncharitable. Bad for her priory for sure, and who was to say that this Soldier of God and his brothers didn't know any of the dismissive canons? What price then the continued existence of Esteil. She breathed a heavy breath – *Mère* Gisela really had no idea what this journey would be like for her Obedientiary. It all sounded so simple in the quiet four walls of the priory.

Henri beckoned to she and Amée and they clicked their horses on, out of the damply heavy greenery and into the drizzle of the open road. He paid them the respect of asking if they minded that Amoury de Poitous joined them as far as Montbrison. Cécile said nothing but Amée said,

'No, although my lord, I am very old, very grumpy and very sick of the rain. So do not expect me to entertain you with witticisms. *Soeur* Cécile and I just want to get to the Benedictine *dorter* in Montbrison so that we can dry our bodies and rest our aching bones. Henri, *aching*! Do you hear? Get us there and soonest!'

Cécile wondered if Amée had just acted the part of the termagant for the Templar's benefit. For sure, she, Cécile looked forward to a cot in the *dorter*. Even so, as they formed into a line with Petrus in the front, Cécile and Amée abreast and then Henri and the knight behind, she felt as if the Templar's eyes burned through her ribs and that he could see what she kept concealed from the world.

She wanted so badly to ask Henri what he thought of the

Templar's presence. To ask Petrus who would be as black and white as ink and ivory. By the Holy Mother's robes, she would be glad when all this was over and she back to her ordered world within the cloister.

Amée claimed they could move on at a trot, perhaps even a canter. That Cécile would be perfectly safe as she had a nice deep saddle with padding strapped to it and a handle to which she could cling to if she needed. Offering a prayer to any of the Holy Family and saints who may be listening, Cécile grabbed the wooden handle of the saddle frame tight as her horse snorted and followed the quickening gait of the others.

As far as she could see, the faster pace prevented speech between the knight and anyone else and for that she was thankful and besides, she knew the distance between Givors and Montbrison was not far – a few leagues of discomfort at most.

The drizzle hung over them in a depressing veil even as they rode through the gates of Montbrison and the bells rang for Sext. Cécile eased one buttock from the wadding of the saddle and then the other, sure that she would never be able to sit in comfort again. Wryly, she thought of all that she had gone through to secure this relic and that she must surely have earned an indulgence or two when the time came.

The Templar left them at the gates of the Benedictine convent where the women would stay. As he rode alongside the Vizézy away from them, Cécile watched him, expecting him to turn back to acknowledge them but he rode on, his wide white shoulders rocking in time with the long gait of his horse.

'Well!' said Amée. 'That was a time of silence that I won't get back in a hurry. Henri, why did he accompany us?'

'He says he must deliver a message here…'

'But?'

'But indeed.' Henri helped her down from the horse. 'Too many of them were on that boat that passed us on the sea and I suspect they have been cast to the winds like seeds, to grow into a thick thatch and catch the unwary. But Amée, we will give them nothing to latch onto. Will we?'

'Of course not, you silly man,' she said waspishly. 'Now, help *Soeur* Cécile and let us get out of this damp or you will find we have caught an ague and are unable to travel anywhere!'

Petrus and Henri had settled the women and found a livery for the horses and an inn for their own needs. Henri would like to have stayed within, but Petrus urged him out and he reasoned if he kept away from the domus of the Forez on the right bank of the Vizèzy, he should be safe. Seen by no one and none to be seen. The drizzle had eased and the late afternoon sky had lightened to the nacreous shade of a pearl with the faintest sight of blue between. Perhaps tomorrow would be drier.

They walked until they came across a row of foodstalls and purchased rabbit pies which were warm and fragrant and settled in Henri's belly like pillows of comfort. They bought wine too, at a tavern where patrons sat easing the aches of the day. No one noticed Henri but everyone stared at Petrus and again, Henri wondered at Adam's decision to send someone so obvious on such a journey.

He glanced across the town and saw the stone ramparts of the castle perched above the streets, remembered the many days and nights of his early life spent in stables with the horses. He never had a dwelling to call home after his mother died – the serving woman who passed through the gates every day to work in the kitchens or the hall, and he a crawling creature left in the kitchens while she worked. He was handled by any and everyone and smiled at all. Very early on, he learned that a quiet demeanour, a smile and willingness produced the best results. His mild congeniality had sent him on his way. That and the fact he could be trusted. Nothing changed – it was what had drawn him into the Gisborne ben Simon fold after all – the affability he had affected at the Gigni Hunt long since.

'Henri, Petrus will walk.'

By which Henri knew to leave the big man to his own devices and to be honest, he relished being alone, just for a little. To think more on the Templar and what prompted a message so urgently contrived, to come to the Forez.

Part of him felt it was just that. A contrivance.

And by consequence, they would be watched every inch of the way to Esteil. Better to think that than to be lulled. His hand moved to the hilt of the sword hanging from its belt. He found comfort with it beneath his hand and turned along an alley which would take him to the side of the Vizèzy. The small river pushed its way through the town, tumbling over stones and here and there breaching the banks. But it was a pleasing rush rather than a roar and Henri dallied, resting his arms on the stone parapet of a small bridge. A few people passed by but then disappeared and Henri's only companion was a tow-haired child throwing sticks over one side and then rushing to the other to watch them reappear. He had no adult with him and presently he ran up the alleyway and Henri was once again thrust into the past with no warning.

He hated the memories of his mother dying with a rambling fever that sweated every bit of life from her. Hated remembering the pauper's grave. Hated recalling how grateful he was that *Père* Ademar who had taught him letters was kind enough to take him to the grave and pray for his mother without asking for payment.

He hated his father for ignoring the by-blow that was his ill-gotten son, and how as a child he had been bullied black and blue for being just that – a by-blow. But then, unbidden, he remembered the exact moment he had learned that spontaneity and charm could win battles and how his life had changed.

More than twelve and fed mostly by *Père* Ademar, he was bruised and with a black eye from another street fight. He dreaded returning to the church; the priest would chide him with strong words before passing him a quill and an ink pot and ordering him to practice his letters so he delayed and tried to walk off his stiffness.

A loud shouting sounded around a corner close by the entrance to the Forez domus and he hurried to see what happened. Some of the younger nobles were yelling at two youths who grappled with each other. A fight, no less, thought Henri as one was knocked flat. No skill, he observed. Just brash thuggery as the other jumped on the lad on the ground and had begun to punch – head, neck, belly. Rage filled Henri – maybe it was the defencelessness of the youth on the ground or maybe just insipient anger that finally boiled like hot oil. The others stood round yelling but making no move and so Henri strode across, pushing at shoulders and arms until he stood above the fighters, yanking the aggressor off. Surprised and off-balance, the fighter had turned slowly as Henri balled a fist and undercut to a half-turned jaw. The face whipped away, spraying blood, and Henri punched again – an ear this time. Punched again and squashed a nose as the face flipped this way and that and all the time the fellow was staggering backward. Finally, with one last wrathful punch to his head, Henri laid the youth out and there was ringing silence. Henri's knuckles throbbed and he shook them, noting the blood skinning the top of each one, but not sure if it was his or the youth's he had knocked out.

He turned, walked back to the noble on the ground, observing a mashed face that he thought he recognised in between the swelling and bruising. He held out a hand to help the fellow up, steadying him. Bowing slightly, he said, 'Henri de Montbrison, at your service, sir,' and began to walk away.

But he was pulled back by the collar and expecting the worst, he gave no resistance.

'Henri, you say,' the youth, spitting out blood between split and swollen lips. 'Then I thank you. I am Gui de Forez, and I am grateful for you doing what these louts could not. That...' he searched for the word and someone passed him a square of linen. 'That *brute* had me at a disadvantage and *they* made no move. Shame on you!' he yelled, eyeing them off. 'Henri is my liegeman from this day forth and any who think otherwise shall feel my family's wrath. Come, Henri...'

Henri knew Gui de Forez, had known since he developed memories that the young noble was a distant cousin to a bastard whelp but he kept the knowledge secret. He learned quickly that the only way to exist in the milieu was to be likeable and apparently transparent, all in one. He had slipped into the group and learned to fight with finesse as he attended combat lessons, had learned there was an art to nobility and much of it unlikeable. All the while his father ignored him and he never acknowledged his father. He continued to learn Latin and letters from his priest and to be mocked for it, but the youths of the domus knew his worth as a fighter and it was half-hearted teasing.

He left Montbrison as a young man with the sad blessings of *Père* Ademar and sought employment as a sword for hire. When the time came for fighting men to follow Philip Capet to the Holy Land, he became part of the Forez family's levy to their king. He was not privileged enough to ride forth on a horse like those he had trained with and thus walked with common men. He didn't mind. He had tired of the entitled view of the nobility and preferred the earthiness of those who sailed with him across the seas. He never saw any member of the Forez family again and had no wish to.

Which was why he wanted to leave Montbrison swiftly and without a ripple.

The river played across the stones, a noisy churning, and the light had softened, the burgeoning sun warm on his back – so easy to take a moment, just one as the bells rang for None. The traffic through the alley and across the bridge dribbled to nothing as folk headed to Mass or to other business in the centre of the town and he revelled in the solitude.

He stood watching the rushing river for perhaps a heartbeat too long and sensed rather than heard the soft footfall behind him. He ducked and the sword stroke that should have sliced into his shoulder, instead cracked off the stone parapet as he crouched down and then scuttled out of range. The bridge was empty apart from his attacker and no one loitered in the alley and he cursed himself for dropping his guard, ripping his sword from its scabbard and eyeing off the fellow who came at him furiously. No style, no skill – just an ordinary man with a big blade. It was easy for a former crusader to take one step forward and block a strike, the sound dissolving into the None carillon.

Henri followed through with a swift return swing, movements that came as naturally as breathing. It didn't even allow the attacker to blink as the air filled with hissing, singing speed. The sword sank its cutting edge into the fellow's side, through the thin cloth of his tunic to slice into flesh, fat and muscle. With the hefting power of his sword, Henri cut deathly deep and just to be sure, he twisted the blade. The fellow yelled, eyeballs wide and Henri pulled his sword out, grabbing the stunned man and pushing him over the bridge into the Vizèzy. Terrified eyes locked onto Henri as the man scrabbled at his side, trying to hold the wide slash together. Then he swung around in the current and drifted away, a bloody stain following him.

Whoever had orchestrated this wanted to reduce the guards to one and that one minding two old women.

It had begun…

Chapter Twenty

The horarium had helped Cécile settle herself. It was a form of anchoring, there was no denying, and the discipline of rising through that night and attending the prayers with the Benedictine sisters lessened the stiffness in her body. She had not changed her robes – why bother? They would be in Esteil maybe two days hence if the weather held.

Two days!

In two days, she could pass Amée and the astonishing relic over to her prioress and return to her cell, cast off her travelling clothes and with the pulling on of her old habit, take up where she had left off. Even as she thought, so she could hear the doves on the roof of the cloister outside her cell burbling their dulcet song and she crossed herself in anticipation.

But take off where she had left off? Perhaps not.

She had been through so much in this short time that she knew she was probably irrevocably changed and it must be accepted. She was more worldly; how could she not be? But there was one thing that remained as inviolable as Holy Law. Her faith was as powerful as it had ever been – nay, even stronger. She could never have achieved this venture without it and thanked the Holy Trinity.

She had just stretched out on her cot in the *dorter* when she heard the door open. A benign light wobbled across the room along with the shush of sandalled feet through the rushes and she sat up.

'*Soeur* Cécile?' a voice whispered. Cécile could just make out the features of the gatekeeper nun and her heart jumped. 'Sister, there are two men at the gate with your horses and they ask that you pack forthwith and leave. It is almost Prime and the sky lightens.'

Now, she thought? But it had been agreed *after* Prime and *after* breaking their fast.

'Now?' she asked in hushed tones in order not to disturb the other women who slept in the *dorter*. 'Then I must wake *Madame*. I thank you...'

She pushed herself off the bed, taking the extra candle lamp from the nun, knowing something must have happened. '*Madame* Amée,' she whispered.

'Quiet!' growled a woman traveller sleeping next to Amée's cot.

'*Madame*,' she shook Amée's arm and with a snort the woman's eyes flew open. Cécile held two fingers over her lips. '*Madame*, we must go. Henri has sent a message. Say nothing.'

Amée rose with speed for such a short rotund woman. It was possible to see how she had led the house of de Clochard through momentous times and though her eyes were wide and she huffed as she grabbed her sack and cloak to hurry after Cécile, she no doubt saw the need and followed without a word. In the passage, torches lit the way, jibing in the cool air of dawn and there was a fragrance of freshness and possibility in the air.

Cécile wondered for whom? Not them, else Henri would have kept to their agreed timetable.

'*Soeur* Céc...' Amée began.

'Not now, *Madame*,' Cécile cut her off.

The gatekeeper let them out of the entrance swinging the gate open on silent iron hinges. Petrus held the horses and Henri gave *Madame* a leg-up and she settled herself in the saddle. Then it was Cécile's turn and her body stretched across the hips as if to split apart into two equal halves.

'Henri?' she whispered.

'Later, Sister. After we leave if you will…'

They clopped through the town, passing under the arch and through the gate heading west along the well-used road to Ambert.

Turning to survey that the road behind was empty, Henri began.

'My apologies to you both, but we had no choice.'

'Henri! Don't obfuscate,' grumped Amée, straightening her veil and then taking her reins back off the horse's neck. 'Are we in danger?'

'Yes, *Madame*. It has begun.'

Cécile's heart banged against the taut cloth wrapped round her chest and her hand slid up, rubbing back and forth as if to sooth her precious cargo. 'Explain,' she ordered and noted the old unambiguous tones of the Obedientiary of Esteil.

'I was attacked at None, yesterday. It was deliberate.'

'You say!' gasped Amée.

'*Messire* Henri!' Cécile felt weak, glad that the horse carried her and that she wasn't walking. Whilst she had been told this might happen, maybe in her heart she had thought it unlikely. Stupid woman!

'The bells were ringing, the path I was on was empty and I had been followed.'

'But,' said Amée. 'He did not get the better of you. You survived to tell the tale. He presumably,' she finished succinctly, 'did not.'

Henri grimaced. 'Exactly so, *Madame*.' He cast a quick look at Cécile and she frowned at him.

'You killed him?' she said.

God above, here she sat, talking calmly about a life taken. She, *Soeur* Cécile, Bride of Christ.

'I am sorry to say it, Sister, but I did.'

'And you feel no shame or guilt?'

'Sister!' Amée turned on her. 'How can you say so? Henri fought for his life. Indeed not just for his life but for yours and mine and for the relic. We must thank God.'

Cécile thought on that and realised Amée was right, but she did not reply. A life was still a life. And yet in her dim recesses, she was sure she had thought she too would kill if she had to. What did that make her in the sight of her Holy Father?

'But Henri had further issues,' said Petrus. 'Which is why we left with speed.'

'What else?' Amée asked. 'I swear I wish I could fly to Esteil like a bird and miss the road altogether. My heart will cease with all of this …' she held a hand to her chest whilst Cécile rode on, her face beginning to set in stone. The thought that she would arrive whole and alive in Esteil two days hence began to dissolve like a fine dream vanishing when one wakes.

'I hurried back into the centre of the town and was endeavouring to get back to the inn when a voice called my name and I turned to find the knight, Amoury de Poitous. He, charming as always, asked why I was rushing, was it not a peaceful afternoon to be enjoyed? I told him I looked for Petrus with a message from *Soeur* Cécile. Lies, I know, but all I wanted was to get out of sight and mind of any in Montbrison.'

He told me he had just been to the Forez domus, and received news that a valuable relic had gone missing, stolen from a Templar ship in Marseille. It was called the *Cloth of Marie,* he said and asked if I had heard of it. It was all so innocent in the asking and I told him I knew of no such relic. That I was not a churchgoer and had no faith in relics; that my belief was in God's will…'

At this Cécile's eyes closed to slits as Henri looked directly at her. Liar, she thought. On whom I depend for my life…

Henri continued, telling them that he had asked what the

relic was like and what should they do if they came across the thieves. Indeed, was the knight or the Forez family even sure it came this way? To which the knight demurred. "Not especially, no." Worse, he also said that as I was asking of de Tremelay in Givors, that he had news the knight was staying at the Chateau Neuf de Drac. So you see, I believe he knows about the cloth, maybe even that we carry it and that he is under orders to unsettle us, panic us, if not directly to maim us. We have only one way out and that is speed. We must push on at a gallop. Sister?'

Cécile winced. *Deus!* 'If I must, then I must. I have faith that the Holy Mother will protect me.'

'Petrus will stay close…' the big man said.

She looked at the Byzantine guard and God help her, her eyes filled and she nodded shortly, embarrassed.

They dug their heels into their horses' sides, gave them rein and the animals leaped away, excited to be galloping. Petrus guided Cécile's horse to the less rutted part of the road, so that there were no stumbles, that the horse could keep up its pace. The mounts were all geldings, and it was with surprise that Cécile noted the pack horse had been left behind with its luggage and that Petrus's and Henri's saddlebags carried very little.

'Petrus,' she called. 'We are not stopping at Ambert, are we?'

Petrus looked across from the back of his large grey, the horse's hooves thundering. 'The goods for the convent will be sent on, Sister, do not fear. We will bypass Ambert and take the forest paths to Esteil. It has to be done.'

She said nothing, just changed hands from left to right upon the handle of her saddle and leaving the horse to trust in its partnered grey as the trees sped by, the leaves floating in their slipstream. The words of Luke's Gospel flooded into her mind:

*'Behold, I have given you the power to tread upon serpents
and scorpions and upon the full force of the enemy
and nothing will harm you.'*

Henri's gut roiled with a premonition.

As his horse sped alongside Amée's, he had the most
God-awful feeling that no amount of speed, no amount
of surprise would make a difference and that one of the
Templars – de Tremelay, de Poitous, whomever, would
shadow their footsteps right to the gates of Esteil, if not
into the priory itself. There had been no time to talk with
Petrus about it and the man was so damned phlegmatic that
he couldn't imagine they would have sweated a plan. For
Petrus, it would always be alert, armed and ready to fight.

In truth, Henri knew they could do nothing more.
Keep the women safe and fight like dogs if they had to. The
thought of sending them off into the Forez to make their
way with stealth back to Esteil whilst he and Petrus manned
the frontline was surely a dream. He looked at Amée. Her
veil had gone, her grey hair blew back and exhaustion began
to lengthen lines on her face, dark pillows beneath her eyes.

'*Madame*?' he called.

'Tired, Henri!' she yelled back. 'Can we stop? Afraid of
losing my balance and falling…'

The age of the women was not lost upon him and he
knew they must rest. Against his better judgement, Henri
waved his arm in the air, pointing off the road to the leafy
surrounds. Petrus reached down and took *Soeur* Cécile's
reins, easing her horse to a canter, then a trot and finally a
breathy walk as they bent beneath the trees. Amée was quite
adept and slowed her horse expertly and when they were
finally under the trees, she leaned forward, laying her head
along the drooping horse's neck.

'Henri, my horse is as exhausted as I. We cannot continue
at this pace…'

'You're right,' he admitted. 'We'll rest within the forest for as long as it takes and then pick a safe way down into Esteil from the plateau. Sister, are you familiar with the woods and any likely concealed way into Esteil?'

The nun had slid from her horse, Petrus grabbing her and easing her to the ground. She made no fuss of his manhandling and attempted to smile her thanks. Henri was aghast at her colour – she was as grey as her robe and her lips seemed almost blue. He could ask no more of her, he knew. Whatever leagues remained must be done at a cautious creep through the forest.

'No, Henri. Not this far away. The sisters and I would venture to the edge of the woods outside Esteil for nuts, *ceps* and berries but the first time I saw the forest near Ambert was on my way to Lyon…' Petrus had passed her a costrel filled with unwatered wine and she drank it off without restraint and colour began to return to her cheeks.

Amée slid down from her own mount, holding onto the stirrup as she reached into one of her saddlebags for her costrel, unstoppering it and throwing back the contents unashamedly. 'Lord, I'm not as young as I once was,' she muttered. 'Give me strength for this next, I beg you…'

Perhaps Henri was not meant to hear her. He loosened the girths on Amée's mount and looping up the reins safely, he left the animal to graze. The horses shook themselves with a great rattling of leather and metal and blew down their noses. There was a tiny streamlet lacing through the damp grasses and the animals drank off a little, ate more grass and then drank again.

The women sat with their backs against the smooth boles of mountain ash trees, the budding yellow flowers ready to burst in the warmth of a better day. Henri briefly thought how ironic that they took shelter between trees commonly referred to in the country as *trees of life.*

'We will journey carefully, moving easterly all the time and because we're in the forest, it will be by nature slow…'

'Henri, can we walk for a little and lead the horses?' The nun was almost plaintive in her request. Poor woman, never ridden a horse until she ventured on this plagued journey.

'Yes. We'll eat now, get some food into our bellies and then walk our horses for a little. But I confess, Sister, we must mostly ride in order to put distance between us and any who follow.'

'Well,' said Amée, looking skyward. 'At least the weather is clear.'

Yes, clear, thought Henri. Hoofprints marked indelibly in drying mud. He jumped up and grabbed his horse, tightened the girth and leaped on. 'Eat while I'm gone. I'll be back forthwith.' He raced through the forest to the road, looking in both directions and listening. No sound of hoofbeats, no birds flying up in alarm. He began to circle his horse in all directions and then to ride it back and forth east and west, making a melée of prints for some distance each way, checking his path onto the road and widening the circle of prints round and round, up and down so that one set of tracks leading into the forest became enmeshed with more and more tracks leading out. And then he cantered off the way they had come, westerly toward Montbrison, finding a stony, dried part of the road and circling up between rocks and back into the forest.

To a wily tracker, his efforts would be for nought but if pursuers followed at speed, he hoped they would gallop on. He trotted back to his companions and settled his horse again.

'And?' asked Petrus.

'No sight no sound,' Henri replied. 'Rest easy.'

Cécile was standing, pulling at her robes, straightening them. Amée slept unbelievably, her mouth ajar, a little snore emerging. Henri grinned at Petrus in response and then took a swig of wine from his costrel, chewing on some of the stale bread that Amée had insisted they pack. It lined the gut; it was all that mattered.

'We must make steady progress – even at a walk,' Henri said. 'Sister, I'm so sorry to inflict all this upon you...'

'Do not chide yourself, *Messire* Henri. What must be done, must be done. What will happen will be God's will.'

Henri turned away. This old woman disturbed him and to an extent he realised he was in awe. Her devotion to her Faith, her strength. By the stars above, her strength! As sure as the Saints were his witness, he would keep her safe.

He looked over to Petrus but the man was busy, checking the flap on his daintily worked leather purse and tightening the wide girdle at his waist. He was like a river of slippery ice – cool, unbreachable. One wondered what he would be like in a thaw. Henri could barely make head nor tail of the man. He was the first of Gisborne's men with whom a bond was tardy in forming. Did he trust him? He grimaced slightly as he led his horse to the stream. Because Adam and Gisborne did, he felt he had no choice but occasionally he wondered how much of anything Petrus did was for Petrus and no one else.

And yet... and yet he and the nun seemed to have formed the strangest bond. That was an enigma he would love to solve when there was time. 'We must wake Amée and move, I think,' he said. 'We need to be beyond Ambert by dark.'

'Are we to sleep in the forest?' the nun asked. Her face had resumed a healthy colour but behind her eyes there was a shadow. Tiredness? God only knew, thought Henri with some irony.

'Possibly, Sister,' he replied as kindly as he could. 'I am sorry. But we can't risk yours and *Madame's* lives trying to ride down from the forest in the dark.'

'When shall we be in Esteil?' she said as she struggled to tighten her horse's girth.

Henri helped her as Petrus woke *Madame* Amée. 'Between Sext and None perhaps, if we have the Saints on our side.'

'Then I shall pray that we do, *messire*. And not just the Saints but the Holy Family as well.' There was a degree of lemon-sour tartness to her voice but he was becoming used to it and strangely, it didn't diminish his admiration for her.

Cécile cursed her manner. It seemed that she had learned nothing about the art of equanimity on this journey. She respected *Messire* Henri in truth. His beliefs worried her but she could not deny his care of the companions as they rode. But Petrus was her earthly saviour and she liked his silences, as if he knew that speech was unnecessary and that kindred spirits could exist as well in silence as not. It was what she and Benedicta had together – that rare thing where silence was golden and filled with like heartbeats. Mary, Jesus and Joseph but she was counting every breath until they passed through the gates of the priory.

She pulled on her reins and her horse tore at the last strands of grass before stretching its neck to follow her. Petrus, Cécile, then Amée and finally Henri in single file. Above them through the beeches, rowans and pines the birdlife of the Forez chirruped and called –

shrikes, larks, stonechats and there, she thought she heard the delicate sound of a linnet! She loved linnets for the simple joy of their call and it gave her hope that home was not far away.

When she looked up through a gap in the pines where a beam of what she called God's light streamed to the forest floor, she saw a kite and liked to think it was God's way of seeing them safe.

She rubbed her chest, pushing at the tight-wrapped *byssus* and praying as they walked. It was a rhythmic meditation and it calmed her. Occasionally Petrus would tread on a fallen branch and a sharp crack would sound, birds flying up in alarm, but then all would fall into the crystal-clear chatter of forest life and Cécile's heart would settle back into a calm cadence.

She thought on Petrus. They had formed the strangest alliance. She trusted him implicitly. They thought along the same lines – he with his Greek Church beliefs and she with her Faith. He had told her a little of himself when she lay bruised and battered in Lyon – his mother who had been an Imperial servant in Constantinople, and his father part of the Varangian Guard and so it was natural for him to follow in his father's footsteps. His father subsequently died from a fever of the bowel and his mother entered the nunnery of Xylinites and Petrus was left unencumbered by family responsibility. But things went awry when he was wrongfully accused of a theft within the Guards' quarters. His Fate would have been sealed if he had stayed to meet it – hands chopped off, left to bleed to death. But before they could condemn him, he escaped, running with hand-chains through the city in a raging storm. Pitching up in the Venetian Quarter and being found by Gisborne's shipmaster.

In time, and encouraged by Ahmed, the afore-mentioned shipmaster, he began working for Gisborne, finally landing in Lyon where he did whatever was asked of him – if it suited. His reputation of being a law unto himself grew as quickly as his blond mane and most knew never to question his history if they valued their lives.

How Cécile had inveigled this from Petrus was a miracle, she knew. But then she returned his favour by telling some of her own story from between her swollen and split lips and they rubbed along as saviour and saved.

'Sister,' said Amée, startling her from her thoughts. 'Can we mount now? Have you walked enough? I for one am tireder for the walking than the riding.'

Of course you are, thought Cécile uncharitably. But then you are fat and unused to walking, whereas I… She stopped. *Lord forgive my unkind thoughts…*

'Of course, *Madame*. I am ready. My apologies but I am such a novice on horseback.'

Petrus and Henri helped the women mount and presently, they walked smartly along, covering twice the ground than before and Cécile knew without doubt from Henri's manner that he was glad that they could gain more distance.

The day passed without incident and Cécile fingered her beads in gratitude.

To you Lord, we give thanks...

She meditated on the Paternoster as her horse picked its way over root and leaf and the day moved toward None. She thought on the None prayer where she could ask for perseverance, and the strength to cope with whatever demands came her way, rubbing at the pressure at her chest. The *byssus*, silk of the sea, reminded her of her responsibility. It was only since she had been attacked that she'd begun to feel such pain in her chest and mostly, that venerable cloth would ease the strain and she would think *another miracle* and her thin mouth would turn up slightly into a small complicit smile.

Sometimes though, the chest ache would remind her of dear sweet Benedicta and she wondered if there had been such a thing for the nun as she drifted toward the end and her ascension to Heaven. Was she, Cécile, experiencing the same thing? Was she like some threaded needle, the silk thread running out after stitch upon stitch? Her life source reduced to a series of ripples against the chest wall?

But of course not. This was merely the bruising from where she was kicked with such venom. She must rub some arnica cream into her skin when they stopped. She had a small pot with a scrape left in it.

Eventually, as their stomachs began to growl with hunger, *Messire* Henri signalled a stop and Cécile slid gratefully from her horse, holding tight to the stirrup leather to prevent falling backward. Petrus came up behind her and steadied her, saying,

'All is well, Sister?'

'As well as it can be till the morrow, Petrus.' She sank onto the ground, sighing, as Petrus led their horses away to unsaddle and water the animals. The one thing about this wetter-than-usual spring was the ability to find water wherever they went. The horses dipped their mouths into the pool, slurping and then clinking their bits as they swilled the water, dropping mouthfuls to splash on the ground.

Cécile too felt thirsty but would much have preferred the crystal water of a running stream than a dank water hole with the lengthening shadows of the forest. Amée folded beside her and Cécile asked, 'Do you think we are safe, *Madame*?"

'In a word, no. Not until we ride through the gates of Esteil and they can be barred behind us.' Amée smoothed her hair back from her face and began to plait the length at the back. Obviously a veil was just a hindrance and Cécile was inclined to agree as she had pulled her own into place any number of times on horseback. Perhaps she should discard it and ride in the firmly tied wimple. But no, for a nun it was unseemly. She would hold onto it as best she could.

'Madame,' she said. 'If we are in danger because we carry the relic, one wonders at the price. I fret for my sisters and the priory once the world finds out what we hold.'

It was true. Every second thought brought her back to this concern because she knew that no matter the miraculous nature of the relic, no matter the fact that it lived within a hallowed precinct, it had been proven to matter little as lives were lost in the hunt to possess it. There had been Saul ben Simon in the first instance and maybe even more before that, in Constantinople. Then the man who had attacked Henri. Her own battering. It was too much!

'The thought has crossed my mind,' Amée admitted. 'Sometimes, I think the safest place for the relic to reside is back in Christ's cave or even at the nunnery from whence it came.'

'A nunnery, you say?' Cécile was surprised. She'd never once given its journey to their own hands a thought. To her it just happened, and apart from the miracle with Gelis, she found its presence almost a threat. At such a thought, she racked herself with guilt. A cloth with Christ's blood and shed with such pain! If she could perform a penance, she would.

'Yes. It was pilfered in an ivory casket from an Orthodox nunnery in Byzantium and the name was carved into the ivory.'

'I did not know…'

'A strange name,' mused Amée. 'X… Xyl…'

'Xylinites?' Cécile's face had chilled to ice and she found herself gazing at Petrus. Had he heard? But he was too far away at the waterhole and was talking with Henri. Small mercies?

'Meh, possibly,' Amée shrugged her shoulders. 'Many Greek names sound the same to me.'

Cécile's hand moved to where the *byssus* encircled her chest. God is testing me, she thought and immediately after, she recalled Benedicta's imagined words from a lifetime ago: *You have been chosen…*

Chosen in more ways than one, thought Cécile. Such responsibility lay on her shoulders – even more so now with Amée's words. It lay across her like a chain of iron and she closed her eyes at the very thought, looking for a prayer of help – searching through her mind.

'*To thee I have recourse in the daily dangers that surround me…*' and then she prayed the Paternoster for its simplicity and grace. She rubbed away the tears that formed in her eyes. By Our Lady but she was worn down.

'Peslières is somewhere over there,' Henri pointed. 'And Issoire. I believe the domus of the Drac family is situated on the edge of the ravine between the two. *Seigneur* Bertrand du Drac was the founder of the priory but I know nothing more of the family.'

'There is no help to be had there? Should it be needed?'

Henri frowned as Petrus rubbed his horse's wither and then untwisted his and *Soeur* Cécile's reins. For Petrus to even hint at help being required was startling. 'No. Let us assume that the women rely completely on us, Petrus. Christ,' he sighed. 'We can't even plan a defence. It's like fighting in a fog.'

'Perhaps then,' Henri's companion said, 'if we are attacked, we form a wall and send the women on.'

'I can see no other way,' Henri replied unwillingly. 'Do you sense we are being watched?'

'Yes. From a distance…' Petrus spoke as if it was of no consequence.

Henri looked around as he pulled the two horses from the waterhole and they lurched up the bank. He tied their reins to a branch of a pine and they grazed. But he was uneasy. He studied the women – Amée was playing with her thick grey hair, trying to plait it again, out of the way. She seemed lethargic but not as much as the nun who leaned back against the tree, her eyes closed, her mouth moving as she no doubt prayed. Such strength in the old woman and to think she carried the most valuable artifact in the Christian world upon her person. If he had any connection with God, he would ask that this frail Bride of Christ should receive sainthood.

'You are worried for them,' Petrus murmured.

'Not so much for Madame whom I think could readily go to war. But for *Soeur* Cécile. She has the fire of the archangels running through her but she is worn down by us all and if we come to a fight, I cannot conceive what will happen. *Madame* would handle a knife I think, or some dirty blade play. But the sister has been pushed to her extremes and so yes, I worry.'

'Then, Henri, Petrus says do not. The sister will have the sword of a Varangian guard to shield her and a Varangian guard does not give in to anyone. Least of all a Templar.'

'A Varangian, you say!' Henri hid his words from the women.

'Do not pretend you did not know, Henri.' Petrus grinned.

Henri chuckled, despite his unease. 'If you say.' He pulled dates from his saddlebags and pieces of stale almond cake. 'When this is over, will you tell me?' he asked with sincerity, because trust in the man had finally burgeoned with that one admittance.

'Perhaps. If we return to Lyon together.' Petrus was non-committal and in truth, Henri had the feeling that once their time in Esteil was done, Petrus would disappear like dust on the wind.

Chapter Twenty One

She was done riding.

If she never got on the back of a horse again after reaching Esteil, she would be content. It wasn't what nuns did, after all.

They'd remounted after eating a few dates and the crumbling oatcakes and quaffing wine from their costrels. She liked the unwatered wine. It softened the hard edges for a little. Not long enough though and she began to understand why her betrothed, back in her youth, had spent much of his days with a wine jug held to his lips or a mug of ale by his side. The man escaped from all that was distasteful. No wonder he fell dead in his mill.

Thankfully…

She crossed herself and begged God to understand that her entry into the convent had breathed new life into her soul and from that day, she revelled in the service and duty required of her. She became the person she was meant to be – God's handmaiden – and she came willingly.

'Sister?' Petrus's deep voice pulled her from her contemplation.

'Yes?'

'You are comfortable?' He had ridden up close by and their legs touched, stirrup to stirrup.

She waggled her head from side to side. 'I'm not a born rider, Petrus.'

His voice dropped to a murmur that she strained to hear. 'Sister, we are being followed. Don't turn, you must pretend all is well. Henri is telling *Madame*. We sensed them when we stopped. In a moment, we will begin to speed along the track. We are between Issoire and Peslières and if you head toward the sun, you will eventually connect with the road to Esteil. When Petrus tells you, you ride like you have never done. Petrus and Henri will drop back and shield you, but you must ride as if the Devil licks your heels.'

She frowned at him but knew better than to argue and made sure her gown folds wouldn't chafe her legs. She would not admit her fear, not to God nor Petrus, but he leaned over and placed something cold in her fingers. She looked down and found that her palm had curled round a mean *misericorde* and at that moment her heart froze.

Whilst Petrus held her reins, guiding her horse, she knotted her girdle tighter, slipping the knife between the taut knots, hoping to the Holy Spirit that riding would not cause her to lose it.

Armed!

What did that make her?

Would she kill?

And then she thought of Saul ben Simon and the men who had attacked her and something visceral began to rise and her back straightened in consequence. She took the reins back from Petrus and shortened them and then Petrus hissed 'Go!'

Her heart jumped but she dug her heels into the horse's side and it squealed and then leaped forward, nearly unseating her, but she held hard to the wooden pommel and gave the animal its head as it raced after *Madame* and Henri.

The rutted track flew beneath her but she didn't look down, afraid to lose her balance, conscious of the others racing in front and the canopy thinning as they headed for the road to Esteil.

Were they so close to the convent?

Had Petrus or Henri misjudged how far they had yet to travel?

She didn't know. The verdant surrounds of Esteil looked like any other forest and she had only ever ventured out when one or two of the other sisters could not accompany the novices to collect food. *Christ God!* She railed against the circumscribed life of the convent, of her narrow view of everything…

With leaves whipping away and the crack of branches smashing as the horses galloped, she broke free of the forest, the ravines of the Drac demesnes rising up at her side.

'Sister! Do not look back!' Petrus yelled. 'Go!'

Henri had yanked on his reins and turned his horse back as Amée spurred her horse harder and Cécile leaned over her own horse's neck, urging him on.

Father, help me…

Henri flew back past her and she knew that he and Petrus would form a protective shield, allowing she and Amée to ride safely to Esteil whilst the men engaged the pursuers. Shouts and the clash of blades flew on the air, but as she had been ordered she did not turn back, focusing her gaze through the horse's ears, thinking only of getting to the convent and the gates sliding shut behind her.

Her head jerked back as her veil was grabbed from someone at her side. But she used one hand to free it from her head, her wimple strings almost choking her as the veil loosed. She yelled at her horse and it lifted its momentum and she thought she was free.

But something … someone … nudged her horse's hind-quarters and the horse snorted, shying away. Cécile nearly fell, holding the saddle pommel tighter but in the corner of her eye she saw a horse's head move up, then it's shoulder, then a masculine hand reaching to grab at her reins.

She reached to her girdle, working at the dagger, ripping it out, still holding onto the saddle with one hand.

God forgive me...

She stabbed once on the hand pulling at her reins. The dagger was deadly slim – a narrow pointed blade which could have been at home in a solar, it so represented a needle. The blade pushed deep through the top of the hand and into the palm but the man held tight and stayed close, yelling at her.

'Bitch! Spawn of the Devil!'

She flung a glance at him, recognising the Templar serjeant and yanked at the blade, pulling it free. With no thought she stabbed again, this time his thigh that banged against her own as he kept pace with her terrified gelding. High in the thigh, a deep stab. The blade stuck and she relinquished it as her horse tried to turn from the other animal banging at its neck, snaking at its head and trying to bite.

The serjeant howled after her but his horse dropped behind and she slowed her mount, aghast at what she had done. Her heart pounded as if it were charged with horses' hooves and she panted in time.

She...

A nun...

She pulled at her horse, the animal shaking its head wildly. In the far distance, she could see Amée galloping out of sight and her mount danced and half-reared, desperate to pursue.

Instead, she turned to face the serjeant as the dour folds of his cloak settled around him. He looked at the blood trickling from the leg wound and she knew as well as he that the minute that needlepoint released from the leg, the blood would pump freely. A pulsing fountain as his life dripped to the ground and in no time, he would be dead, slumped over his horse's shoulder. Already the animal sidled at the smell of gore beginning to stain the leather of its saddle.

The horses panted, sidling back and forth and Cécile slid from her saddle, her legs like shreds of torn cobwebs. In the distance she could hear shouts and the noise of weapons but for her there was nothing but this familiar man. The one who had captured her, imprisoned her and then beaten her.

A rage scourged every bit of her body.

She began to walk toward him but his horse jumped and swirled and then gave a small half rear and she could hear the man cry out. A noise like a child – high-pitched and filled with fear.

The bloody dagger released from the wound and fell to the ground and the serjeant rolled off his horse to lie curled around himself, his hand pushed hard into the unstoppered cut as blood, as beautifully red as the cinnabar-tinted ink the sisters used in the scriptorium sprayed the ground. It pumped at first, the serjeant whimpering as he looked at Cécile. She gazed back as his life's blood slowed to a trickle and his hand fell away. He collapsed back against a boulder and whispered,

'Help me, Sister. I beg you…'

Help him? The man who had kicked and beaten her?

But he continued to plead and because she was God's chosen, she mouthed words in a soft murmur. She performed a ritual because it was right, not because she wanted to, and with that feeling she felt as empty as a weathered and worn husk of barley.

'Lord of life, we walk through eternity in Your presence.
Lord of death, we call to You in grief and sorrow.
You hear us and rescue us.
Watch over us as we mourn the death of Your servant, precious in Your sight, and keep us faithful to our vows to You.'

She performed the sign of the cross as his eyes fixed upon her.

'In nomine Patris at Filii et Spiritus Sancti. Amen'

She knew the serjeant was dead as his eyes stared, set in a plea of horrified and fearful forgiveness. What could she do? It was her lifelong role to forgive, surely?

She collapsed to her knees and clasped her hands together, begging for God to forgive *her* for the sin she had committed.

'*Soeur* Cécile...'

The voice of an archangel spoke to her and she shuddered. A golden voice filled with a deep and sustaining warmth. But she knew it was, in truth, the voice of the Devil and as her hand slid up to her chest, to the relic, a magnificent ache grasped her, as if God held her heart in his hands.

She sighed, falling to the ground as the world faded to oakgall black before her.

Henri could hear vague shouting but a bend in the track and a flange of pines blocked his view. He jammed his heels into his horse's side and leaned over its neck for more speed.

His body filled with raging fire as he rounded the corner, approaching a wider clearing. It was bound on one side by a *causse* rising out of the chalky ground and by pines edging the sides of the road and creeping up the side of the *causse*.

Somewhere close by was the Chateau du Drac and that alone caused his heartrate to lift further as he recalled that Gilbert de Tremelay was rumoured to have gone west to stay with *le Seigneur* de Drac. Therein lay the brimstone within his belly. This attack was deliberate he had no doubt, and if it was the last thing he did, he would avenge Saul and Ariella.

A piercing neigh cut through the air and his horse slid to a stop, so that he could leap from the saddle to approach the fight on foot. Henri knew his best chance in the fight was on the ground. Swords on horseback were beyond his experience and he had a brief, coloured flash of de Tremelay galloping toward the little child, swinging his sword back and...

But no! Not now!

He approached the clearing in time to see Petrus' sword

gliding in an even arc from one side of his body to the other, keeping the three attackers at blade length, never turning his back to them. He towered over them like some god of a bard's song and his fluid movement was a thing of great beauty. Henri thrilled as he drew his own sword, hefting it in his hand. It rarely felt right but this time it fitted like a fine chamois glove. He grasped it low on the pommel with his thumb laid over the cross-guard to steady his swings, pulling his dagger from his belt to hold in his left hand.

No one noticed him as he moved in from behind, so focused were the attackers on Petrus. Sliding in and swinging low, Henri slashed hard across one man's calves, almost severing the legs. As the man screamed and folded, the flames of Henri's fire leaped higher.

'You are here at last!' called Petrus as he advanced, still sweeping his sword left and right and forcing the men backward. They had turned as their companion yelled, hearing Petrus call to Henri and displaying empty, unshielded backs to the Varangian.

Petrus pulled back his sword, elbow bent sharply and then stabbed forward through one back with such force Henri thought the point would emerge on the other side. He advanced with speed and drove his own sword into his opponent's chest.

All done so neatly by the two Gisborne men that they looked at each with surprise.

'That was quick,' said Henri, bending to roll the bodies over.

'Petrus could see they had no skill. Easy pickings.' He walked to the almost legless man that Henri had killed as he entered the clearing. 'Well aimed, Henri. They had no clue. Do you know them?' He wiped his sword on the man's chest, and again on a tussock.

'No.' Henri grabbed the loose folds of a dead man's bloody tunic to clean his own blade and shoved his sword in its scabbard. He began to run toward their horses which had paired up to crop the tough grasses at the side of the track calling over his shoulder, 'We need to reach Madame and the nun. Come on!'

Their horses raced.

They flew on the wind and found de Tremelay suddenly, past the bend in the track. He was plainly dressed; no fine white cloak of the order, nothing to identify him as a Templar. He leaned over *Soeur* Cécile and further away, the body of the serjeant lay in a pool of darkening and congealing blood. Henri wanted to run the knight down – slit him from end to end.

'Leave her!' he shouted.

De Tremelay spoke lazily as they jumped off their horses. 'You do a poor job of guarding the women back to the convent, *messires*, which I gather is your job. I find this nun in a grievous state and my serjeant dead.' There was no evident concern at Jean de Laon's death; the knight lacked any sort of compassion, even for the nun lying at his feet, and his cool remove carved Henri to the core.

Soeur Cécile lay still, her chest barely rising. Her face had faded to ivory, her mouth tinged almost the colour of an old lavender flower. Past its prime, like the nun.

'I said *leave* her!' Henri repeated.

'If you please. My lord.' De Tremelay sneered. 'Respect,' he poked Henri's chest and the condescension in his manner provoked Henri to boiling. 'Respect. If you please.' He nodded at the nun. 'The woman needs help. And swiftly if I am not wrong. Let us take her to the Drac domus and then I can find the cur who has killed my serjeant and injured this precious religieuse.'

Henri's hand flew to his sword pommel. He hated that the man was unruffled. That he could shrug off murdering innocents. That he spoke with a voice that could charm angels from on high.

The knight's face was unlined and yet he must be near fifty years, and like any Templar he was slim and muscular, carved from the Order's Rule of ascetic living. Henri had no doubt his swordsmanship would be as honed as his frame.

'No,' Petrus growled, slapping a hand hard across Henri's chest and addressing the knight from his full height, talking down deliberately. 'Leave her. *I* will take her to Esteil, which is her home. Henri, go after *Madame*. Make sure she reaches the convent safely. I will follow.'

Henri hesitated. Now was surely his time with no witnesses and with Petrus by his side, especially as the Templar replied with calm insouciance.

'As well the sister's death will be on *your* conscience than mine.' He shrugged, holding his hands palm out and stepping back. 'She is yours, *messire.*'

Henri's hand let go the sword pommel and began to pull at his dagger. If the Templar noticed, he gave no sign.

'Henri, go!' Petrus kneeled at the nun's side.

Henri gritted his teeth, left his dagger in its sheath and swung up onto his horse, heeling the animal's sides. As he left, he heard the Varangian say, 'Petrus believes it is better, my lord, that you take the body of your serjeant to the Drac domus and leave the nun in Petrus's care.'

He had no idea what the Templar answered as he urged his mount on, reaching a full gallop into the glare of a late spring day. His head swirled with questions as his unquenched hatred of the Templar became even more parched.

Why did he not deal vengeance right then? The time had never been better.

He howled at the sky as he raced along the track and kites circled like threats above his head.

He thought of Cécile lying unaware, her chest barely rising.

Who had attacked her? And the serjeant, what of him?

The knight? Why would he attack the man? What would he stand to gain from his serjeant's death?

No, someone else killed the serjeant. Henri recalled Jean de Laon's hose and the bloodstains over the lacing of his right leg. He had been stabbed through the life-blood vessel in his thigh.

Could *Soeur* Cécile do such a thing? The old nun?

But then she had a spine of iron⁊

He spied Amée in the distance, her horse trotting awkwardly and he urged his mount faster but then gasped in horror as Amée's mount fell in mid-stride to its knees. Amée flew from the saddle and lay still in the chalk dirt of the road to Esteil.

'*Madame, madame*!'

He threw himself off his mount and knelt by her side – her eyes were open and she blinked at him. A graze on her forehead oozed bright blood.

'Ouch⁊' was all she said as she fingered the wound. A lump was emerging, pushing brazenly against her pale skin. 'Pity I didn't wear a wimple,' she managed. A sharp sound from her horse made her turn to the animal lying on its side. 'Henri, his leg is broken⁊'

Henri begged her to stay still as he smoothed a hand down the horse's leg. He felt the bone moving, and shielding Amée from his action he quickly dispatched the animal. He removed the saddlebags and attached them to his own saddle and then knelt back by Amée's side.

'Can you sit up?' he asked and as she nodded, he eased her gently, grabbing her against his legs as she moaned and wavered.

'I'm a little dizzy⁊' she admitted.

'*Madame*, I must get you to the convent. If I lift you, can you slide into the saddle?'

'Lift me?' she muttered. 'Me?' She indicated her ball-like size and began to shuffle. 'Help me to that rock.'

She was a lot less strong than she pretended and her footsteps were unsure and Henri was concerned that a more profound injury lay in her skull. In time, she sat hunched in the saddle and Henri hauled himself up behind her, pulling her to sit in his lap and clicking his horse on.

A slow trip by necessity and Amée dozed against his chest. As they walked, he thought back to the encounter with de Tremelay and he marvelled that the man had avoided justice.

But it would come. As sure as seasons followed each other and days came around, so would vengeance be done and the thought gave him pleasure.

That the knight would appear at Esteil was a given, so obsessed was he with the veil.

And then…

The sun moved ahead of the horse and its load and was on the late afternoon side of the sky when Henri finally spotted smoke above the trees. The thump of wood chopping hung on the air aside the ringing crash of a hammer against an anvil. A dog barking spoke of a pastoral domicile and if he had been a believer, he would have crossed himself in thanks.

Esteil…

The smell of the cesspit reached them first and it woke Amée.

'We are here?'

Henri, relieved that she made sense, replied, 'Almost at the convent.'

They passed a mill, the noise of a wheel being turned inside – a beast walking in a circle and timbers creaking. Along with dust drifting out of the open door, the smell of cracked wheat heads reached them and Henri longed for fresh bread. Children leaned against the frames of doors or ran alongside and a dog snapped at the horse's heels, Henri snarling at him.

The convent was not hard to find. Esteil was a small village dominated by the stone building with its bell tower. The belfry could house three bells which was unusual for such a small convent, surely. In any case, *Madame* had only ordered one, so one would have to do, when it arrived.

If… it arrived.

Henri eased *Madame* back into the saddle off his lap, urging her to hold tight as he slid down over the horse's hindquarter, glad to be at the convent at last, unable to resist a look back along the road in a vague hope Petrus would not be far behind.

He lifted his hand, grabbed the doorbell rope and rang it loudly, then hammered on the gate. It was opened swiftly, a young novice, wide-eyed and unsure, gazing back at him.

'Sister, this is the prioress's cousin. Can you fetch *Mère* Gisela?'

The wide eyes had barely blinked and Henri wondered if she was simple.

'In God's name,' snapped Amée from horseback, 'you stupid girl! Fetch Gisela!'

The novice ran off, her faded robes dragging on the ground.

'Jesu,' said Amée. 'Her robes are poor and don't fit, there are no bells in the tower, the gate is cracked and weathered. Gisela is managing a house that is the very *embodiment* of poverty.'

Henri doubted Amée was badly injured if she could observe and pass commentary. *Soeur* Cécile on the other hand…

The gate was flung wide and the prioress rushed out. 'Amée, my dear Amée. Holy Mother, what has happened? Oh, *Deus*, you're bleeding!'

'Well may you ask what has happened,' Amée said as Henri helped her dismount. 'My horse broke its leg and I fell. That was the last of a litany of issues.'

'Come to the infirmary,' Gisela said. '*Messire*, if you lead your horse through the gate, we have a stable…'

'Thank you,' Henri replied.

He followed the two women, the gatekeeper still wide-eyed as she closed and barred the gate behind him. The prioress was nothing like Amée – tall, slim, an unlined face with clear eyes. The way she led her cousin, her upright back and squared shoulders – she was a strong woman and Henri could see why poor Cécile would have had no say in orders to journey to Lyon.

But he was angry that the prioress had no understanding of the danger into which she had thrust her Obedientiary and wondered what she would say when she learned how frail were the links with which the elderly nun held on to life and he chafed for Petrus's imminent arrival.

For the first time in many years, Henri felt a need to ask a Divine favour but he swung away from it uncomfortably as he entered a small stable with two stalls, an ass in one and the other empty. There was clean straw piled up against a wall and some hempen bags of feed. Oats? Barley? He wondered what this convent could afford.

He tied his horse at the door, filled the stall with straw and then led the tired animal in, sliding a pole across to prevent it escaping. He liked tending to the horse, pulling off its gear, fetching water from a well in the yard, finding some good hay stacked next to the straw. He grabbed a wisp of the straw, dampened it and knotted it off, then wiped at the sweat on the horse as it shifted with something approaching comfort as the dried salty marks were wiped away.

Not once had he seen any other nun and assumed they were perhaps in chapel. Without a bell, he was not attuned to the hours. It would explain the empty yard, the deserted cloister. He wandered to a gate and observed a field filled with healthy grass and a path scythed through to an orchard at the far end and then a stone wall. The orchard was in leaf, and the apple, pear and olive trees were robust. Against the wall stood two skeps – he guessed they had been woven by the sisters for the benefit of the refectory. Homegrown honey must surely be one of the few luxuries, for how would they afford to buy it?

'*Messire*…'

He swung round at the sound of the prioress's voice.

'*Madame* Amée?' he asked.

'A nasty knock but our infirmarian suspects nothing worse. She is abed as we speak. *Messire*, she tells me you are Henri de Montbrison and she spoke of danger…'

Henri frowned but refused to hold back. The woman argued with prelates on a regular basis Amée had said, so she was strong and he would not give her quarter. '*Mère* Gisela, the journey has been fraught. We have been chased and attacked because of the relic we carry and S*oeur* Cécile has borne more than she should ever have. She was severely bashed before we left Lyon and most recently has been subjected to another attack. Believe me when I say she holds life by a thread.'

The prioress's hand flew to her mouth. 'Where is she?'

'Petrus, my friend from Lyon, has appointed himself her protector and he is travelling slowly behind us. Prioress, I must ask you – why did you send her to Lyon?'

The prioress had the grace to look away. She also crossed herself as if that would give her strength. Finally, 'To buy goods for our convent, to accompany my cousin to her retreat. And to choose a relic. She is the most wise and sensible of our number.'

'You did not think to go yourself?'

'*Messire*!'

'I am sorry, but she *is* wise, as you say, and could surely have dealt with the issues of the convent with you away, whilst you, who are so much younger, could have travelled to Lyon to escort your cousin back to Esteil.'

There was a charged silence between the two and then the prioress answered. 'You blame me for her parlous state?'

'In a word, yes. That woman has had the courage of Daniel in the lion's den. She never faltered. Always, she would pray for succour as she was beaten down again and again. But she continued on because you asked her to and she believed she owed it to the convent. Tell me, why should she be placed in such an invidious position?'

Gisela had flushed with anger, plainly not used to being spoken to so baldly. She began to walk back and forth, her hands clenched until she slipped them into the wide sleeves of her grey robe. Three times she walked away and when she returned to Henri the final time, she said, '*Mea Culpa…*' and Henri was pleased to see her eyes had filled.

'*Messire*, never think that I was selfish in this matter. I felt I could hold off the prelates who seek to absorb us into other houses. They are vicious men and no matter how much I beg Fontevrault to drag them off, in the end, it is our Sisters' efforts within the scriptorium and the solar that have kept our heads above water. Cécile has great knowledge for what we need to continue, and I felt she would choose well. As to the relic, it is a blessing to have been offered one by Amée. I have no idea what it is and relied on Cécile to make a wise choice…'

'You have no idea?' Henri raked a hand through his hair. 'Jesu!'

'Then do me the kindness of telling me.'

'Prioress, you have the greatest…' The bell halted his words, followed by a thumping that could have almost knocked the door down. Henri began to run. 'It is Petrus!' He moved the young wide-eyed nun aside and slid the bar off the gate, opening it wide. Petrus was settling the nun is his arms. Her head lolled against his chest, her eyes closed, her pallor still wretched.

'Cécile! Oh, Mother of God! Cécile! *Messire*, this way!' The prioress led and Petrus carried the nun as if she were a wisp of air.

Henri watched them head across to the rose and vine draped cloister and then reached for the horse's reins. He nodded at the surprised young nun at the gate, led the horse through and tied it at a stake in the yard, pulling off the gear, wiping the horse down, giving it a drink and then turning it into the field. He watched it fold its legs, drop to the grass and then roll. Back and forth and again. When it stood, it shook itself, looked around, neighed with ear-splitting strength and received an answer from Henri's horse. It stood as if digesting the reply and then began to graze.

Life is so simple for you, Henri thought, rubbing his hand down the slick grey neck. You have no knowledge of God, no feelings of guilt or hubris. He leaned against the wall and somewhere behind him, he heard the nuns singing prayers for None.

O God, come to our aid.

O Lord, make haste to help us.

Glory be to the Father and to the Son and to the Holy Spirit, as it was in the beginning, is now, and ever shall be, world without end.

Amen.

The words wound into Henri's heart and squeezed so that he was sure he must be feeling Cécile's pain and he leaned, winded, against the stone wall. Unwilling to admit that he wanted God's help. That he wanted God's love to enable this Bride of Christ, Soeur Cécile, to survive. That he wanted her to be able to continue here in this far-flung village where she might be safe and could recoup.

He crossed himself – unwilling fingers touching his forehead, his chest, then left and right.

He refused to tell God that he would make sure the nun was never under threat again. That was for his mind and soul alone.

Chapter Twenty Two

'Henri!'

Henri turned to see Petrus striding toward him. He tried to read the Varangian's face but it was devoid of anything. Nothing like the unetched ice of de Tremelay. More the calm of a shaded glade where secrets lay deep amongst the wafting shadows.

'And?' Henri asked.

'They have settled her in her cell and the infirmarian is doing whatever she believes will help. Petrus thinks they will pray and offer masses all night if it is necessary. The prioress is like a startled rabbit.'

'Good. She had no idea of what she was thrusting her Obedientiary into. Had *Soeur* Cécile been left to run the convent whilst the prioress collected Madame and the relic, then she would not be bargaining with God for the nun's life right now. I told the prioress as much.'

Petrus chuckled, a volcanic rumble. 'Petrus will not tell Cécile what you have done.'

They both laughed but it was short and Henri followed with, 'What is wrong with her, Petrus?'

Petrus sighed as he leaned against the wall. The big grey poked his nose over and nuzzled the man's shoulder and Petrus held out his hand to let the horse lick. 'She is exhausted. Her soul has been laid bare. She has been pushed to the limits of her endurance and her heart suffers. There is no obvious wound, but something lies deep and Petrus believes she needs time and rest. If she has those things, and good, nourishing food, then she may pull through. And prayers, of course.'

'Have you asked God for his help?'

'In fact, yes. Petrus is a Believer, Henri. His mother is a nun in Byzantium.'

'You say?' So much made sense now and Henri knew why the man had taken to the nun and protected her as best he was able. Simply, she reminded him of his mother. A knock against his shoulder drew him from his thoughts. 'I'm sorry,' Henri said. 'You were saying?'

'What about you, the disbeliever?'

'How do you know?'

'*Soeur* Cécile told Petrus…'

'I see.' He was loath to admit that he had prayed for the nun's safety and health, but this was Petrus who had already delivered much in such short conversations. 'The nuns were singing None and I…'

'Then Petrus is sure God heard you,' Petrus said, pushing himself away from the wall. 'Petrus needs food and will eat in the village. The prioress says we can sleep in the *dorter* but the nuns are not to be disturbed in any way. Huh, Madame Amée will shake this place from the paving stones to the very tiles on the roof.'

He chuckled again as he began to walk across the yard and Henri took it as a sign that *Soeur* Cécile was in good hands and would recover. He pushed at the grey who was now nuzzling his shoulder and hurried after his companion.

'Petrus, de Tremelay will come.' Henri had just swallowed the last of a herb-filled pottage and broken the remaining piece of warm barley bread into two halves.

'Yes.' Petrus reached for one half of Henri's bread, having demolished his own.

'We will be ready…'

'Yes…' Petrus chewed, obviously relishing the food after days of dried meats and stale cheese. He offered nothing more and Henri knew when to back away. They would both be ready. One thing he was sure of was that the Templar wouldn't enter Esteil as anything other than a man of the Order.

They walked back to the convent in silence, entering the street entrance of the *dorter*, which was lit with a meagre candle tree. They were relieved to find no other travellers occupying cots and Henri threw his saddlebags on a spare cot, sitting on the one opposite. As they settled themselves, the prioress knocked and entered.

'*Messires*, I want to thank you.' She was diffident and her tell-tale hands moved within her cuffs.

'For what, exactly?' Henri asked.

'For getting my cousin and my loved Obedientiary to us. Amée is well, if tired. Our infirmarian has said she is only bruised and needs some quiet and she will be herself. She asks for you both, and I will make an exception and allow men into our cloister.'

'And *Soeur* Cécile?' asked Henri.

The prioress rubbed at her forehead as if to push an ache away. 'She has woken from whatever place she sank to and had a tiny bowl of soup and some unwatered wine. It gave her cheeks colour and I think her general pallor is improving. She is asleep again but she breathes deeper and our infirmarian is more content. We will pray for her through the night.'

'Prioress,' said Henri, pulling flat packages and a linen bag from his saddlebag. 'We have goods here that are yours. We tried to bring a little of what Amée and Cécile had chosen for your convent. The rest will follow. Petrus has a bag of monies.' He spread the goods on the opposite cot. 'There is some silk cloth and a bag of silken threads. Parchment, ink, and more silk is following. And Madame has purchased a bell...'

Mère Gisela fingered things and held a packet in her hand as if weighing the real and unfortunate cost of it. Clearing her throat, she said, 'Thank you. Help me carry these and I will take you to Amée.'

They followed her down the shadowy stair and through a heavy door which she locked behind them. Along the sweet-smelling cloister to the far end near the refectory where a flambeau jumped in the dusk air. She knocked on the oaken door of a cell.

'Come.' Amée's brusque tones called and the prioress pushed the latch, the two men entering behind her.

'I will leave you, *messires*, and take the goods to the solar. I will return forthwith to take you back to the *dorter*.' She left and her sandals click-clacked on the stone paving.

'Can you believe I am here till almost the end of summer?' Amée said. 'I don't think I will cope with the lack of comfort. Henri, here is a list which you must take back to Lyon and the goods must be sent and soonest.' She passed him a small packet. 'Petrus, do you return to Lyon with Henri?'

Yes, thought Henri. Do you? He waited.

'Perhaps,' Petrus said. Nothing more.

Amée shrugged. 'They told me you please yourself. I have no quarrel with that. The sister and I are still alive thanks to you both and to God. I gather *Soeur* Cécile is improving. Let us hope by the morning that she is well enough for us to see her, eh? Now, I am tired. Thank you for what you have done and I will see you on the morrow.'

Summarily dismissed, they walked along the cloister to await the prioress.

'No lasting damage there,' muttered Henri.

Petrus didn't reply as the prioress's footsteps approached.

Henri lay sleepless. Over and over in his head he tried to foresee how the Templar would try and claim the veil as his own. Short of upturning *Soeur* Cécile and ripping it from around her body, Henri could see no way. But he was sure the man would have an argument. Eventually, to the low snores from his friend, he dozed fitfully.

The nuns singing Lauds woke him but he rolled over and sank into a heavy sleep. At Prime, as their clear voices sang, he woke properly, rubbing the sleep from his eyes, swallowing against a dry throat and stretching his limbs. He pushed back the blanket and rolled toward Petrus's cot.

The man wasn't there.

Nor were his saddlebags.

Henri shrugged, guessing he'd gone to the stables to feed the horses, for they would be on their way soon enough and the horses must be fit.

Soon enough…

But not before the Templar had come.

He took his empty saddlebags up and walked to the door the prioress had locked the night before. It lay open now, allowing the smells of the cloister to drift in with light-beams from the rising sun. The golden beams striped the floor and motes of dust circled lazily, as if the day would be soft and kind. Chickens pecked in the gardens, a half-hearted scratching as they waited to be fed. Bread was in the oven in the refectory and the sunlight suffused the entire space. He stood for a moment and breathed in the peace and then walked on to the stable.

Inside, his horse turned its head and nickered. The ass showed no interest. Henri's gear lay neatly on the floor with the bridle hooked over a nail embedded in one of the wooden beams that formed the stalls. Petrus's gear was nowhere to be seen.

Perturbed now, Henri hurried to the field. It was empty of the stately grey.

Had Petrus just gone to hunt in the forest, to bring back a deer for the priory, a hare even?

Or had he disappeared for good? Because Petrus did what Petrus wanted.

'*Messire* Henri,' a woman's voice called and he hurried back toward an elderly nun. 'I am Melisende, the infirmarian. *Soeur* Cécile wishes to speak with you.'

'Of course...' He was at odds, perturbed at Petrus's absence and wishing he'd washed his face before crossing the yard. As he followed the quick sandalled footsteps of the nun, he grabbed a handful of cold water from the fountain in the middle of the cloister's garden and scrubbed at his face. He raked through his hair, tidying it and pulled at his tunic, as yet ungirdled and with no sword strapped at his side.

'Did she sleep well?' he asked.

The blue-eyed infirmarian turned and waited for him to catch up. 'In fact, yes. She has more life in her face now. She is still very weak and her heart struggles I am sure, but with God's help, she will be well. She was quite adamant about seeing you this morning which is a good sign as she is a very adamant woman. I had to deal with her forcefulness when she asked to see your friend after Lauds.'

'After Lauds?'

'I did not agree, but she would not be dissuaded and slept better after her brief meeting with him.'

Henri had woken at Lauds, had not heard Petrus move from his cot. He was curious now. More than curious.

They entered Cécile's cell, the door of which was wide open.

She shifted on the bed, pushing at the fur that *Mère* Gisela had insisted she cover herself with last evening. The pillows behind her smelled of lavender and she breathed in the fragrance. It settled her as she felt for the wooden cross that lay on a leather string round her neck. Bless Benedicta that she should have left it for her sister. For there had been none other in her whole life who had felt like her true sister.

She looked at Henri and his strong face creased into a half smile. 'Greetings *Soeur* Cécile. You look better.'

'I am, Henri. Before much time has passed, I will be on my feet. The novices are no doubt counting the days. In fear, I might add, not joy.'

He liked hearing her speak so. It gave him pleasure that de Tremelay had not done for her. The knight had no clue of her inner strength.

The infirmarian stood at the door. 'Not long, Sister. I will return when I think you have had enough.' She closed the door behind her and Cécile patted the stool at the side of the cot.

'Sit, Henri. I have a lot to tell you.'

He sat, and she could see from the frown across his brow that he knew he would not like what she had to say.

'Henri, Petrus has gone.'

He said nothing, as if he knew the truth of it. He had unusual eyes, a deep hazel tinged with spring green and as honest and clear as the day is long.

'He has taken the relic.'

'Sister!' He stood and she grabbed his sleeve.

'Sit and be quiet, dear man. I feel I can call you dear because you have watched out for myself and Amée with such diligence and we will be forever grateful. Now listen to me and say nothing. I gave him the veil in the night and he has taken it to where it will be safe. It doesn't belong amongst we at Esteil. It belongs where it was endowed so long ago.'

He shook his head, aghast. 'Sister, all that you have been through…'

'Yes indeed. But is that not the way of travelling on the roads? Danger at every turn?'

He huffed impatiently.

'You are right. I jest. 'She pulled herself further up the pillows. 'The veil was given to the Xylinites Convent outside Constantinople a lifetime ago. It was kept in an ivory casket but not long past, maybe two years, the casket was stolen. It pitched up in the market in Constantinople where your minstrel found it and bought it. I would bet my life that he had no idea of the contents.'

'How do you know?'

'Petrus's mother became a sister at Xylinites, Henri, and he told me the story in Lyon. To me, it seemed right that he should return what belongs to his mother's convent. It's as simple as that.'

'But is it, sister?' He was quite forceful as he spoke, the hazel eyes darkening with shadow. 'Simple?'

She sighed. 'Perhaps not. You saw that *my* life was forfeit for the veil. And I was afraid for my sisters' lives if we kept it here. We are not a big group of women and rely on Esteil's good people. Why should anyone be in danger because there is one foul man who wants what is not his?'

He nodded. Understanding, she thought.

'No one can hurt Petrus. He is strong and fleet and I dare say he will be on the coast and on a boat before the Templar knight knows what has happened. As far as I am concerned, if the knight asks, I shall deny I ever carried a relic. Amée as well. I am sure Gisela will prevent him from searching the convent but the prelates are another thing altogether. By the time he has done all that, Petrus will be halfway to Constantinople and I will breathe freely again.'

'Sister, I am… astonished at what you have done.' He stood and walked around the cell.

'You disapprove?'

He thought and then answered carefully. 'Possibly not. Does Madame Amée know?'

'Not yet, but she will.'

'What do you think she will say?'

'Oh,' Cécile laughed, sinking back against her pillows. 'A lot. But Henri, I think of Gelis, who lives with her infant because of that veil. That miracle. And if that is the only miracle, I am content.' She could feel the strength draining from her and knew Melisende would return imminently. 'I also think of Ariella's father, who died needlessly. Of all those who have died on this journey and I am disconsolate.' She held tight to the cross. 'I think of what I did and am ashamed.' She wondered at herself, talking to this man that she barely knew as if he were her confessor. But the truth was she trusted him more than any priest who might attend Esteil. She continued on, despite her body feeling as heavy as lead and her eyes dry and sore. In her soul she felt a shifting weight and it mattered. 'Do you remember we talked of Faith, once?'

Henri nodded, sitting again, his attention centred upon her.

'In Lyon, after the attack and before we left, I went to the convent on Presque'Ile. I needed peace to talk with God and so in their chapel, I asked God how He could let such a thing happen to me who had been so obedient to his Holy Law and who had never faltered in my devotion to Him. There was no answer, Henri. No sign. And I realised that it was because I was confronting Him, challenging Him. And so I prostrated myself on the stone floor, the bruises and cuts punishing me. I *begged* for His forgiveness. Staying there until the nuns returned to chapel. Still there was no sign.' She took a shaking breath. 'Yesterday, when de Laon grabbed me, every single belief I had that God would see me safe vanished in a heartbeat.' She sucked in a sob and Henri grasped her hand, wrapping his warm fingers around and she held tight. 'I realise now that God would not have come to aid me anyway. He gave his *Son* to show us the way. What we do with His word is our mistake to make. He will be judge and jury when it is time. But, He expects us to repent and ask for forgiveness at the very least. Thou shalt not kill, Henri, and I did.'

Henri looked down at their joined hands. 'Sister, fear is like drowning. One sees nothing else, hears nothing else, remembers nothing else. There is just an elemental need to survive. If God was watching, He would see His handmaiden carrying His son's mother's veil – a veil that carried His son's blood. He would see His terrified handmaiden finding the will to live and carry on working in His name. He would forgive.'

'But I took a *life…*'

'Sister, de Laon would have taken yours. I think God did not want that to happen. You could say that God guided your hand.'

She wiped her eyes with one hand, needing Henri to keep holding the other. The warmth and strength of his touch reassured her. Finally, she whispered. 'Thank you.'

He smiled. A beautiful smile filled with honesty and kindness. 'Sister, He *will* forgive.'

She gave a tired snort. 'It is my most fervent wish. But I also have another. I wish for you to be safe in your confrontation with the knight.'

'You know?'

'It is written all over you. You tremble with it, I think. Henri, you *must* reconcile yourself with God.'

He shifted on the stool. 'If I become reconciled, it is only to ask for protection for those I love.'

She patted his hand. 'Go now, Henri. I will pray for you.'

His palm moved her hand and he kissed her knuckles, the warmth of a blush spreading across her cheeks. 'And believe it or not, Sister, I will pray for *you*. My time with you has been a privilege.'

'Thank you but I suspect a trial, more like. So, you speak to God, then?' She pushed the point.

'You are persistent, Sister. And since you ask, I will admit I speak to him now and then.' He stood. '*Adieu*. We will not meet again, I think, but send word with *Madame* Amée if you are able.'

She watched him pull the door open and then close the door quietly behind and was content. Much had been achieved.

Henri leaned against the wall of the cloister. All for nothing.

He tried to put everything in some kind of logical order. Would Saul still have died? Probably. Because Toby would have bought the relic anyway and even if it had not been sent to Esteil, it would have been sent elsewhere and Saul assaulted because of it.

The nun was a good woman, honest and committed and perhaps sending it back to Xylinites was her way of securing redemption for killing Jean de Laon. The ways of Faith were beyond his ken, despite that he had asked God to keep her safe.

Had he lied to her about reconciling with God? Yes and no. But he had no time to delve into the detail. Right now, he needed to break a Commandment. Again…

He collected his sword, dagger, belt and girdle from the *dorter*, leaving a small purse for the time at Esteil. Descending the stair, and passing along the cloister, he nodded at a pair of novices. They were not yet experienced enough in the Rule not to lift their eyes to his face and he caught the flushing cheeks on one, smiling to himself as he stepped to the fountain.

The water was still cool after the dark of night and it served to scrub the tiredness away from his mind. He fetched his horse, saddled it and took it out through the field, the leafy apple trees brushing against him and the horse snatching at clusters of tiny fruit. He pulled the horse away, growling at it and then opened a wicker gate at the bottom of the orchard. The gate was freshly woven and fitted the wall well and he wondered which of the nuns was so skilled. Or perhaps the nuns wove it and then a layman fitted it.

God knows, he thought.

The horse followed him readily into the wilder, longer grasses beyond and so he tied it to the branches of a split and fallen oak and watched the animal graze. The nuns' chorus drifted in waves and he sat on the wall, thinking back through *Soeur* Cécile's confession.

What a brave woman. The prioress had no idea…

He unsheathed his sword and realised the bloodstains of yesterday were still evident, seeing Adam's frown of disapproval in his mind. So he grabbed a handful of the grasses and knotted them, scrubbing hard. They moved unwillingly, almost as a reminder, until all that remained was a faint rust-coloured stain in the fuller. Grabbing a corner of the cloak he had thrown over the stone wall, he burnished until the sword shone bright in the early sunshine, a world reflected back in its gleam, thinking as he worked, wondering how de Tremelay might have found out about Xylinites.

He guessed there would have been some sort of trail. Perhaps in the Palace of Patriarch George II Xiphilinos there was a record of relic locations. Perhaps he discovered, through a diplomatic relationship with Patriarch George II, that the veil which had supposedly been gifted to Charlemagne, may have been in fragments. Whilst the largest fragment may indeed have been gifted to the King of the Franks, one of the smaller pieces was no doubt passed on in the form of a benefice to the Xylinites Convent. By consequence, the knight could have learned of the later theft. Perhaps in some sort of hellish serendipity, the Templar had heard of a certain dealer near the waterfront of the Venetian Quarter, who was selling an ivory chest.

Such things happened.

In any case, Henri believed his summation was not far from the mark and everything had bought him to this point. Where he waited at the bottom of an orchard, because he knew de Tremelay would come looking for he and Petrus. Lucky on one count. Not so much on the other.

He weighed his weapon, easing his grip until he felt the wrapped leather of the haft settle into his palm like a lover and he began to move – forward and back like a dance in a lord's hall where gittern and pipe celebrated life. He described glistening arcs and circles, his focus tight at the very sword tip, never wavering.

He felt light despite the news of Petrus. He had *Soeur* Cécile's blessing and Ariella's plea to avenge her father. Anything beyond that would have been greedy. It was a question of…

'If you weren't a churl, lowborn despite your father, I would say you show knightly skill.' The voice of the archangel spoke behind him and he turned, keeping his sword poised.

'I have had good teachers.' Henri spoke without anger. Insults were merely words.

'How is it,' asked de Tremelay, laying his white cloak next to Henri's, 'that a bastard from the great Forez family has spent his whole life un-noticed, unrecognised? Is it because your mother, a lowly maidservant who couldn't keep her legs together, was just disposable?'

'Perhaps.' Henri remained unruffled. He had expected this. He would be goaded to make the first strike, he had no doubt. 'In my experience, nobility views life differently.'

'You say. Do they even remember you in Montbrison?'

'I neither know nor care. But tell me,' he kept his sword pointed at the man's mid chest, his hand easy on the grip, his eyes fixed on de Tremelay's face. He felt no tension, breathing evenly. Good. He needed to remain in control of his emotions. 'How came *you* to know so much of *me*?' He was curious as to why it would matter to the knight. But then surely it was just all bait.

'You have a link to the town by your name, so one asks and finds answers. But now, of course, you have left the Forez,' de Tremelay drawled, 'for that failed knight, Gisborne. Buying and selling. A merchant's lackey. Quite a few rungs lower than the Forez family, I'd wager.' He tutted. 'A seller of goods.' Spoken with distaste, but then with a swiftness that surprised Henri, 'They say he deals in relics.'

Ah, the nub. Henri tightened his grip slightly. He stood well balanced, the sun behind him. It was the position he wanted to maintain if he could. 'Does he?' he answered.

In a lightning movement, de Tremelay pulled his sword from its sheath and struck out. The move was wondrous and any other might have been surprised but Henri had positioned himself perfectly and stepped back out of reach, sensing de Tremelay moving to the right so the sun was not directly in his eyes. Henri moved again, so that the knight had no option but to step back into the sun's glare. Ah, it would be like a chess game if it wasn't lethal.

The Templar grunted. 'Clever. You use the sun to advantage.' And he stepped once, twice, forward, his blade describing an arc and Henri had to back away as the cutting edge sang through the air a horsehair's breadth away from his middle. The knight had positioned himself to the side of the sun and he dove in again, circling round Henri so that Henri had to move, batting the man's blade away as *he* was forced into the sun's glare. He blinked and lowered his head, keeping his gaze fixed on the knight, watching, assessing the mood, sensing the next move.

It came, a lunge. Henri stepped quickly aside but the point pierced his arm, his tunic slit open. Blood stained the torn linen of his chemise.

'Move faster, fool,' the knight said.

Henri did as he was told. Describing a welter of arc, slice, stab and twirl – the gritty sound of iron upon iron singing on the air. He struck once against the knight's mail surcoat, a ringing of metal against metal but it meant nothing. Except that the protective mail was heavy and it slowed the knight so that with a speedy lunge, Henri pricked the man's arm. In the moment of surprise, he jumped into the knight's ambit, close enough for the blades to strike and slide screeching, one on the other, to the very crosspieces. The men pushed against each other – younger brute strength against an older man, despite the obvious fitness of the knight.

The smell of sweat wafted from the Templar and beads of moisture sparkled on his brow. Curiously, Henri felt no heat at all, just a cool calm for which he thanked God.

Now there was an irony, he thought. If only you knew, *Soeur* Cécile. 'Don't you want to know where the veil is before you kill me?' he asked as he fleetly stepped back beyond the range of the knight's sword.

De Tremelay stood with knees flexed, his blade point aimed at Henri's chest. He breathed hard which surprised Henri and he wondered if the man was showing his age. 'The prioress says there *is* no relic. Has never been and is not likely to be. But then she doesn't know, obviously, that the Templars are aware of a stolen relic that has been transported from Byzantium. I assume you have kept it for yourself. You and the grotesque Varangian.

'Grotesque?' Henri's lips turned down. 'You think? I see an ordinary man with an extraordinary love for Christ and his fellow man.'

'A bard, are you?' The knight's breathing eased and his voice assumed the more measured tone with which Henri was familiar. 'Then tell me,' de Tremelay sighed as if bored, 'before I kill you, where *is* the veil?'

'Returned to Byzantium and beyond your reach.' Henri watched that small spark of surprise flit across the knight's eyes and for one brief instant, de Tremelay's attention focused elsewhere. Henri leaped in, kicked his foot against the man's heels and upended him, striking downward with his sword as the man fell. Hitting his arm, watching his sharp blade enter the shoulder. He pushed harder on the grip, slicing down until he met bone and then dragged his blade out. The knight's sword had fallen from his hand as his arm was rendered useless, and blood began to pour from the awful wound into the long grass that lay bent and buckled around him.

His shoulder shed blood like a waterfall. His arm, where it remained attached, hung as lifeless as a dead man's, the inner flesh peeled back and shattered bone gleaming white.

'You are better than I thought,' he panted in stunning pain. 'I am surprised.' He sucked in a breath. 'Byzantium, you say?' He groaned against the agony. 'Jesu! Finish the deed, churl. It is what you want, is it not? Or have you not the gall?'

Henri snorted, shaking sweat that had now begun to roll into his eyes. 'Gall?' His blood began to bubble through his body, fizzing with fury. What was a haze before was now hatred of a size that began to overcome him and his sword trembled as it danced against the Templar's throat. 'Is that what one needs to behead a young child? I saw you in Outremer. Or perhaps one needs gall to kill Jews? I knew Saul ben Simon well, he was a good man and a father, de Tremelay. Or perhaps you prefer to take a nun's life? But then you didn't bargain with *Soeur* Cécile and her faith and strength, did you?'

'It is a knight's calling to have gall, de Montbrison...' De Tremelay's voice was ragged at the edges, like the red and white wound that gaped across his shoulder. 'It is what makes us knights.'

'Then what is it that makes you a murderer? What will the Order say when they discover what you have done?'

'Holy Christ! God take you for the idiot you are! It was *for* the Order, you fool, and for God...' De Tremelay hissed in a breath. 'I acted on the Grand Master's orders. The Order is the greatest weapon that God has and the Order must care for the greatest relic known to the Christian world. Such holy power...'

'Then I stand mistaken, my lord.' Henri would give the man credit for strength, for sure. His arm hanging off, bleeding like a stuck pig and still his voice seduced with its honeyed tones. But his faith was no different in its strength to the nun's and it bore thinking about at some point. 'I offer you an apology of sorts,' he said. 'But you see, there is still the child's life to be avenged, and my friend's life and then the assault on a Bride of Christ.'

De Tremelay said nothing in reply, closing his eyes and Henri thought he perhaps prayed as he travelled swiftly toward Judgement.

But then he reared up and yelled, throwing himself into a sitting position, reaching out, wielding a dagger with his good hand to stripe Henri deeply across one shin, almost to the bone. Despite the pain, Henri lunged forward, stabbing with the length of his sword through the knight's chest over his heart. He rolled his blade, the Templar growling throat deep, showing his teeth like an alaunt about to make a kill. Swallowing a scream that would have come from any lesser man.

A death blow.

Henri pulled his sword out and stood a blade length from the man.

The Templar looked right at him, a half-smile on froth-stained lips.

Henri knew he would never forget that moment because it seemed the knight had seen God and that every terrible thing he had ever done had been forgiven because he believed it had been done in God's name.

Henri waited until the light of life dulled and then wiped his sword on the Templar's cloak – vengeful red stripe across the white wool. Sheathing the weapon, he slit a strip at the hem of his own cloak with his dagger, binding his leg as tight as he dared and swabbing at the slash on his arm.

Untying his nervous mount who backed wild-eyed from the iron scent of blood, he mounted, the sun overhead, and without looking back at the Prieuré d'Esteil, he headed south east…

The End

Author's Notes

The inspiration for this story originally came from the research I carried out for the previous trilogy called *The Triptych Chronicle*. In the process of seeking facts on rare and valuable merchandise that may have been traded in the twelfth century, I came across mention of a silk called *byssus* and which is still harvested in the Mediterranean from a species of shellfish.

The sea mollusc called 'pinna nobilis' was known as far back as biblical times to be the source of the most curious cloth. The mollusc produces a fine filament that can be dried and then spun into silk so fine that a veil could be folded and placed in half of a walnut shell. One of the curious properties of *byssus* is that it can't be dyed or painted upon, and it was an article posted by *Paul Badde,* on *September 29, 2004* in the German daily *Die Welt,* that stirred my imagination.

At the time, he maintained that there was a *sudarium* with the image of a man upon it held in the small church of Santuario del Volto Santo in Mannopello, Italy. The image is rumoured to be Christ's face which is pressed upon unpaintable *byssus*. He also maintains that this is the lost Veronica Veil.

Is this an urban legend?

Despite the world authority on *byssus*, Chiara Vigo, declaring the *sudarium* to be made of that rare silk, no one will know until scientific tests can confirm the cloth and the image, something the Capuchin friars of Mannopello would not allow at the time that Paul Badde's original article was written. He has, since then, written a number of books on the search for the Holy Face.

His original article encouraged me to think about the value of relics to churches and their income, and I started reading about the history of relics. More particularly, I mused on the relic at Mannopello – supposedly made of *byssus*, the obscure cloth about which I had written in **Michael**, Book Three of *The Triptych Chronicle.*

Byssus intrigues me. The ancient nature of the cloth, the strange properties. This is a silk that by its very nature cannot be marked in any artificial way known to Man, so imagine the integral value of the Mannopello veil!

The research pathway brought me happily into the twelfth century where relics held great sway, and where the 'pilgrim way' was a Christian's Gap Year through France, Spain, Italy and on to Jerusalem. The Pilgrim's Way was marked with relics of real and dubious quality which were held not only by the Church, but traded with enthusiasm by merchants from, amongst other places, Constantinople.

When French researcher and my close friend, the late Brian Cobb, found the remains of a little twelfth century convent in Esteil (pronounced Iss-toy), only a few kilometres from the Chemin de Compostelle, I began to have the whisperings of a story.

Add into that a twelfth century trading house with a reputation for finding the exotic, the rare and the secretive and my fingers itched to start writing. The people of the merchant house of Gisborne ben Simon were calling…

At no point did Brian or myself find evidence that the Prieuré d'Esteil had possession of a relic either in the 1190's or at any other time, but I'm writing a fiction, and one could only wonder what the small convent did to survive in those difficult years, with a small agrarian population surrounding it and huge relic-laden abbeys like Conques, further along the road, and which effectively drew crowds of pilgrims who would bypass anything less.

I asked myself what would have happened to the priory if it had acquired a relic? More particularly, with the right sort of relic, what mayhem might have occurred trying to relocate the object from Constantinople to Esteil? Especially a relic rumoured to have been wrapped around the body of Christ.

That was the inspiration for the story.

As the research developed, actual historical individuals began to appear and although there is little detail on their lives, I was able to use their miniscule background to create threads to weave together through the narrative. Some disappeared, not to be heard of again, but in the case of the Prieuré d'Esteil, the Drac family was mildly notable. I have used the exact facts provided by the Prieuré d'Esteil about its donor, but there is very little more to be had in research across the board. This however, always plays into a fiction-writer's hands. Unlike the well-documented king of the time, Philip of France, in whose service my main protagonist Henri de Montbrison fought in the Holy Land during the Third Crusade. History relates much on Philip and one can hardly veer from the truth.

The Third Crusade brings me to the concept of PTSD of fighting men in historical times. Was there such a thing? I would just like to offer up two links which were revelatory to me.

https://sciencenordic.com/
anthropology-denmark-depression/
violent-knights-feared-posttraumatic-stress/1398550

https://www.warhistoryonline.com/instant-articles/
ancient-and-medieval-ptsd.html

A common and simplistic view has been no, there was no suffering because in previous societies, historians say violence was the norm. But many allusions from as far back in time as the Greek ancients to fourteenth century Geoffroi de Charny and beyond, indicate a number of common factors – lack of sleep caused by fear of night-terrors, overwhelming sadness, and mental images that could not be ameliorated. Thus it seemed to me quite possible that my main protagonist, Henri de Montbrison, should experience any one or a number of these, given what he endured in Outremer.

Could he lose his Faith because of the Third Crusade? One would think the Church, which after all approved the Crusade, would be able to provide an ethical and spiritual support to men on their return. But early on, I wanted Henri to be a thinking man, trying to rationalise what he had seen and done with what he had been taught of the overarching power of the Holy Trinity.

So yes, his Faith was tried significantly and found wanting.

The village at which Henri and his friends disembark in Southern France before continuing by road to Lyon is called Notre Dame de Ratis in the narrative, translated as Our Lady of the Boats. This became Notre Dame de la Mer and finally, in the eighteen thirties, it became St Maries de la Mer and is now a popular seaside destination on the edge of the marshlands of the Camargue. It is famous for the Romanesque church which was built between the ninth and twelfth centuries and which can be seen for a distance of up to ten kilometres. In those times, it was used as both fortress and refuge from invasion.

The floods of 1196 did indeed happen and are documented. In March of that year, the Rhône valley amongst other areas, was subjected to an horrendous wet spring. It stopped the fighting between Richard Coeur de Lyon and Philip Augustus. It is said that only alms and prayers halted the rain and helped the waters recede.

I was able to use the subsequent halt of water transport on the Rhône and Saône, to slow Ariella's journey to *rue* Ducanivet in Lyon, so that a fast-tracked, urgent overland message from Italy arrived in Lyon only a day after she herself had passed through the city gates.

Sometimes facts are just meant to be…

The details of Benedictine *Soeur* Cécile's life, have been underlined by the book ***Benedict's Rule: a translation and commentary*** by Terence G Kardong. Liturgical Press, Minnesota, 1981.

For those who may not have read ***Michael***, Book Three of ***The Triptych Chronicle***, the Xylinites Convent which is integral to the denouement of this novel, actually existed. I quote my Author's Note for that novel: 'Judith Herrin's various books (*The Formation of Christendom; Byzantium – The Surprising Life of a Medieval Empire; Women in Purple; Unrivalled Influence*) have been go-to references regularly. In searching for a suitable Byzantine convent … I was concerned by Judith Herrin's prophetic words *"many others are* *noted for a single reference and remain unidentified".* Once again, it seemed I was entering unchartered waters. This is the dilemma that historical fiction writers most often love because it gives them free licence and so I chose to once again make another fiction call, placing one of the "single reference" nunneries, Xylinites, outside the city in a location of my choosing... (I)... cannot find any reference as to whether the convent survived the Fourth Crusade. Being a "single reference" convent, my guess is that it did not...'

Acknowledgements

In writing a book, one has a huge list of helpers along the way – people who bolster one's writing life.

In the first instance with **Reliquary**, I owe the greatest debt to my friend and researcher, the late **Brian Cobb**. Brian's role in my writing life has been documented in detail on my blog https://pruebatten.com/2020/06/07/un-homme-charmant/

With his passing, I am the poorer for lost friendship as we used to regularly go off-piste and share some wonderful chats.

I also acknowledge the steadfast and loving support of my husband of forty five years. He is my rock.

My family – especially our little grandson who has transformed our lives.

With such affection and respect – my peers **Simon Turney** and **Gordon Doherty** who see something in my work that I don't see myself. I owe you chaps more than you can possibly imagine.

My dog – a Jack Russell. 'Nuff said.

My editor – the intuitive **John Hudspith.**

My cover designer and formatter, the amazing superwoman and mountain climber, **Jane Dixon Smith.**

All my online friends – you are so very important to me on a daily basis. Especially **Matthew Harffy** whose work has been such an encouragement to continue with my own stories.

My path along the Pilgrims' Way has been a fascinating journey as I researched this novel. It has also provided more unique nuggets which hopefully will enable me to complete the series, still set in the twelfth century and within the fellowship of the merchant house of Gisborne ben Simon.

I hope you, the reader, have also enjoyed the companionship. If you have, you would do me a great honour by reviewing, either at your point of purchase or on Goodreads (or even gossiping about it over a cup of coffee with friends). My books can only continue their purpose of entertaining readers with your help.

Many thanks for reading my words and I wish you well.

Cheers, stay safe and see you within the words of the next book!

CPSIA information can be obtained
at www.ICGtesting.com
Printed in the USA
LVHW042147170122
708503LV00002BA/33